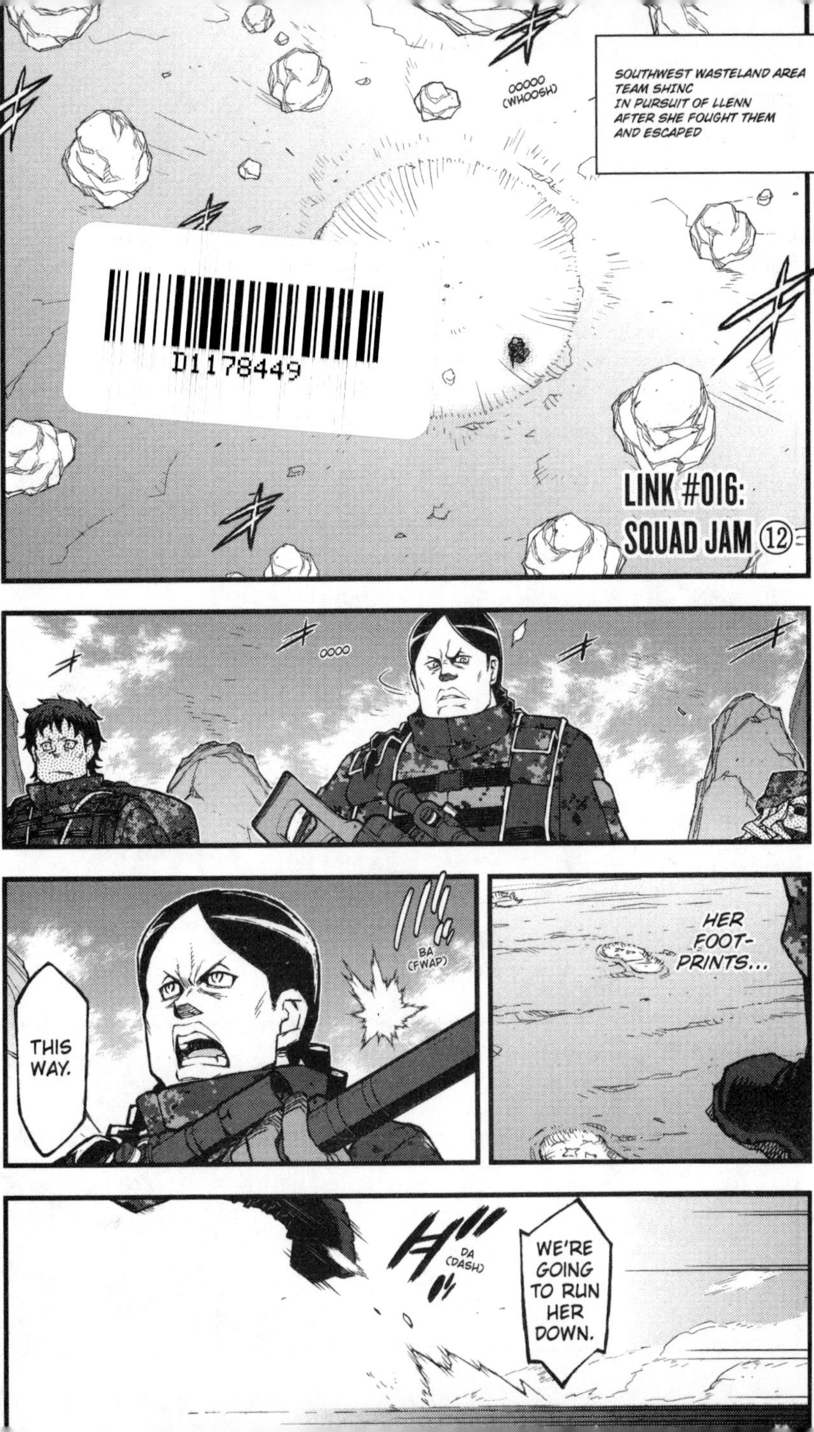
SOUTHWEST WASTELAND AREA TEAM SHINC IN PURSUIT OF LLENN AFTER SHE FOUGHT THEM AND ESCAPED
OOOOO (WHOOSH)
LINK #016: SQUAD JAM ⑫
OOOO
HER FOOT-PRINTS...
BA (FWAP)
THIS WAY.
WE'RE GOING TO RUN HER DOWN.
DA (DASH)

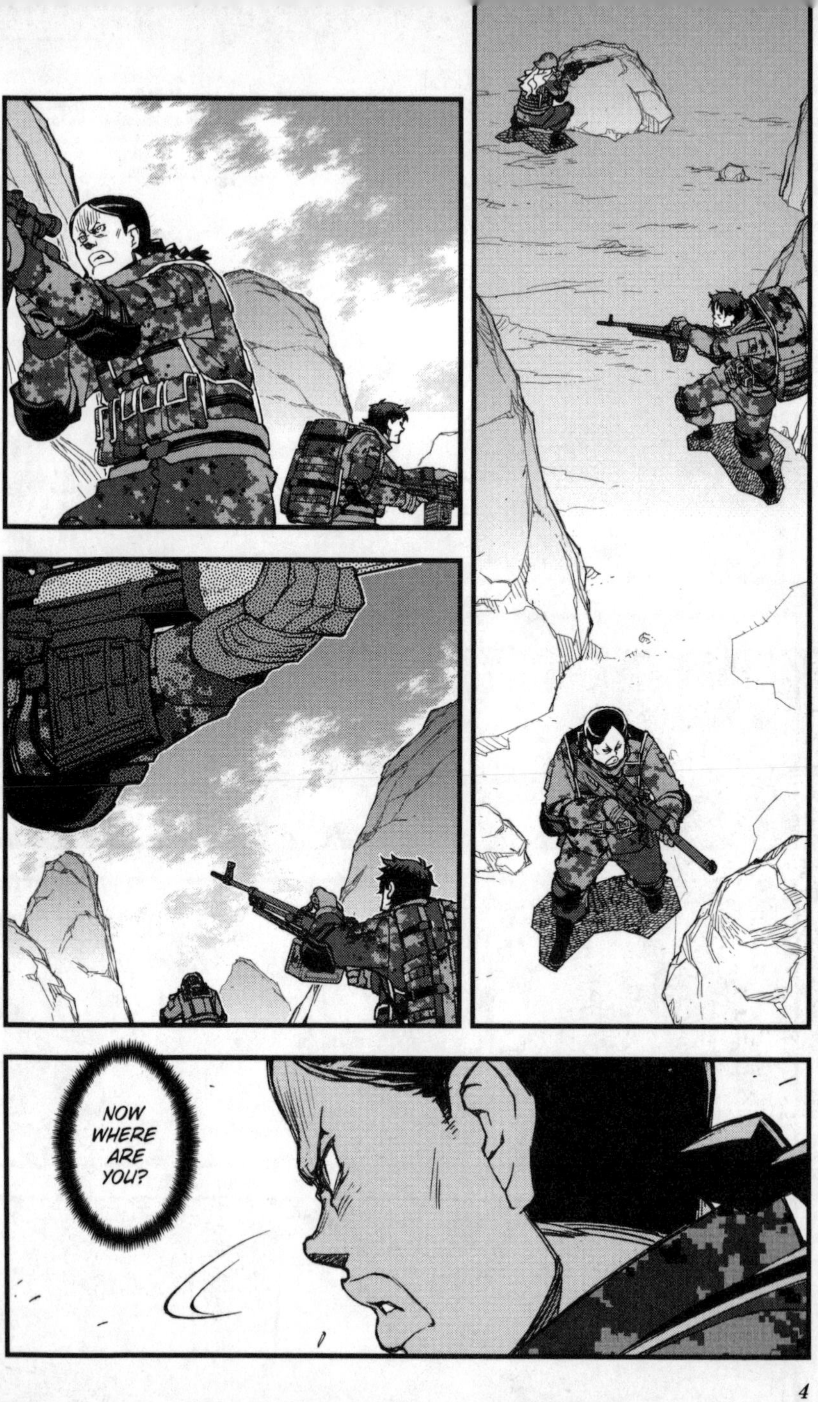
NOW WHERE ARE YOU?

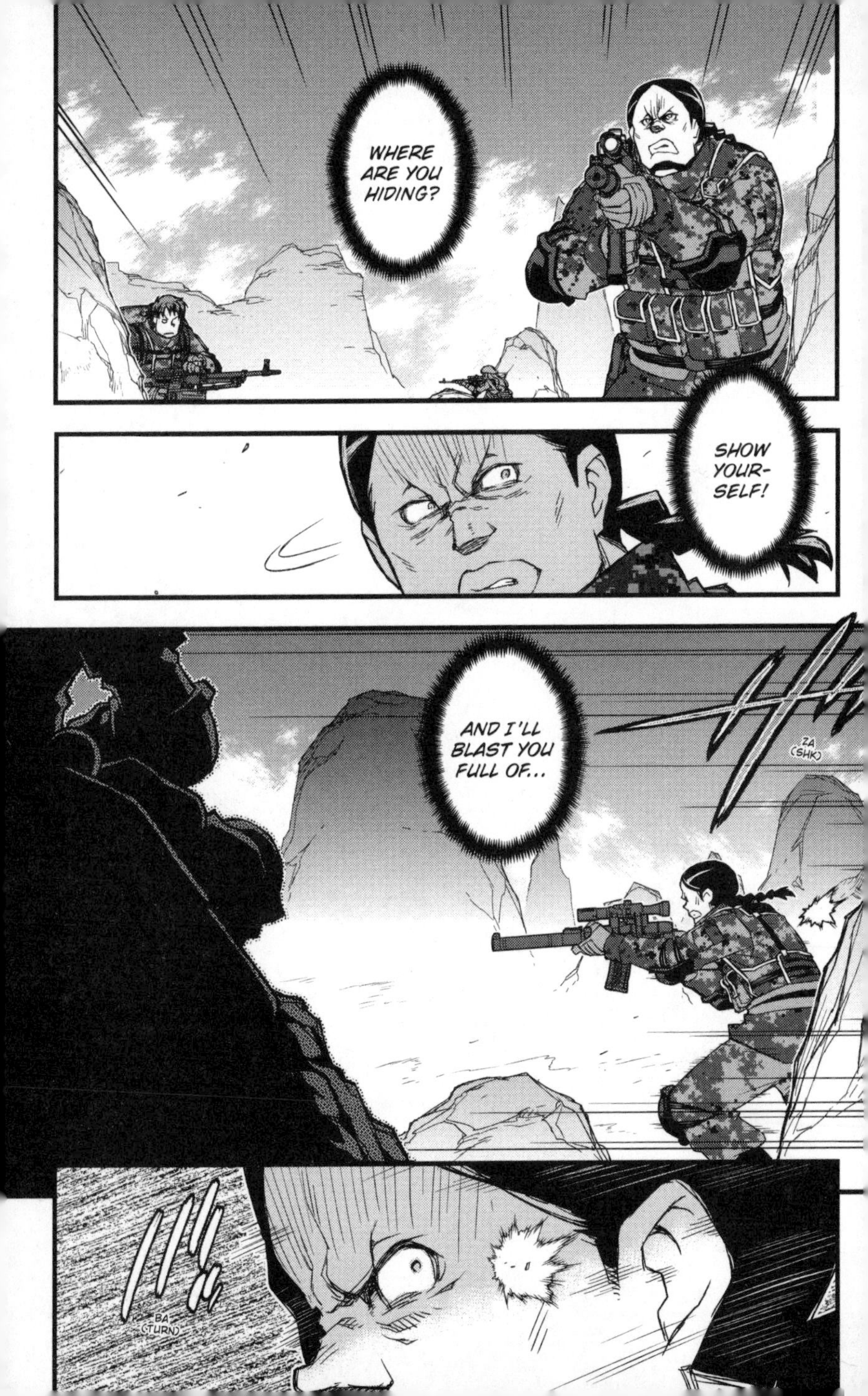
WHERE ARE YOU HIDING?
SHOW YOURSELF!
AND I'LL BLAST YOU FULL OF...
ZA (SHK)
BA (TURN)

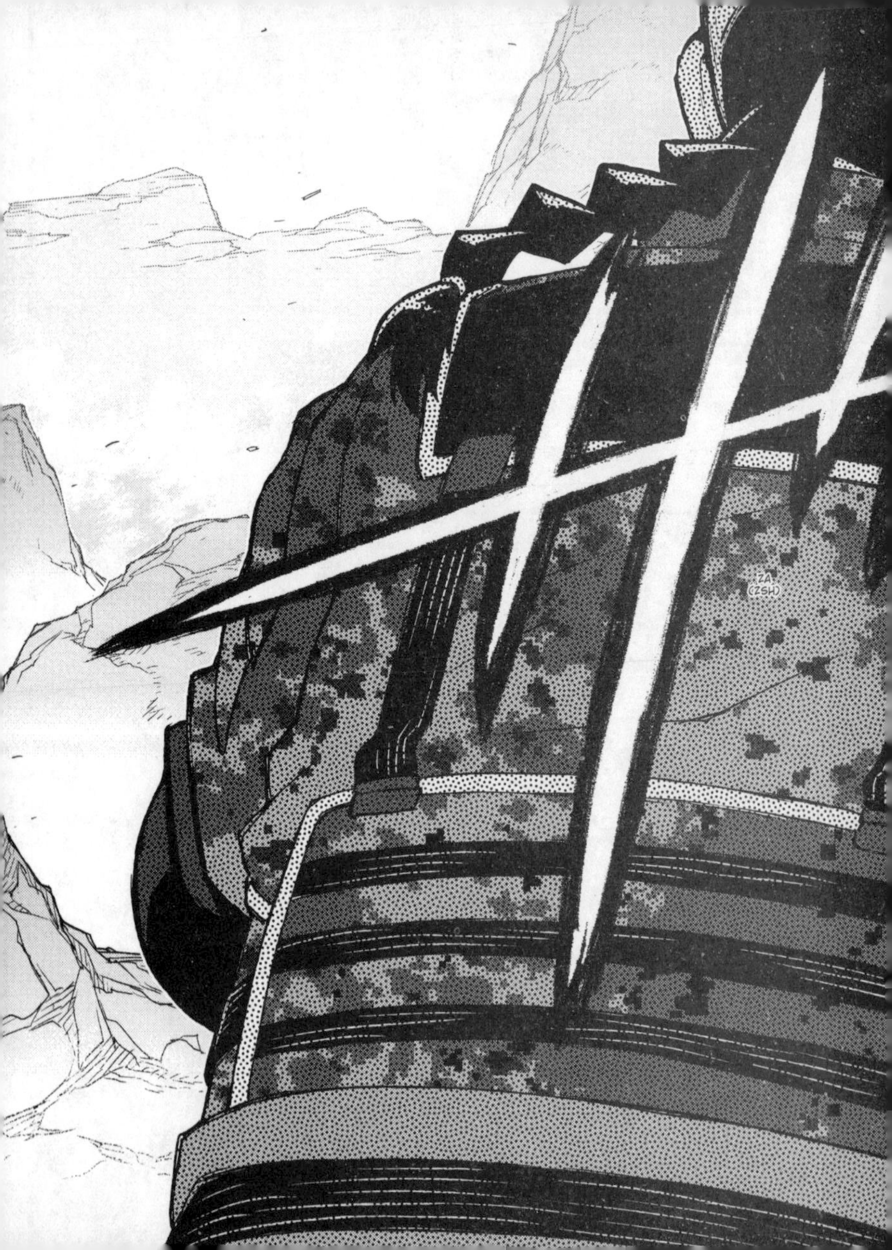
ZA
(ZSH)

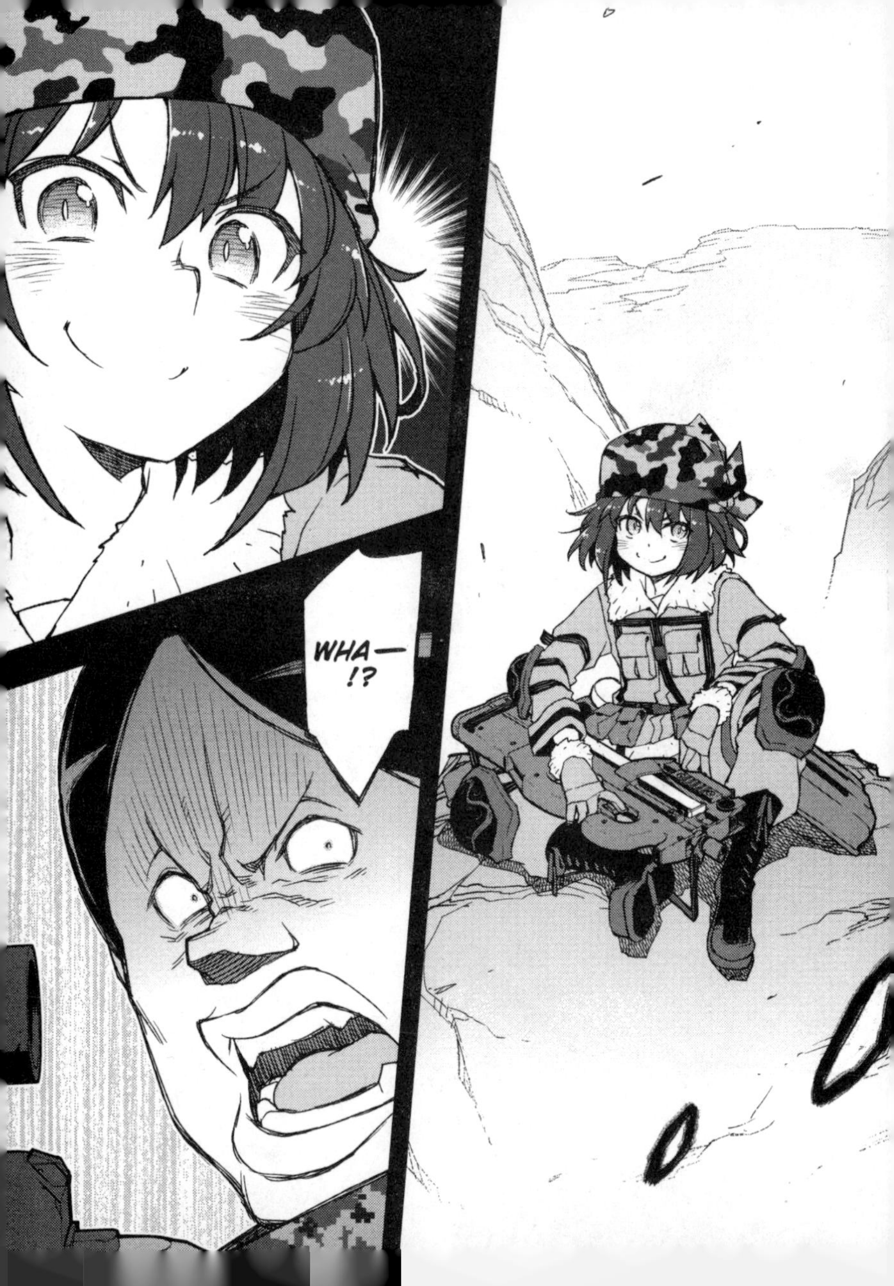
WHA—
!?

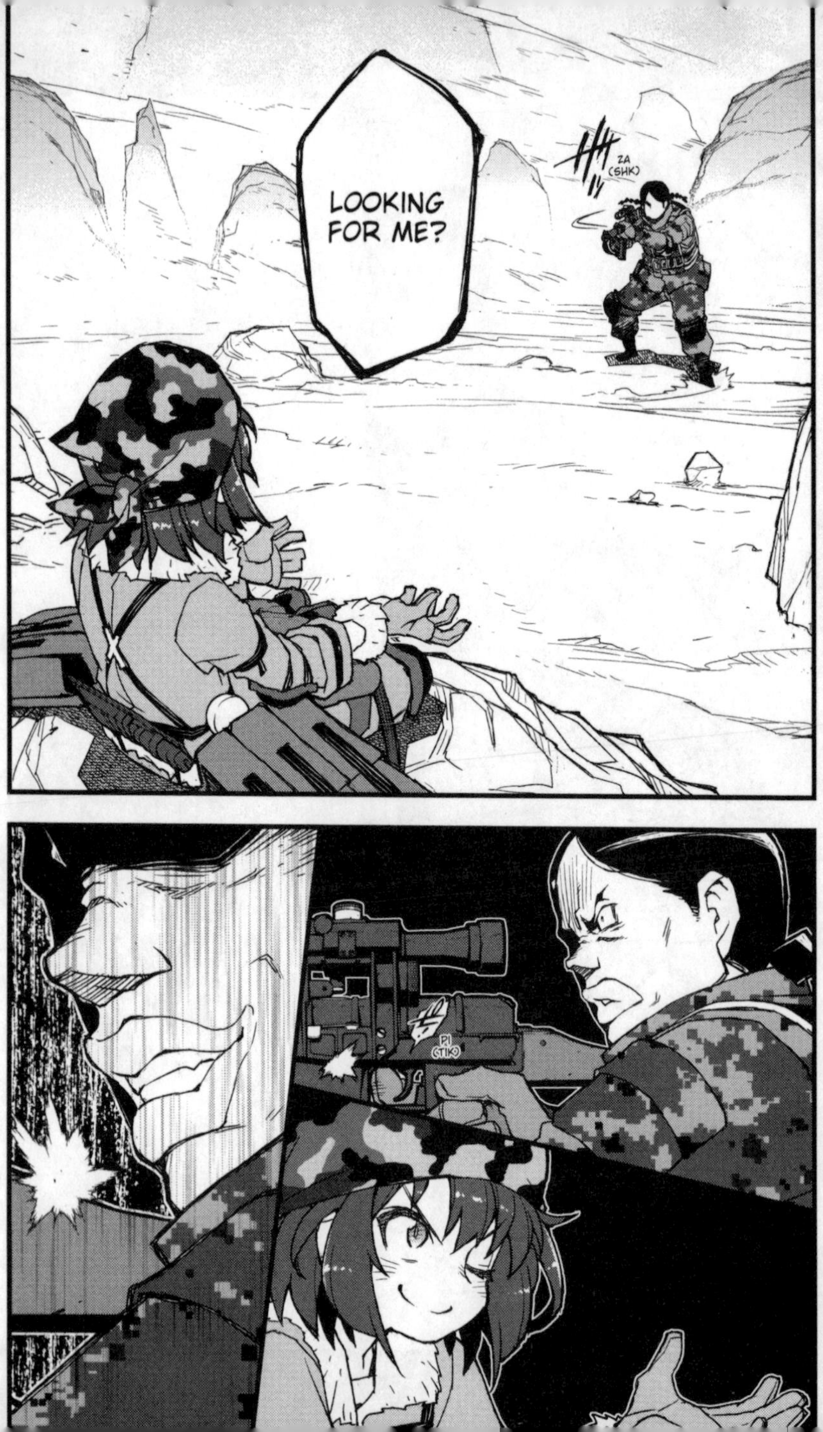
LOOKING FOR ME?
ZA (SHK)
PI (TIK)

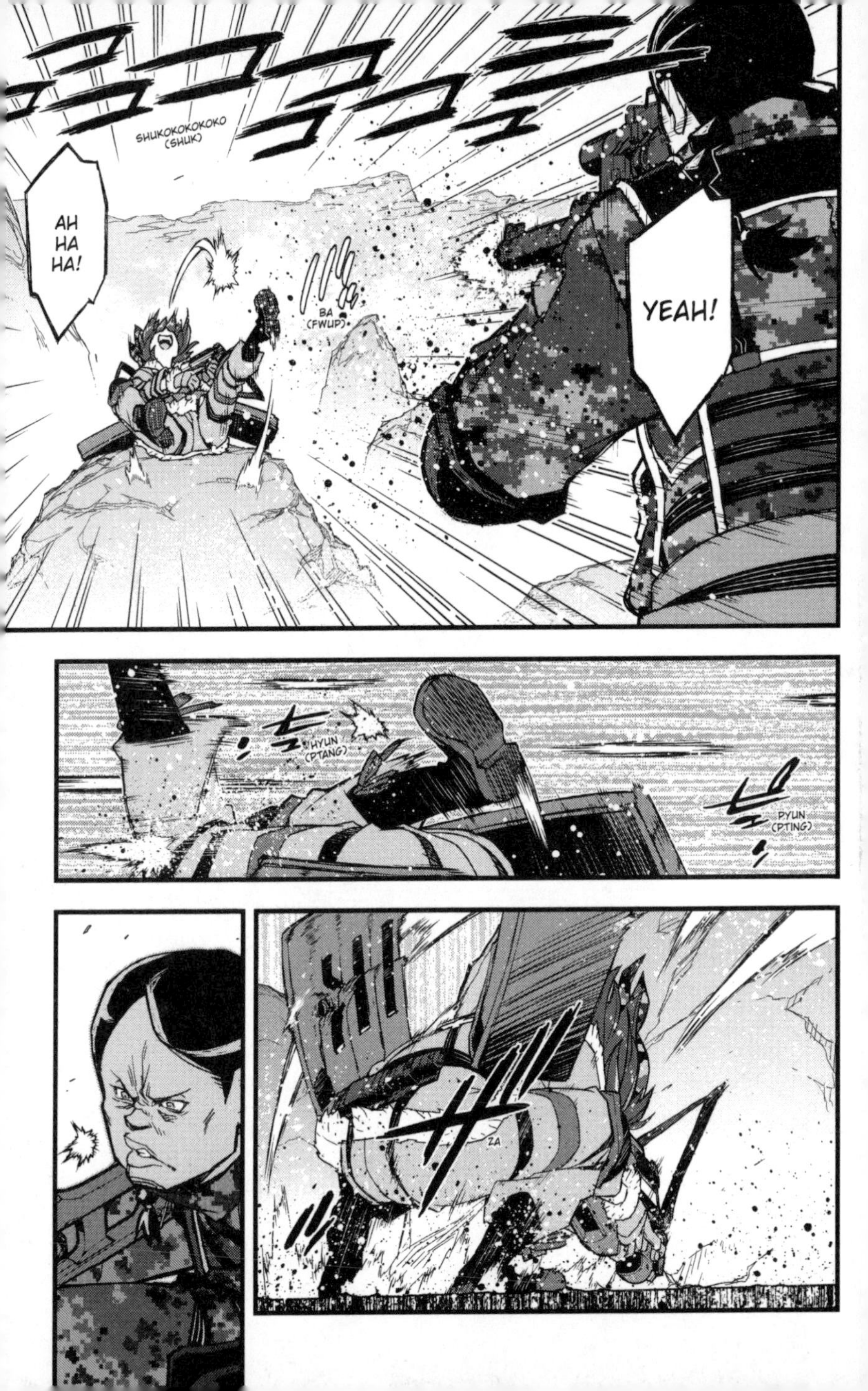
SHUKOKOKOKOKO (SHUK)
YEAH!
BA (FWUP)
AH HA HA!
PYUN (PTING)
HYUN (PTANG)
ZA

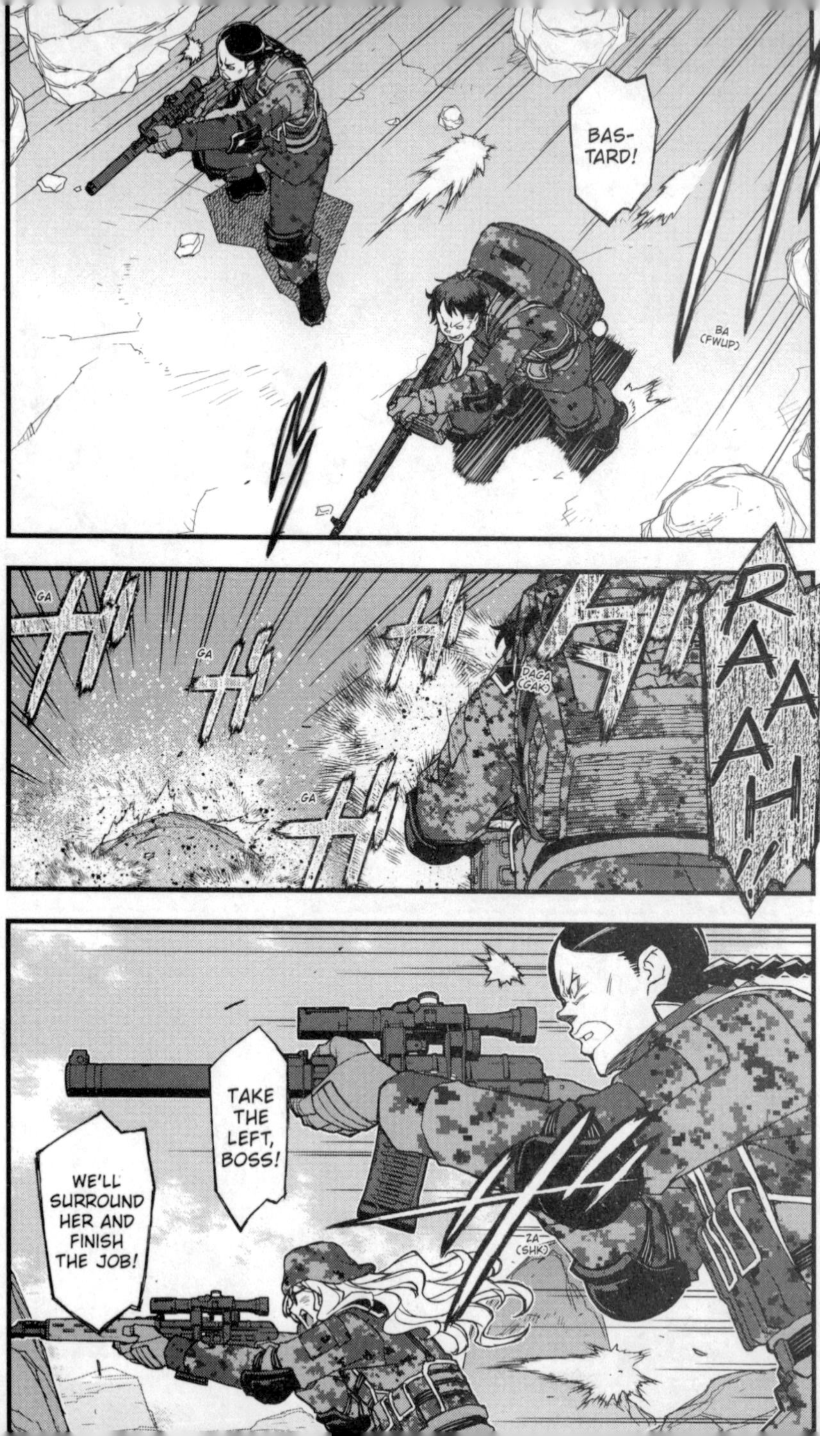
BAS-TARD!
BA (FWUP)
RAAAH!!
DAGA (GAK)
GA
GA
GA
TAKE THE LEFT, BOSS!
WE'LL SURROUND HER AND FINISH THE JOB!
ZA (SHK)

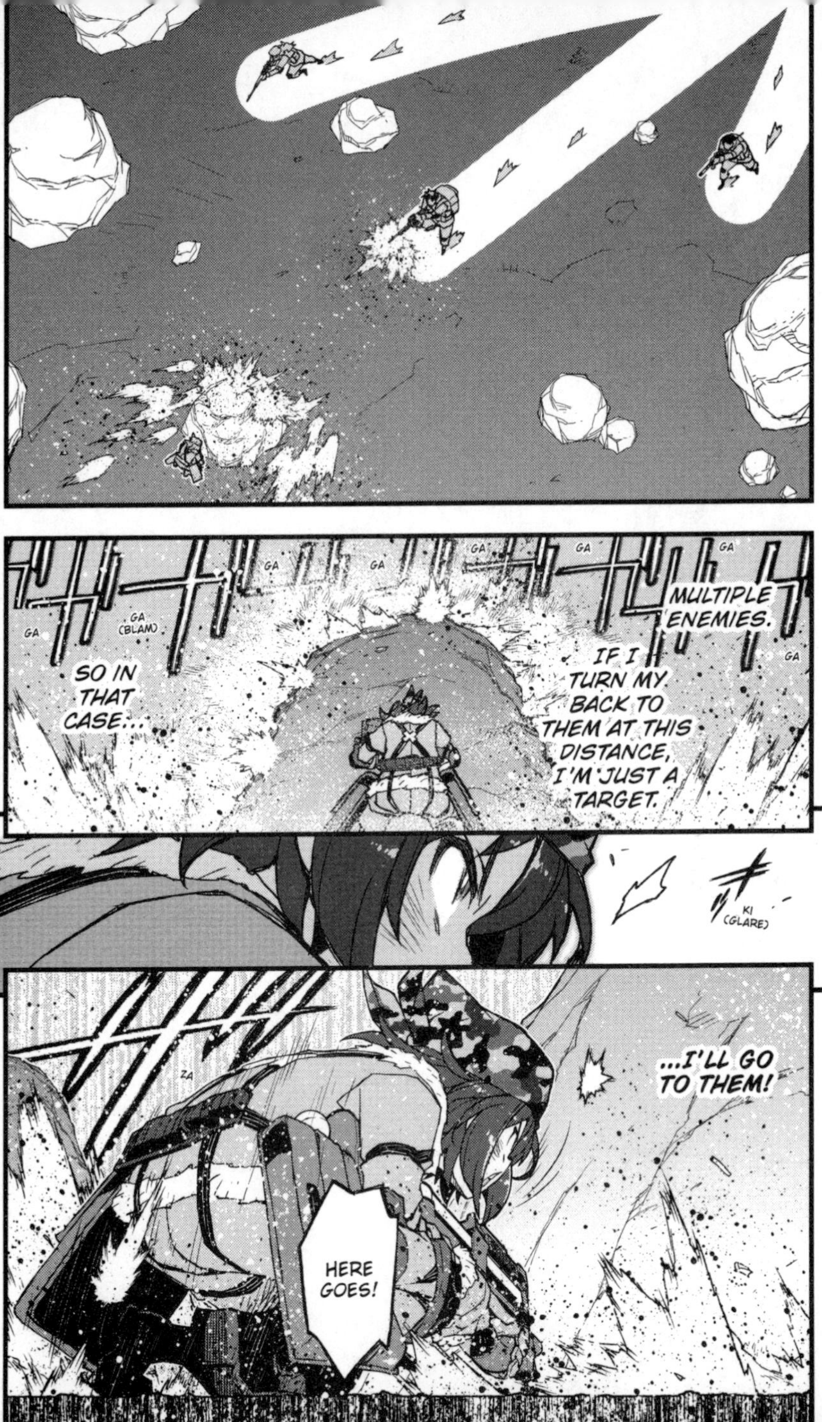
GA
GA
GA
GA
GA
GA
GA (BLAM)
GA
MULTIPLE ENEMIES.
IF I TURN MY BACK TO THEM AT THIS DISTANCE, I'M JUST A TARGET.
SO IN THAT CASE...
KI (GLARE)
...I'LL GO TO THEM!
ZA
HERE GOES!

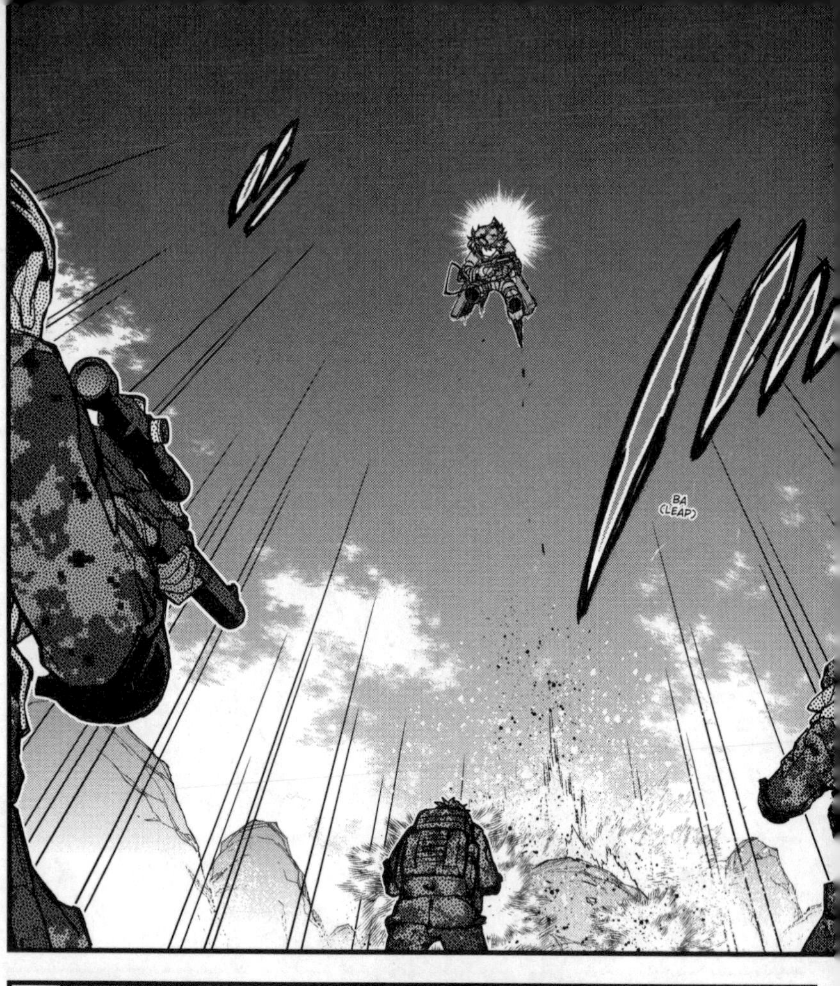
BA
(LEAP)

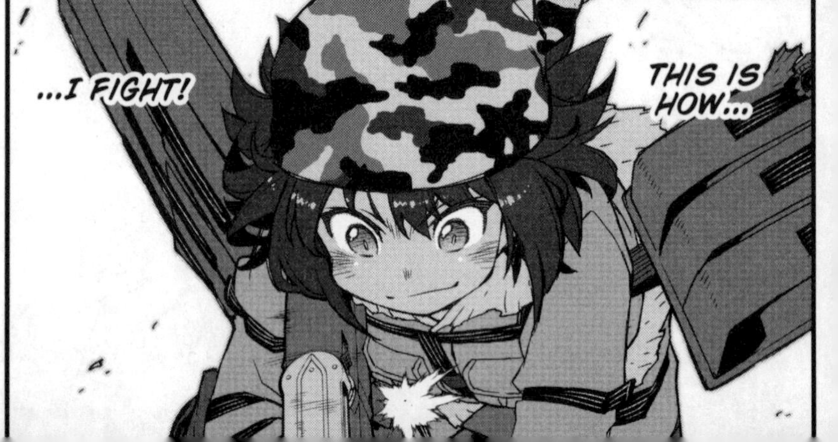
THIS IS HOW...
...I FIGHT!

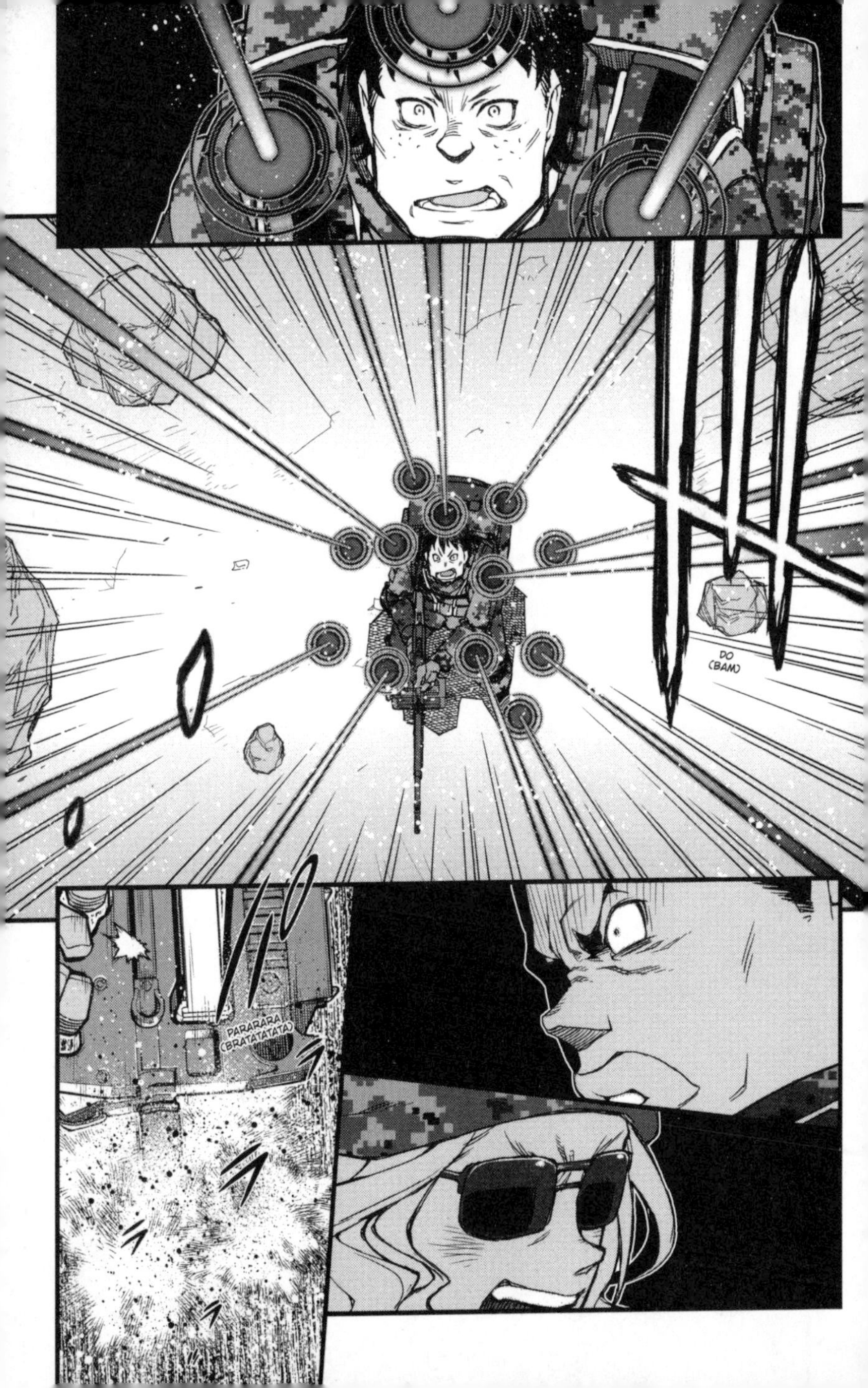
DO
(BAM)
PARARARA
(BRATATATATA)

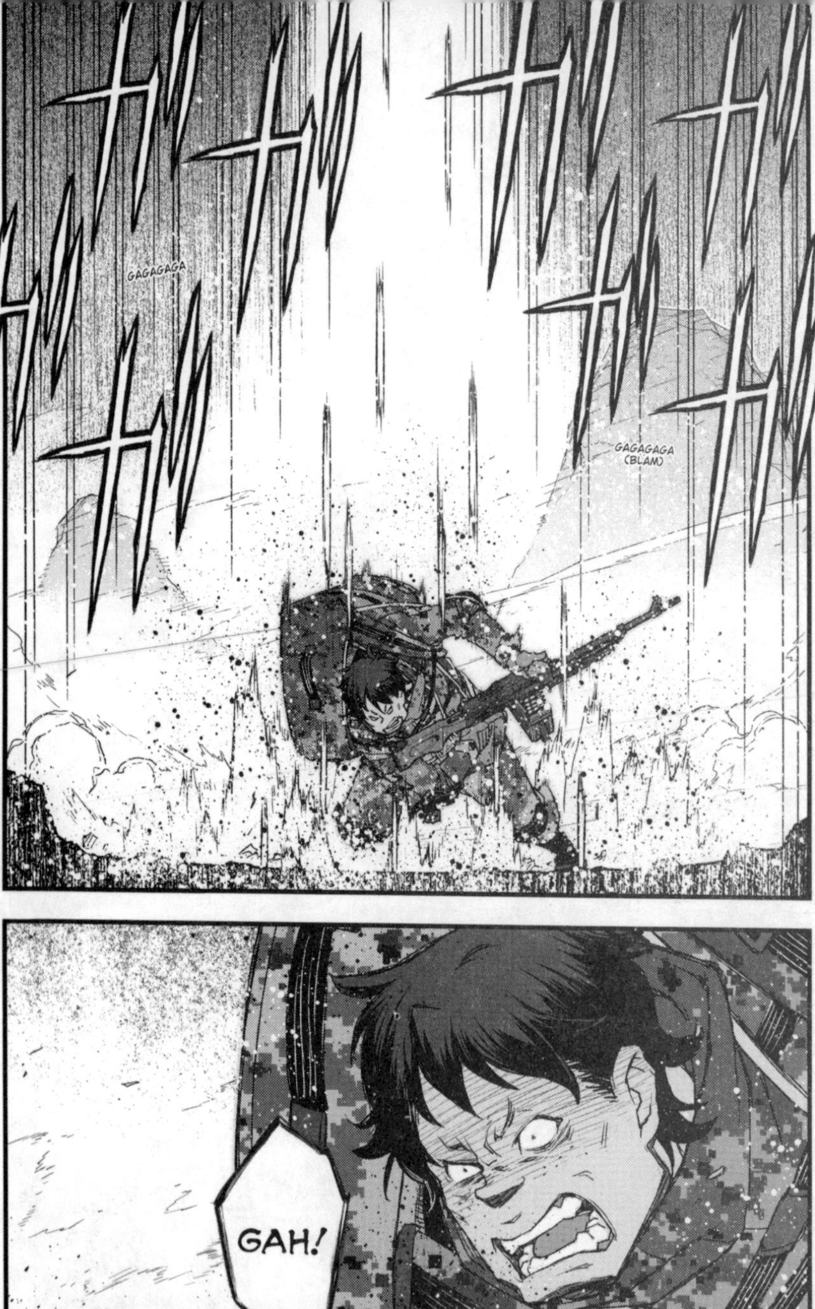
GAGAGAGA
(BLAM)
GAGAGAGA
GAH!

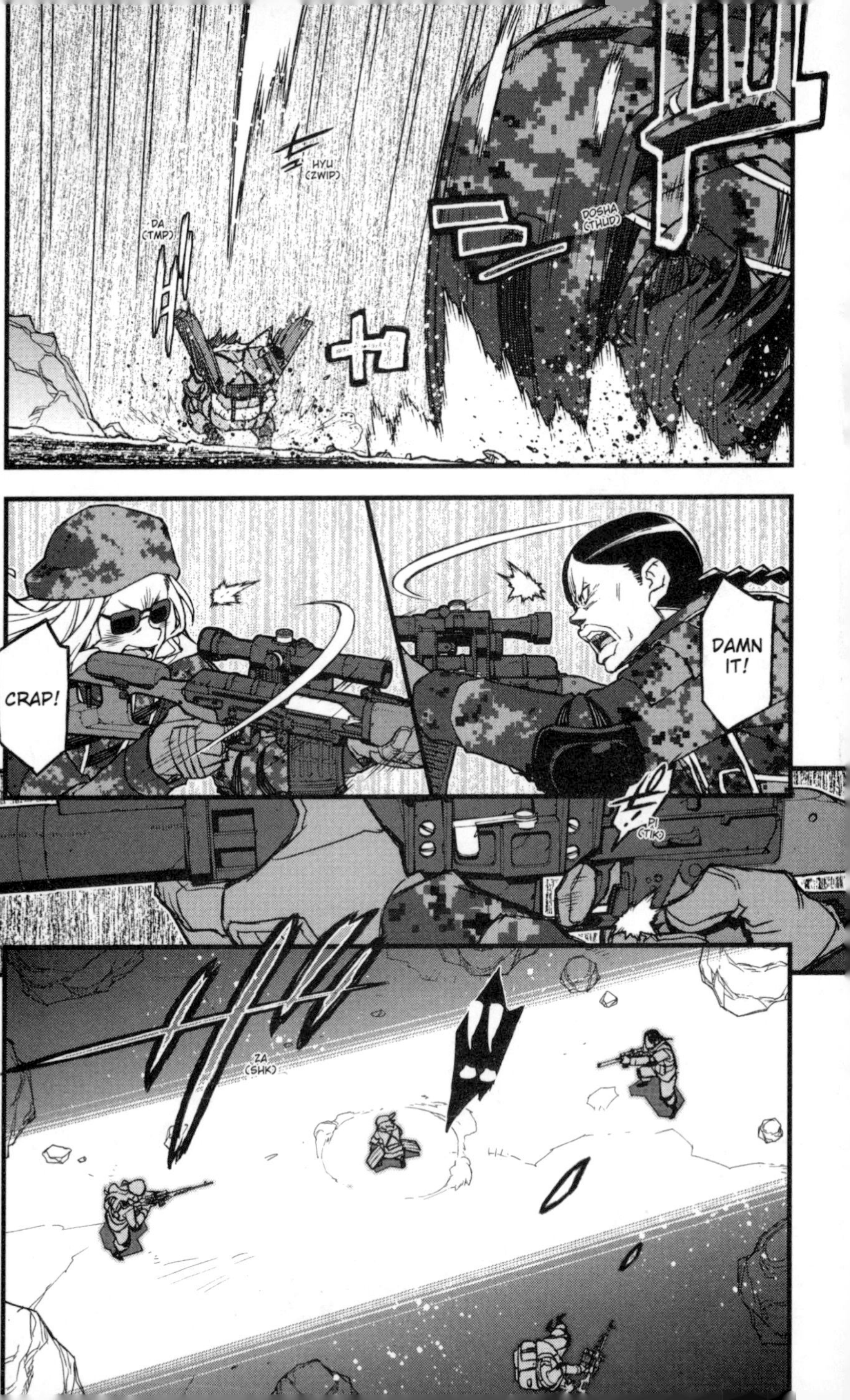
DOSHA (THUD)
HYU (ZWIP)
DA (TMP)
DAMN IT!
CRAP!
PI (TIK)
ZA (SHK)

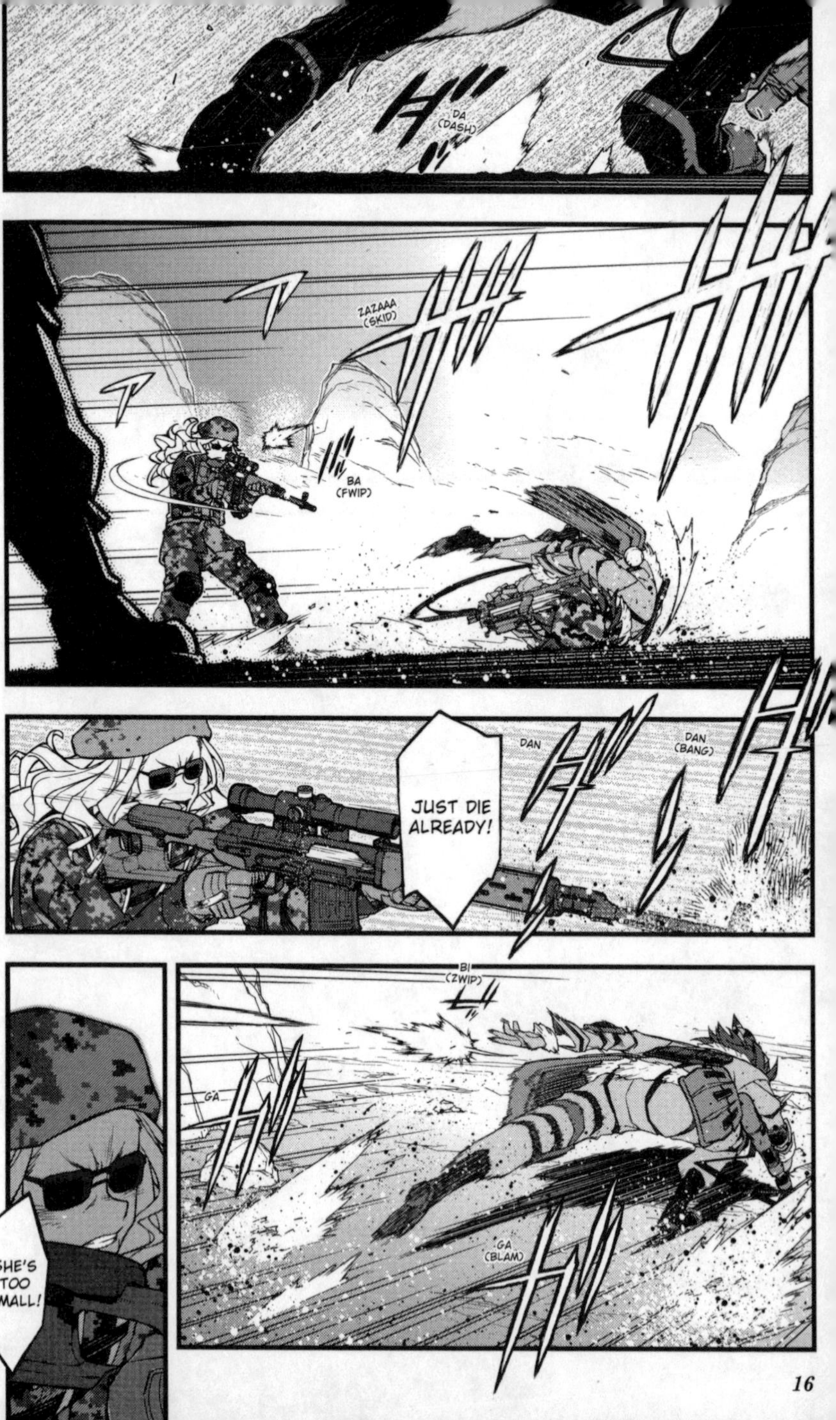
DA
(DASH)
ZAZAAA
(SKID)
BA
(FWIP)
DAN
(BANG)
DAN
JUST DIE ALREADY!
BI
(ZWIP)
GA
GA
(BLAM)
SHE'S TOO SMALL!

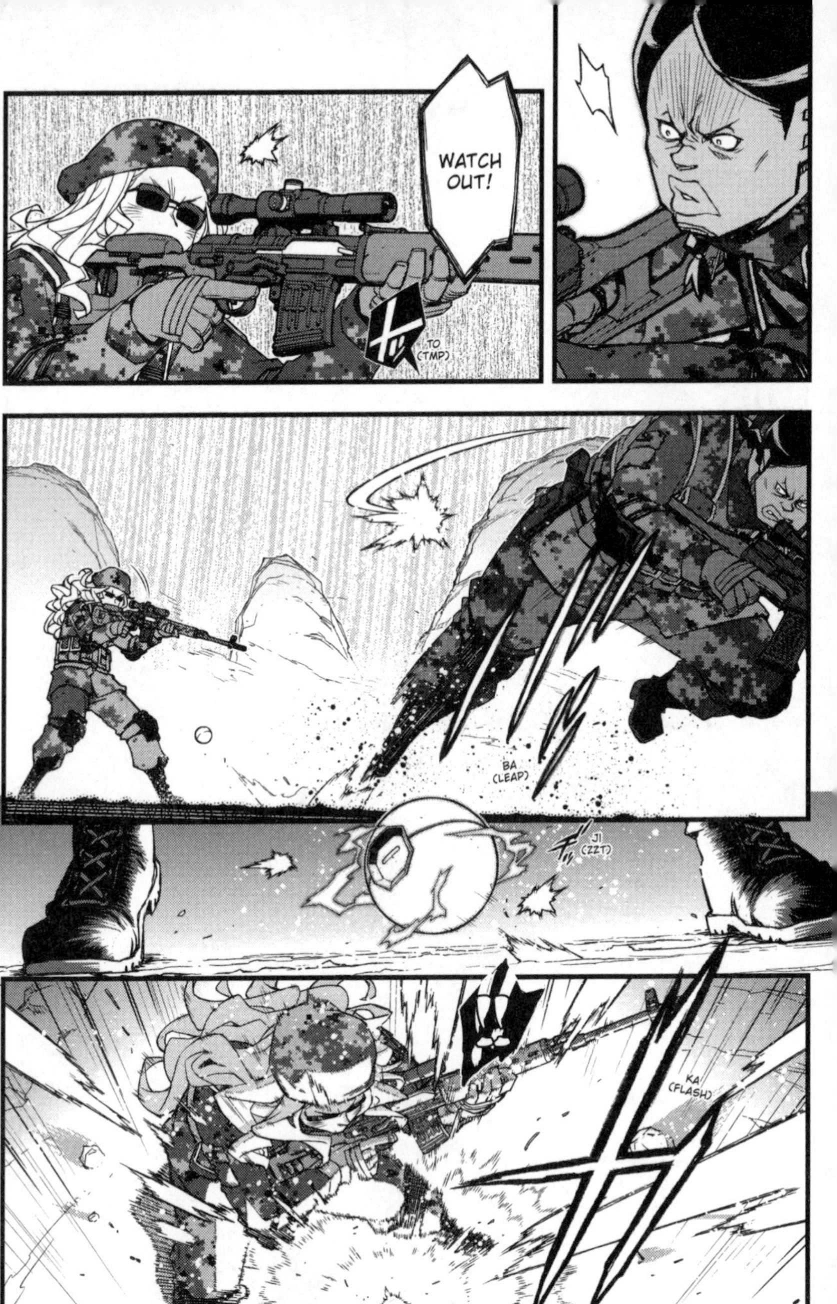
WATCH OUT!
TO (TMP)
BA (LEAP)
JI (ZZT)
KA (FLASH)

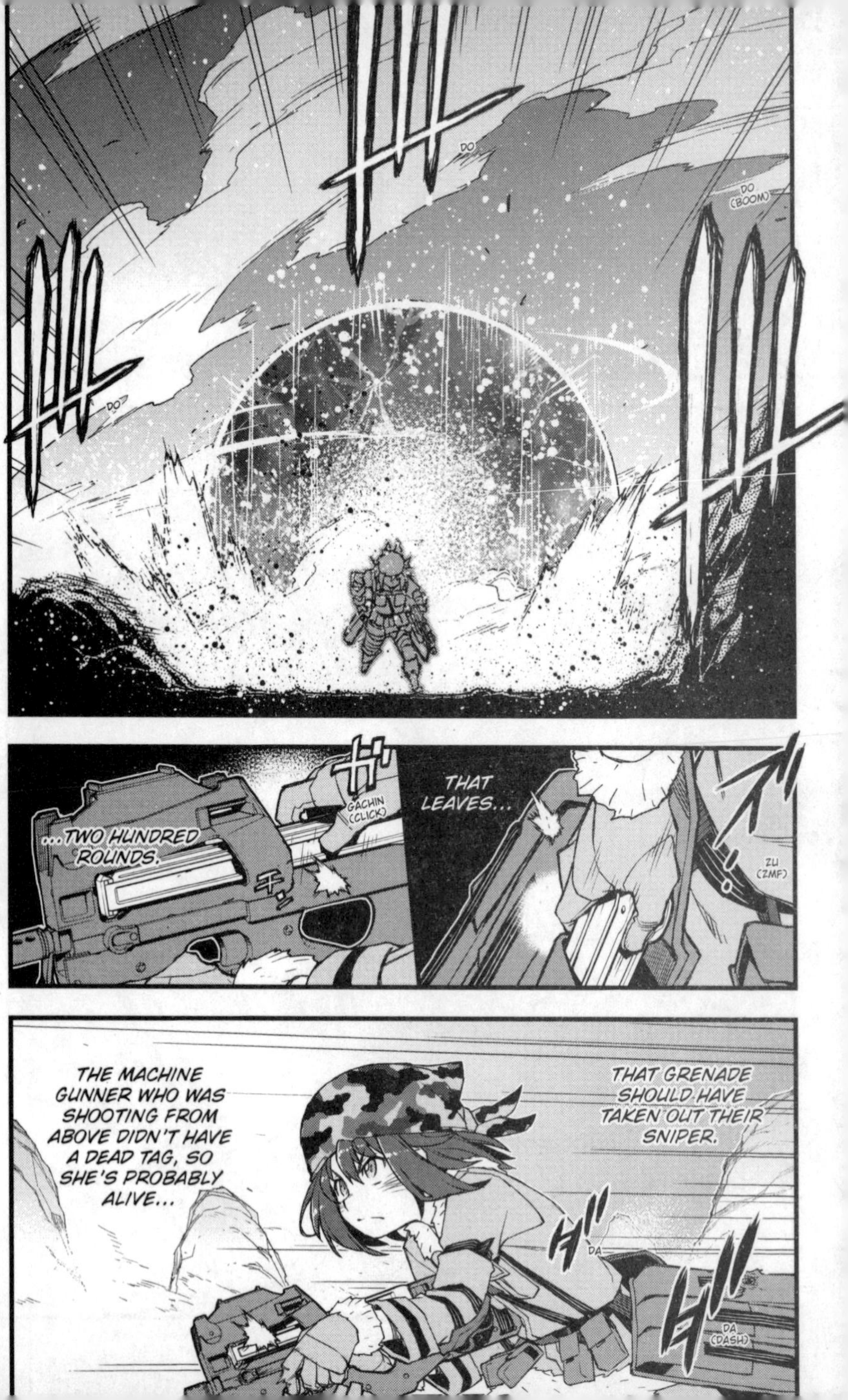
DO
DO (BOOM)
DO
THAT LEAVES...
ZU (ZMF)
GACHIN (CLICK)
...TWO HUNDRED ROUNDS.
THAT GRENADE SHOULD HAVE TAKEN OUT THEIR SNIPER.
THE MACHINE GUNNER WHO WAS SHOOTING FROM ABOVE DIDN'T HAVE A DEAD TAG, SO SHE'S PROBABLY ALIVE...
DA
DA (DASH)

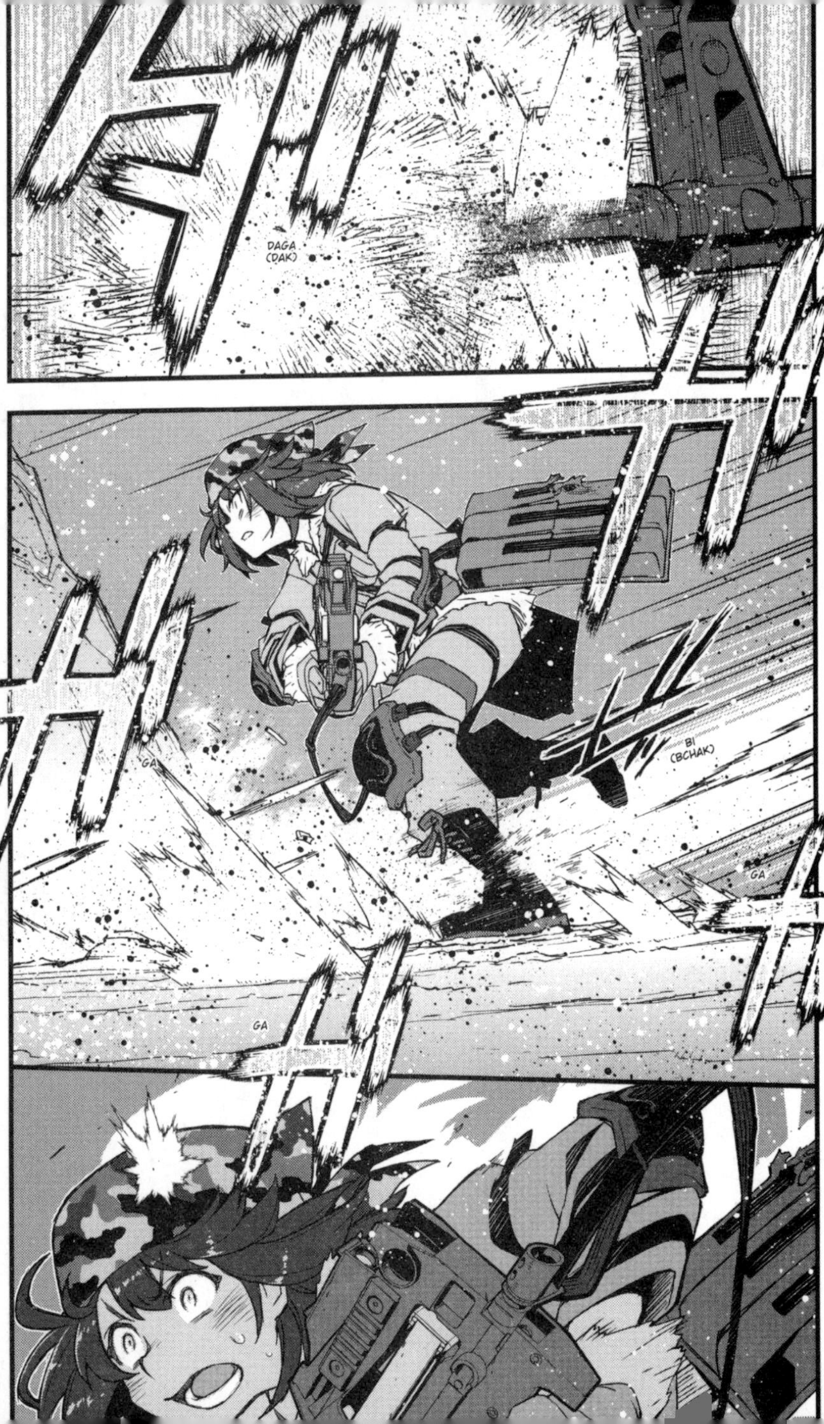
DAGA (DAK)
BI (BCHAK)
GA
GA
GA

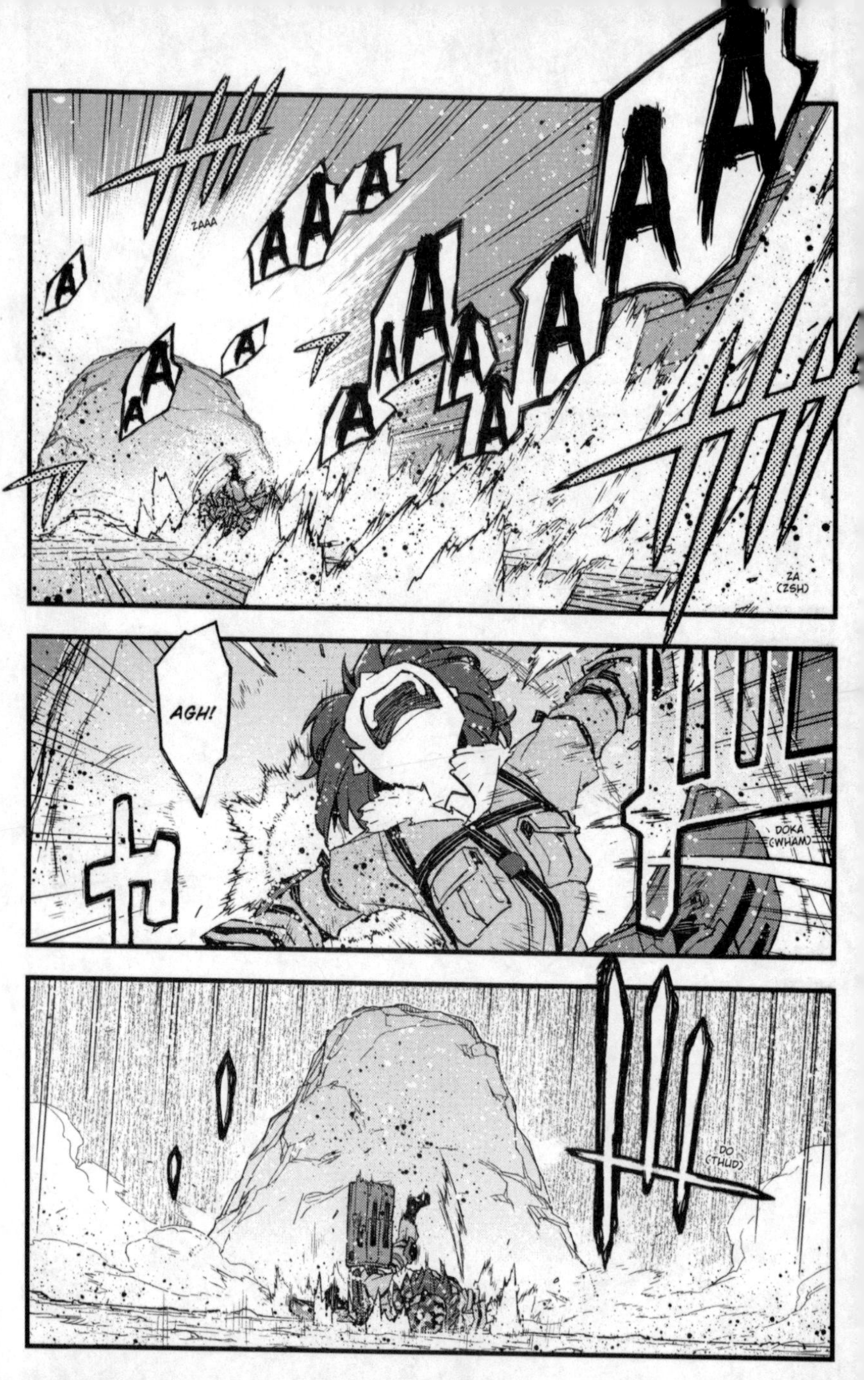
ZAAA
ZA (ZSH)
DOKA (WHAM)
AGH!
DO (THUD)

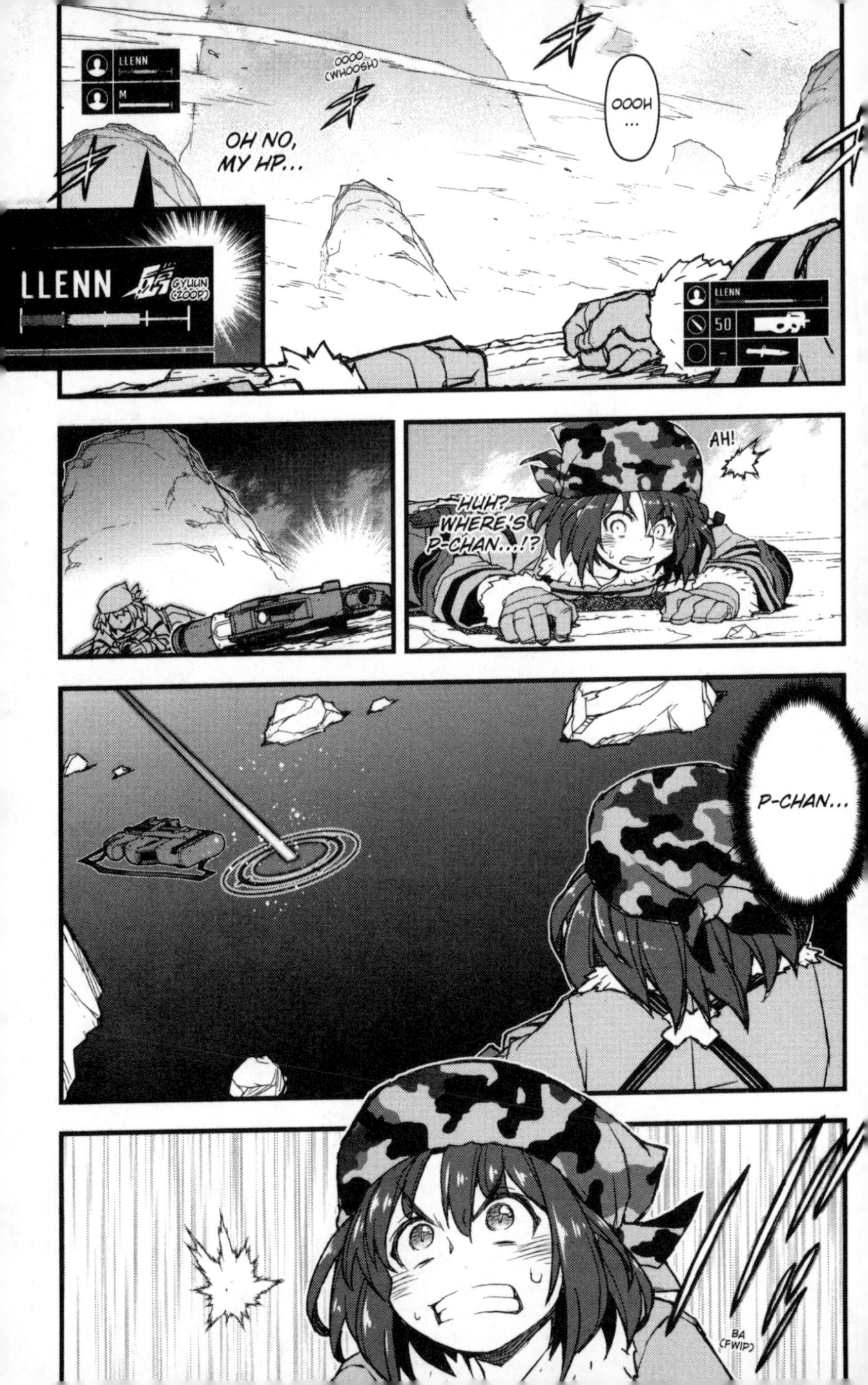
OOOH ...
OOOO (WHOOSH)
LLENN
M
OH NO, MY HP...
LLENN
GYUUN (ZOOP)
LLENN
50
AH!
HUH? WHERE'S P-CHAN...!?
P-CHAN...
BA (FWIP)

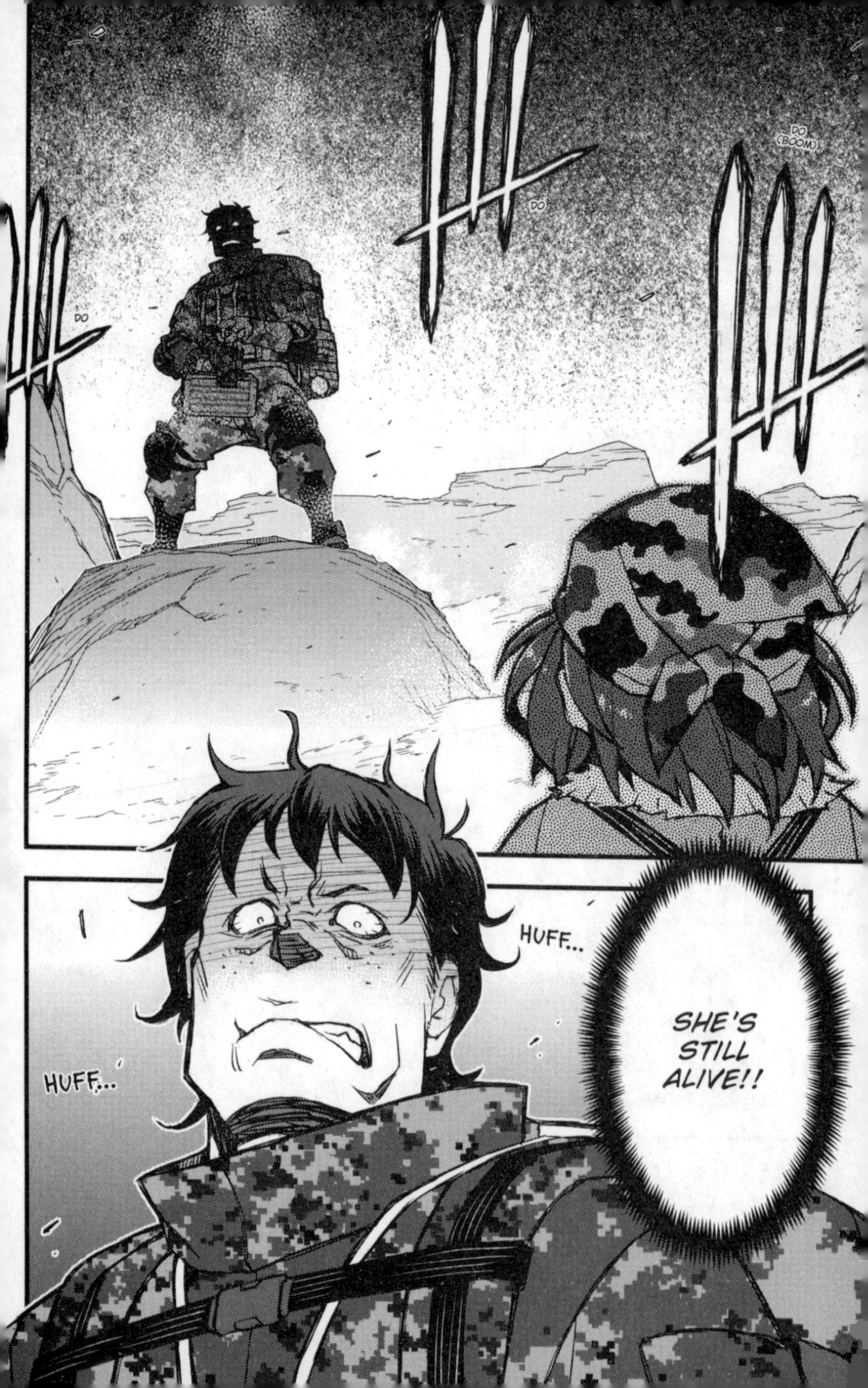

DO (BOOM)
DO
DO
SHE'S STILL ALIVE!!
HUFF...
HUFF...

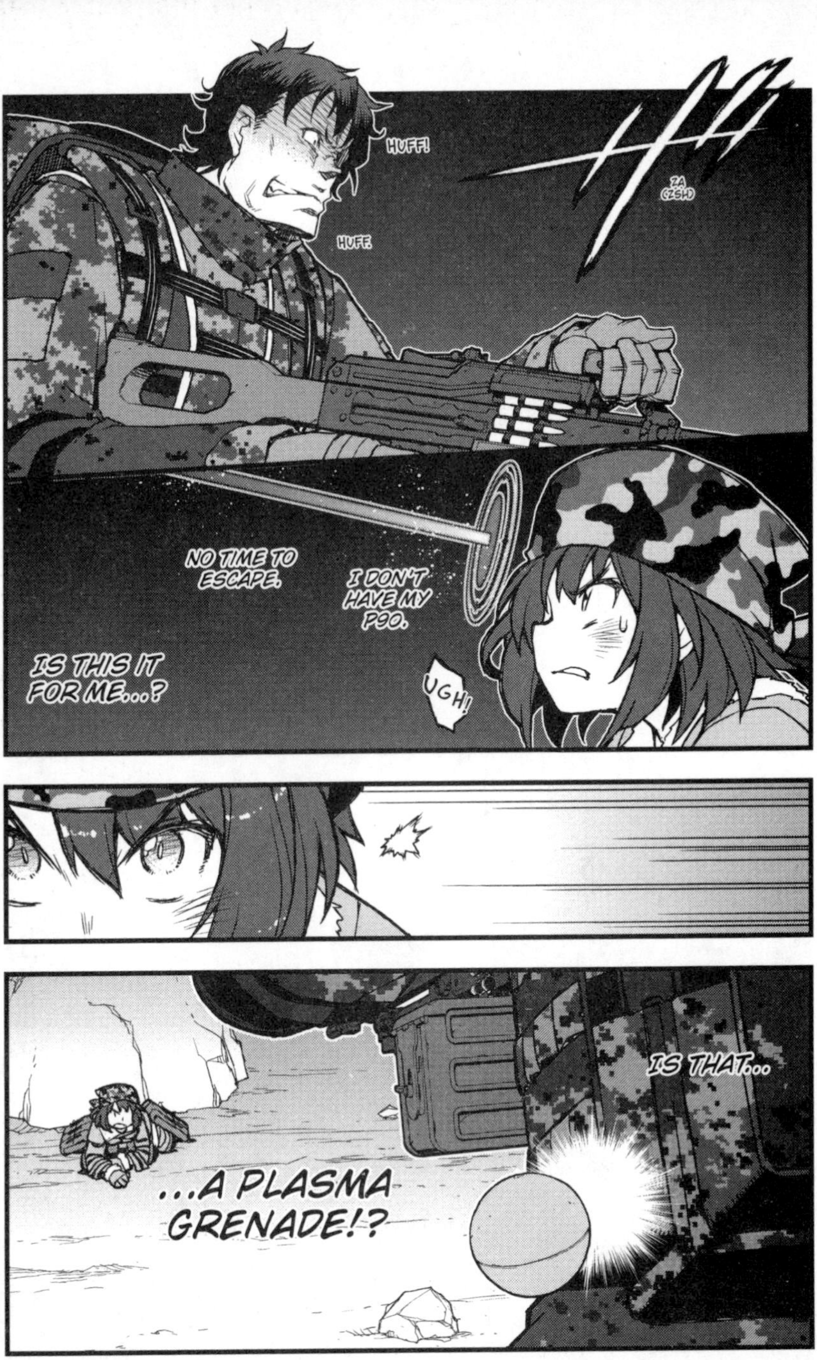
ZA
(ZSH)
HUFF!
HUFF.
I DON'T HAVE MY P90.
NO TIME TO ESCAPE.
UGH!
IS THIS IT FOR ME...?
IS THAT...
...A PLASMA GRENADE!?

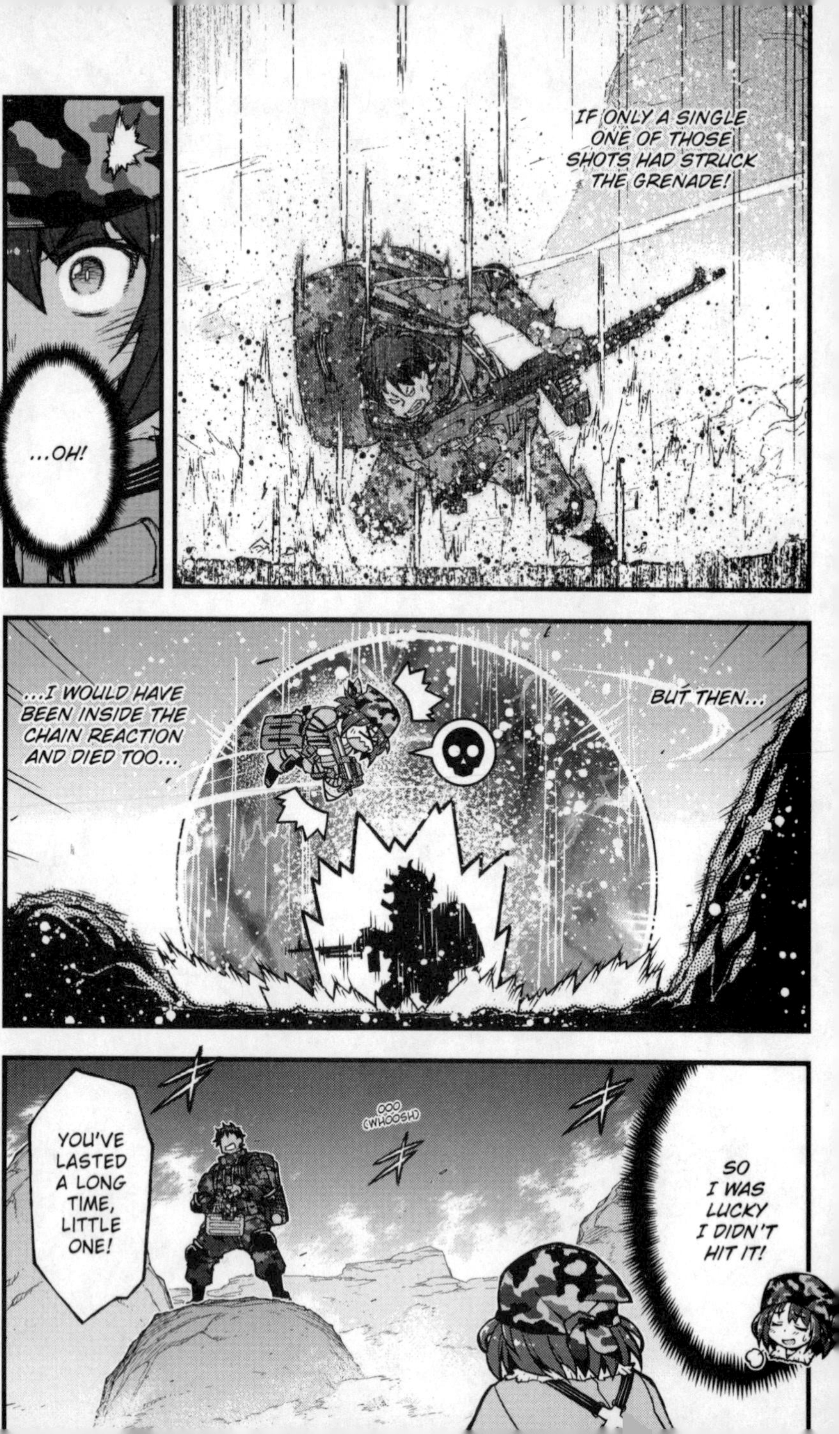
IF ONLY A SINGLE ONE OF THOSE SHOTS HAD STRUCK THE GRENADE!
...OH!
BUT THEN...
...I WOULD HAVE BEEN INSIDE THE CHAIN REACTION AND DIED TOO...
SO I WAS LUCKY I DIDN'T HIT IT!
OOO (WHOOSH)
YOU'VE LASTED A LONG TIME, LITTLE ONE!

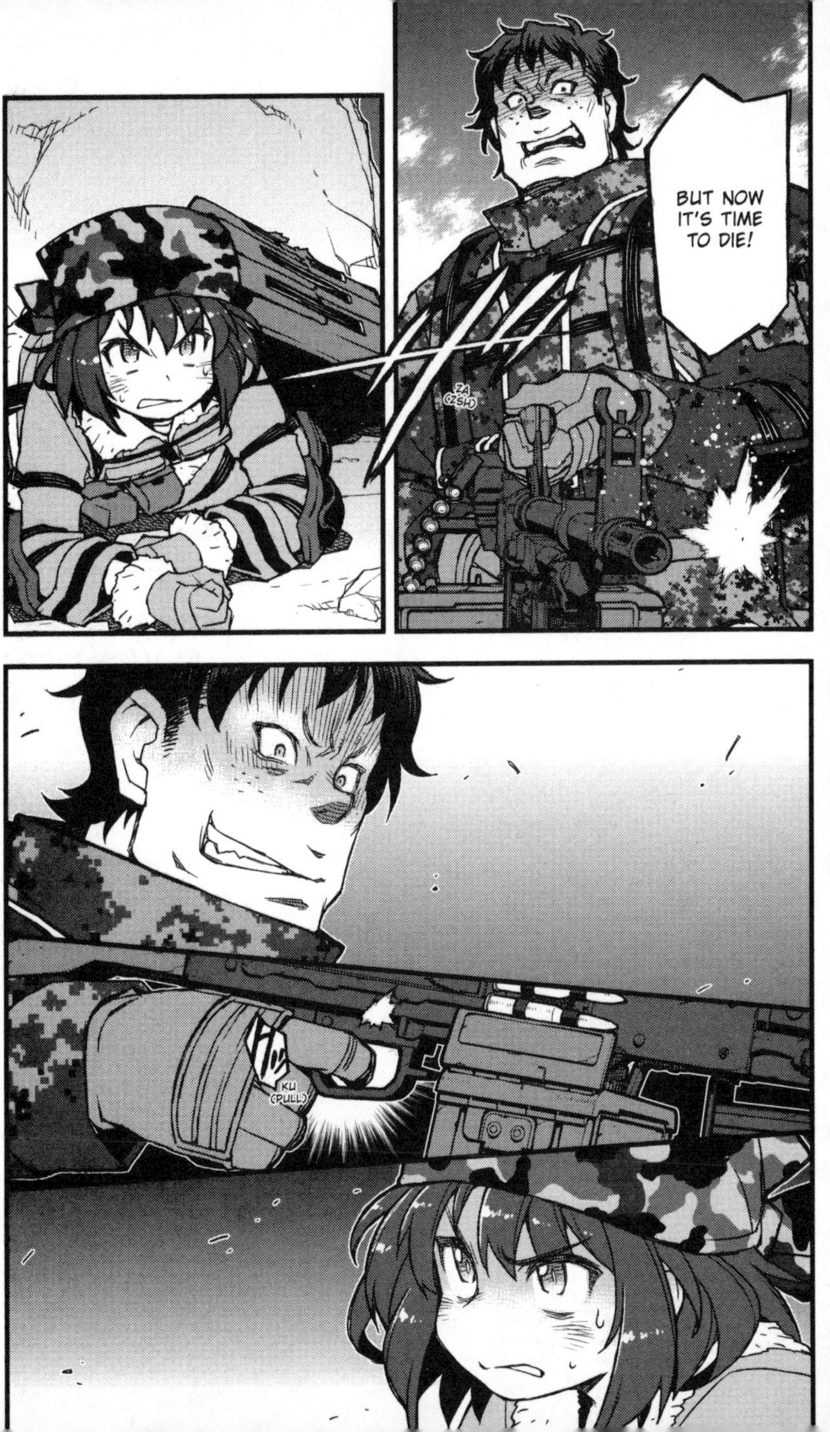
BUT NOW IT'S TIME TO DIE!
ZA (ZSH)
KU (PULL)

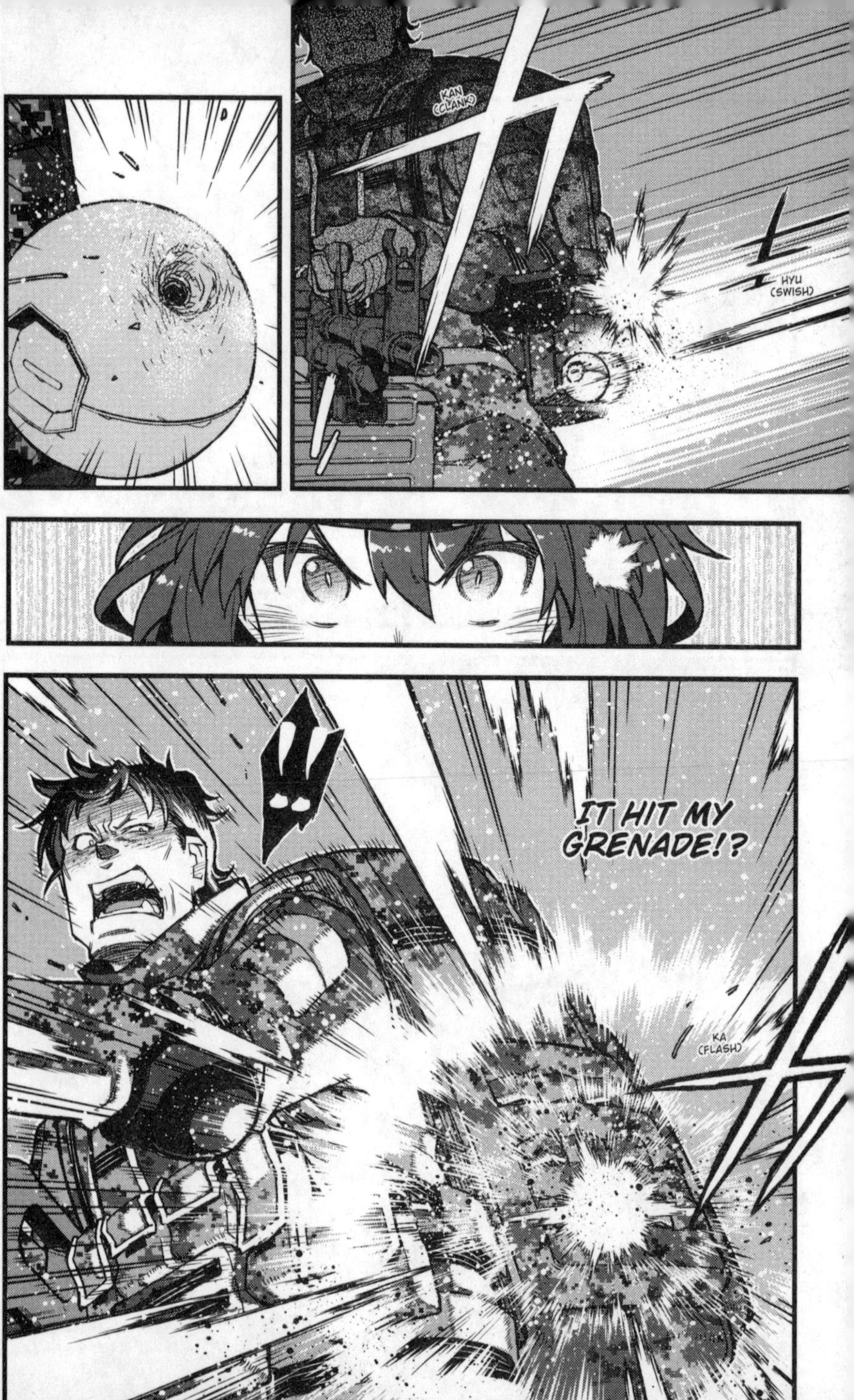
KAN (CLANK)
HYU (SWISH)
IT HIT MY GRENADE!?
KA (FLASH)

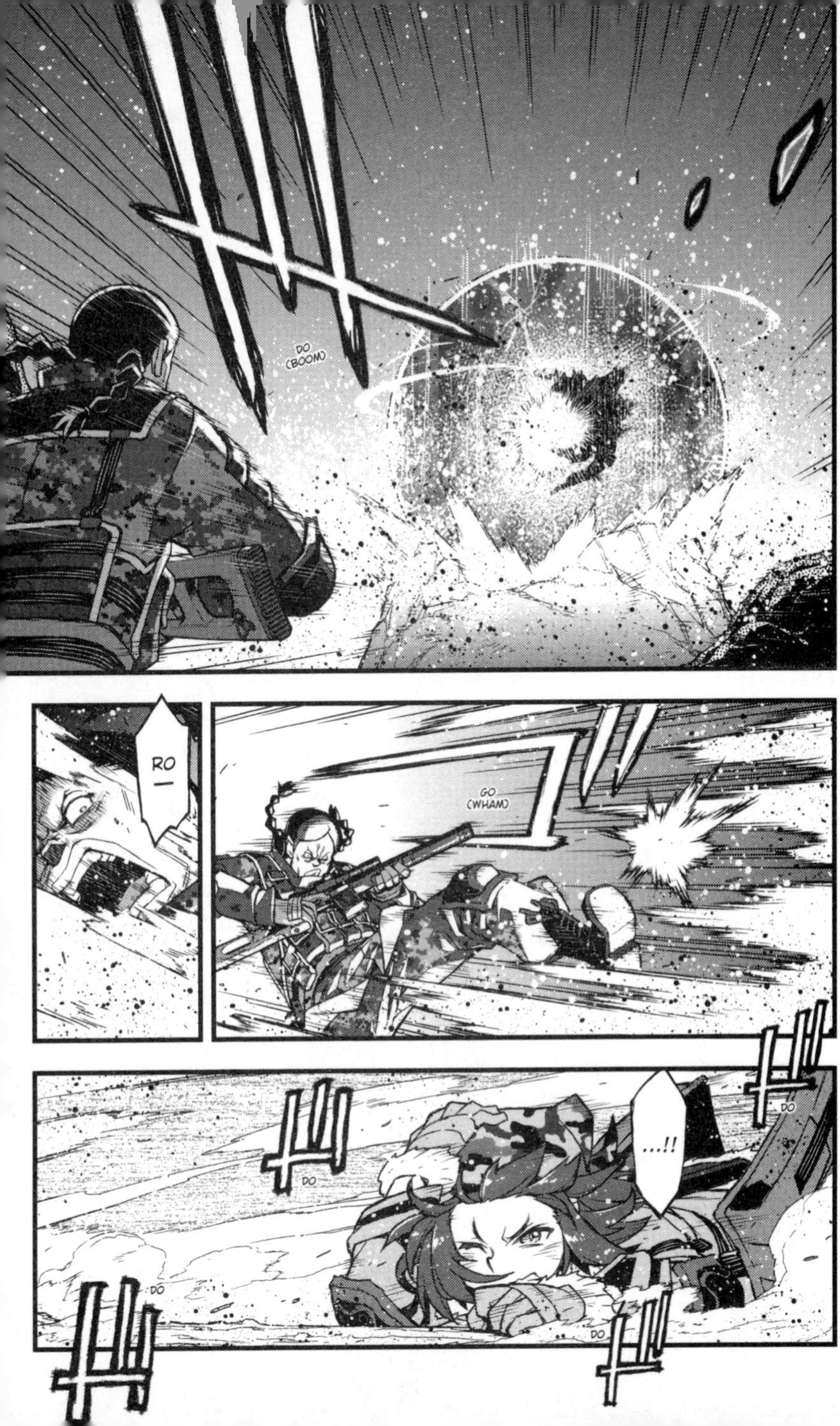
DO
(BOOM)
GO
(WHAM)
RO
—
DO
...!!
DO
DO
DO

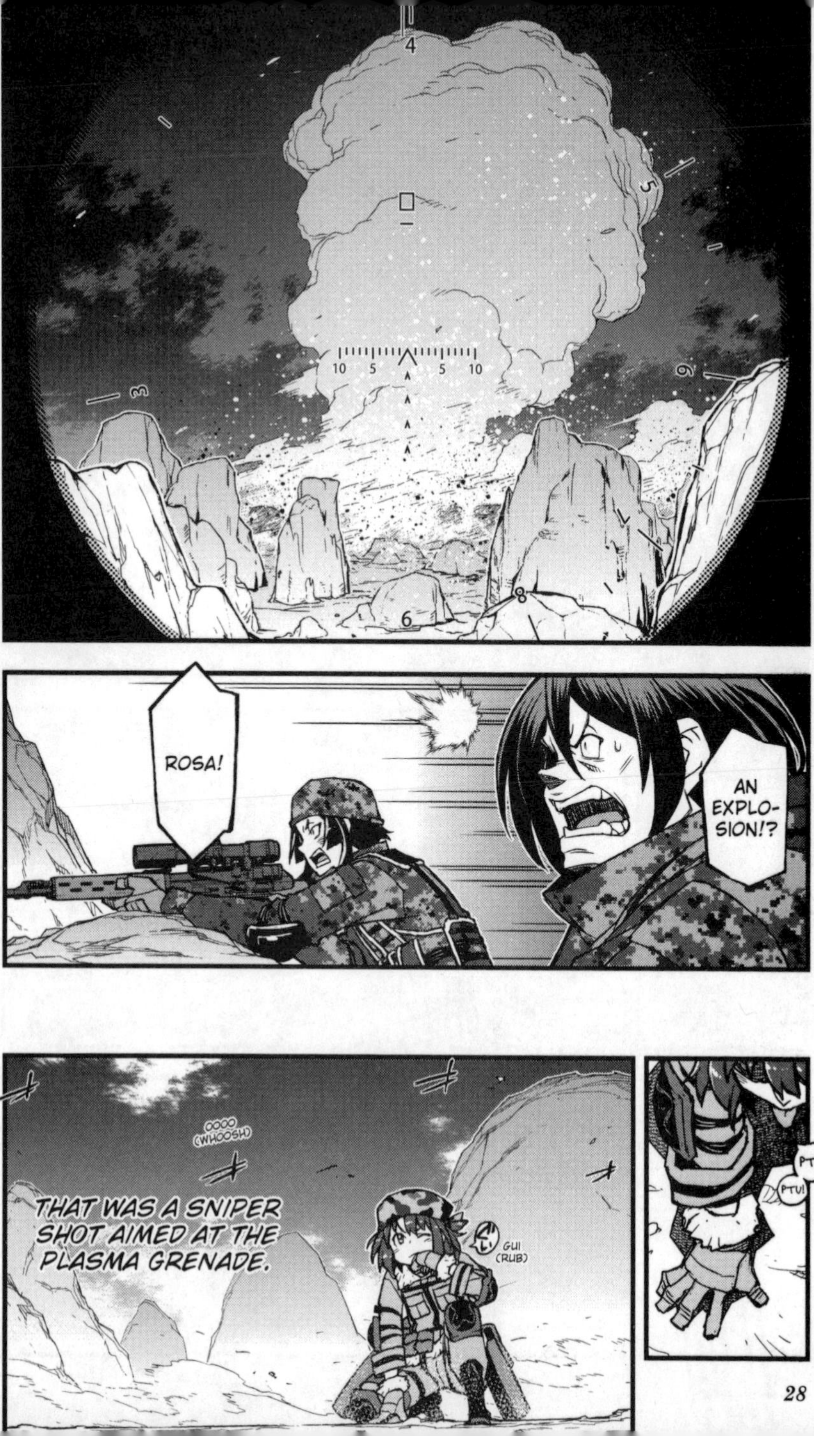
AN EXPLOSION!?
ROSA!
PTU!
PTU!
OOOO (WHOOSH)
THAT WAS A SNIPER SHOT AIMED AT THE PLASMA GRENADE.
GUI (RUB)

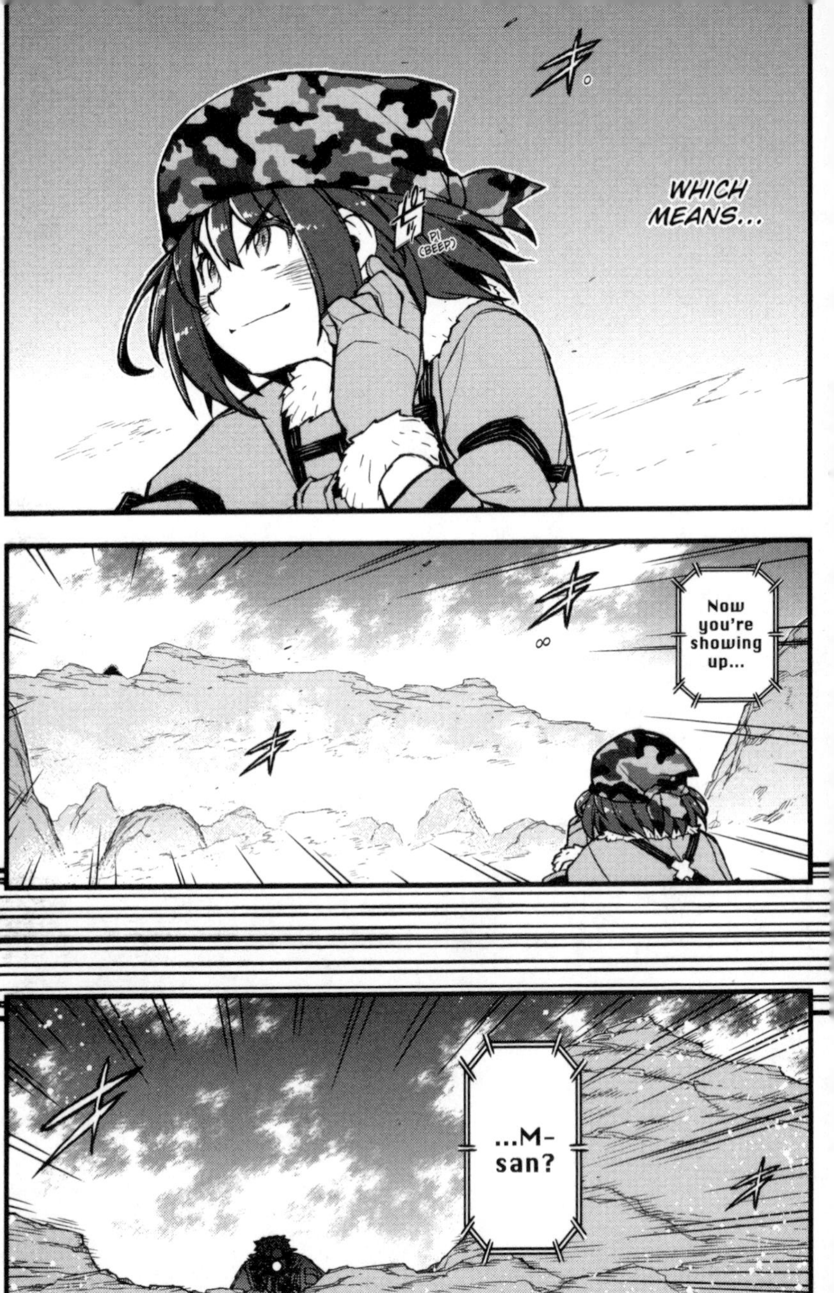
WHICH MEANS...
PI (BEEP)
Now you're showing up...
...M-san?

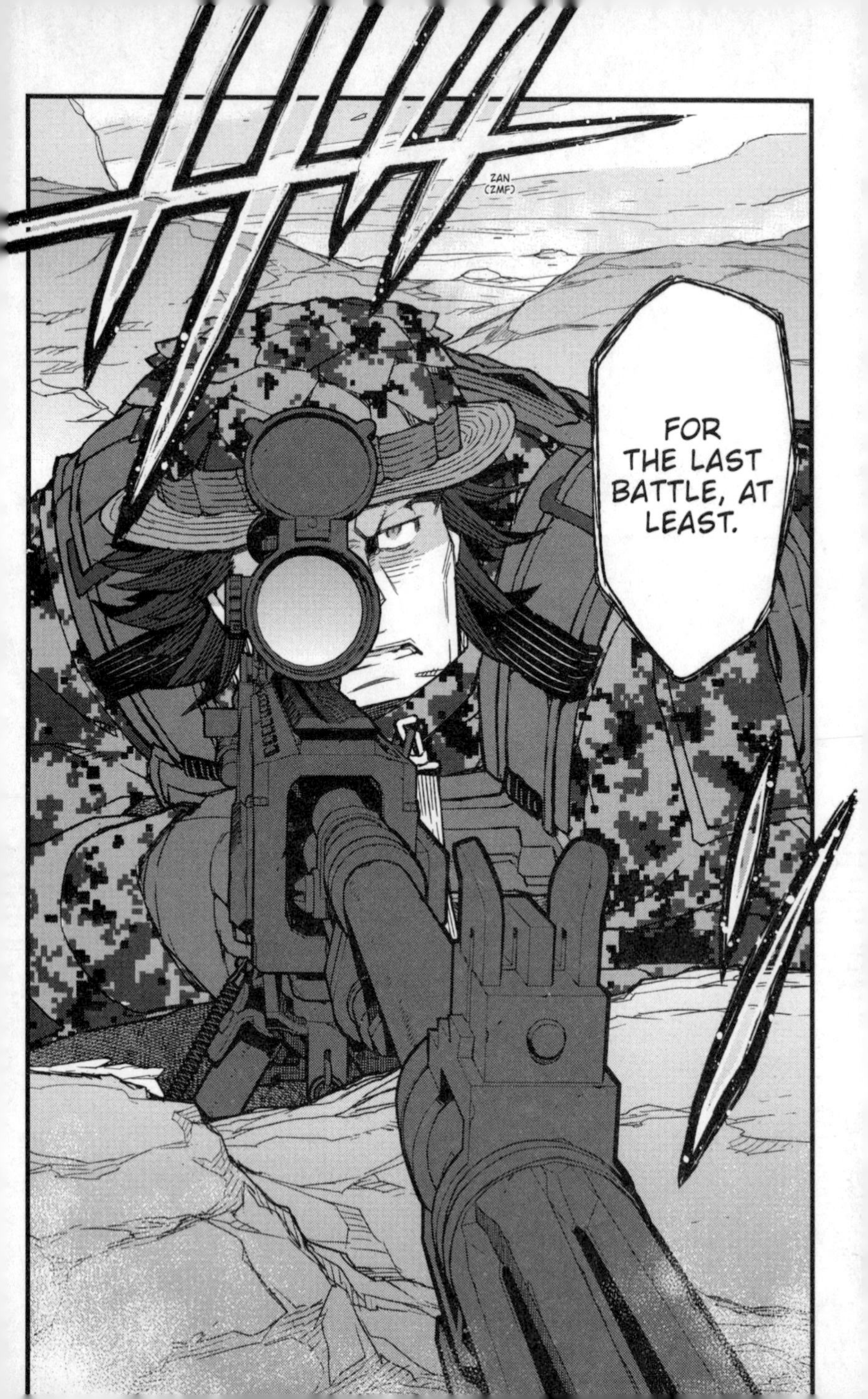
ZAN (ZMF)
FOR THE LAST BATTLE, AT LEAST.

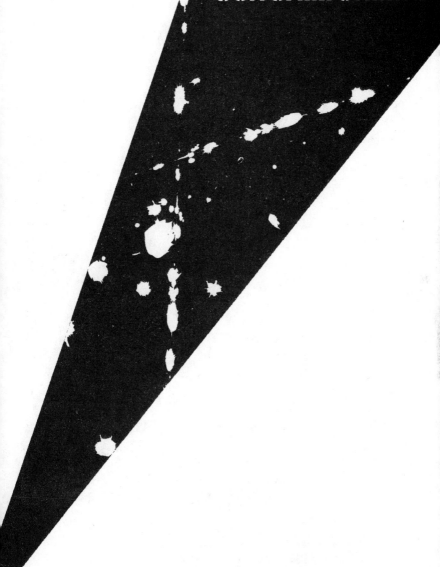

SWORD ART ONLINE ALTERNATIVE
GUN GALE ONLINE

SWORD ART ONLINE ALTERNATIVE
GUN GALE ONLINE

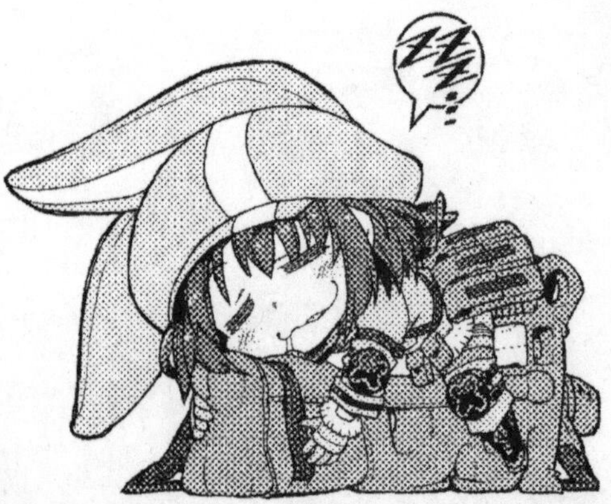
ZZZ

LINK #017: SQUAD JAM ⑬

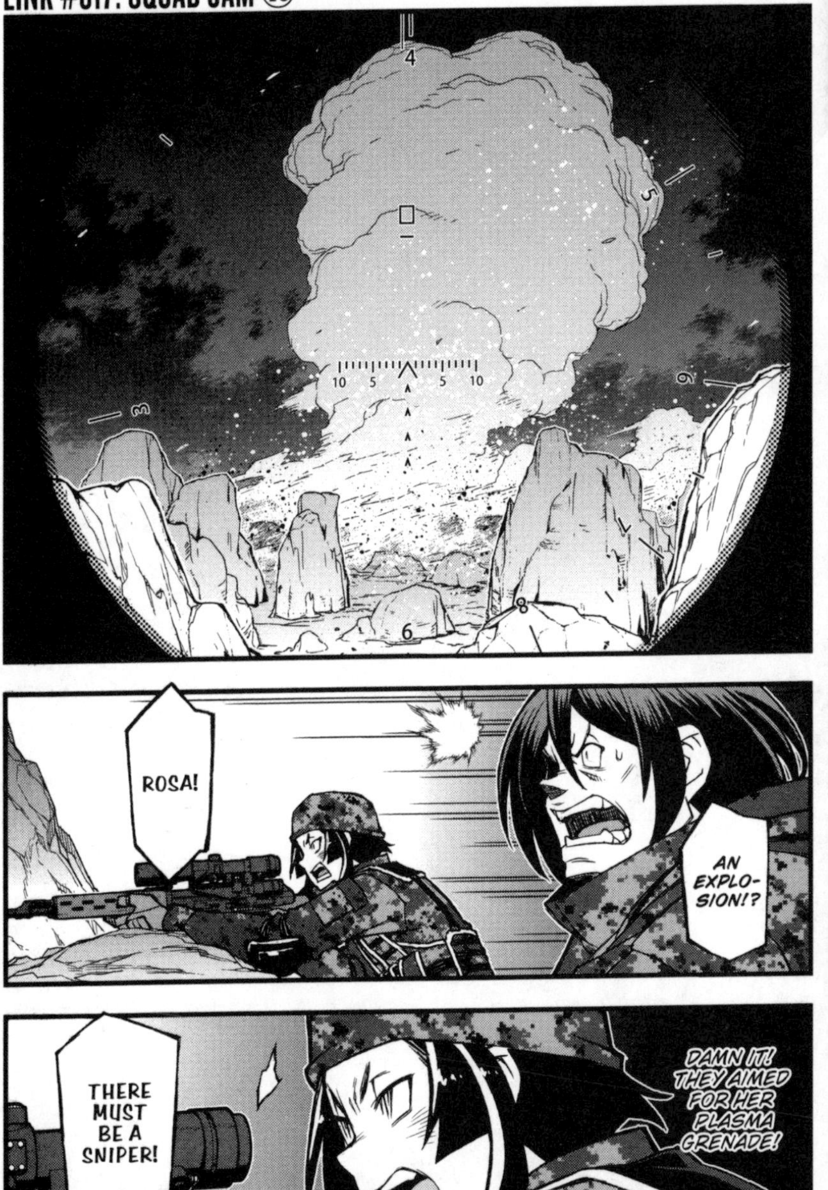
AN EXPLOSION!?
ROSA!
DAMN IT! THEY AIMED FOR HER PLASMA GRENADE!
THERE MUST BE A SNIPER!

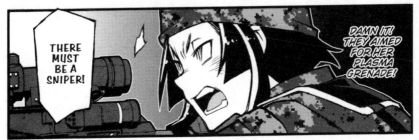

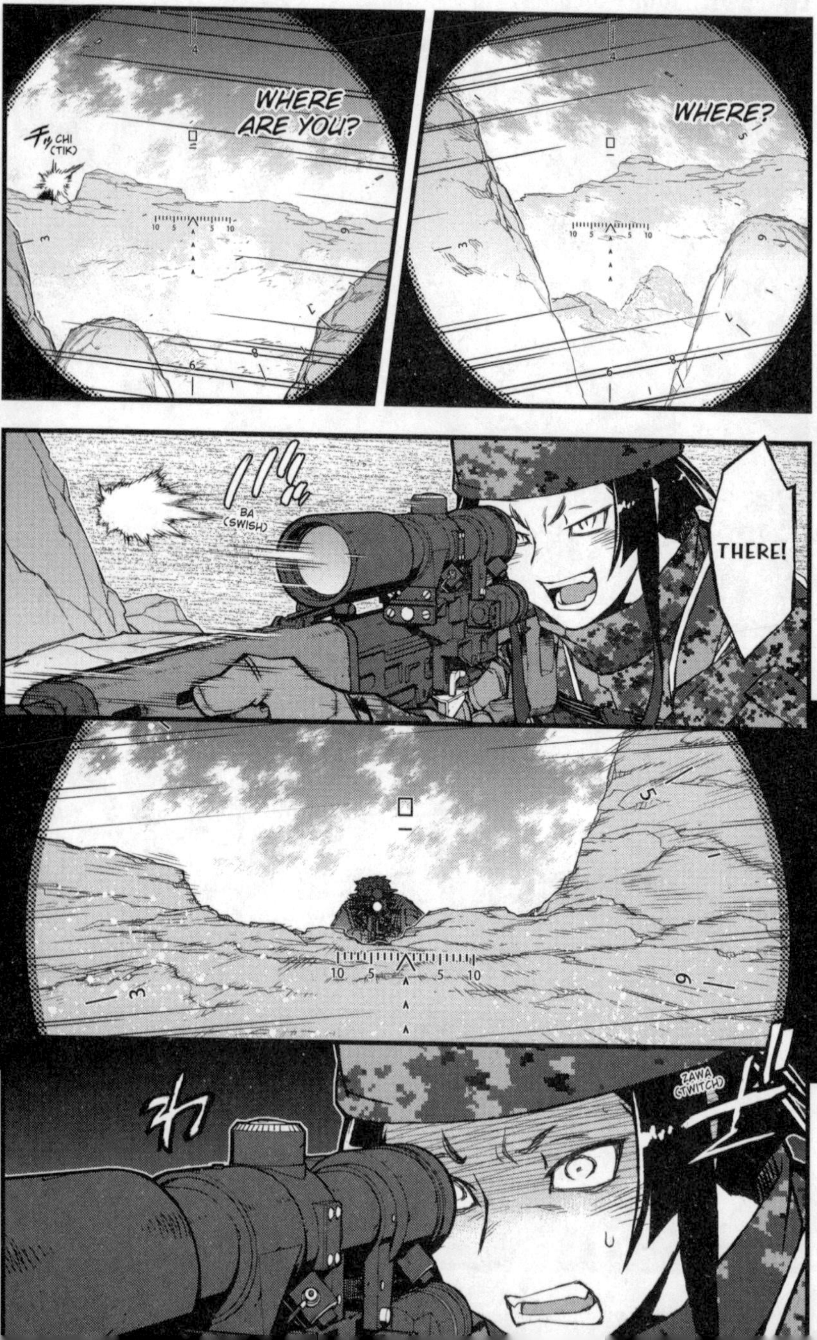
WHERE?
WHERE ARE YOU?
CHI (TIK)
THERE!
BA (SWISH)
ZAWA (TWITCH)

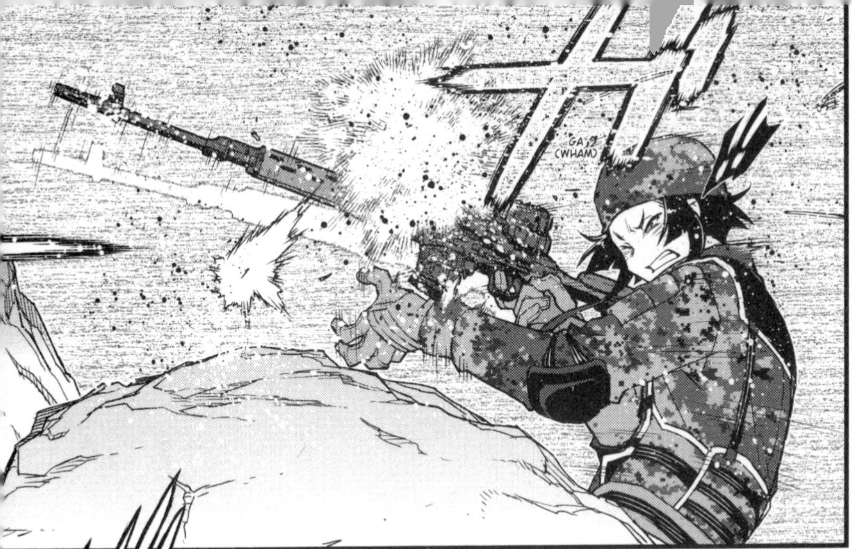
GA (WHAM)

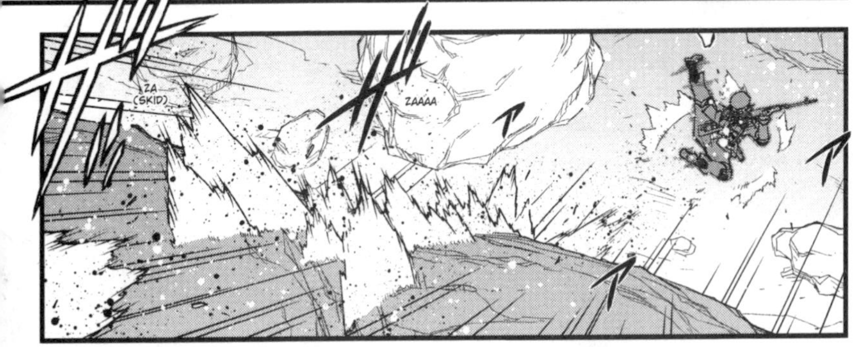
ZA (SKID)
ZAAAA

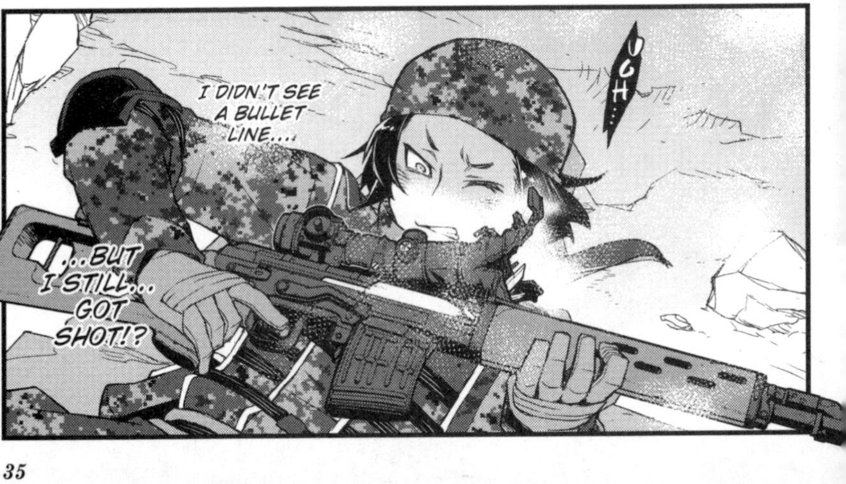
UGH...
I DIDN'T SEE A BULLET LINE....
...BUT I STILL... GOT SHOT!?

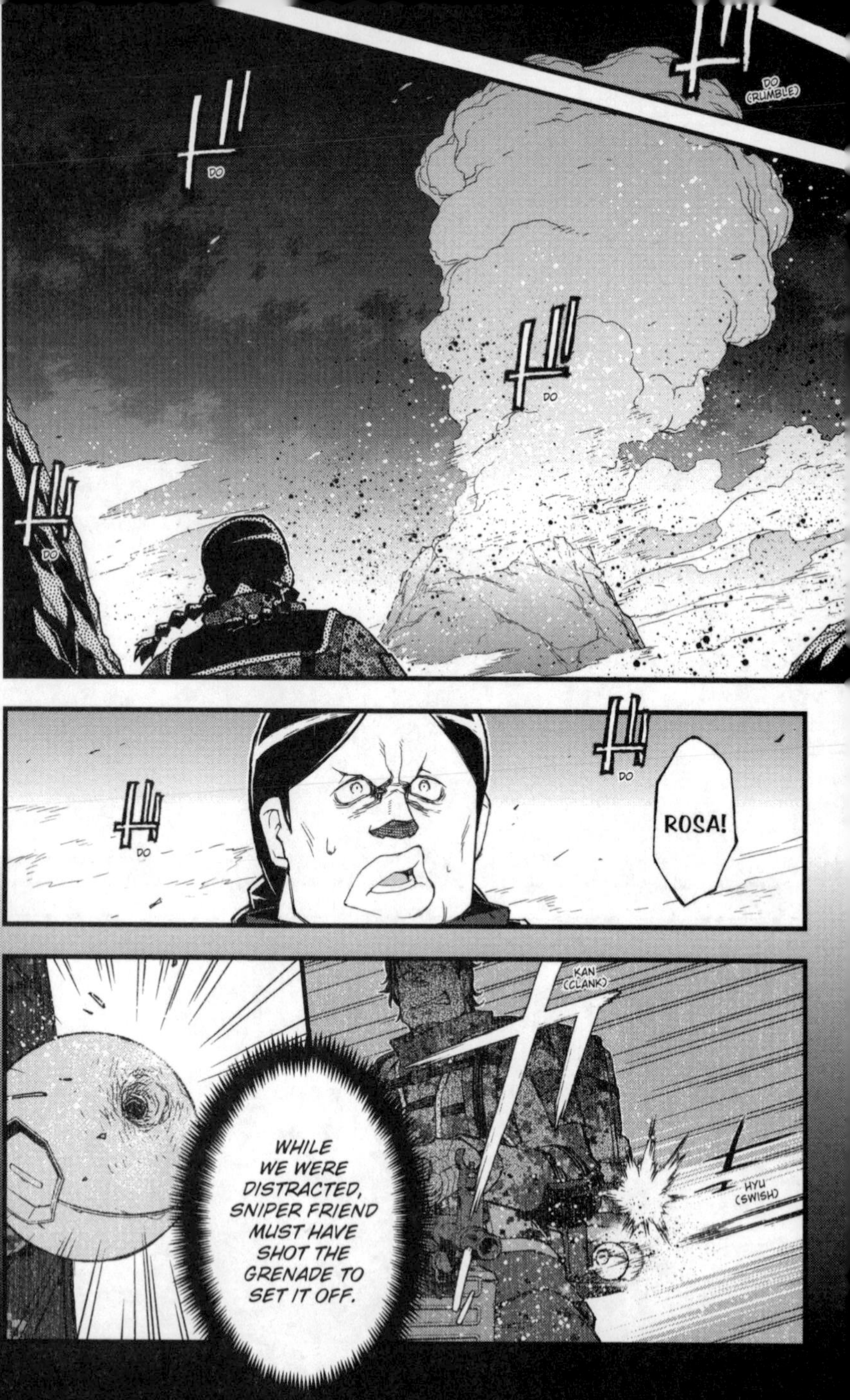
DO (RUMBLE)
DO
DO
DO
DO
ROSA!
DO
KAN (CLANK)
HYU (SWISH)
WHILE WE WERE DISTRACTED, SNIPER FRIEND MUST HAVE SHOT THE GRENADE TO SET IT OFF.

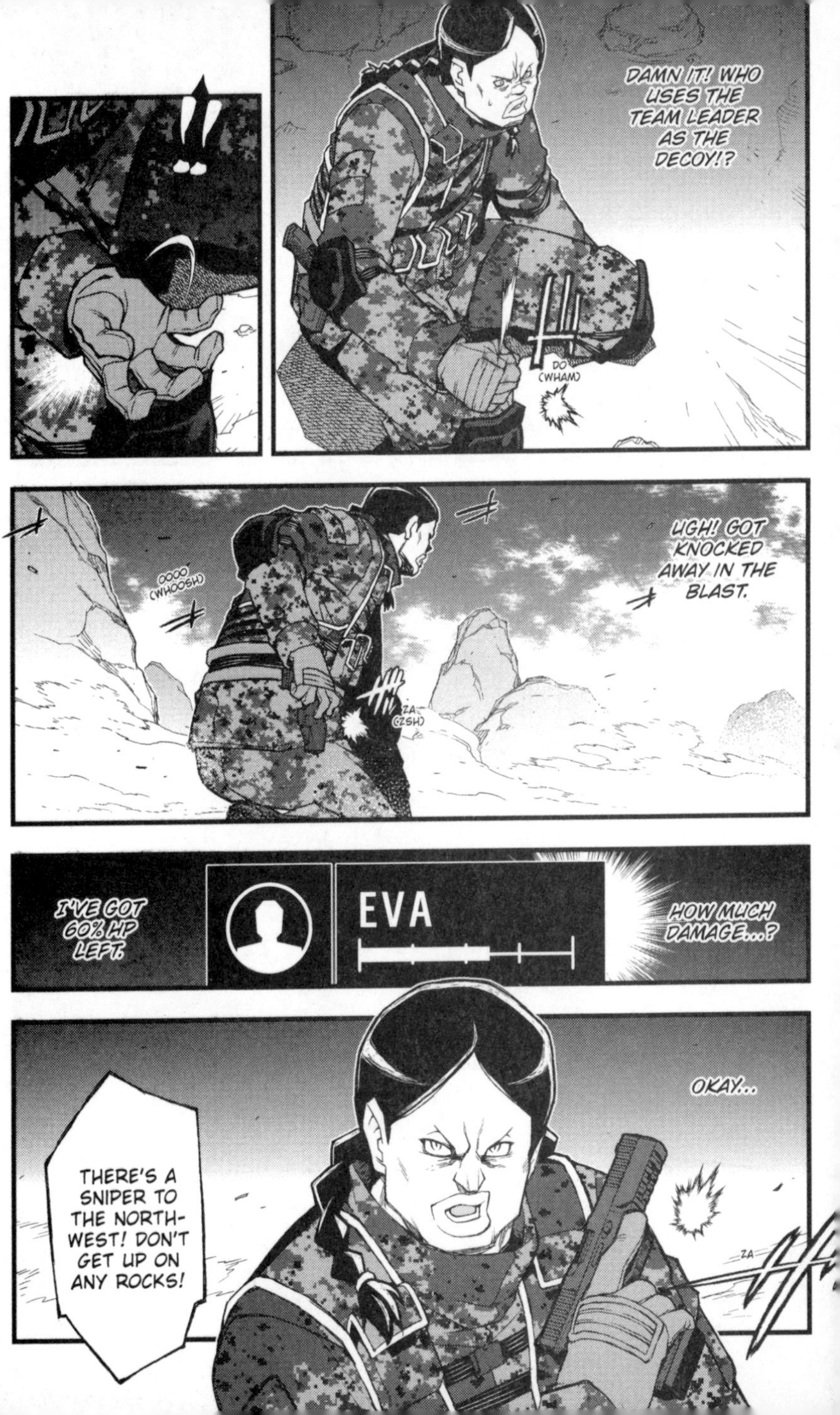
DAMN IT! WHO USES THE TEAM LEADER AS THE DECOY!?
DO (WHAM)
!!
UGH! GOT KNOCKED AWAY IN THE BLAST.
OOOO (WHOOSH)
ZA (ZSH)
HOW MUCH DAMAGE...?
EVA
I'VE GOT 60% HP LEFT.
OKAY...
ZA
THERE'S A SNIPER TO THE NORTH-WEST! DON'T GET UP ON ANY ROCKS!

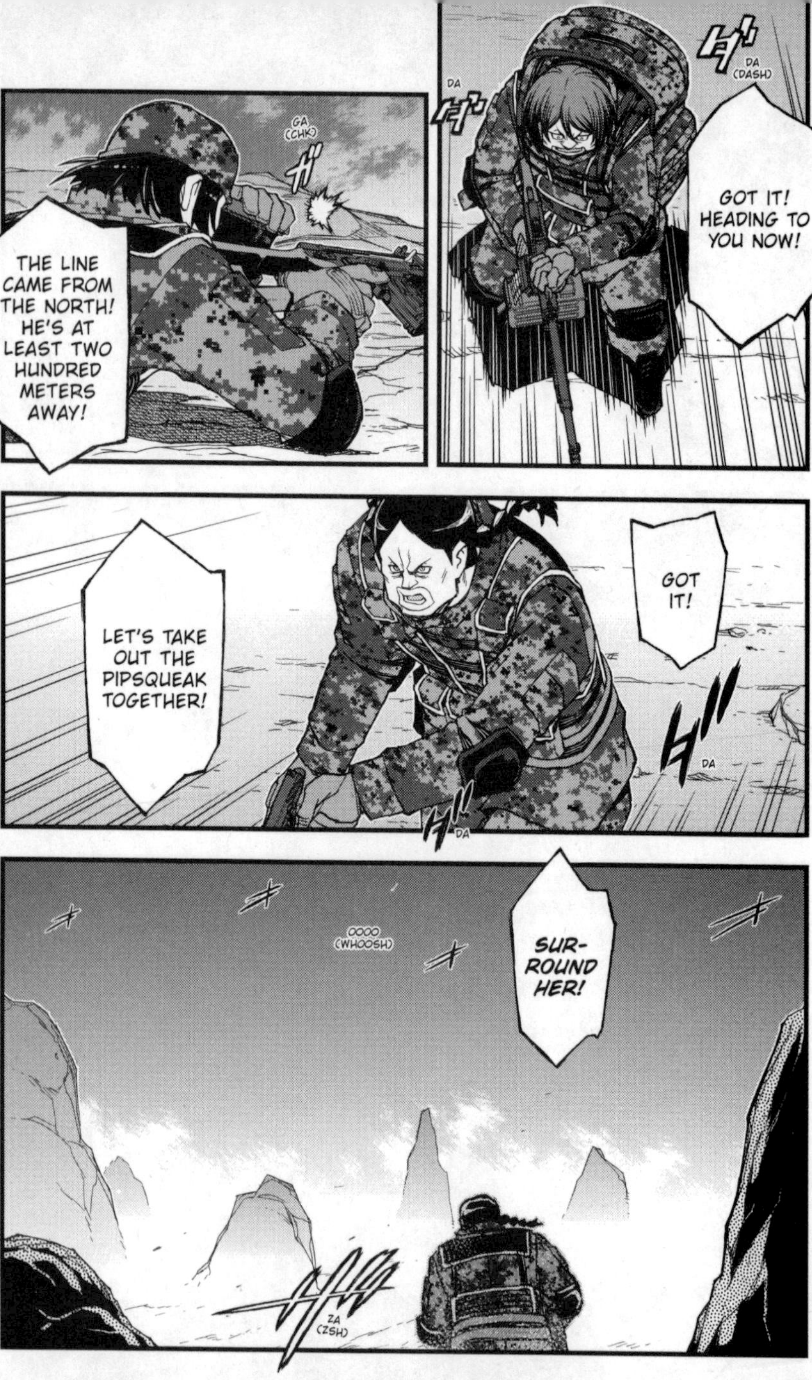
DA (DASH)
DA
GOT IT! HEADING TO YOU NOW!
GA (CHK)
THE LINE CAME FROM THE NORTH! HE'S AT LEAST TWO HUNDRED METERS AWAY!
GOT IT!
DA
LET'S TAKE OUT THE PIPSQUEAK TOGETHER!
DA
SUR-ROUND HER!
OOOO (WHOOSH)
ZA (ZSH)

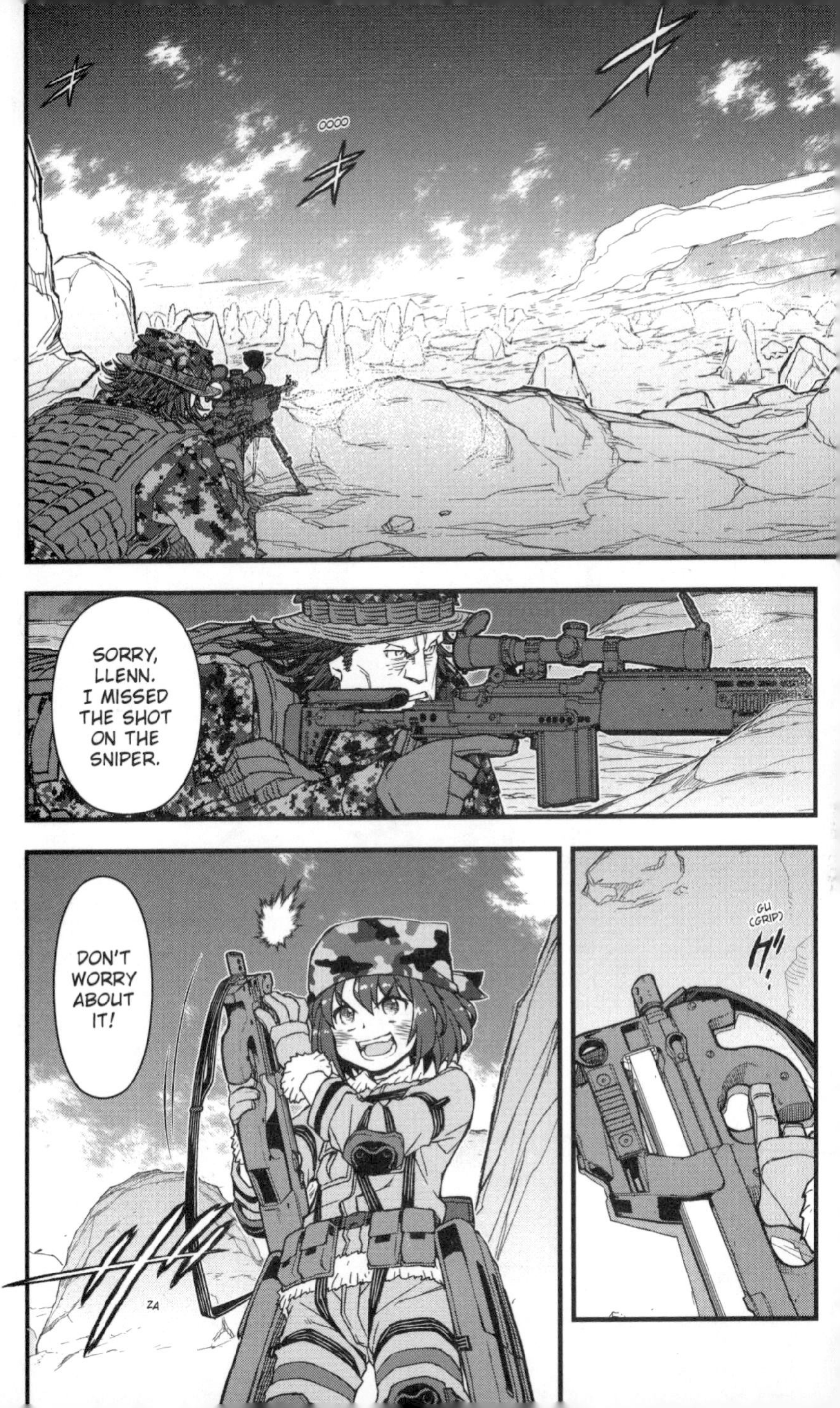
OOOO
SORRY, LLENN. I MISSED THE SHOT ON THE SNIPER.
GU (GRIP)
DON'T WORRY ABOUT IT!
ZA

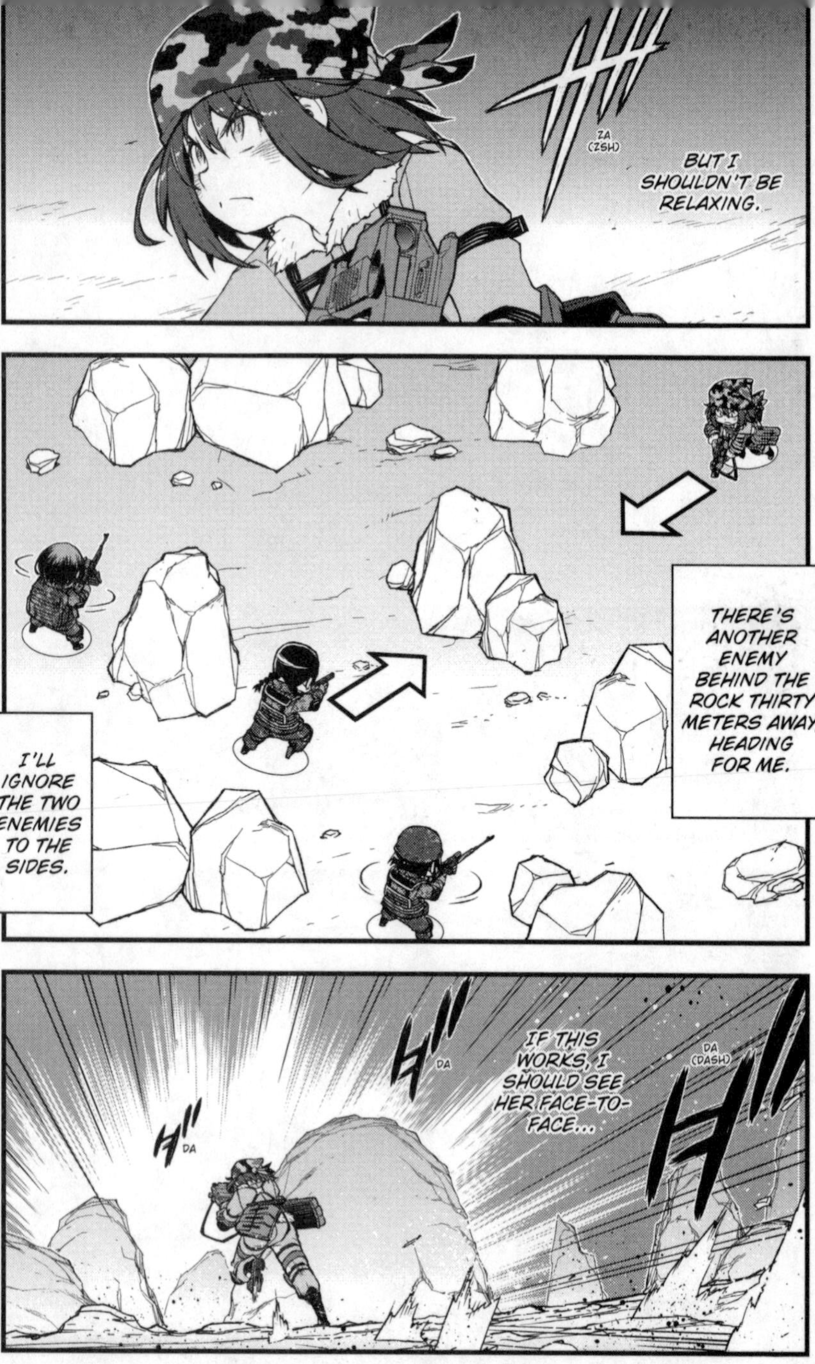
ZA (ZSH)
BUT I SHOULDN'T BE RELAXING.
THERE'S ANOTHER ENEMY BEHIND THE ROCK THIRTY METERS AWAY, HEADING FOR ME.
I'LL IGNORE THE TWO ENEMIES TO THE SIDES.
DA (DASH)
IF THIS WORKS, I SHOULD SEE HER FACE-TO-FACE...
DA
DA

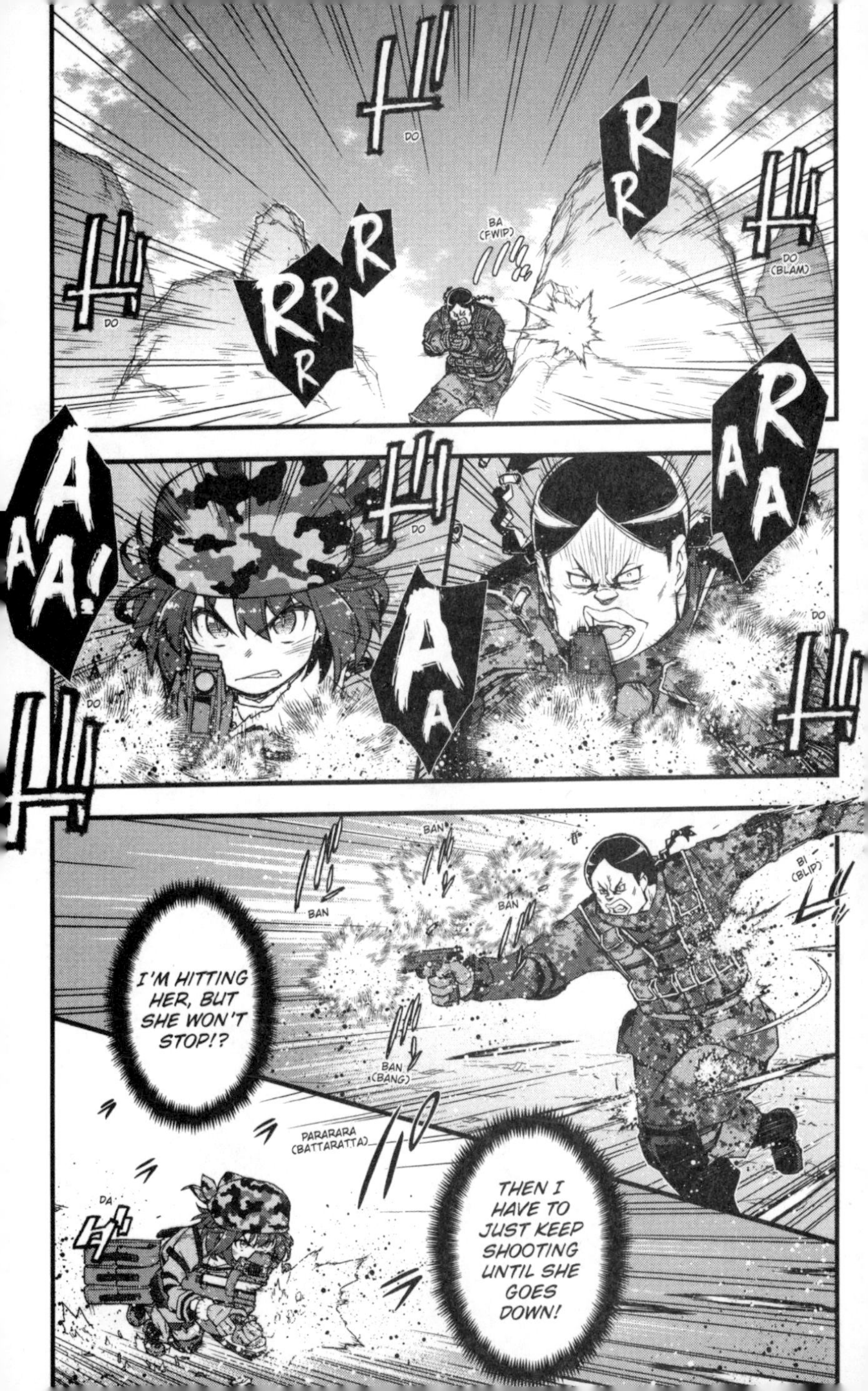
DO
(BLAM)
RRR
BA
(FWIP)
DO
RRRR
DO
RAA
DO
AA
DO
AAA!
DO
BI
(BLIP)
BAN
BAN
BAN
I'M HITTING HER, BUT SHE WON'T STOP!?
BAN
(BANG)
PARARARA
(BATTARATTA)
THEN I HAVE TO JUST KEEP SHOOTING UNTIL SHE GOES DOWN!
DA

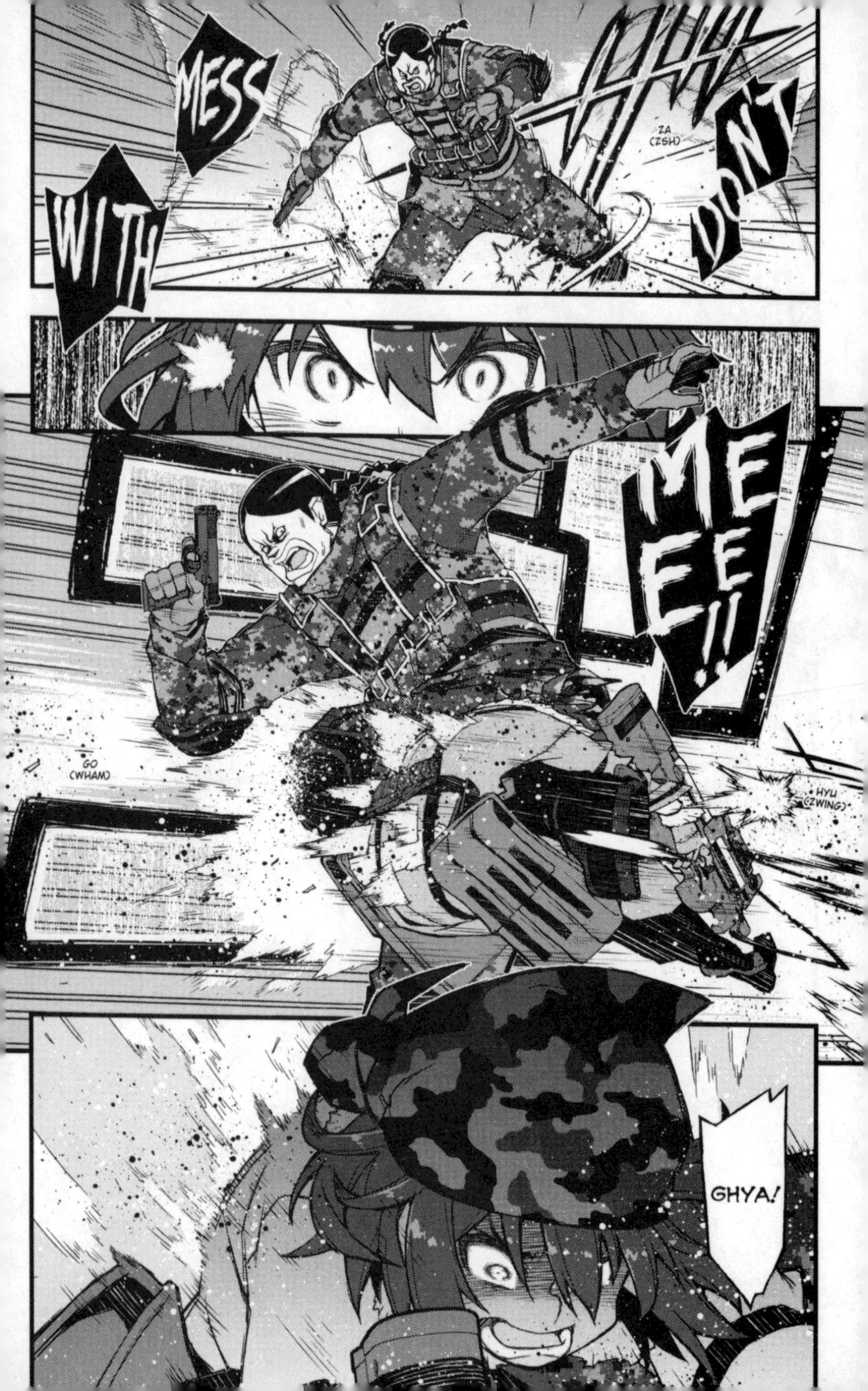
DON'T
AHH
ZA (ZSH)
MESS
WITH
MEEE!!
HYU (ZWING)
GO (WHAM)
GHYA!

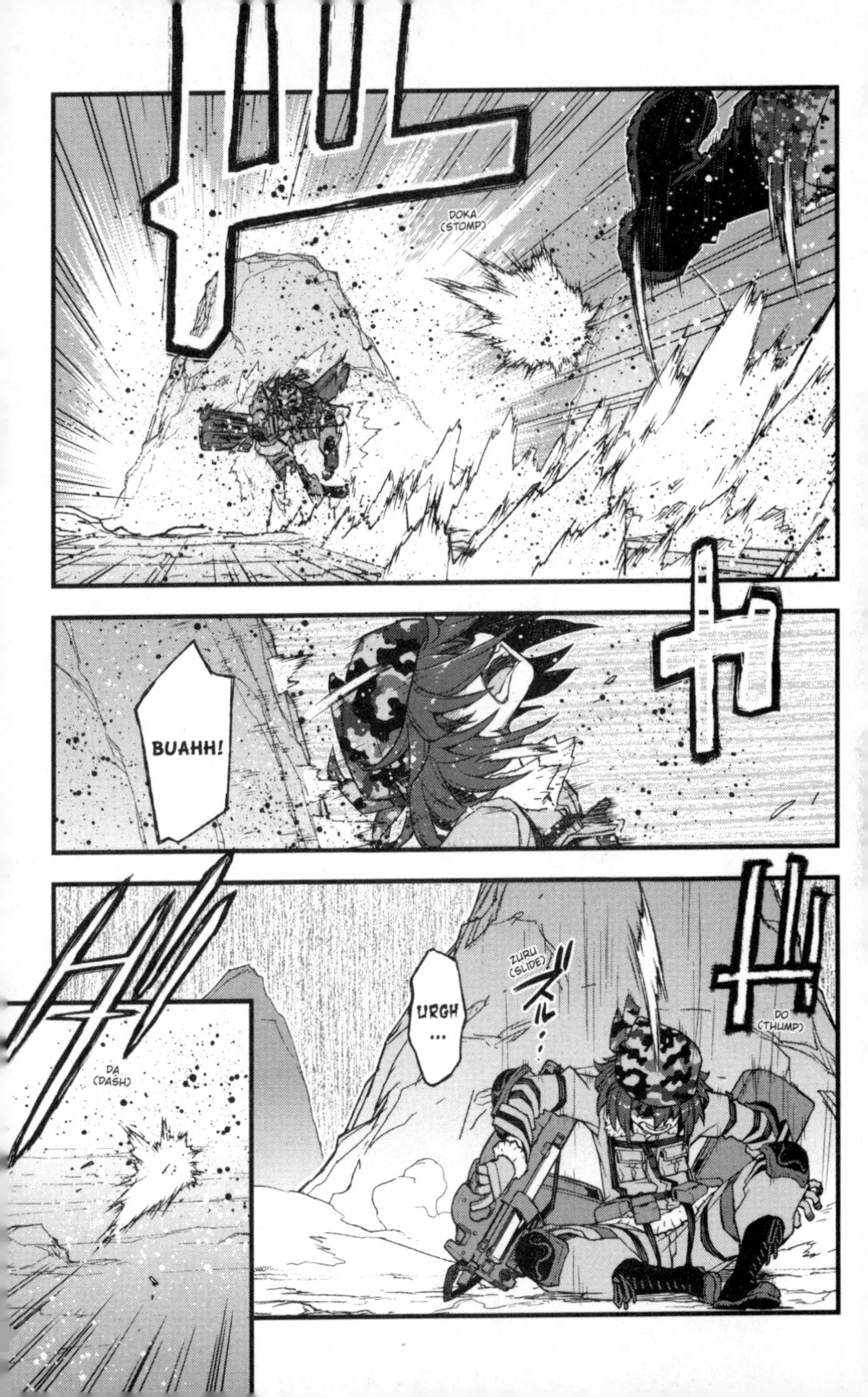
DOKA
(STOMP)
BUAHH!
DO
(THUMP)
ZURU
(SLIDE)
URGH
...
DA
(DASH)

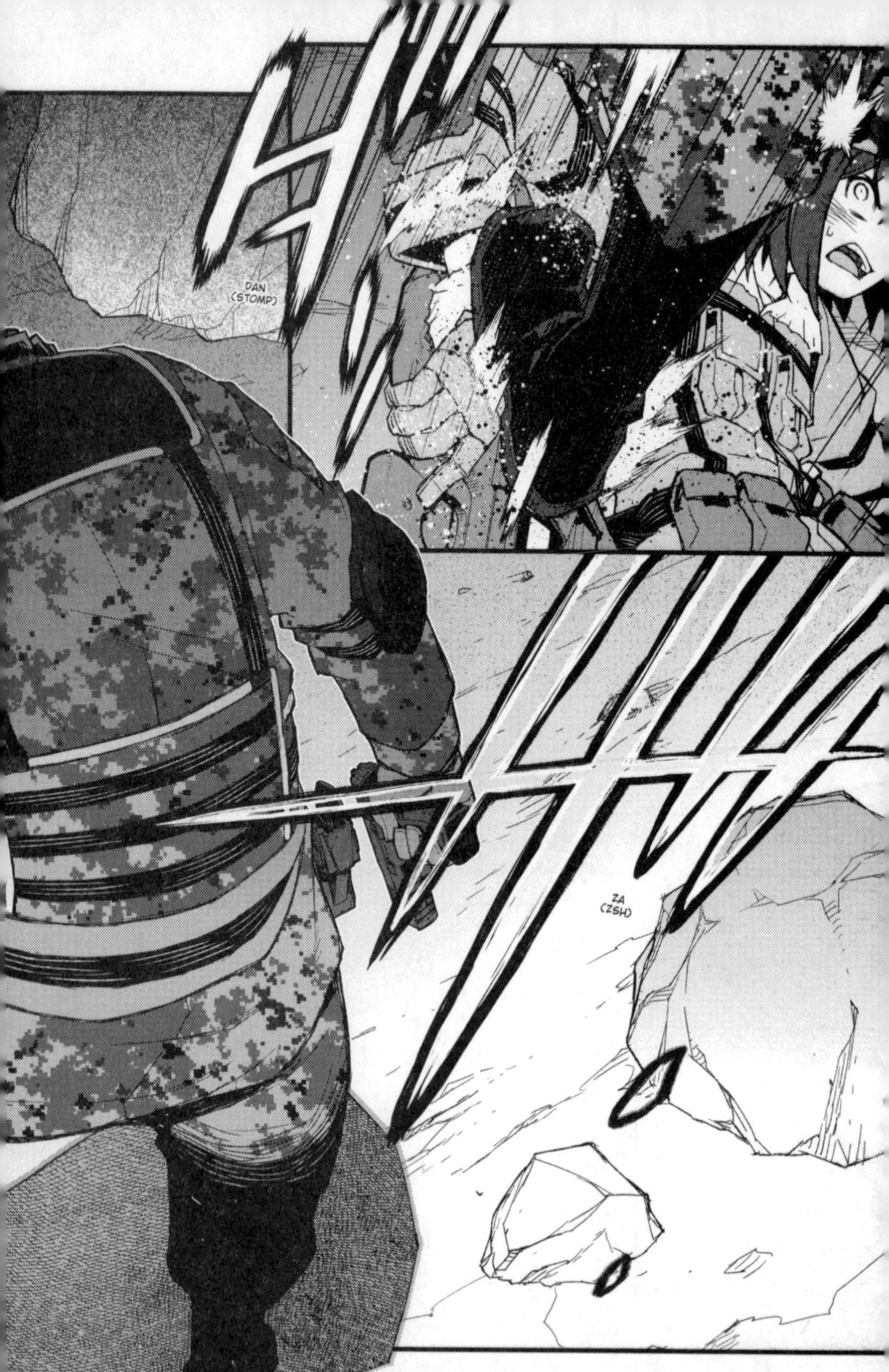
DAN
(STOMP)
ZA
(ZSH)

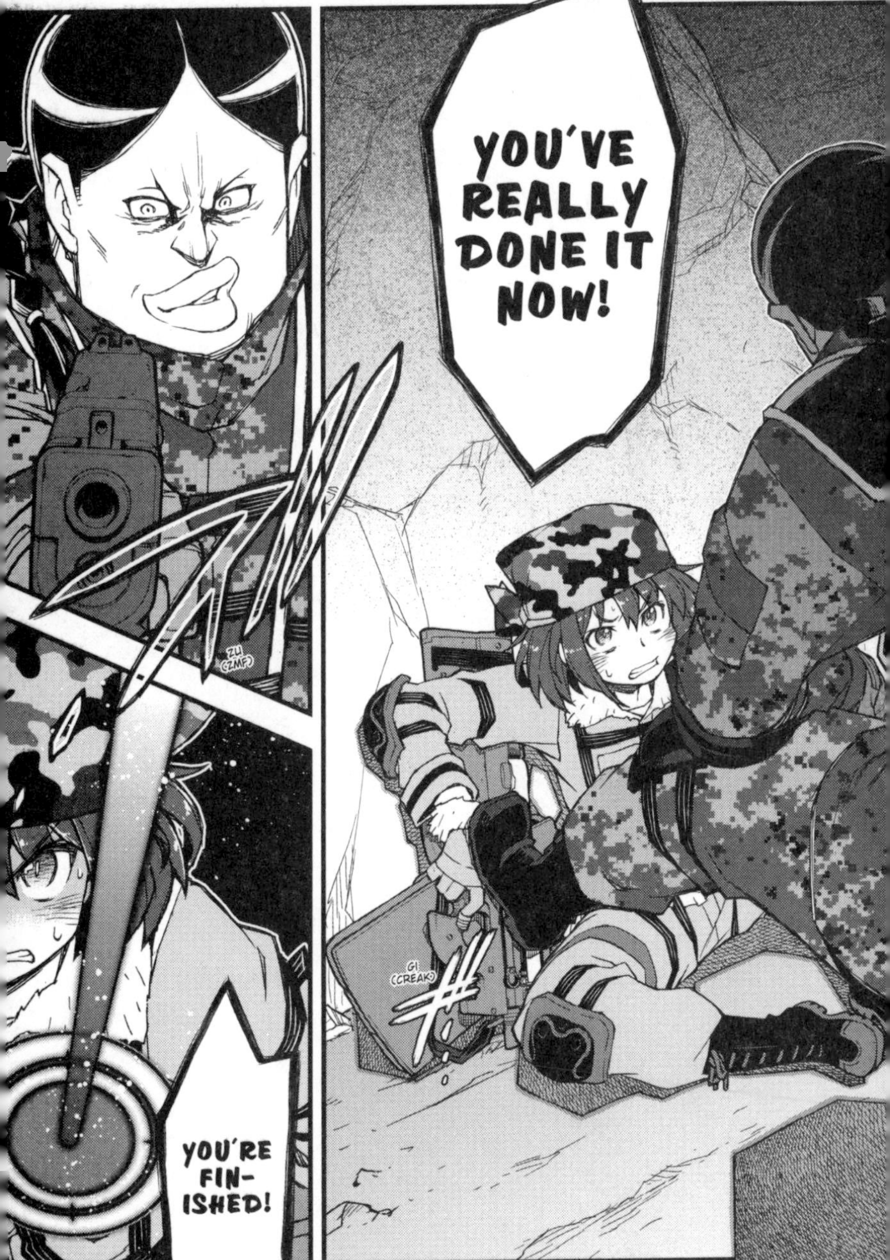
YOU'VE REALLY DONE IT NOW!
GI (CREAK)
ZU (ZMF)
YOU'RE FIN-ISHED!

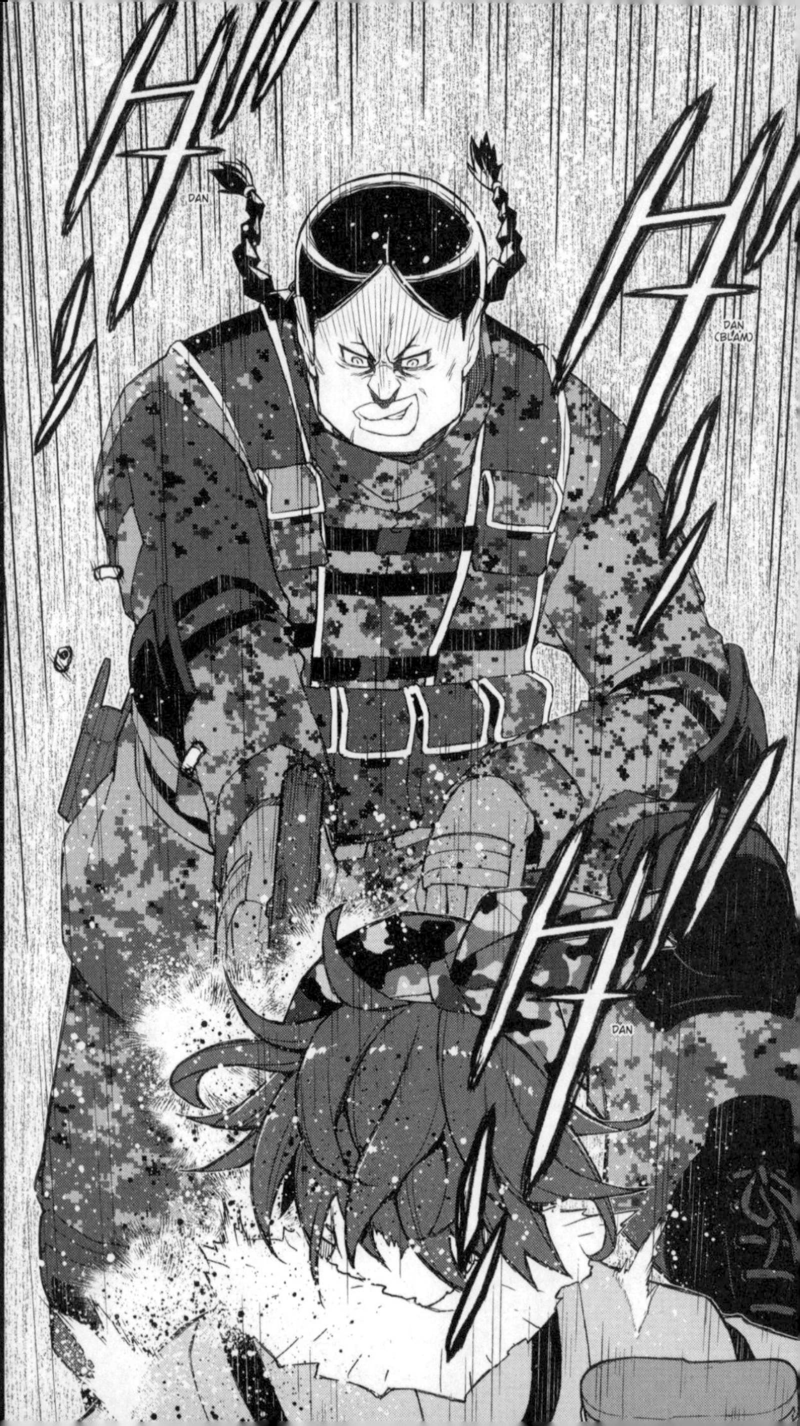
DAN
DAN
(BLAM)
DAN

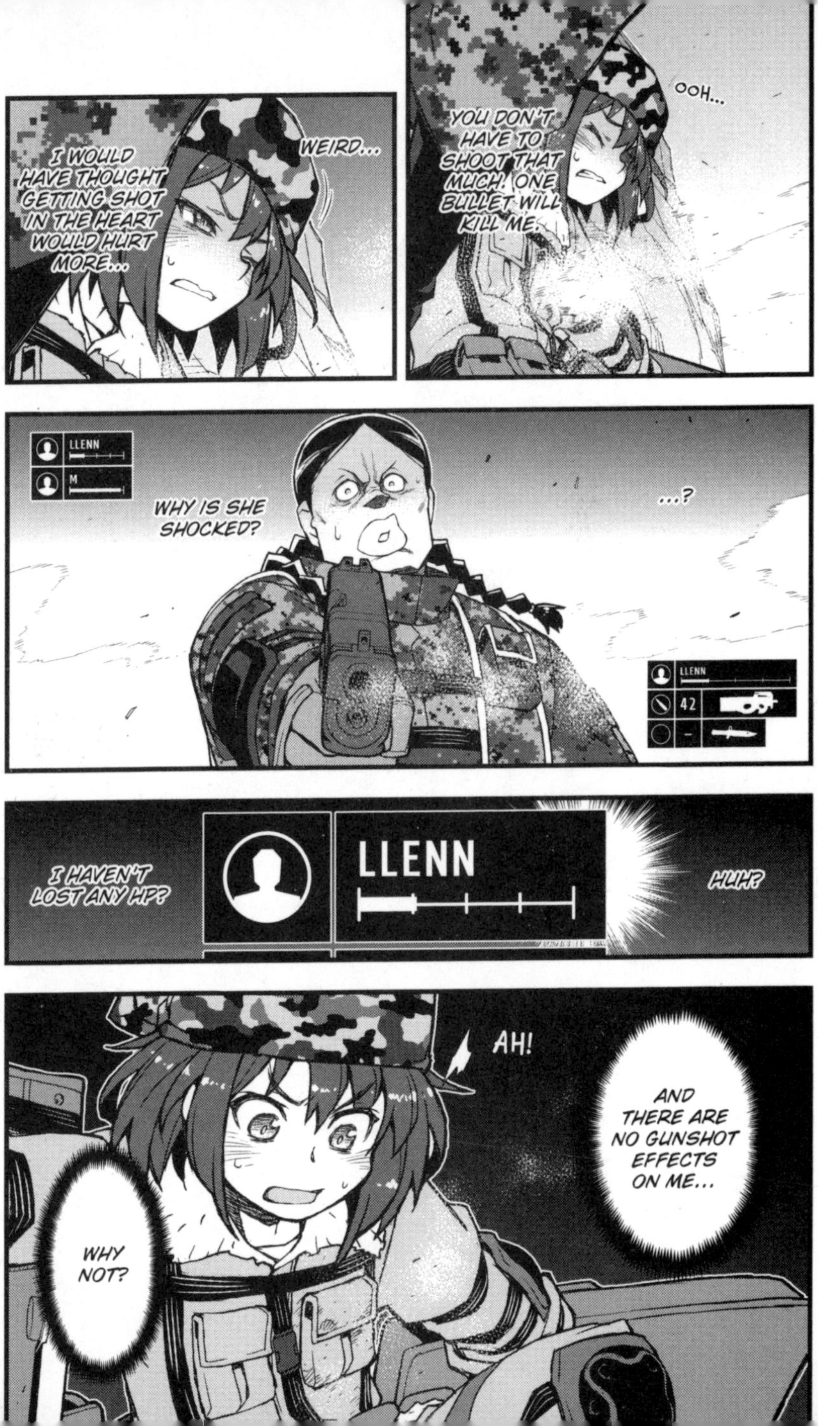
OOH...
YOU DON'T HAVE TO SHOOT THAT MUCH. ONE BULLET WILL KILL ME.
WEIRD...
I WOULD HAVE THOUGHT GETTING SHOT IN THE HEART WOULD HURT MORE...
LLENN
M
...?
WHY IS SHE SHOCKED?
LLENN
42
-
HUH?
LLENN
I HAVEN'T LOST ANY HP?
AH!
AND THERE ARE NO GUNSHOT EFFECTS ON ME...
WHY NOT?

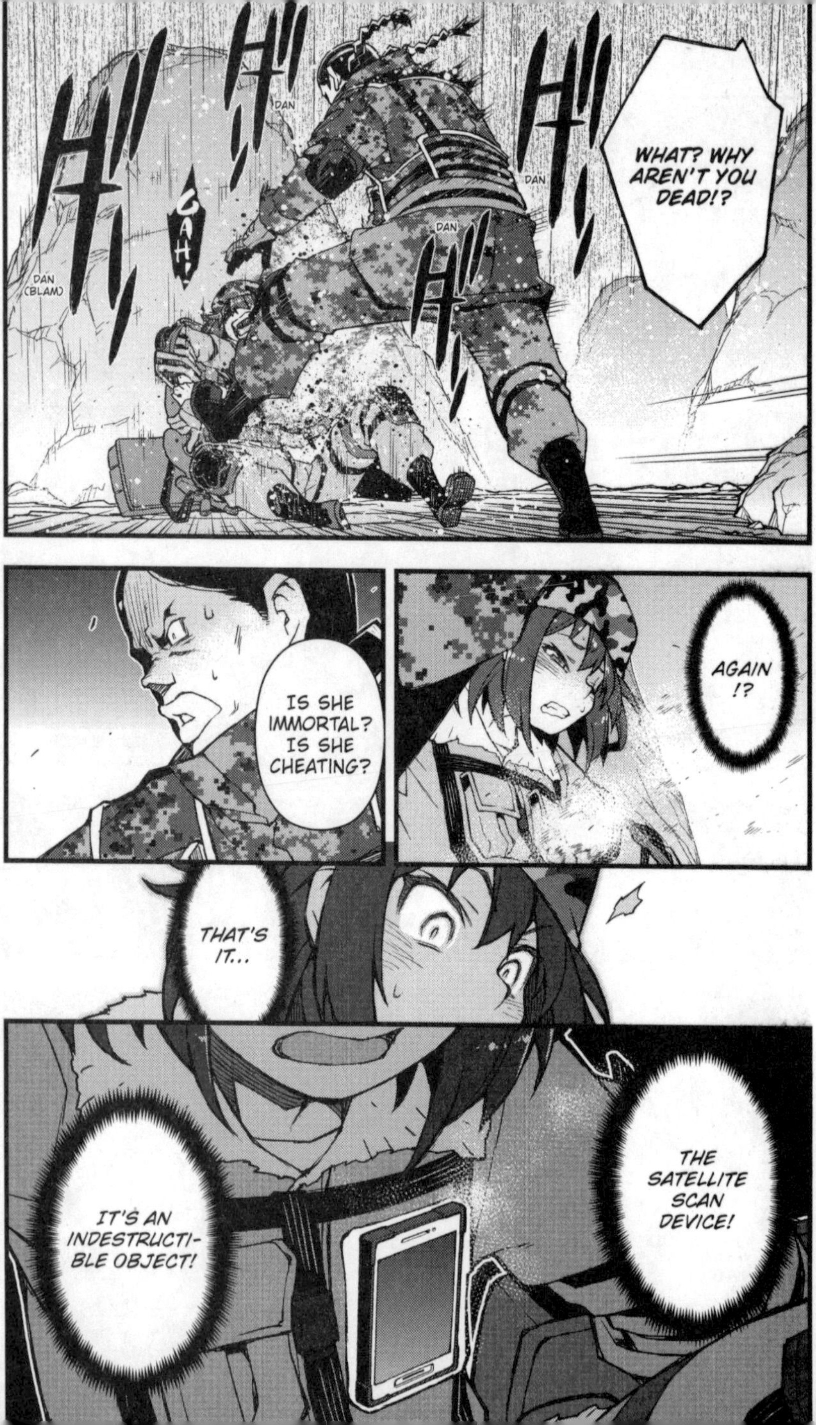
WHAT? WHY AREN'T YOU DEAD!?
DAN
DAN
DAN
GAH!
DAN (BLAM)
AGAIN!?
IS SHE IMMORTAL? IS SHE CHEATING?
THAT'S IT...
THE SATELLITE SCAN DEVICE!
IT'S AN INDESTRUCTI-BLE OBJECT!

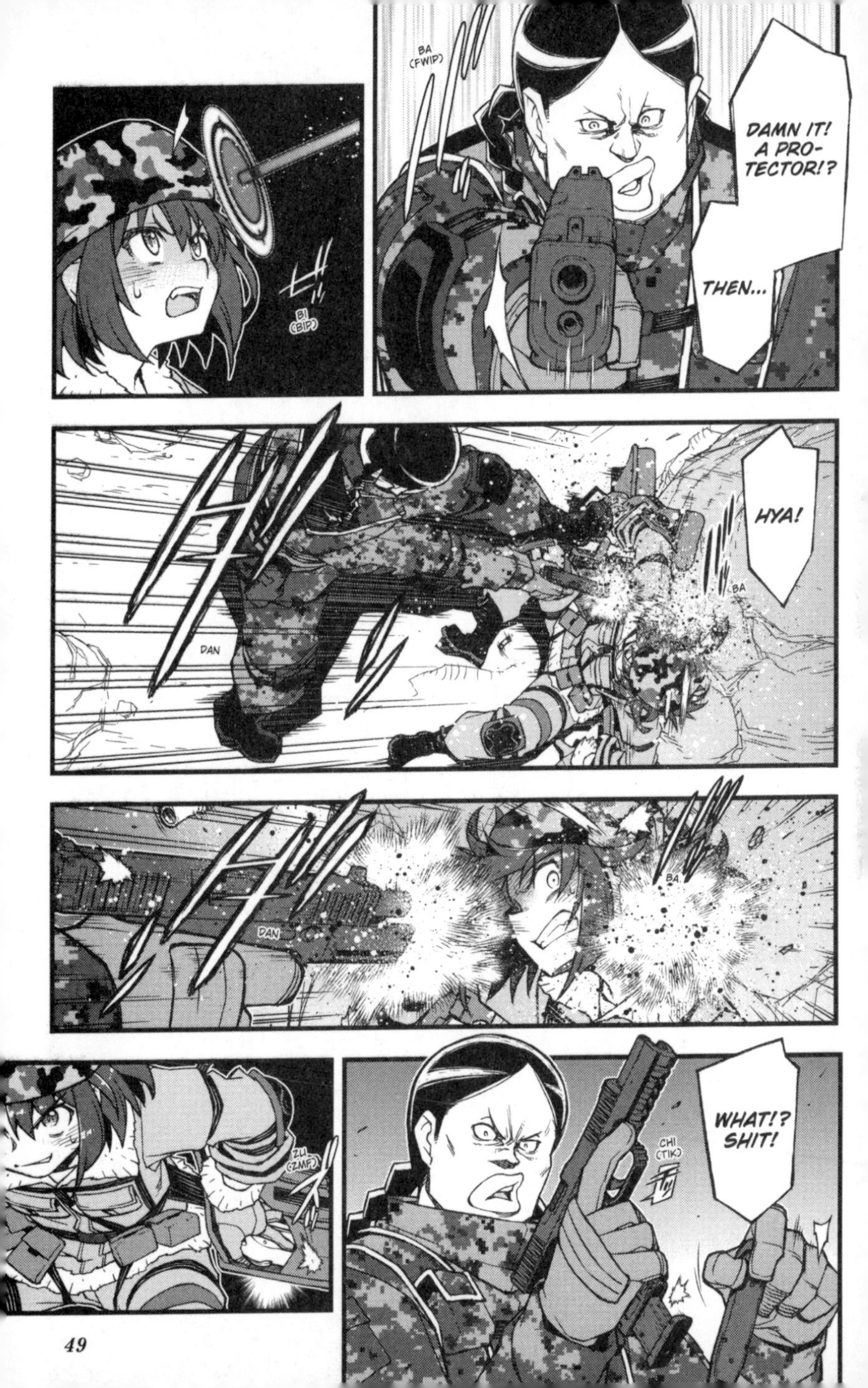
BA (FWIP)
DAMN IT! A PRO-TECTOR!?
THEN...
BI (BIP)
HYA!
BA
DAN
BA
DAN
WHAT!? SHIT!
CHI (TIK)
ZU (ZMF)

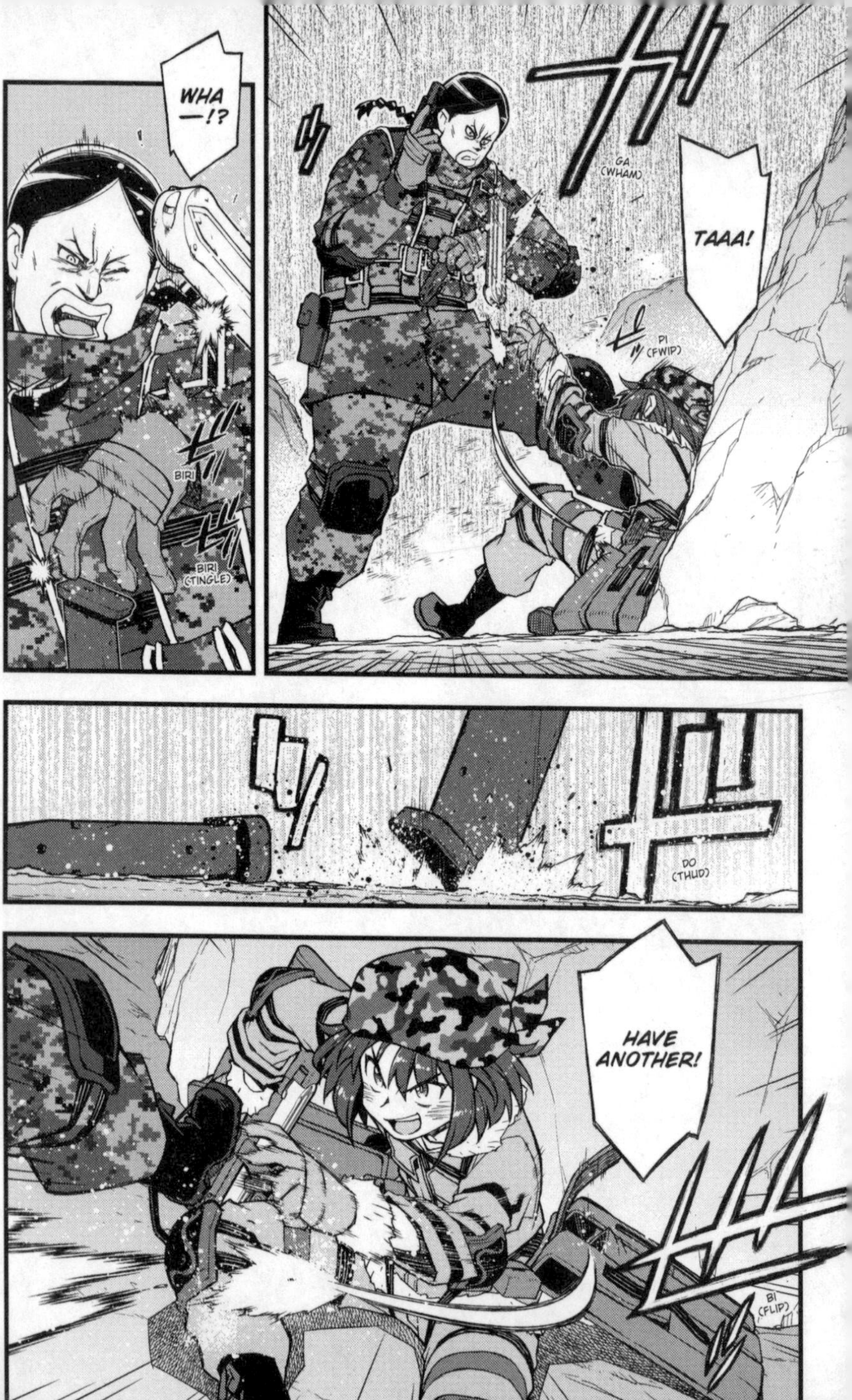
TAAA!
GA
(WHAM)
PI
(FWIP)
WHA—!?
BIRI
BIRI
(TINGLE)
DO
(THUD)
HAVE ANOTHER!
BI
(FLIP)

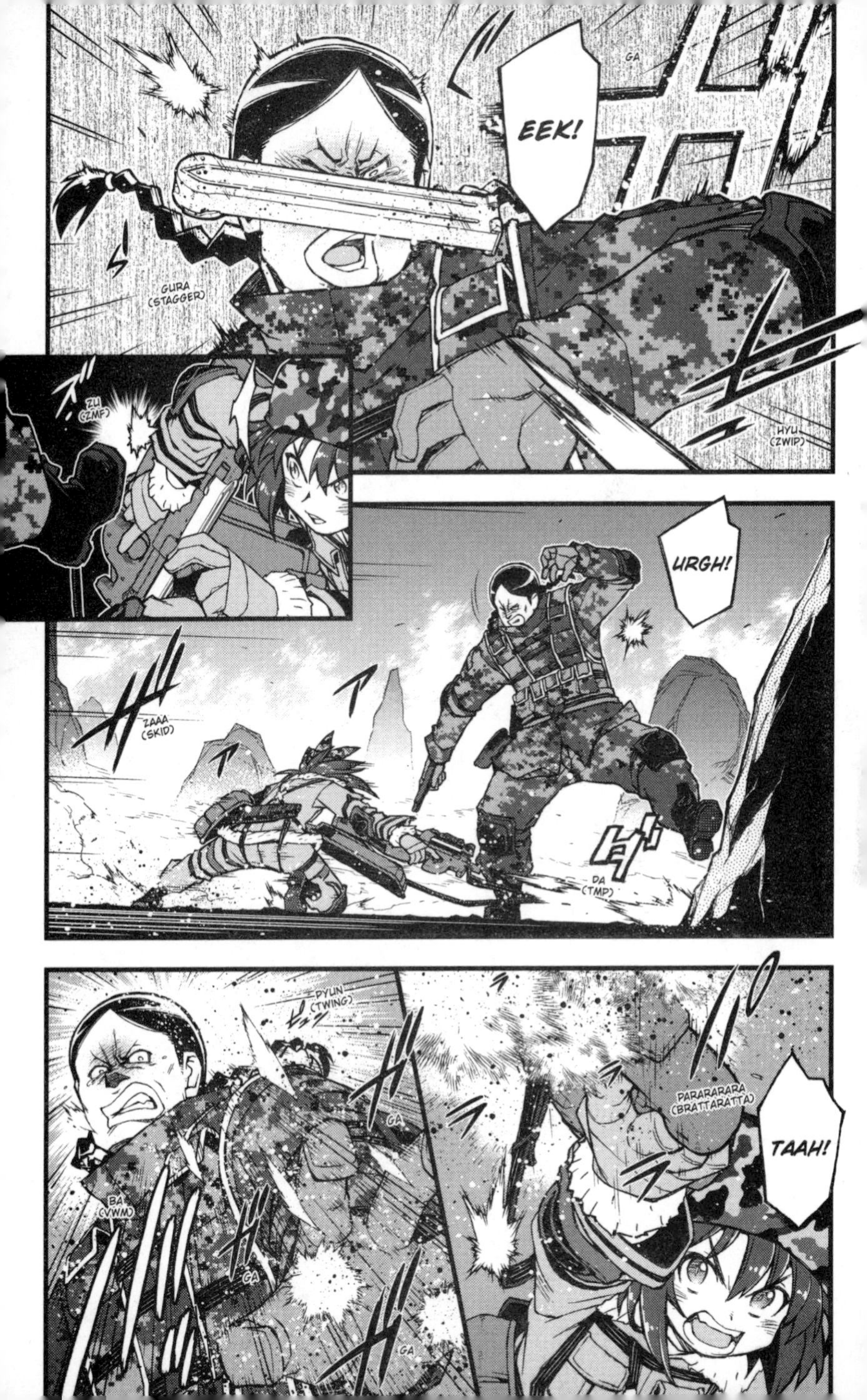
GA
EEK!
HYU
(ZWIP)
GURA
(STAGGER)
ZU
(ZMF)
URGH!
DA
(TMP)
ZAAA
(SKID)
TAAH!
PARARARARA
(BRATTARATTA)
PYUN
(TWING)
GA
BA
(VWM)
GA
GA

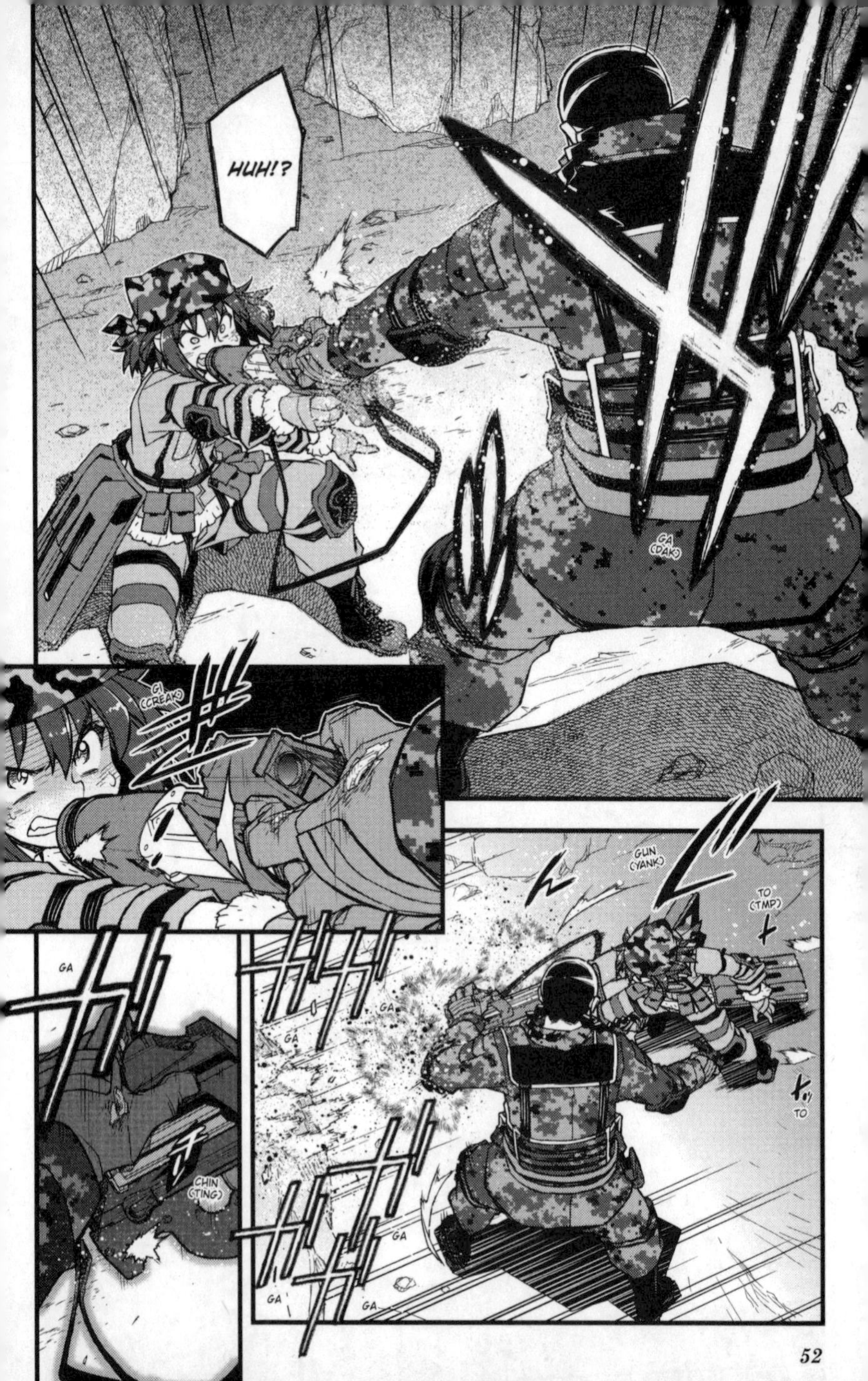
HUH!?
GA (DAK)
GI (CREAK)
GUN (YANK)
TO (TMP)
TO
GA
GA
GA
GA
GA
GA
CHIN (TING)

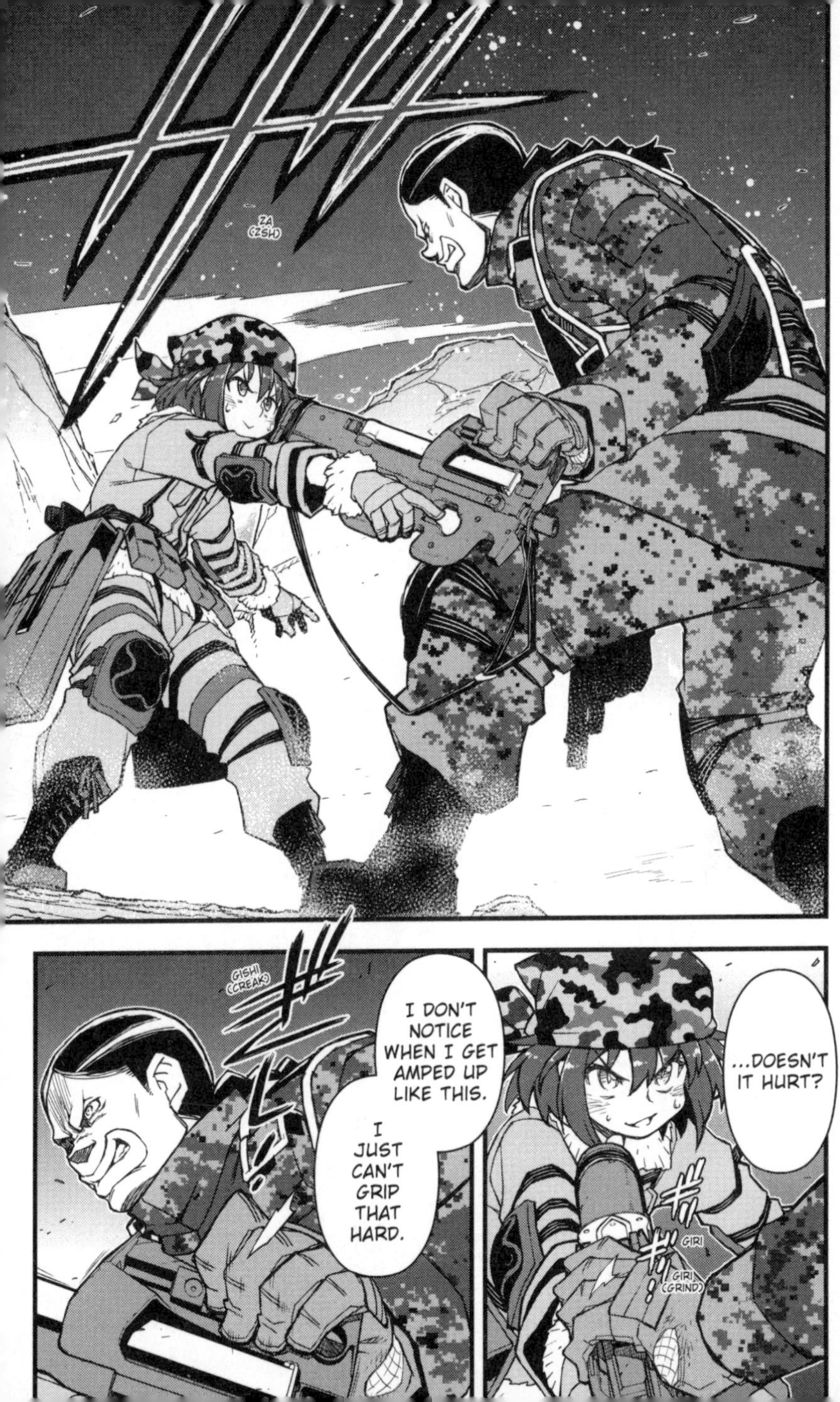
ZA (ZSH)
...DOESN'T IT HURT?
GIRI GIRI (GRIND)
GISHI (CREAK)
I DON'T NOTICE WHEN I GET AMPED UP LIKE THIS.
I JUST CAN'T GRIP THAT HARD.

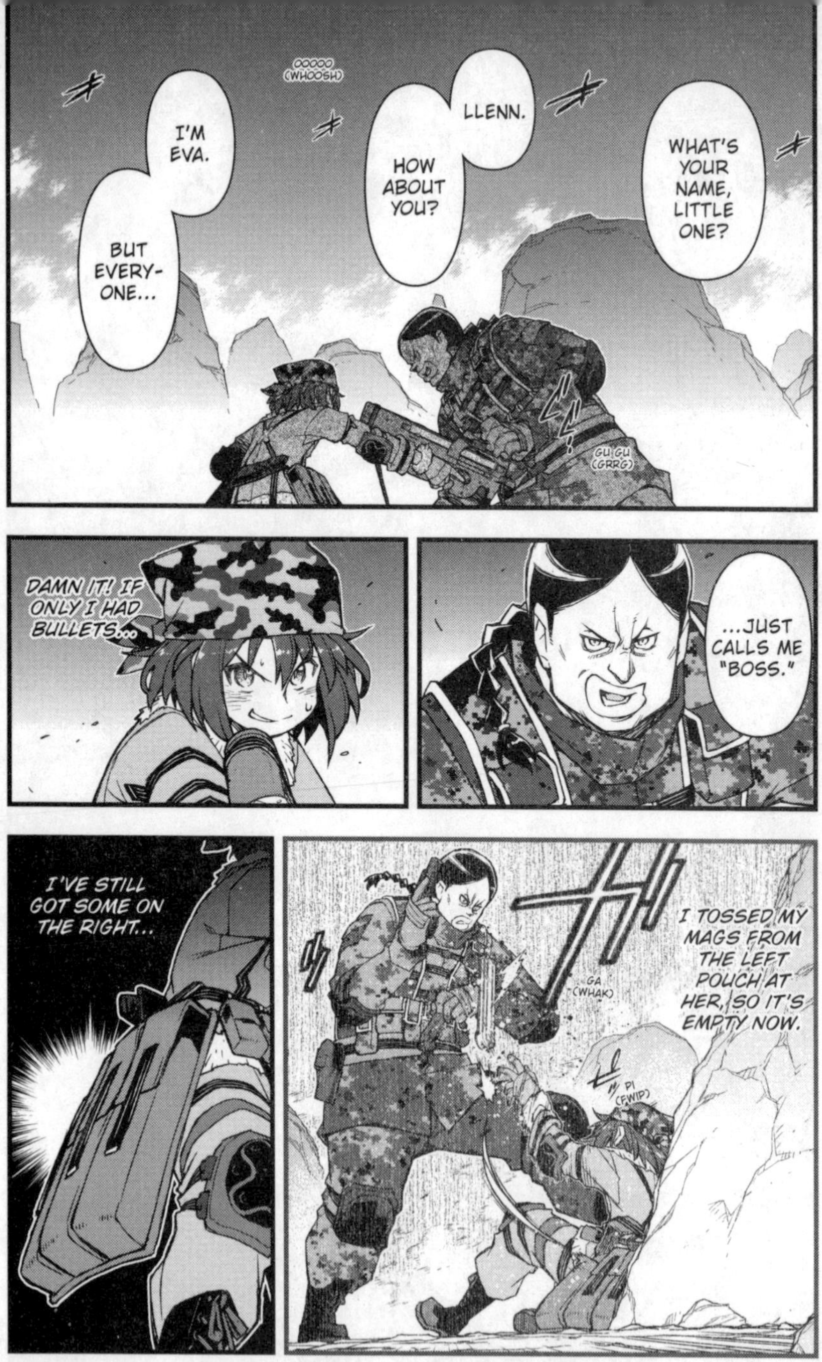
WHAT'S YOUR NAME, LITTLE ONE?
LLENN.
HOW ABOUT YOU?
OOOOO (WHOOSH)
I'M EVA.
BUT EVERY-ONE...
GU GU (GRRG)
...JUST CALLS ME "BOSS."
DAMN IT! IF ONLY I HAD BULLETS...
I TOSSED MY MAGS FROM THE LEFT POUCH AT HER, SO IT'S EMPTY NOW.
GA (WHAK)
PI (FWIP)
I'VE STILL GOT SOME ON THE RIGHT...

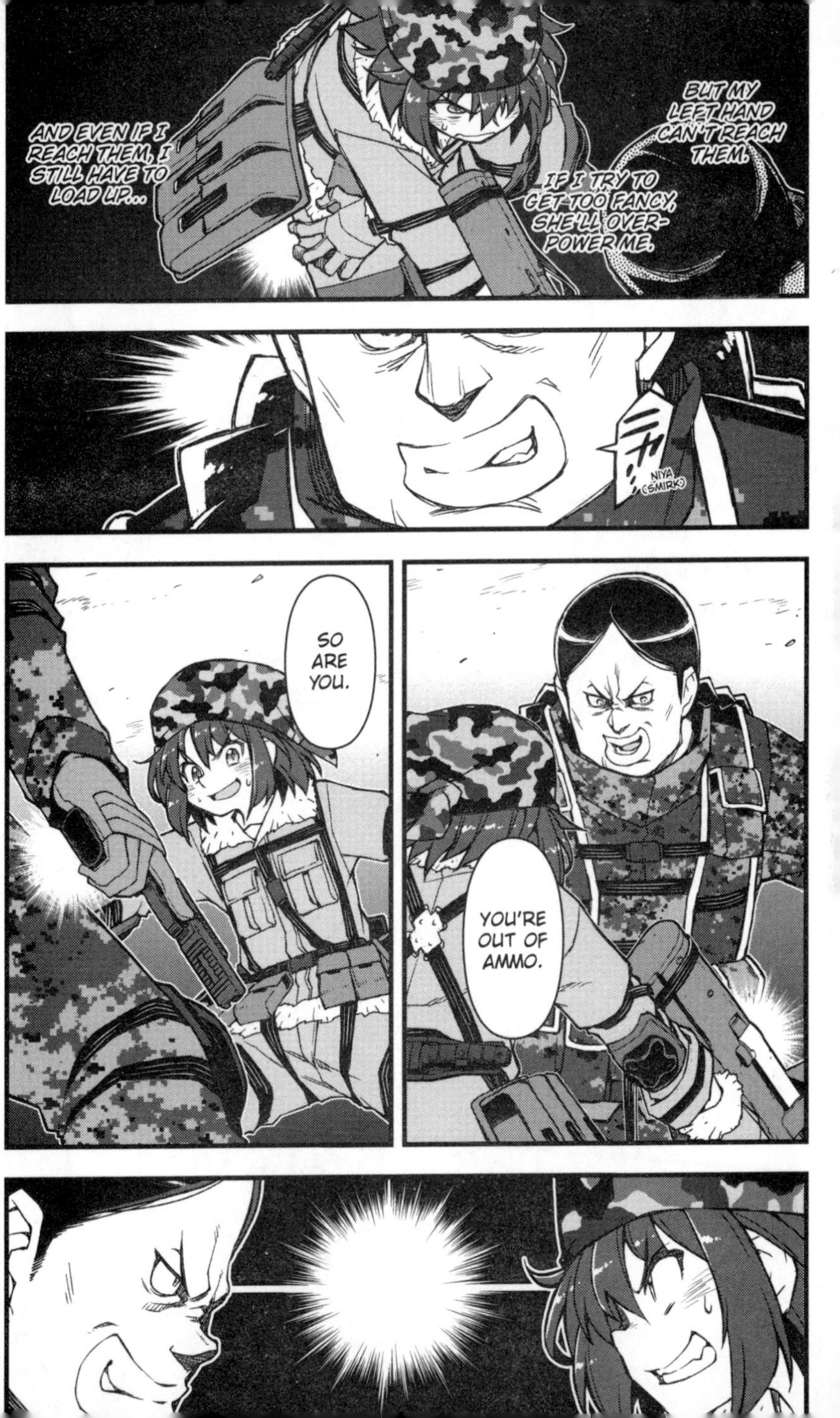
BUT MY LEFT HAND CAN'T REACH THEM.
IF I TRY TO GET TOO FANCY, SHE'LL OVER-POWER ME.
AND EVEN IF I REACH THEM, I STILL HAVE TO LOAD UP...
NIYA (SMIRK)
YOU'RE OUT OF AMMO.
SO ARE YOU.

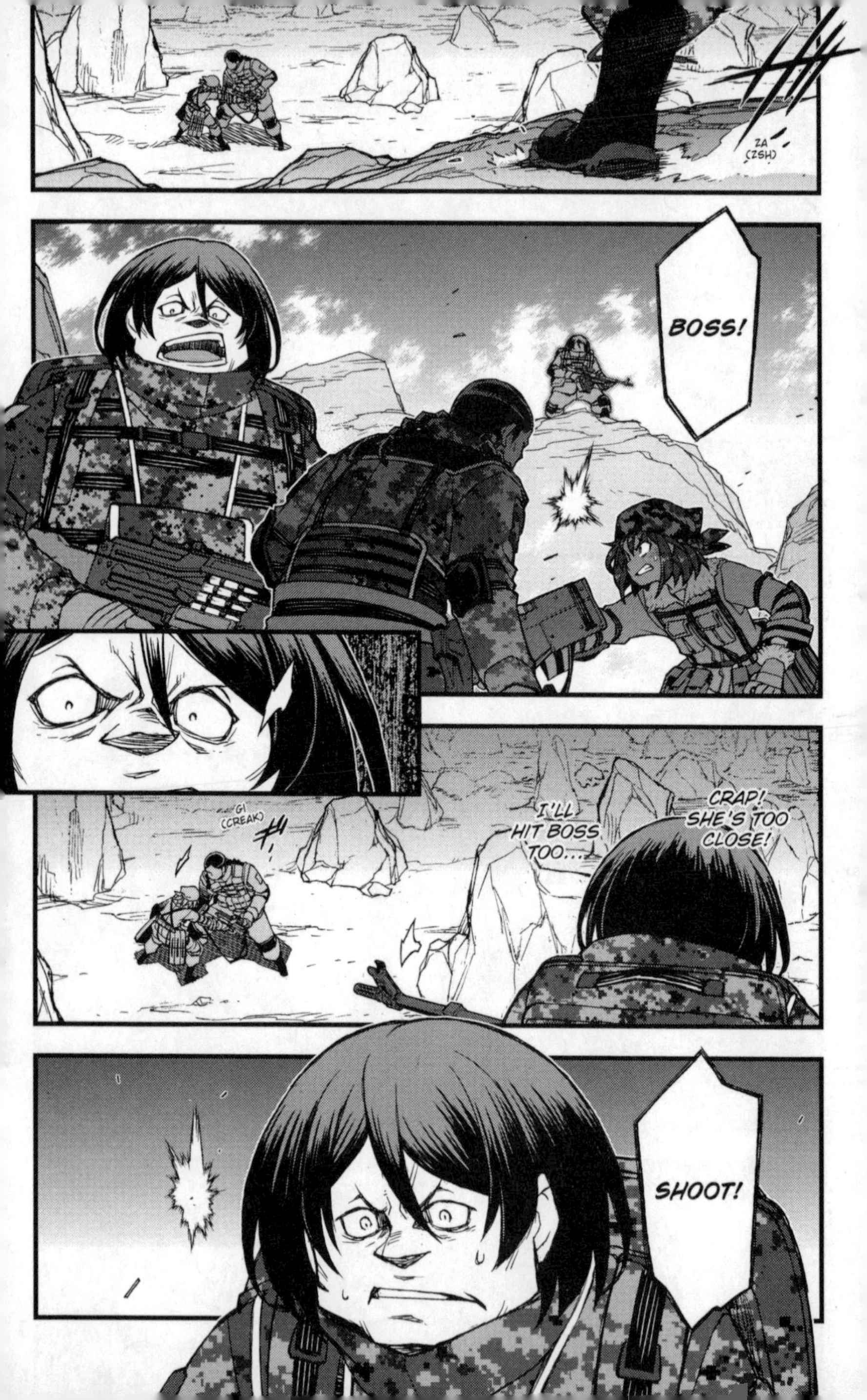
ZA (ZSH)
BOSS!
CRAP! SHE'S TOO CLOSE!
I'LL HIT BOSS TOO...
GI (CREAK)
SHOOT!

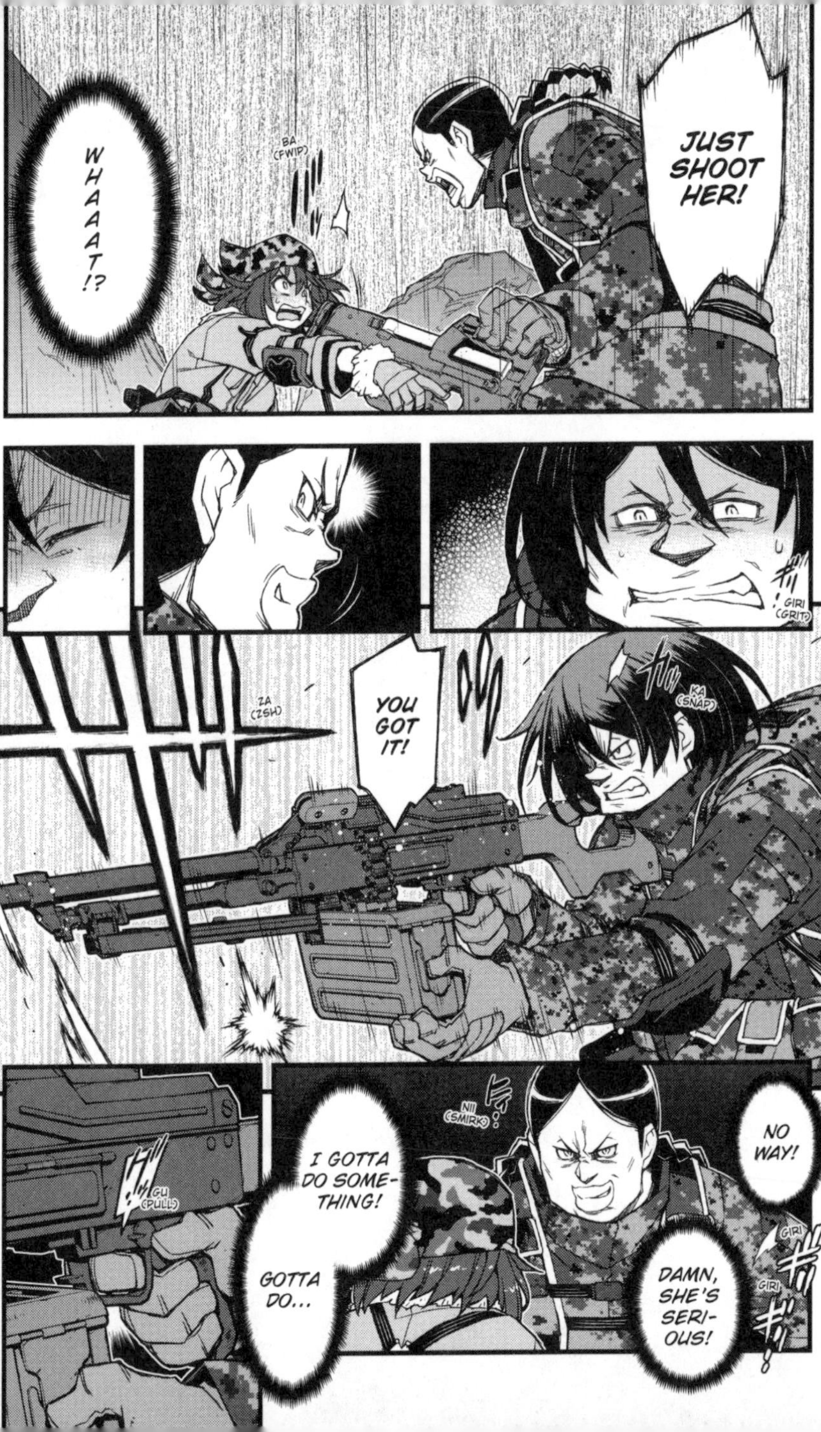
JUST SHOOT HER!
BA (FWIP)
WHAAAT!?
GIRI (GRIT)
KA (SNAP)
YOU GOT IT!
ZA (ZSH)
NO WAY!
GIRI
GIRI
DAMN, SHE'S SERI- OUS!
NII (SMIRK)
I GOTTA DO SOME- THING!
GOTTA DO...
GU (PULL)

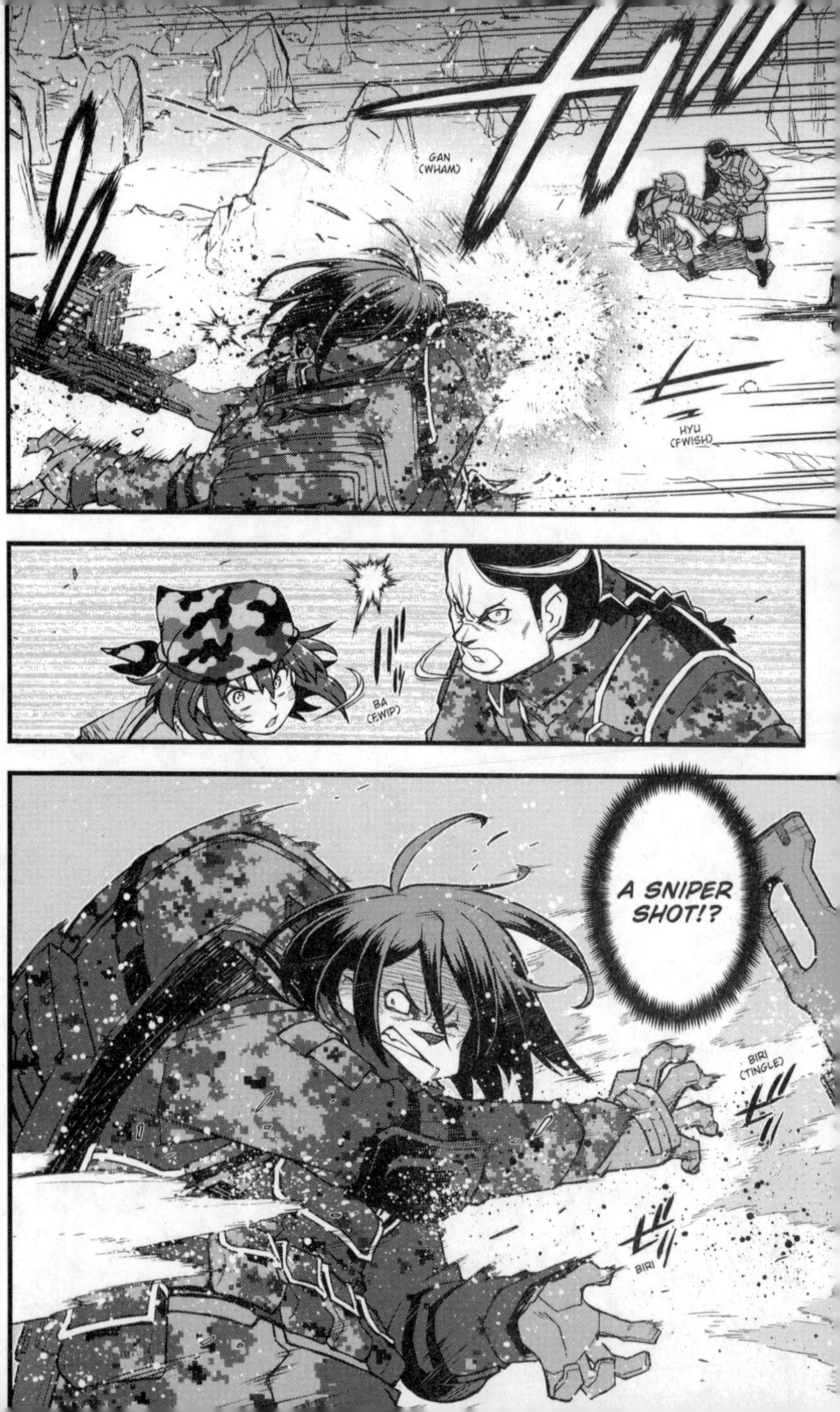
GAN
(WHAM)
HYU
(FWISH)
BA
(FWIP)
A SNIPER SHOT!?
BIRI
(TINGLE)
BIRI

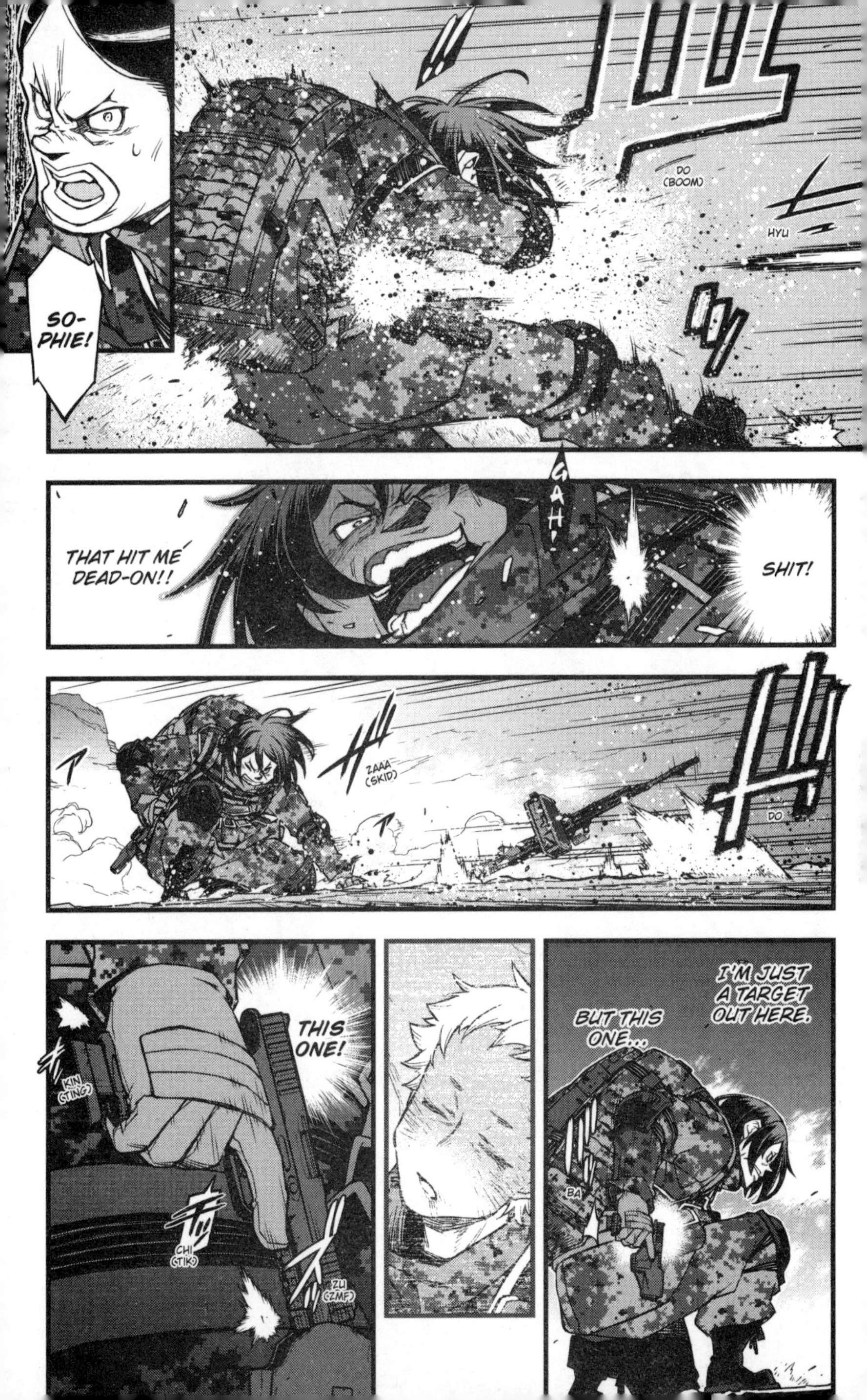
DO
(BOOM)
HYU
SO-
PHIE!
SHIT!
GAH!
THAT HIT ME
DEAD-ON!!
DO
ZAAA
(SKID)
I'M JUST
A TARGET
OUT HERE.
BUT THIS
ONE...
BA
THIS
ONE!
KIN
(TING)
CHI
(TIK)
ZU
(ZMF)

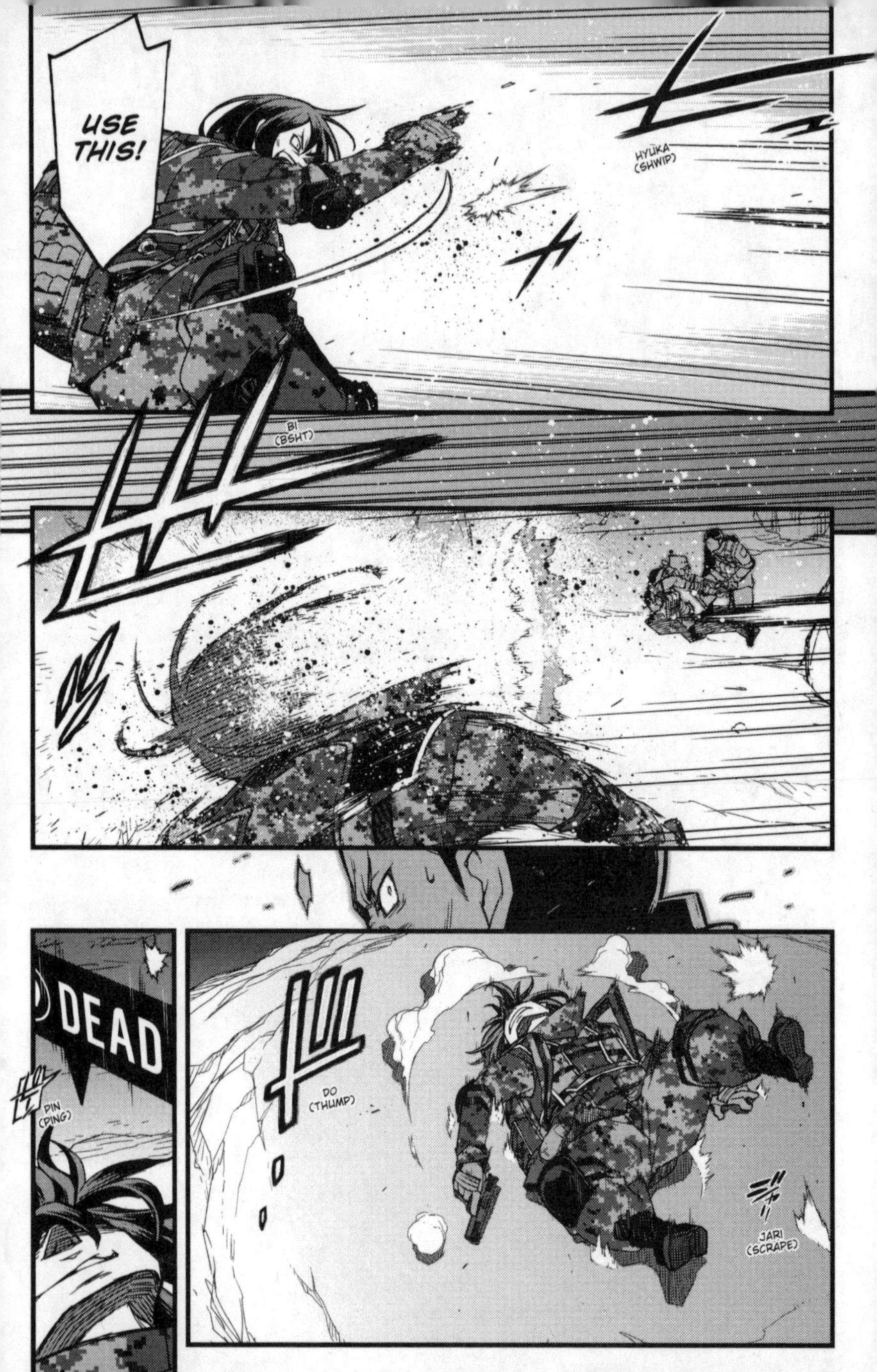
HYUKA
(SHWIP)
USE THIS!
BI
(BSHT)
DO
(THUMP)
JARI
(SCRAPE)
DEAD
PIN
(PING)

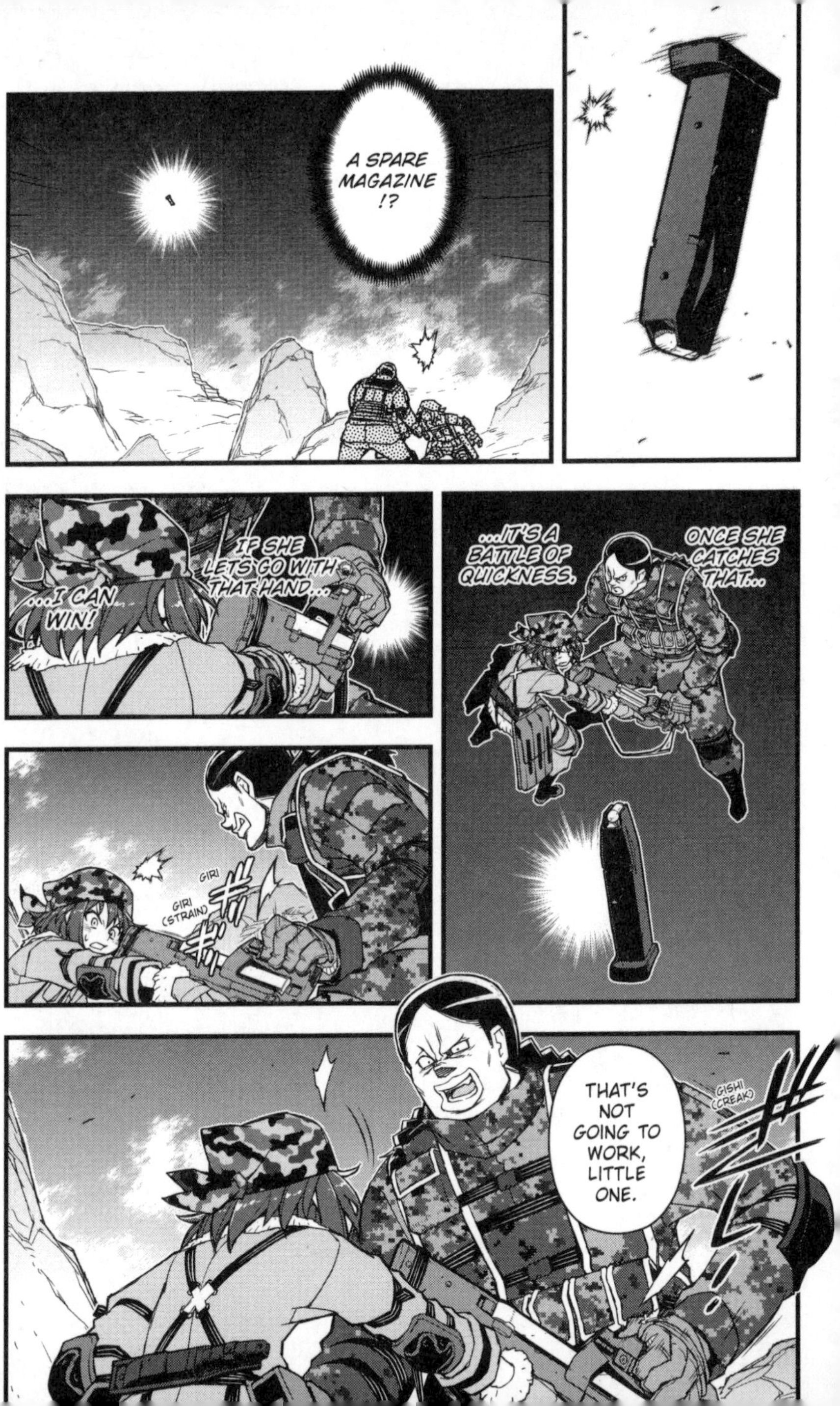
A SPARE MAGAZINE !?
ONCE SHE CATCHES THAT...
...IT'S A BATTLE OF QUICKNESS.
IF SHE LETS GO WITH THAT HAND...
...I CAN WIN!
GIRI
GIRI (STRAIN)
GISHI (CREAK)
THAT'S NOT GOING TO WORK, LITTLE ONE.

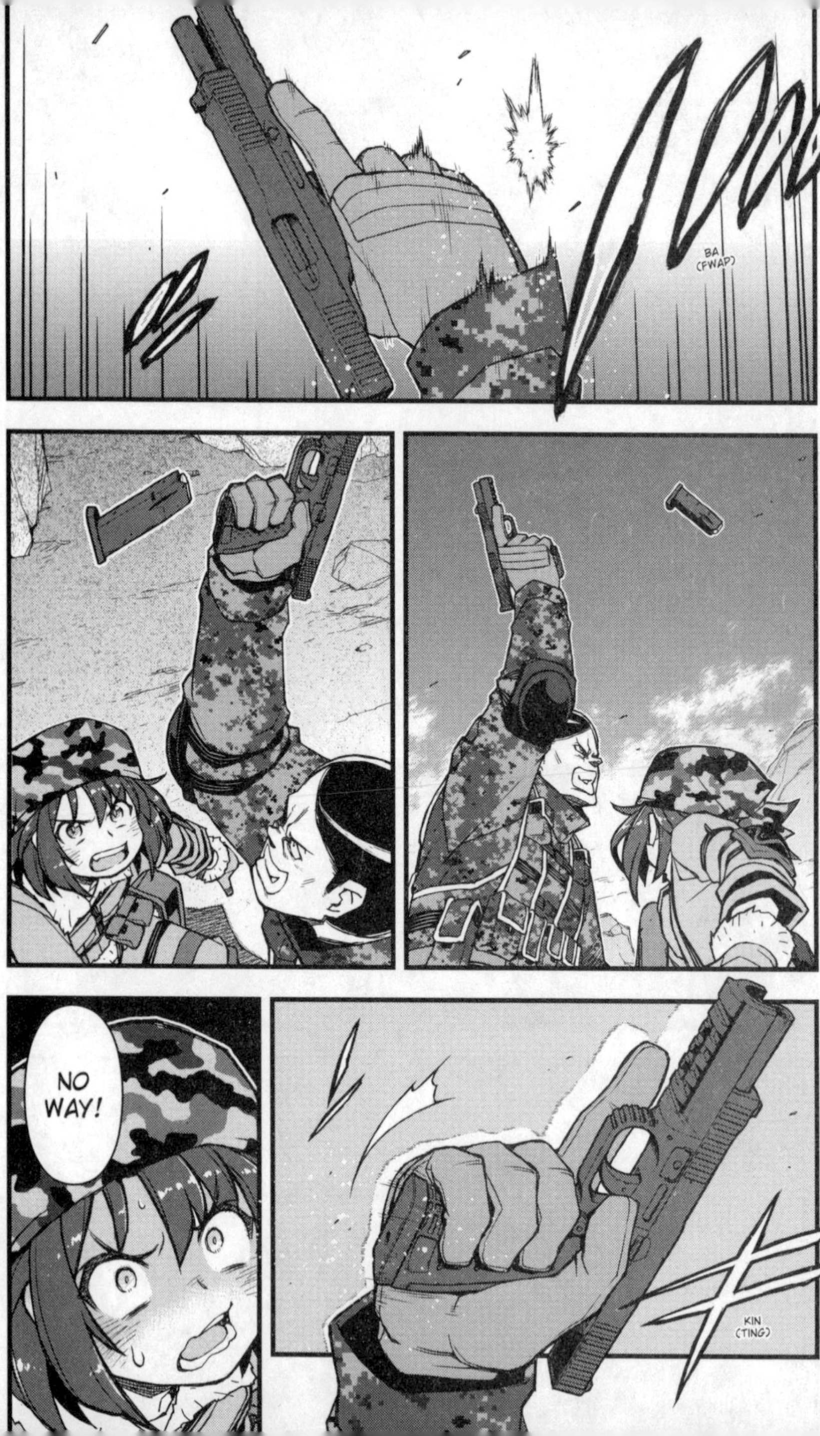
BA
(FWAP)
KIN
(TING)
NO WAY!

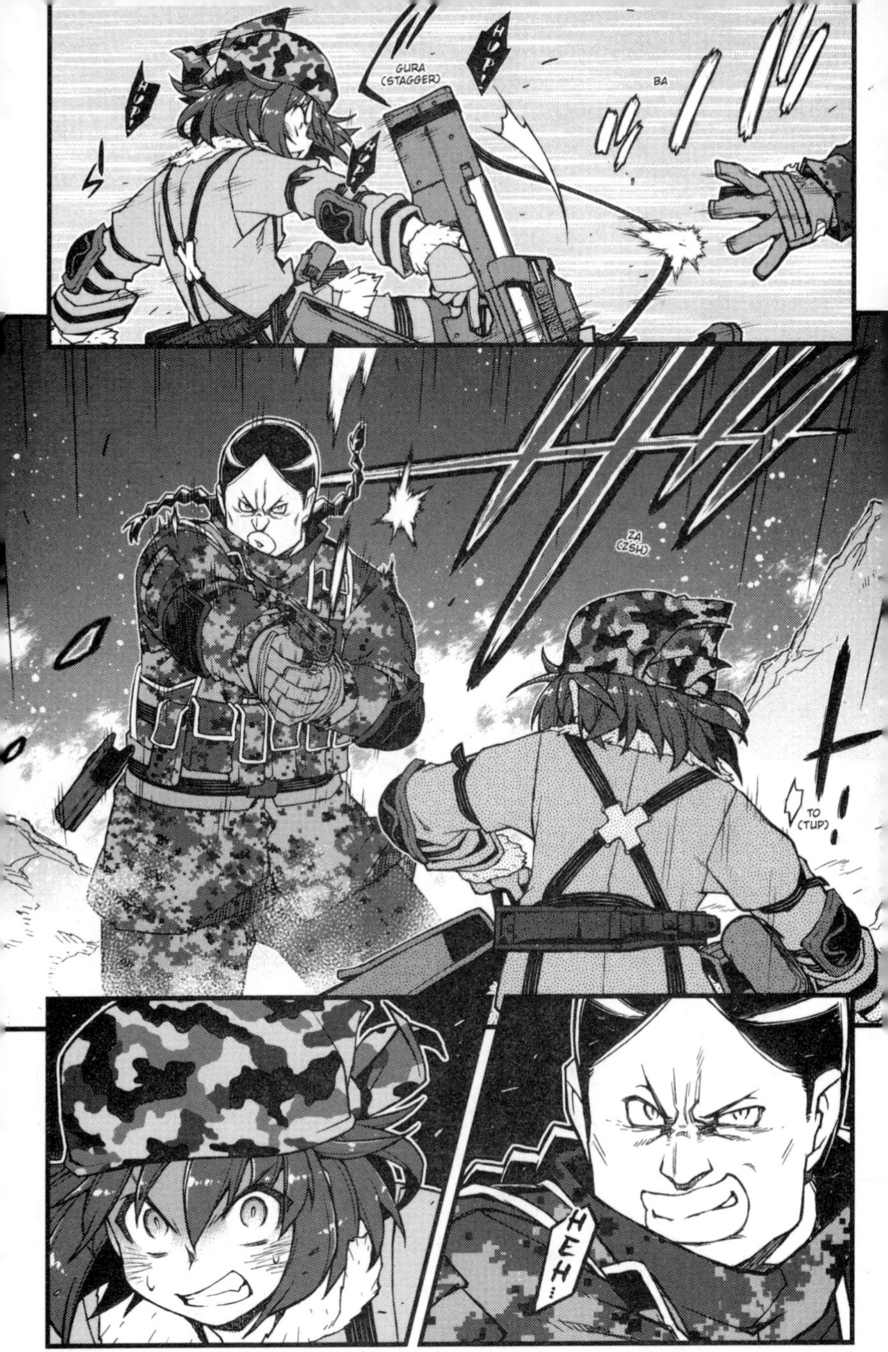
BA
HUP!
GURA (STAGGER)
HUP!
HUP!
ZA (ZSH)
TO (TUP)
HEH...

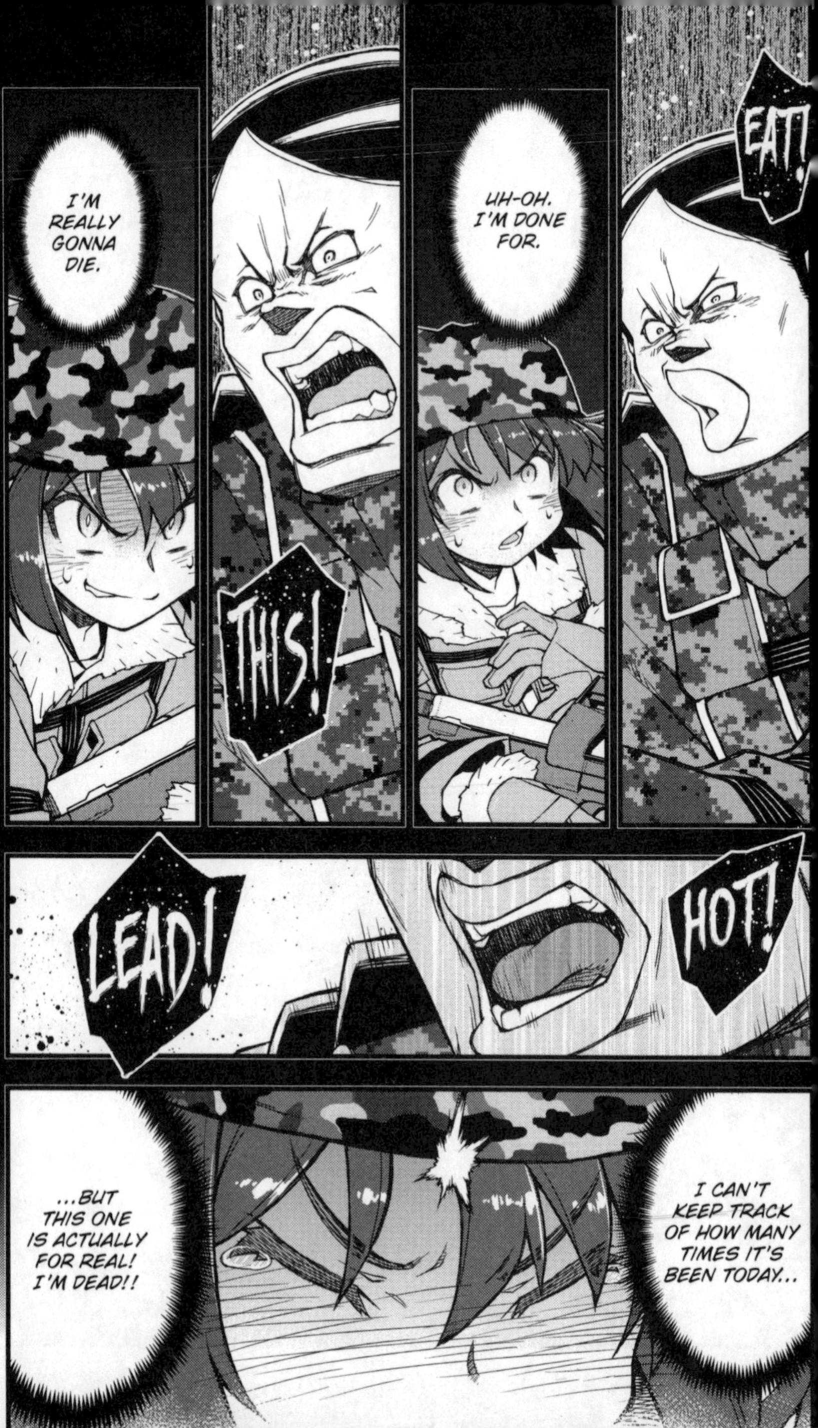
EAT!
UH-OH. I'M DONE FOR.
THIS!
I'M REALLY GONNA DIE.
HOT!
LEAD!
I CAN'T KEEP TRACK OF HOW MANY TIMES IT'S BEEN TODAY...
...BUT THIS ONE IS ACTUALLY FOR REAL! I'M DEAD!!

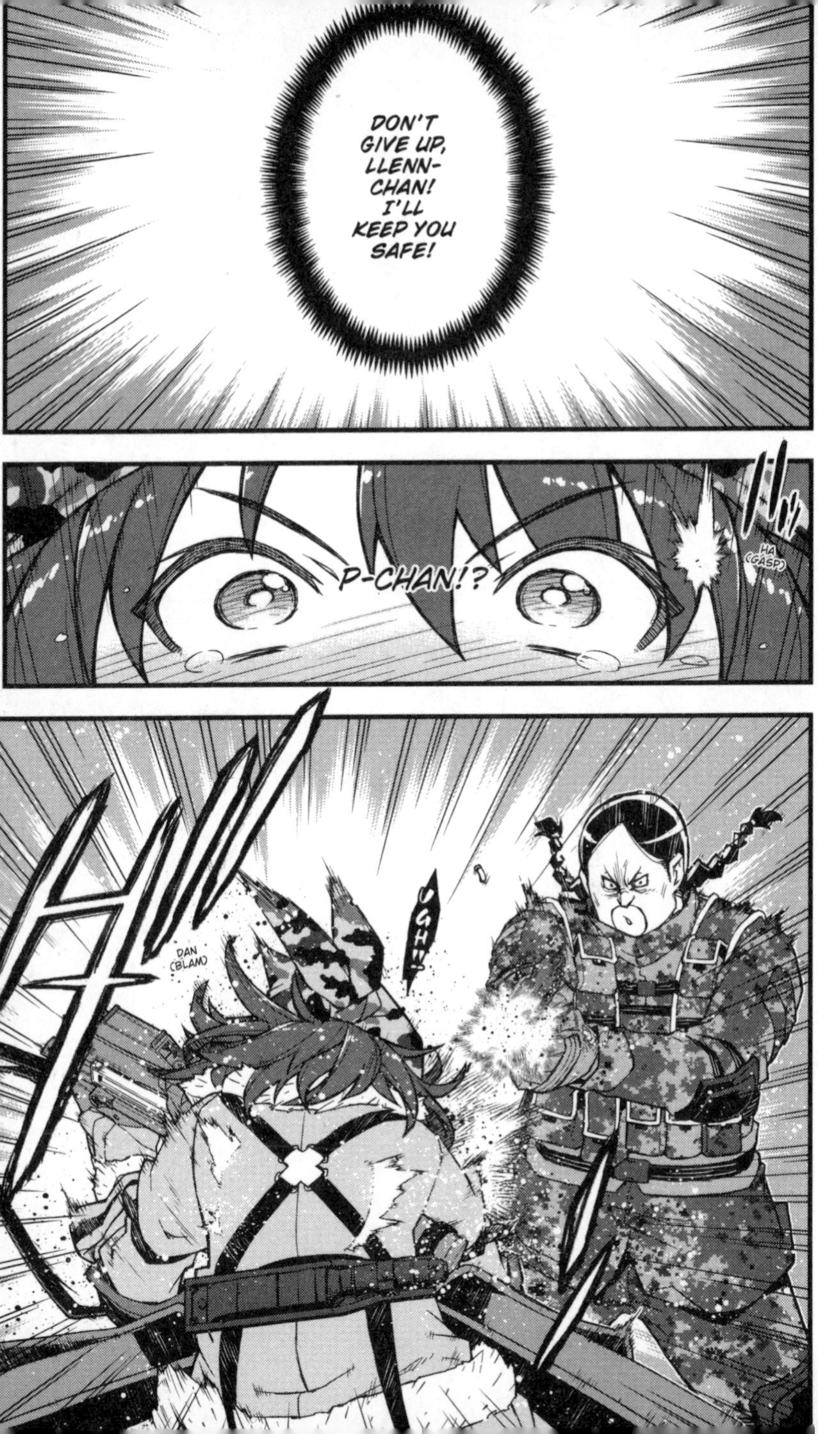
DON'T GIVE UP, LLENN-CHAN! I'LL KEEP YOU SAFE!
HA (GASP)
P-CHAN!?
UGH!!
DAN (BLAM)

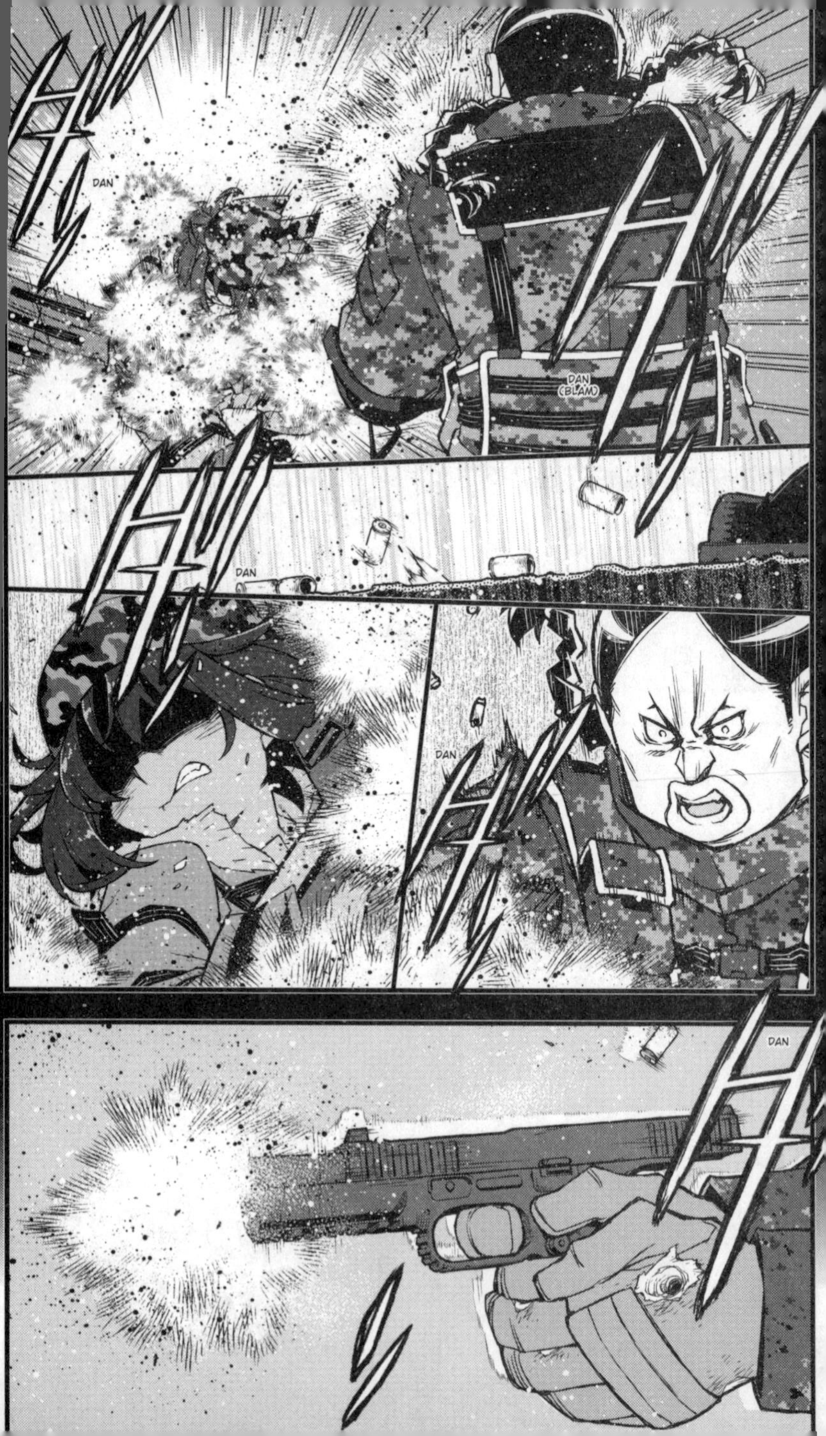
DAN
DAN
(BLAM)
DAN
DAN
DAN

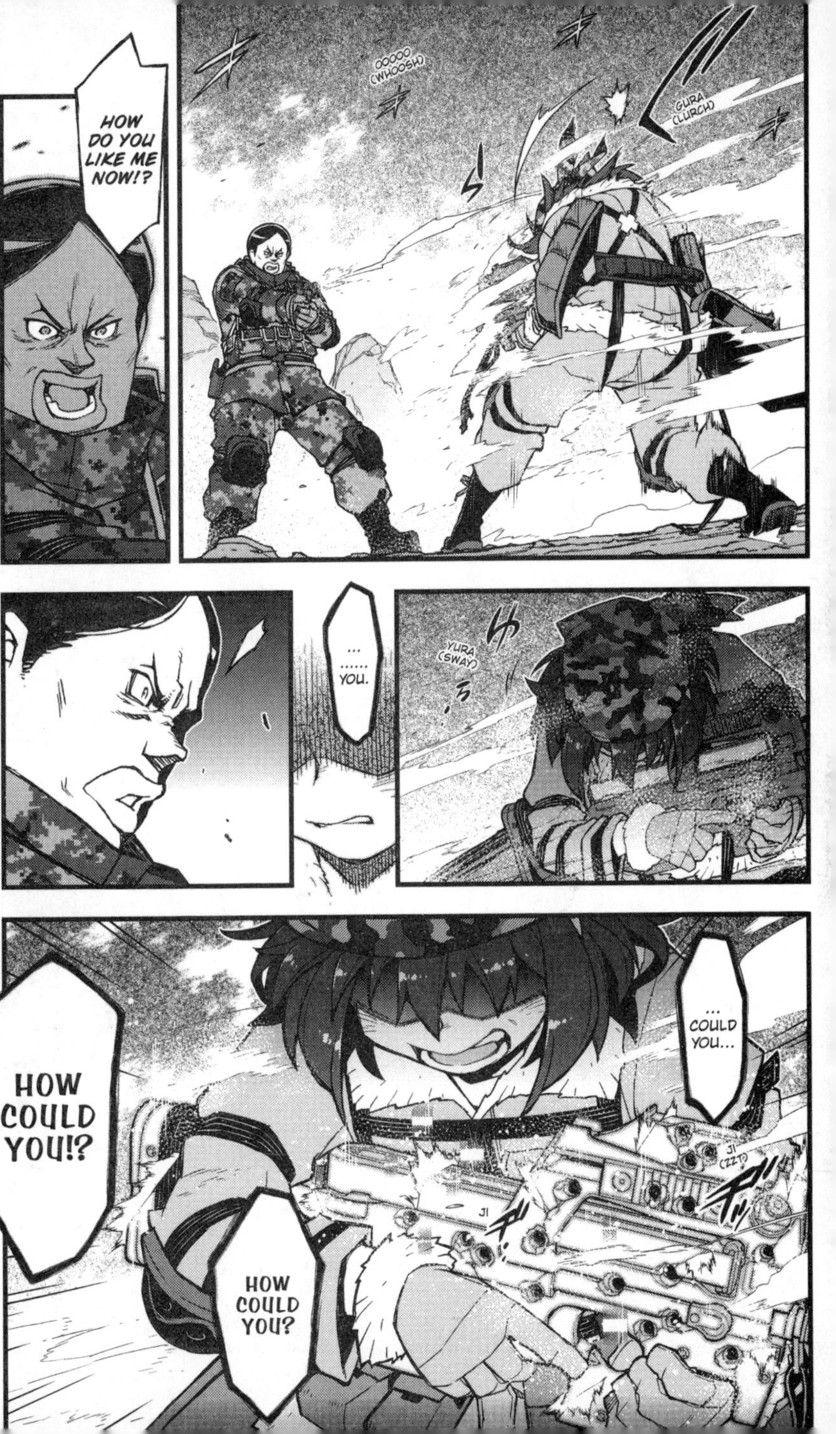
GURA (LURCH)
OOOOO (WHOOSH)
HOW DO YOU LIKE ME NOW!?
YURA (SWAY)
... . YOU.
... COULD YOU...
JI (ZZT)
JI
HOW COULD YOU!?
HOW COULD YOU?

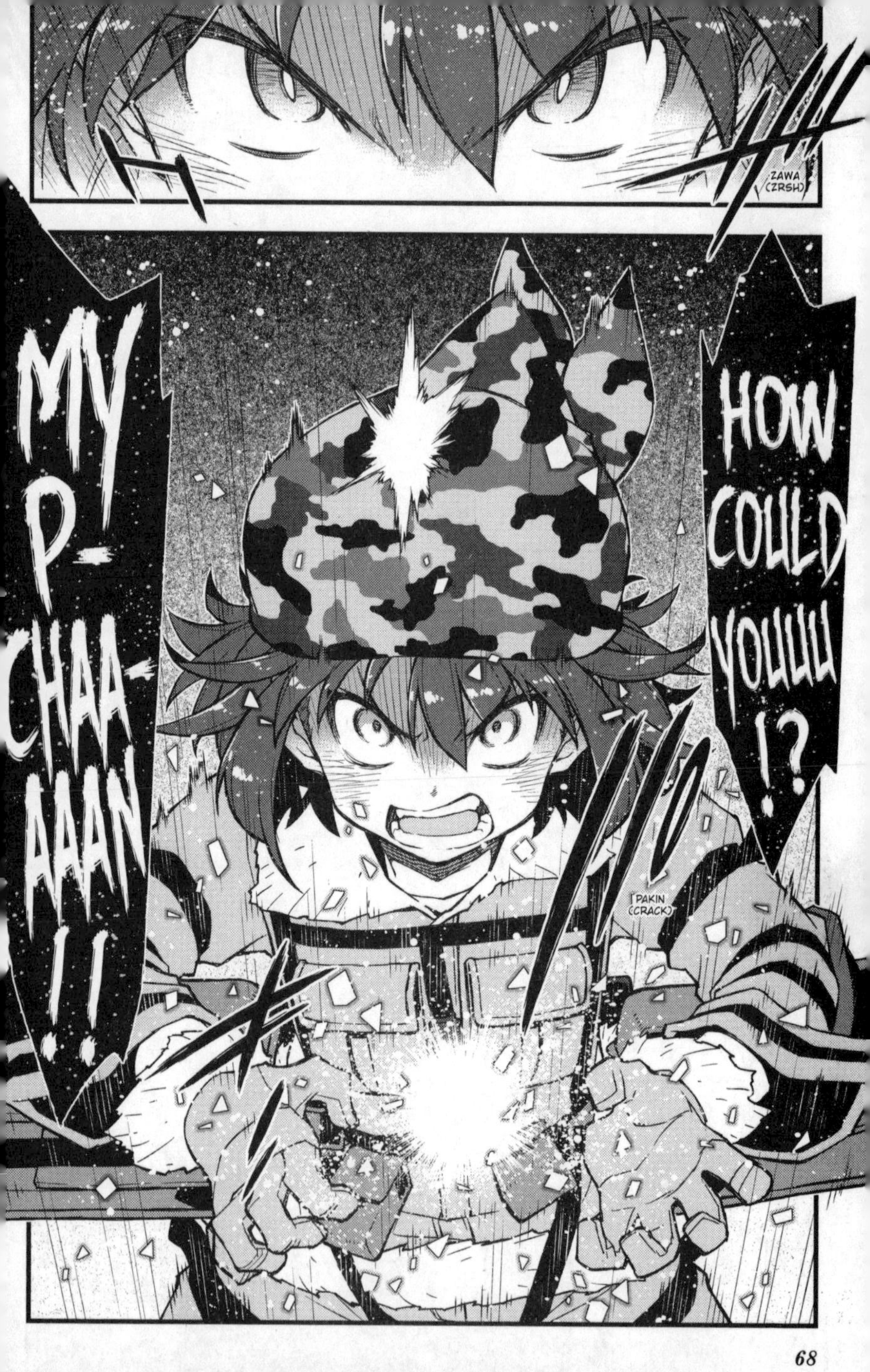
ZAWA (ZRSH)
HOW COULD YOUUU!?
MY P-CHAAAAAN!!
PAKIN (CRACK)

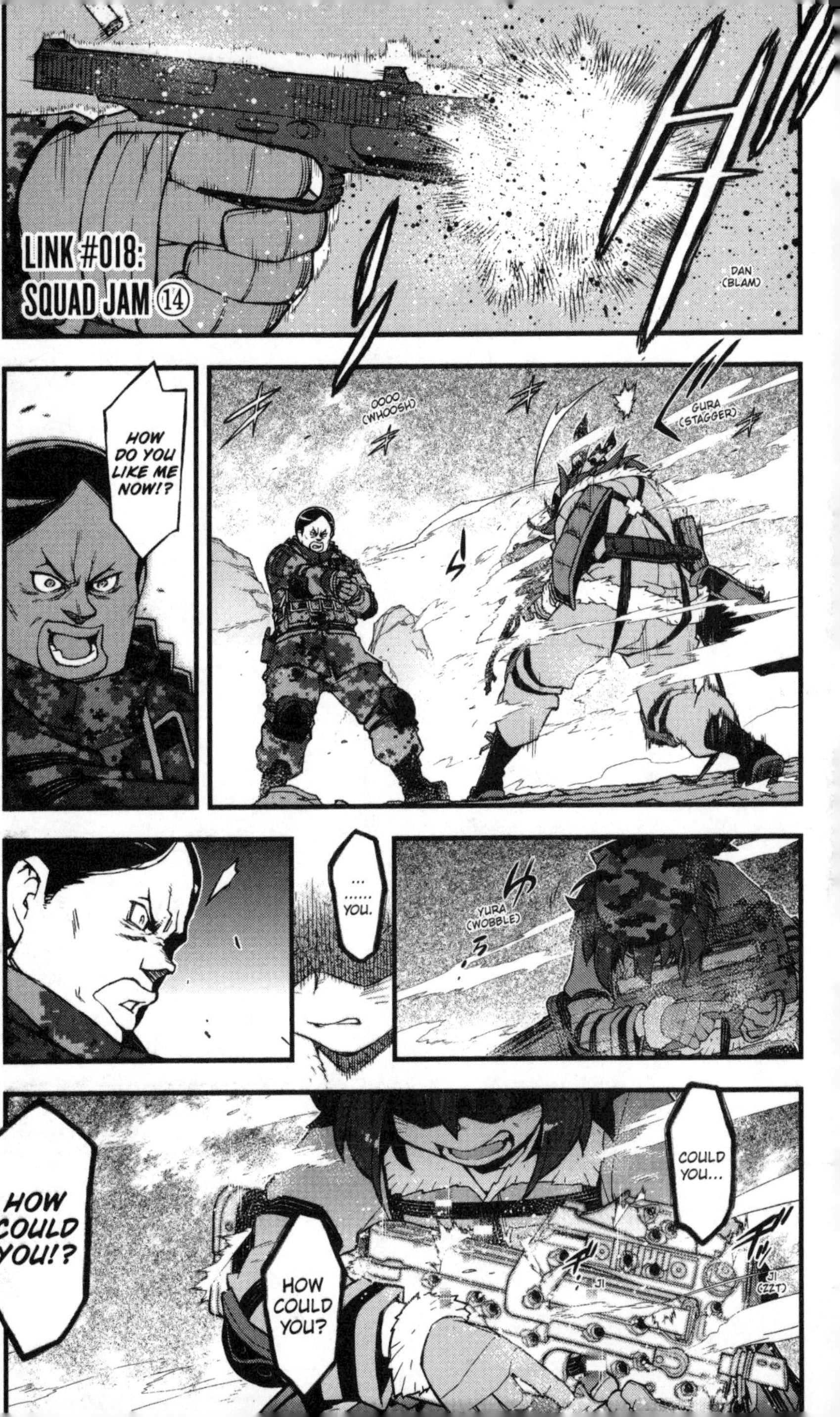
LINK #018:
SQUAD JAM ⑭
DAN (BLAM)
GURA (STAGGER)
OOOO (WHOOSH)
HOW DO YOU LIKE ME NOW!?
YURA (WOBBLE)
... . YOU.
COULD YOU...
JI
JI (ZZT)
HOW COULD YOU?
HOW COULD YOU!?

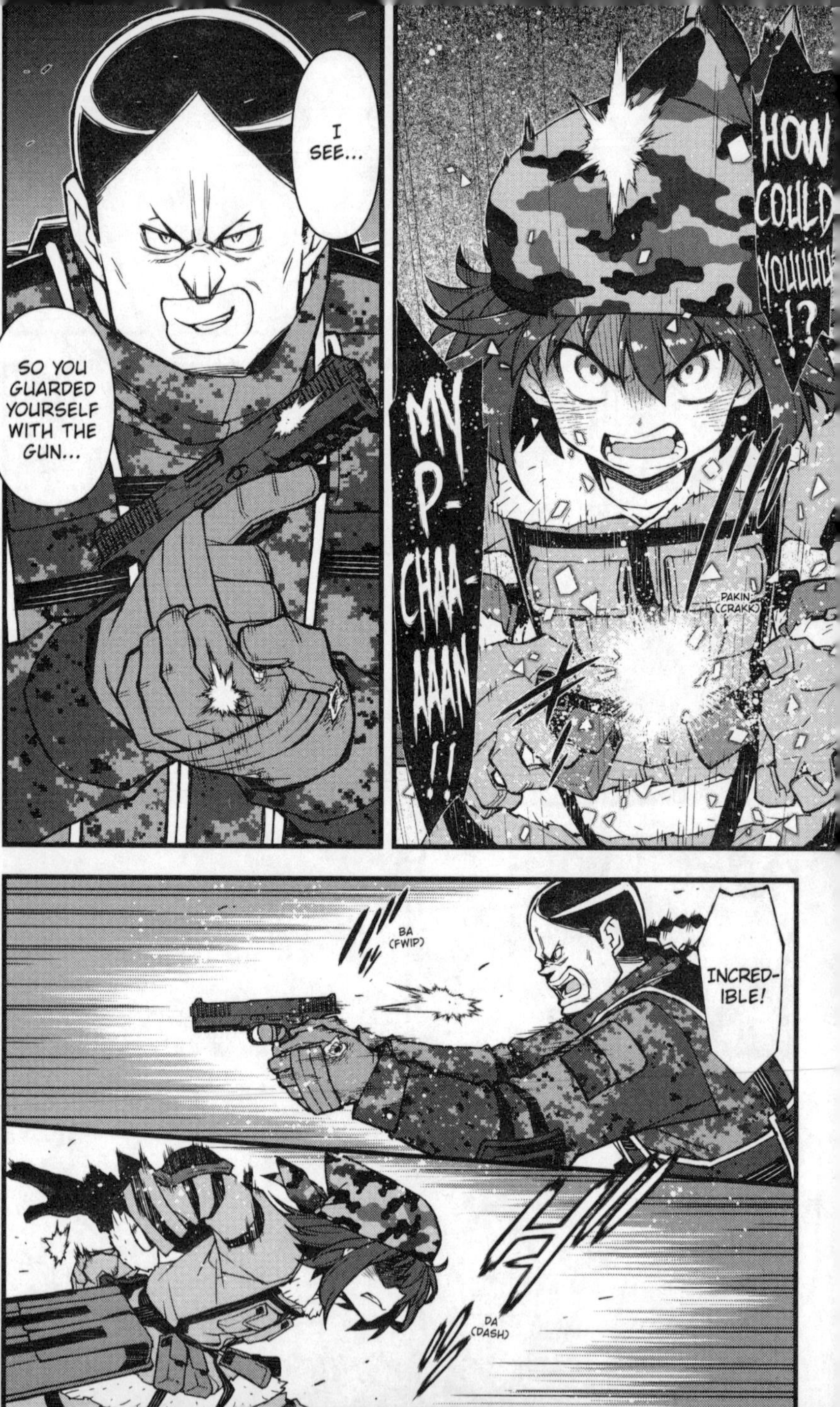
HOW COULD YOUUUU!?
MY P-CHAAAAAAN!!
PAKIN (CRAKK)
I SEE...
SO YOU GUARDED YOURSELF WITH THE GUN...
INCRED-IBLE!
BA (FWIP)
DA (DASH)

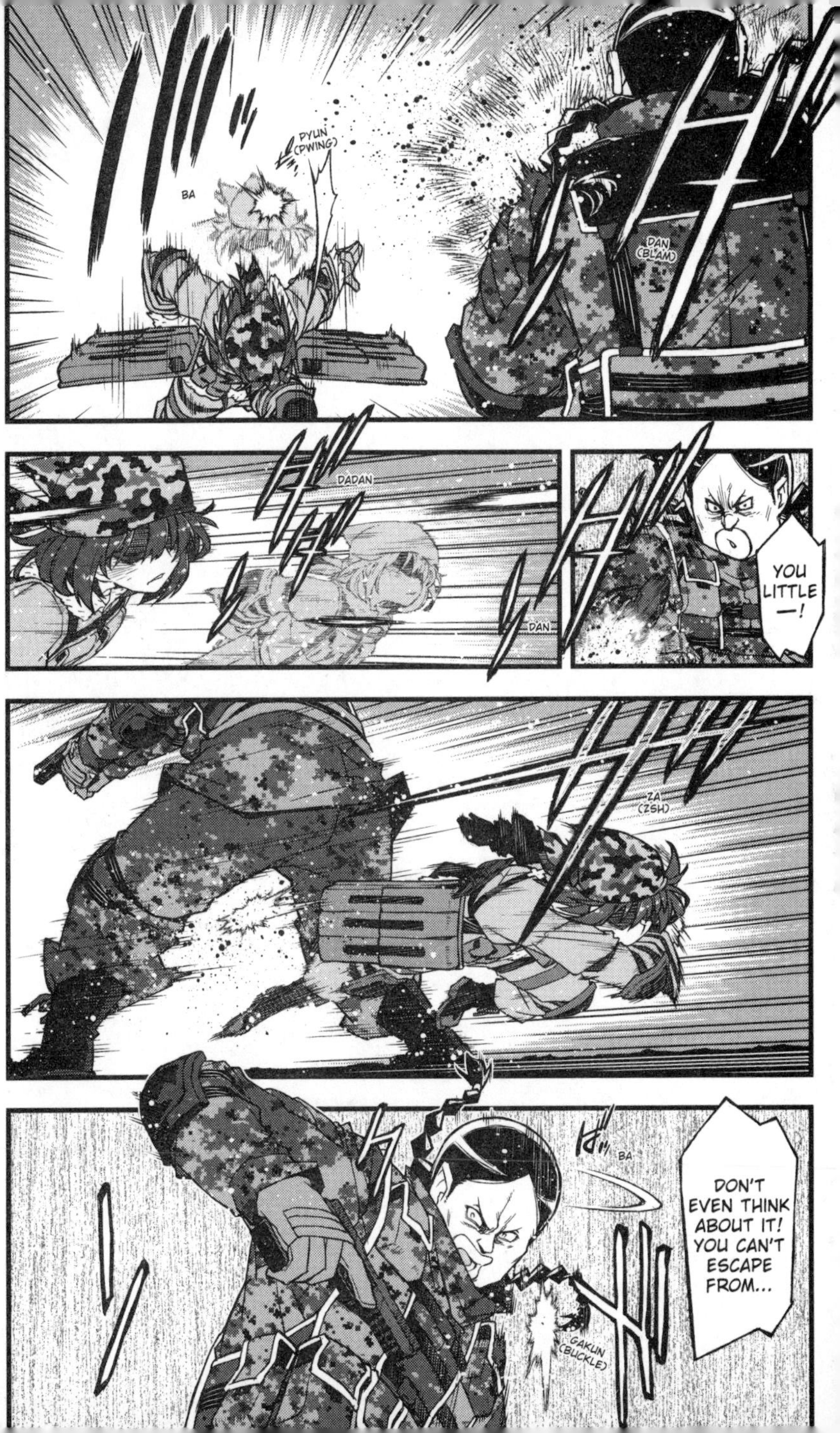
DAN
(BLAM)
PYUN
(PWING)
BA
YOU LITTLE—!
DADAN
DAN
ZA
(ZSH)
DON'T EVEN THINK ABOUT IT! YOU CAN'T ESCAPE FROM...
BA
GAKUN
(BUCKLE)

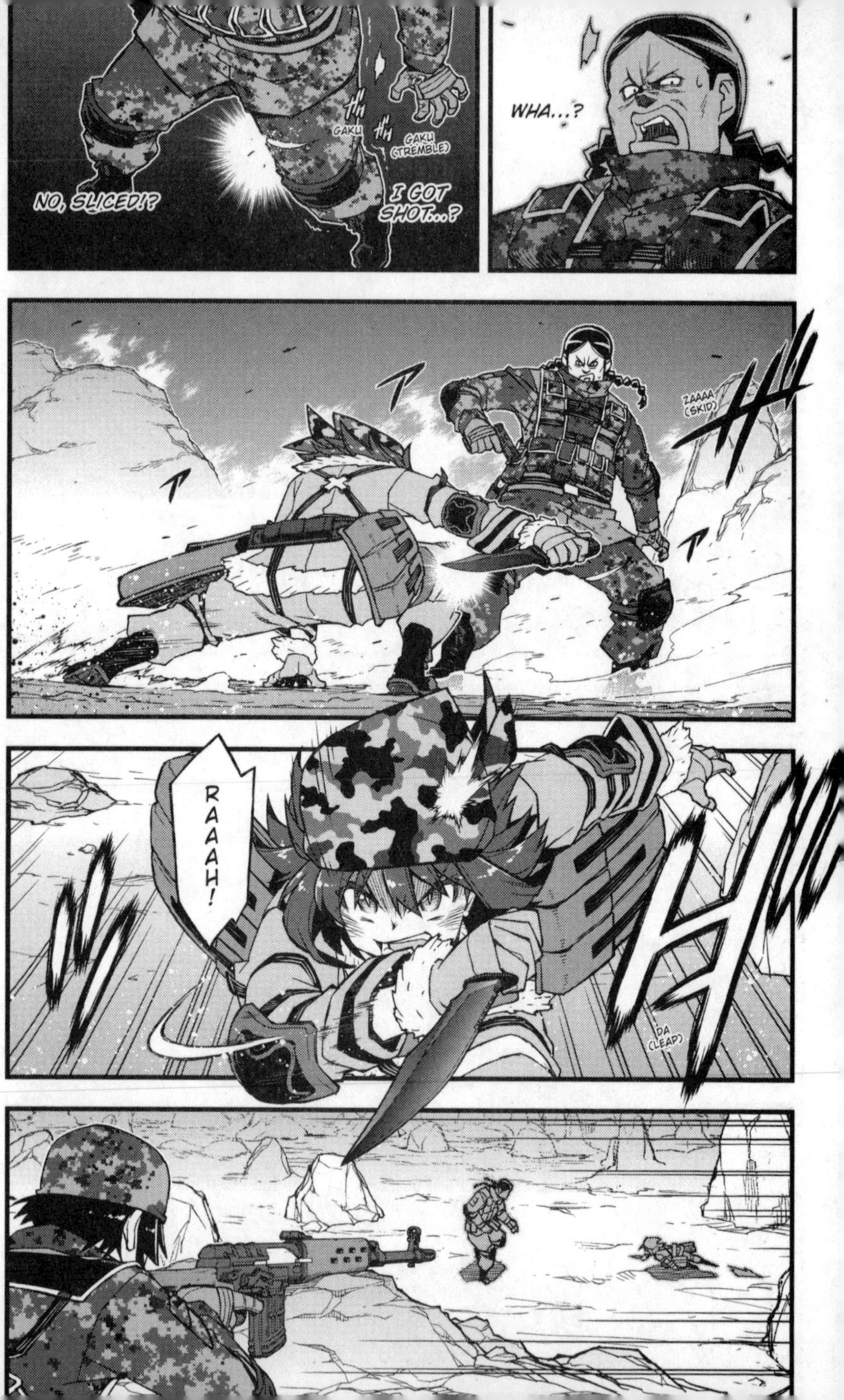
WHA...?
GAKU (TREMBLE)
GAKU
I GOT SHOT...?
NO, SLICED!?
ZAAAA (SKID)
DA (LEAP)
RAAAAH!

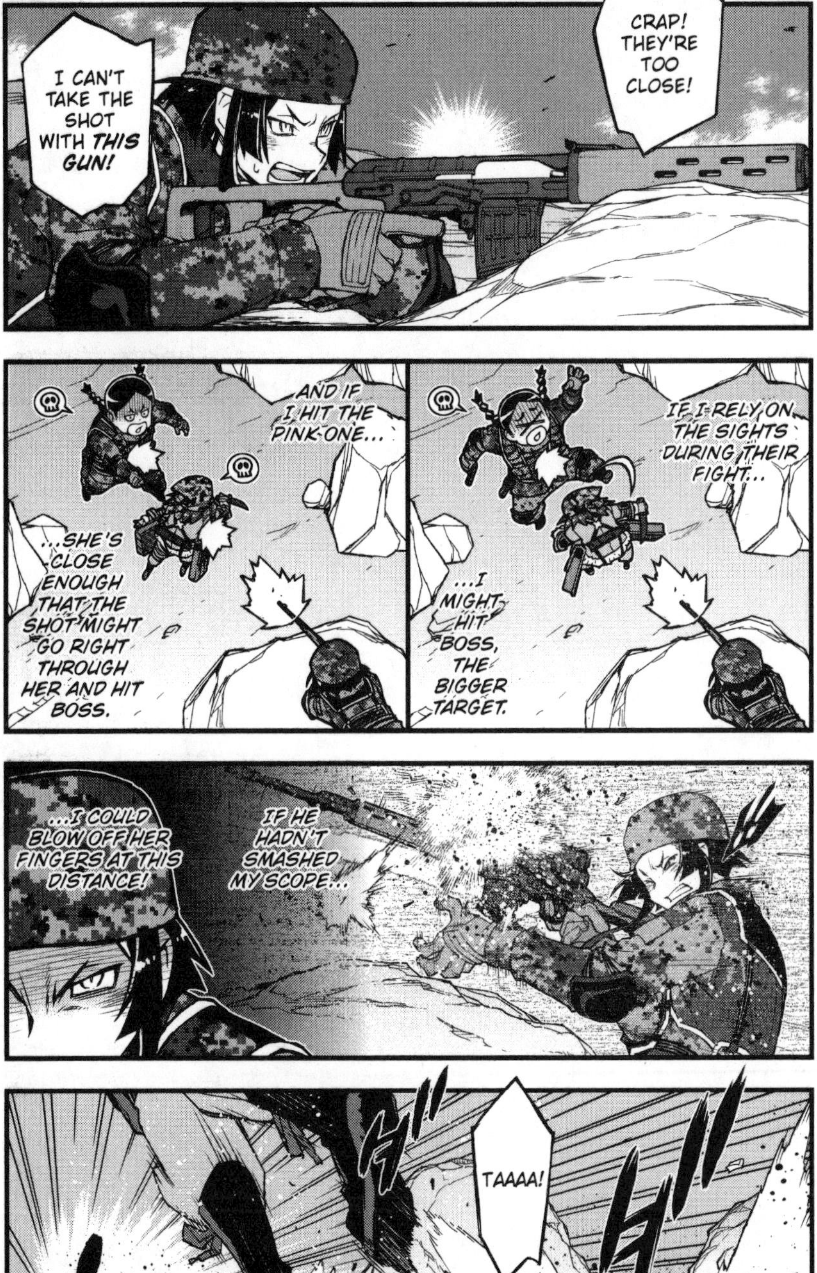
CRAP! THEY'RE TOO CLOSE!
I CAN'T TAKE THE SHOT WITH THIS GUN!
IF I RELY ON THE SIGHTS DURING THEIR FIGHT...
...I MIGHT HIT BOSS, THE BIGGER TARGET.
AND IF I HIT THE PINK ONE...
...SHE'S CLOSE ENOUGH THAT THE SHOT MIGHT GO RIGHT THROUGH HER AND HIT BOSS.
IF HE HADN'T SMASHED MY SCOPE...
...I COULD BLOW OFF HER FINGERS AT THIS DISTANCE!
TAAAA!
DADAN (DASH)

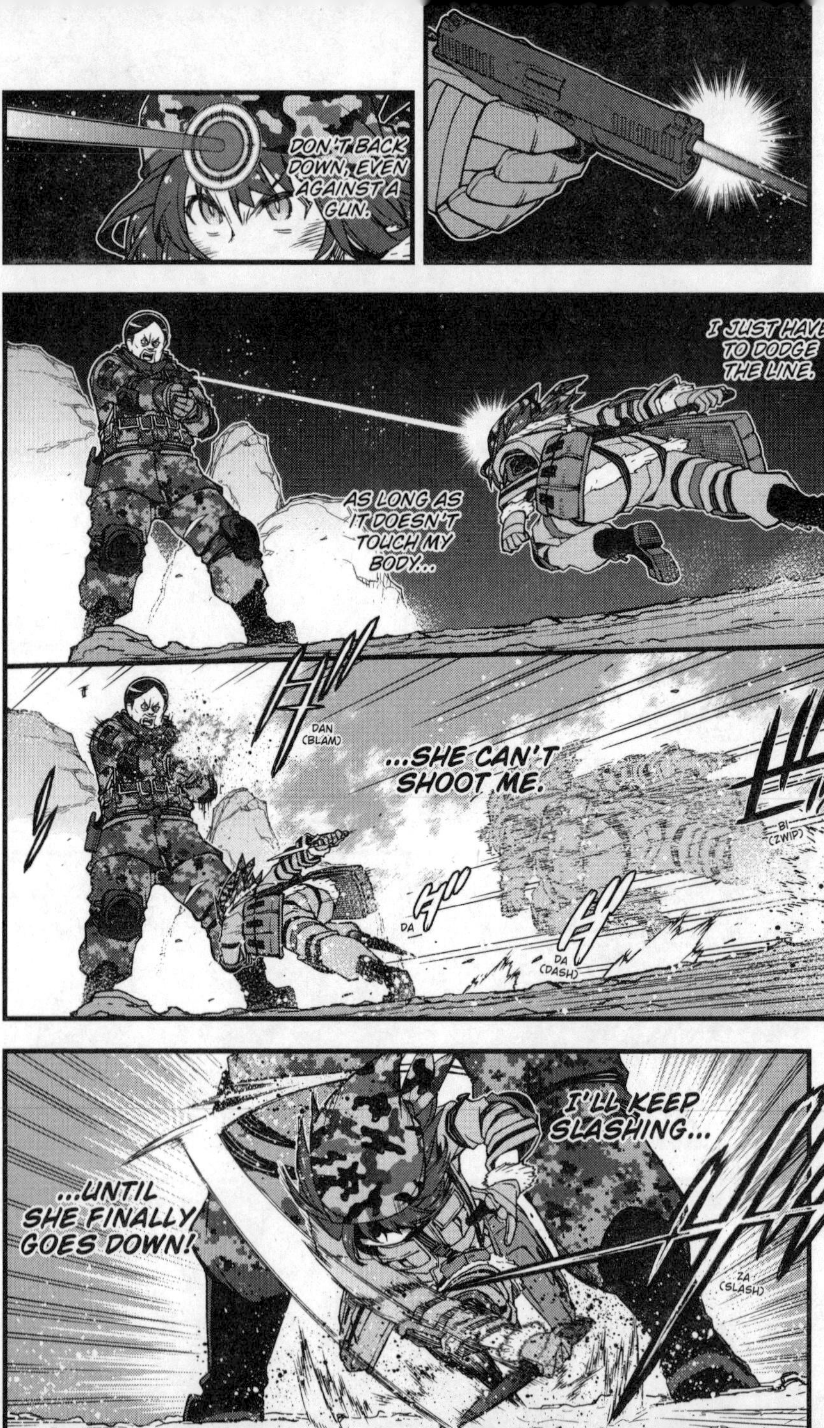
DON'T BACK DOWN, EVEN AGAINST A GUN.
I JUST HAVE TO DODGE THE LINE.
AS LONG AS IT DOESN'T TOUCH MY BODY...
BI (ZWIP)
...SHE CAN'T SHOOT ME.
DA (DASH)
DA
DAN (BLAM)
ZA (SLASH)
I'LL KEEP SLASHING...
...UNTIL SHE FINALLY GOES DOWN!

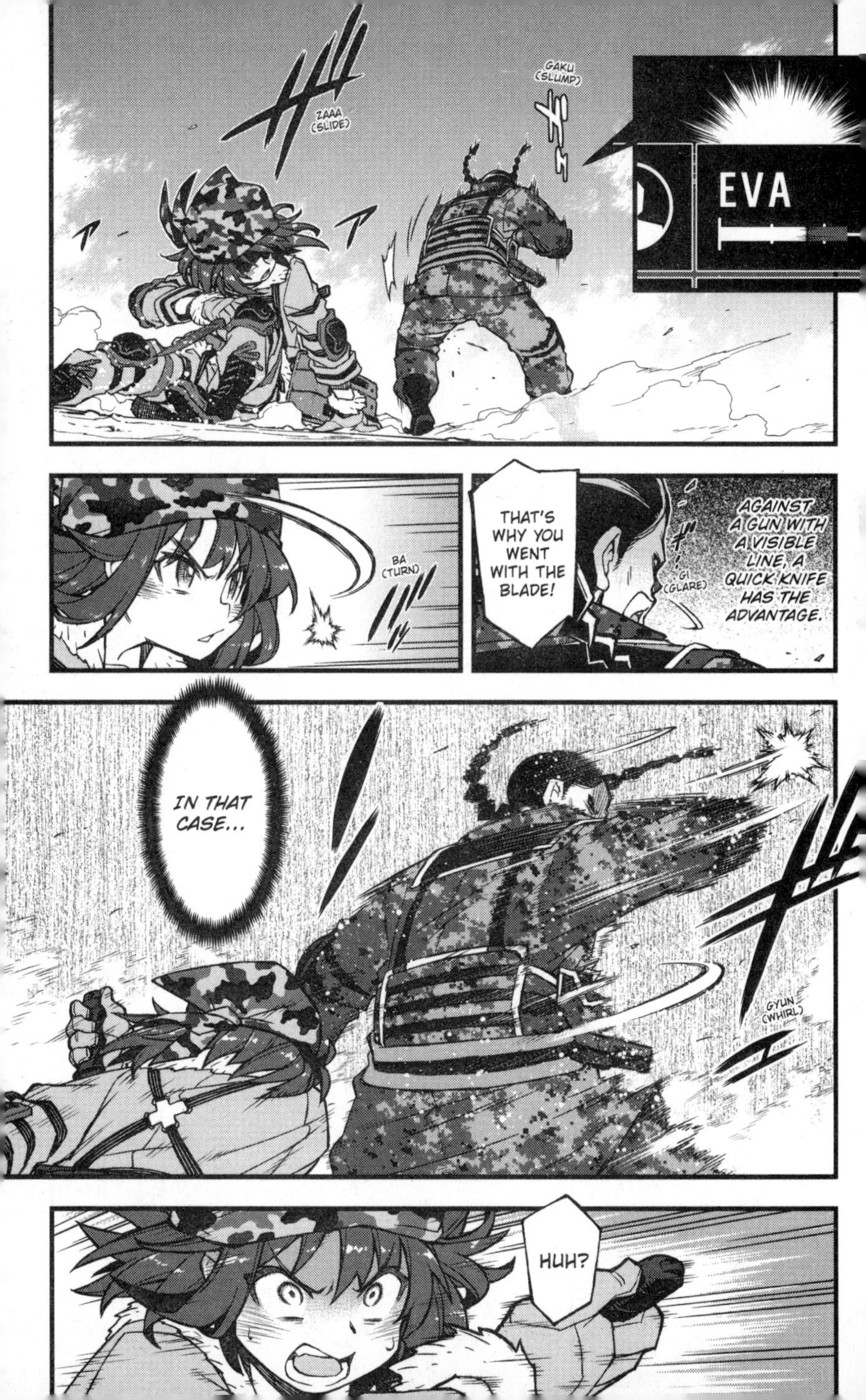
EVA
GAKU (SLUMP)
ZAAA (SLIDE)
AGAINST A GUN WITH A VISIBLE LINE, A QUICK KNIFE HAS THE ADVANTAGE.
GI (GLARE)
THAT'S WHY YOU WENT WITH THE BLADE!
BA (TURN)
GYUN (WHIRL)
IN THAT CASE...
HUH?

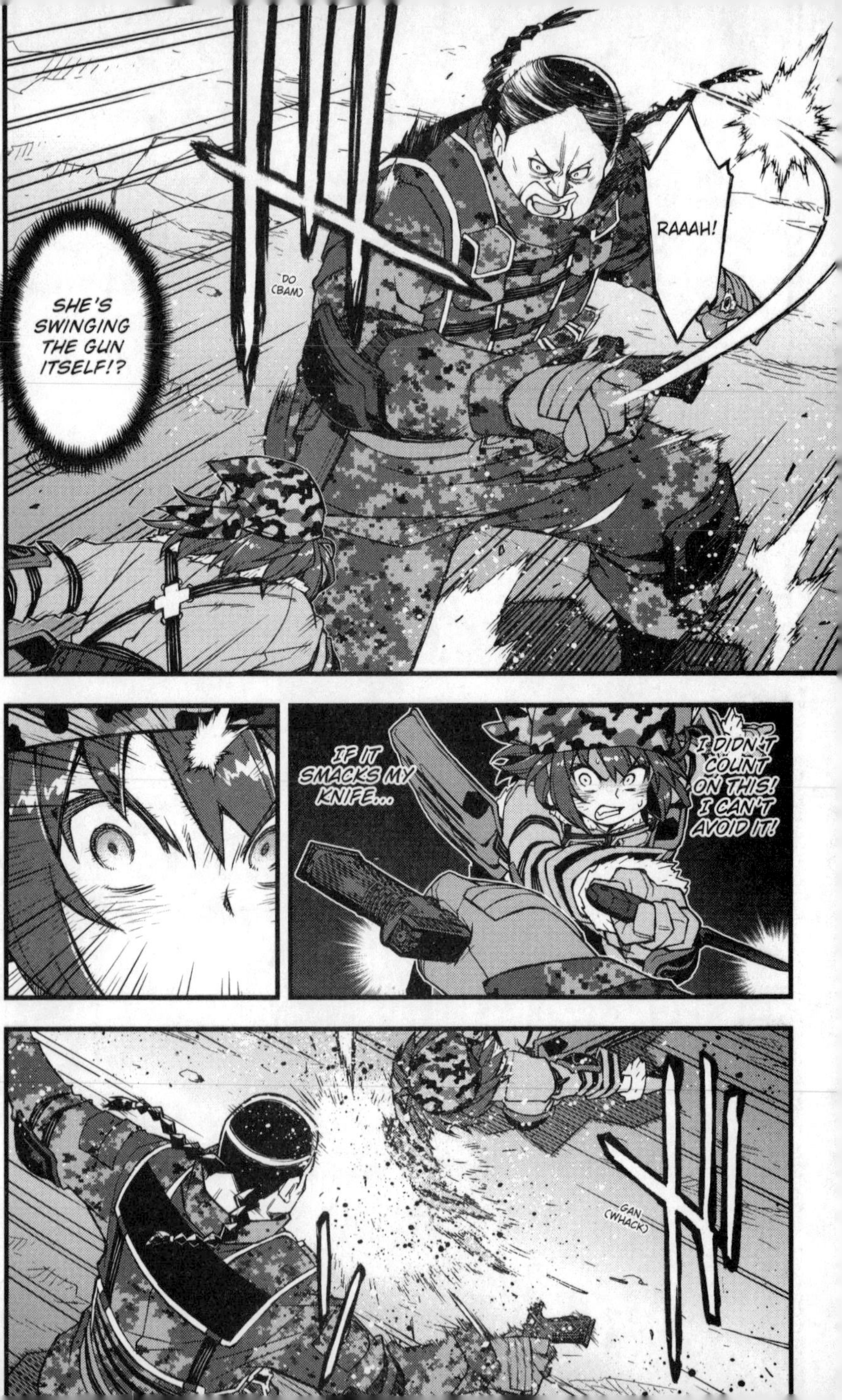
RAAAH!
DO (BAM)
SHE'S SWINGING THE GUN ITSELF!?
I DIDN'T COUNT ON THIS! I CAN'T AVOID IT!
IF IT SMACKS MY KNIFE...
GAN (WHACK)

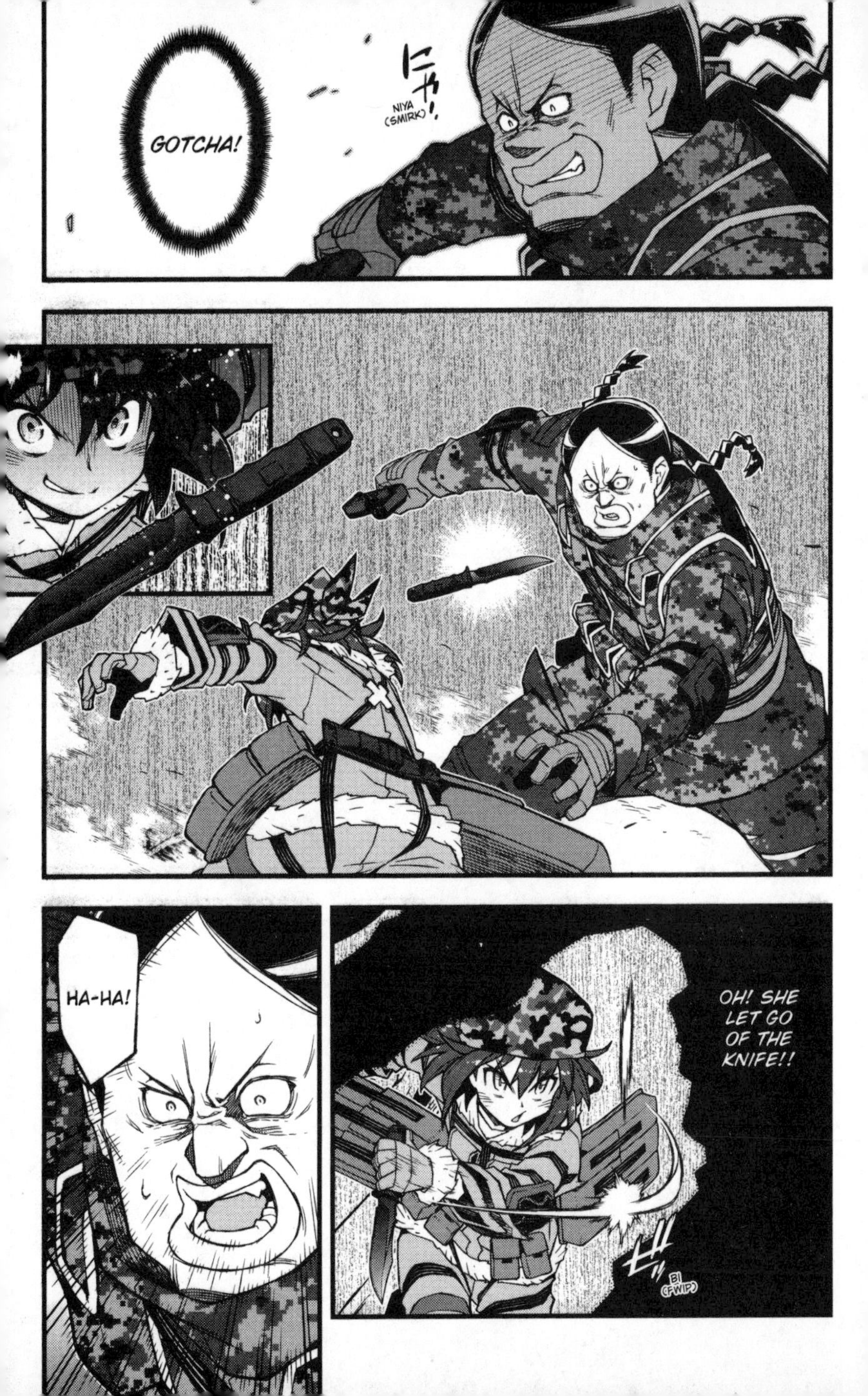

にや
NIYA (SMIRK)
GOTCHA!
OH! SHE LET GO OF THE KNIFE!!
BI (FWIP)
HA-HA!

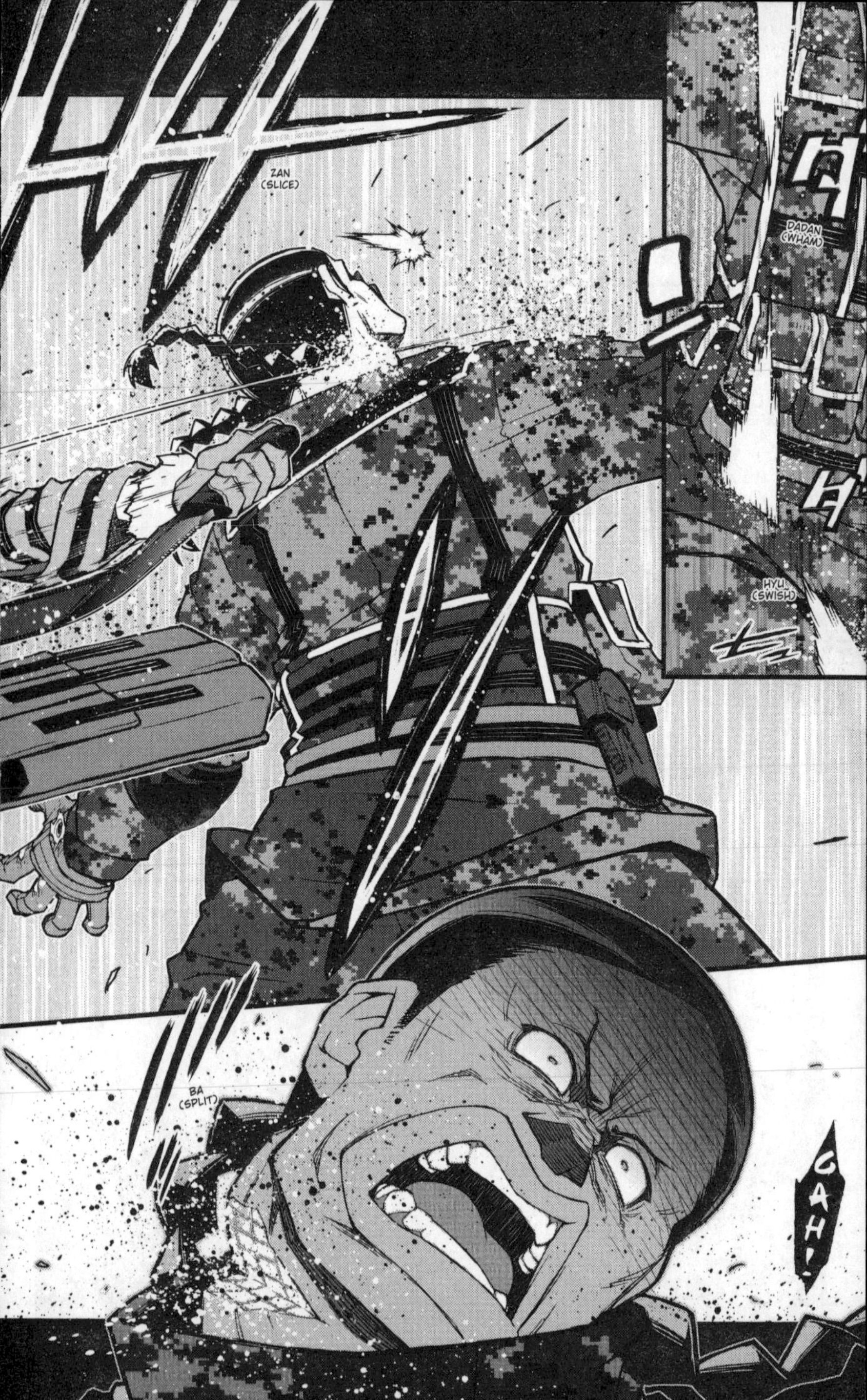
DADAN (WHAM)
HYU (SWISH)
ZAN (SLICE)
BA (SPLIT)
GAH!

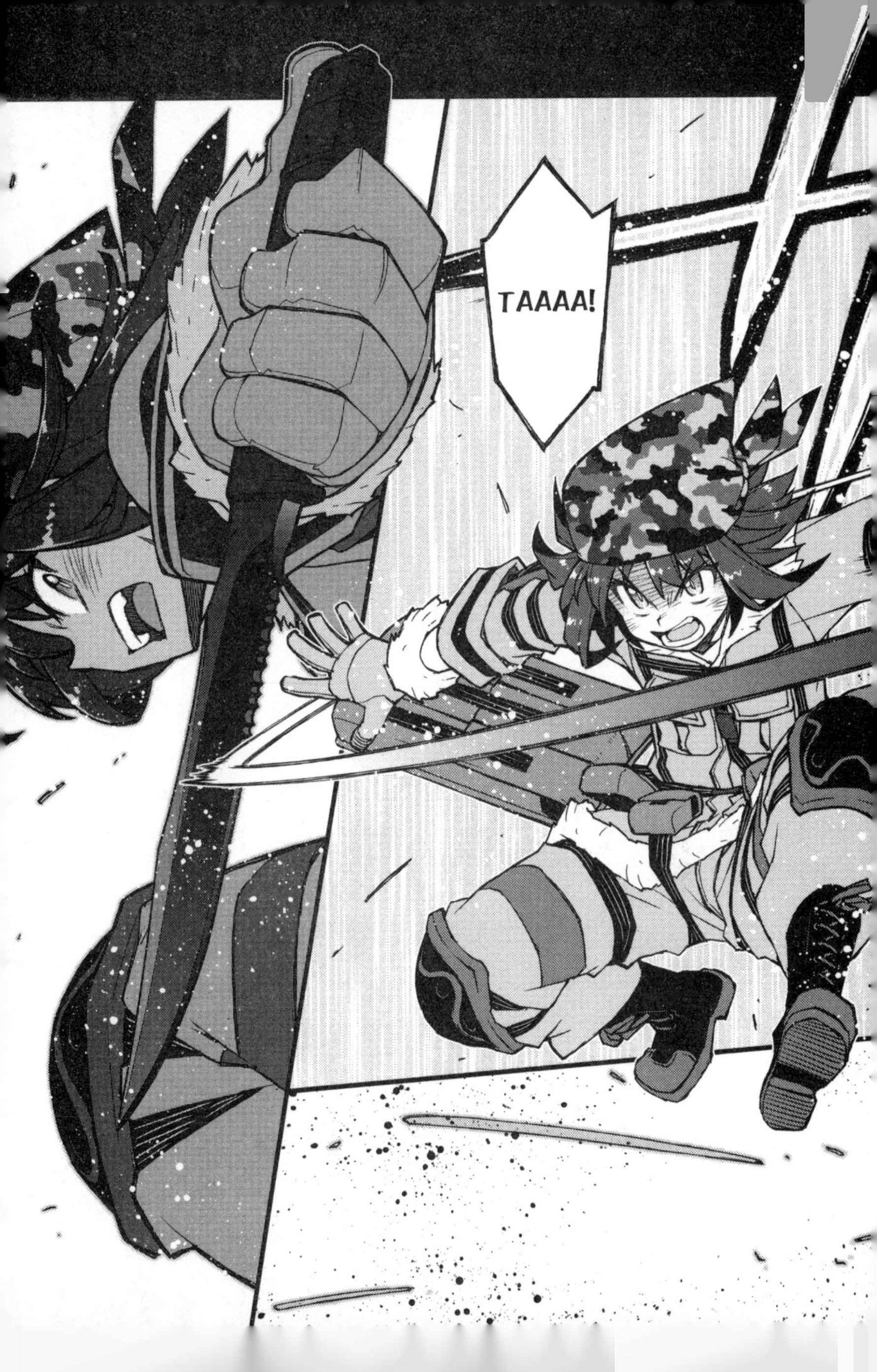
TAAAA!

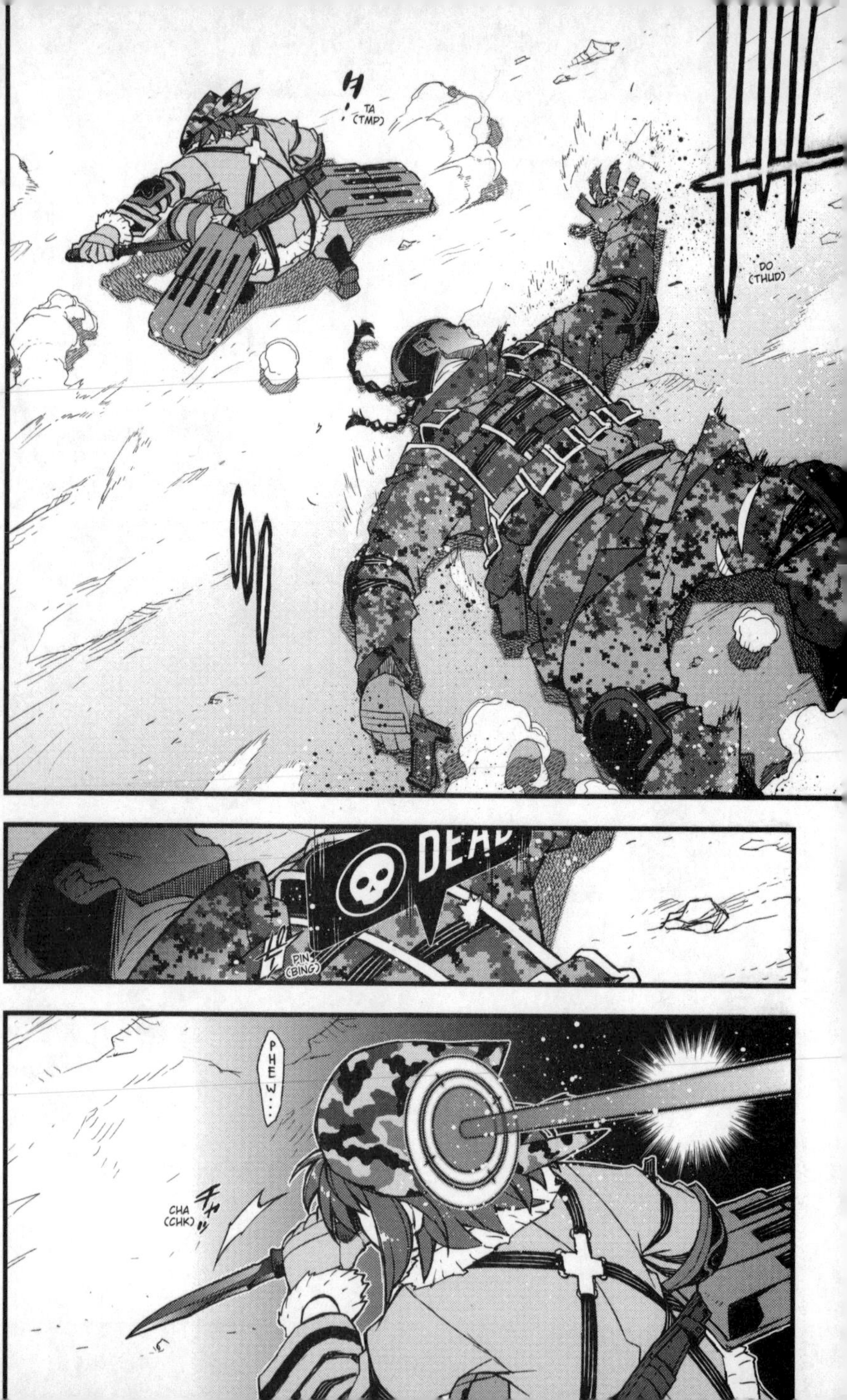
DO (THUD)
TA (TMP)
DEAD
PIN (BING)
PHEW...
CHA (CHK)

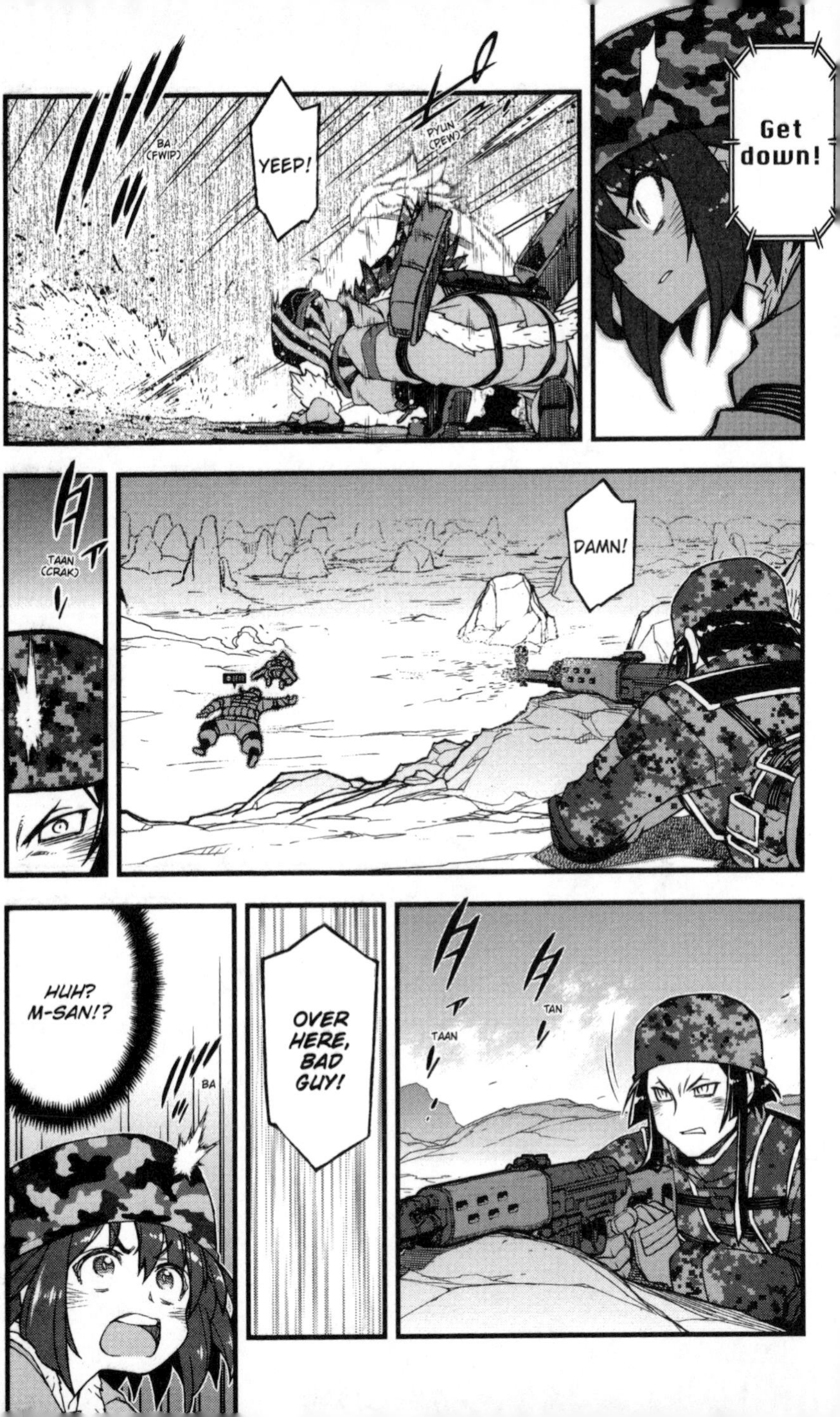
Get down!
PYUN (PEW)
YEEP!
BA (FWIP)
DAMN!
TAAN (CRAK)
TAN
TAAN
OVER HERE, BAD GUY!
HUH? M-SAN!?
BA

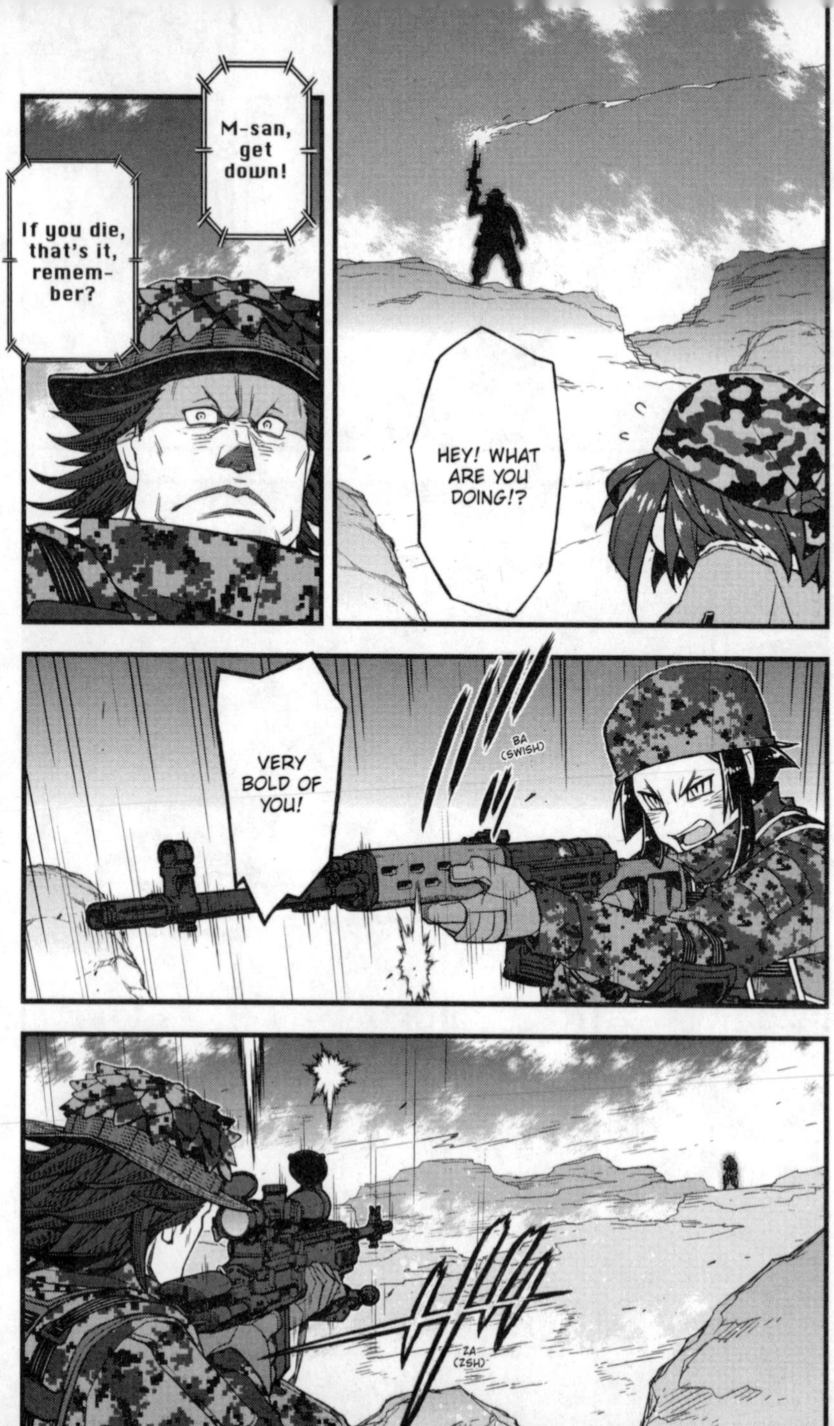
HEY! WHAT ARE YOU DOING!?
M-san, get down!
If you die, that's it, remember?
VERY BOLD OF YOU!
BA (SWISH)
ZA (ZSH)

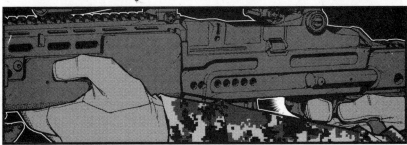

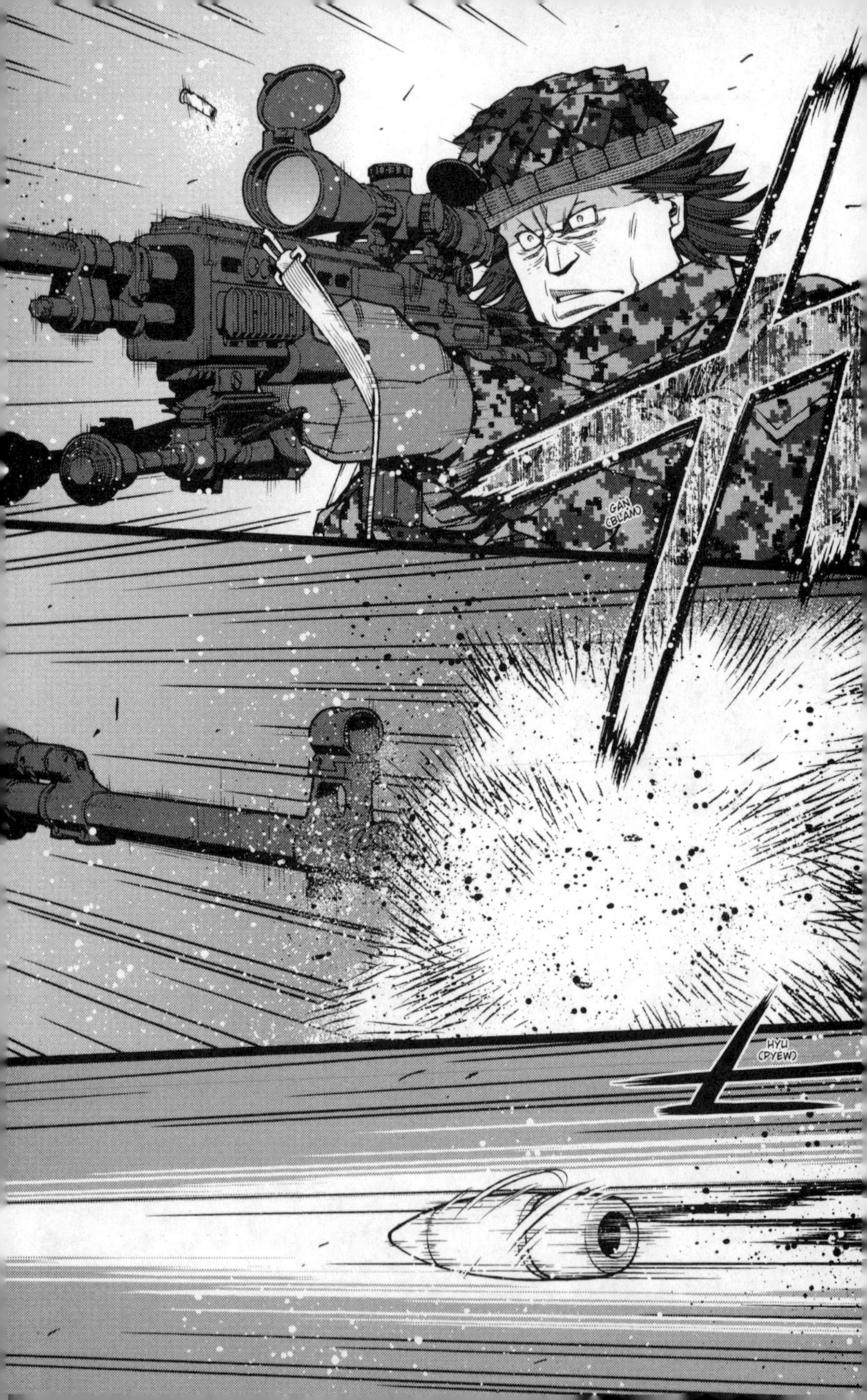
GAN (BLAM)
HYU (PYEW)

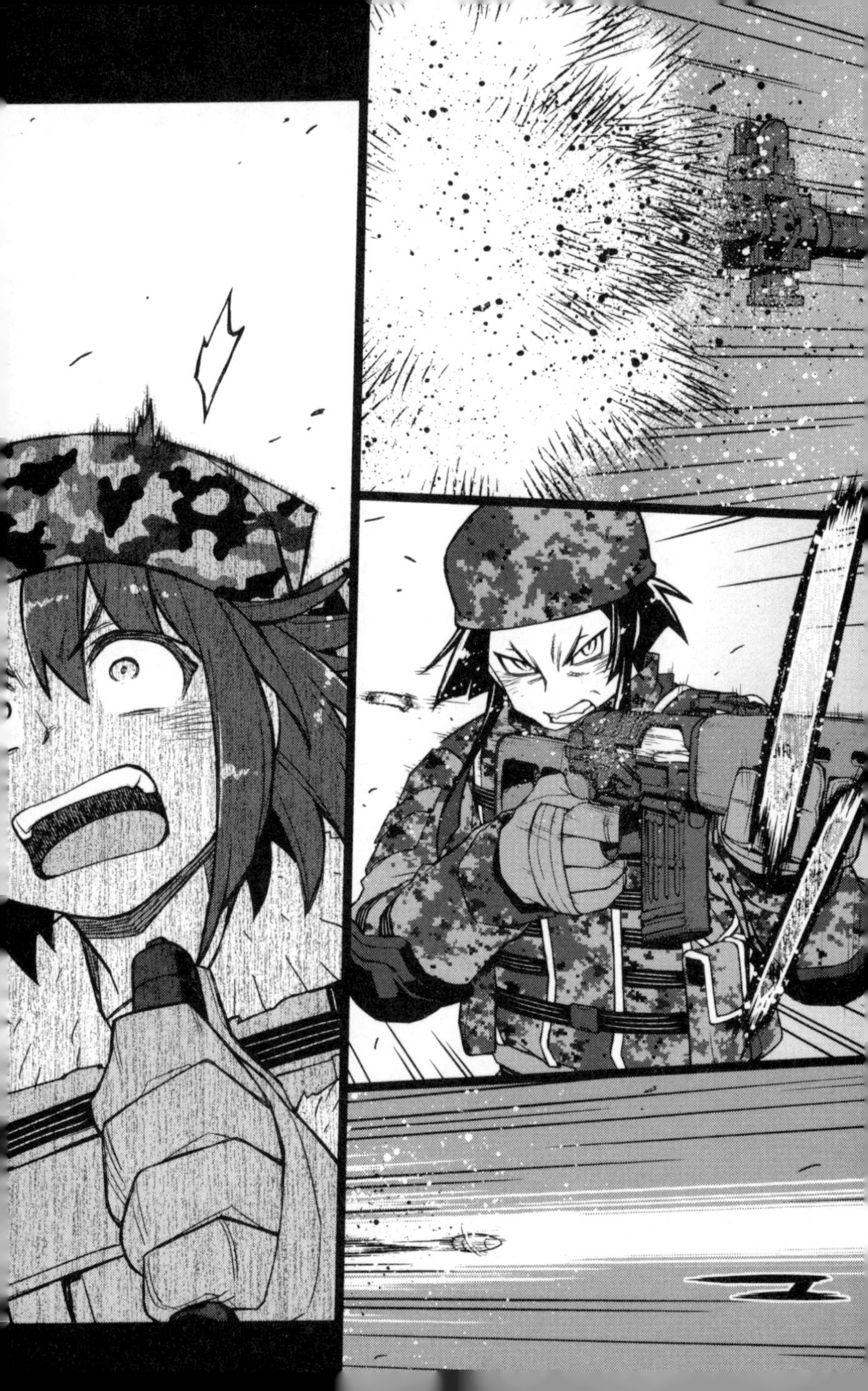

チッ
CHI
(TIK)
DO,
(BOOM)
GAH!
GURA
(STAGGER)
ぐら…!

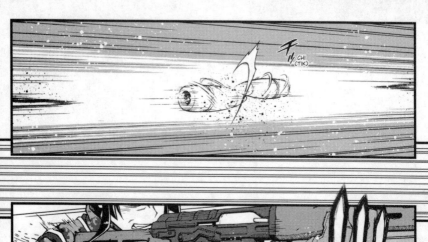

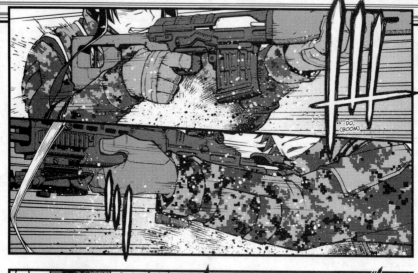

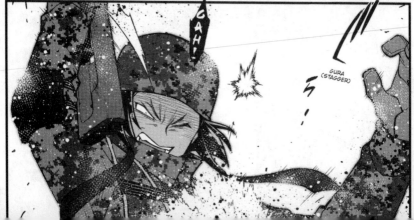

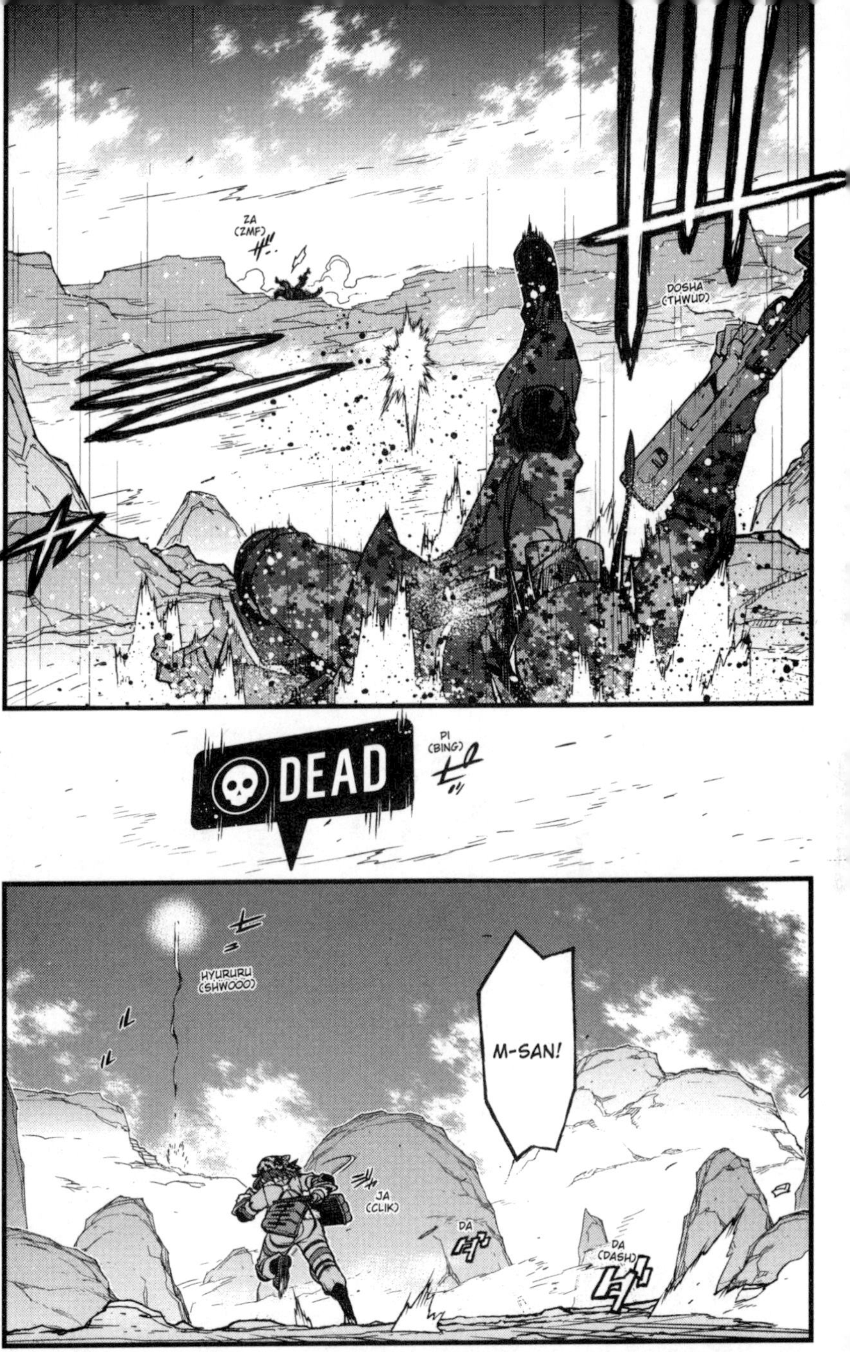
DOSHA (THWUD)
ZA (ZMF)
DEAD
PI (BING)
M-SAN!
DA (DASH)
DA
JA (CLIK)
HYURURU (SHWOOO)

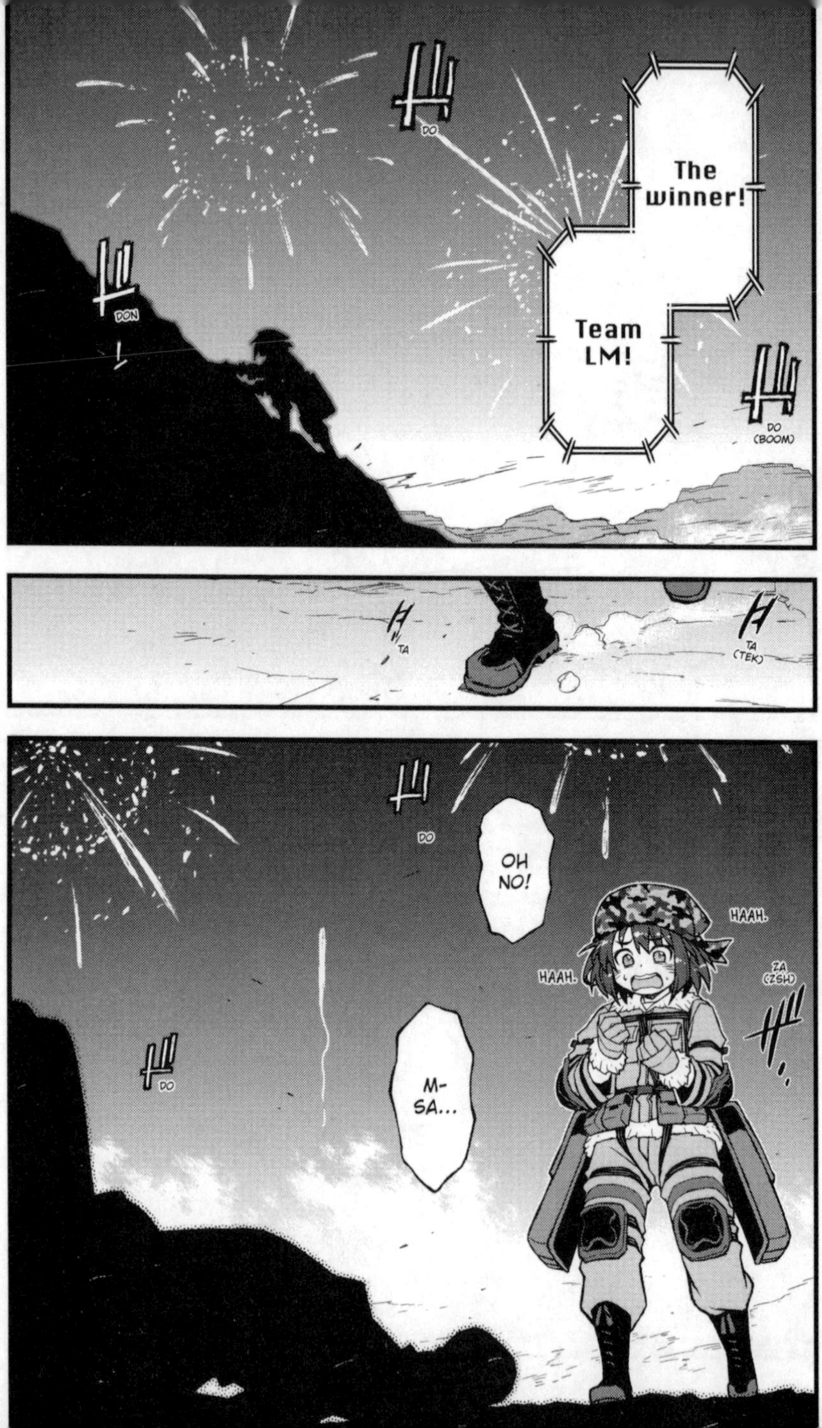

The winner!
Team LM!
DO
DO (BOOM)
DON !
TA (TEK)
TA
HAAH.
ZA (ZSH)
DO
OH NO!
HAAH.
M-SA...
DO

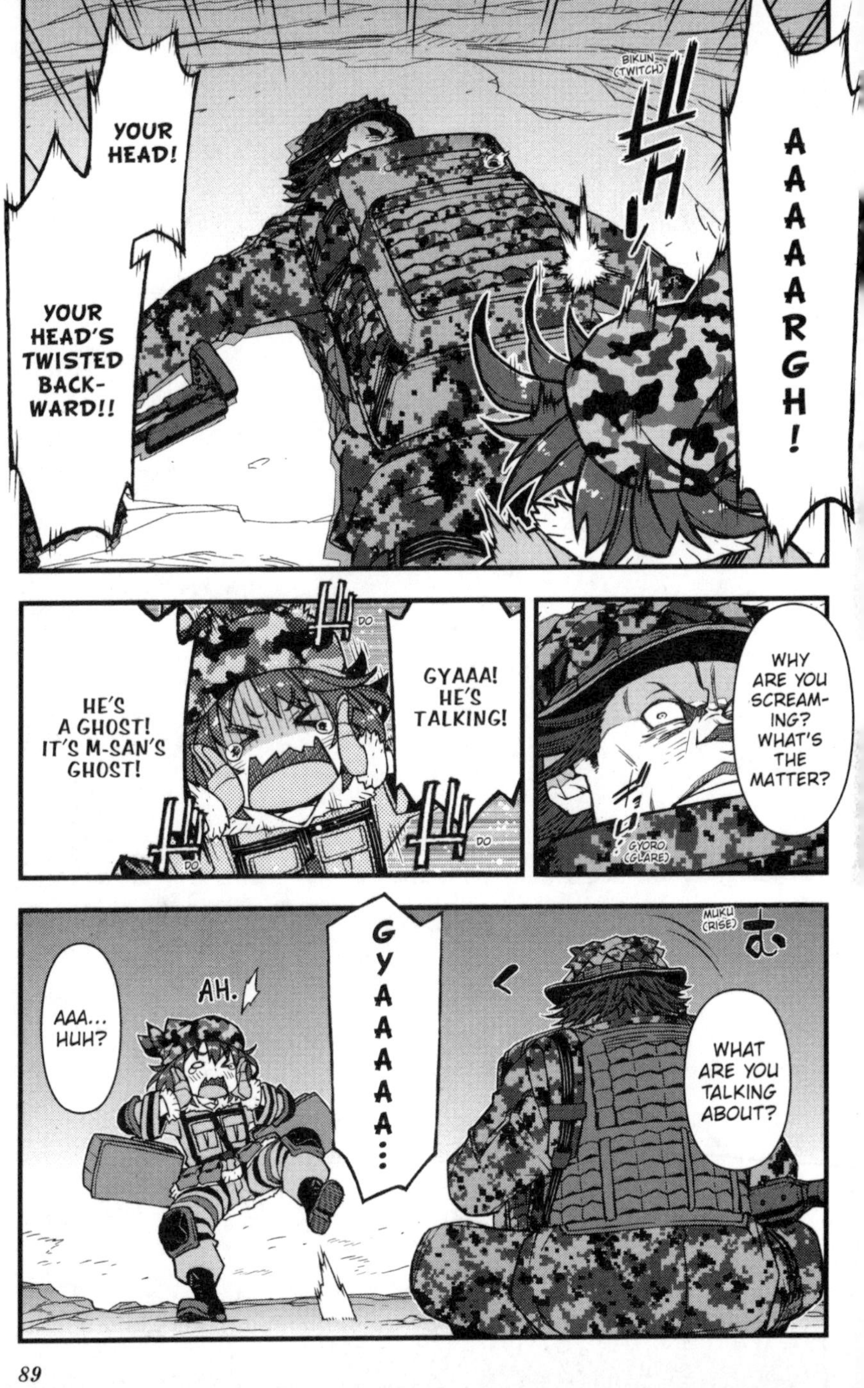
AAAAAAARGH!
BIKUN (TWITCH)
YOUR HEAD!
YOUR HEAD'S TWISTED BACK-WARD!!
WHY ARE YOU SCREAM-ING? WHAT'S THE MATTER?
GYORO (GLARE)
GYAAA! HE'S TALKING!
DO
HE'S A GHOST! IT'S M-SAN'S GHOST!
DO
DO
MUKU (RISE)
WHAT ARE YOU TALKING ABOUT?
GYAAAAAA...
AH.
AAA... HUH?

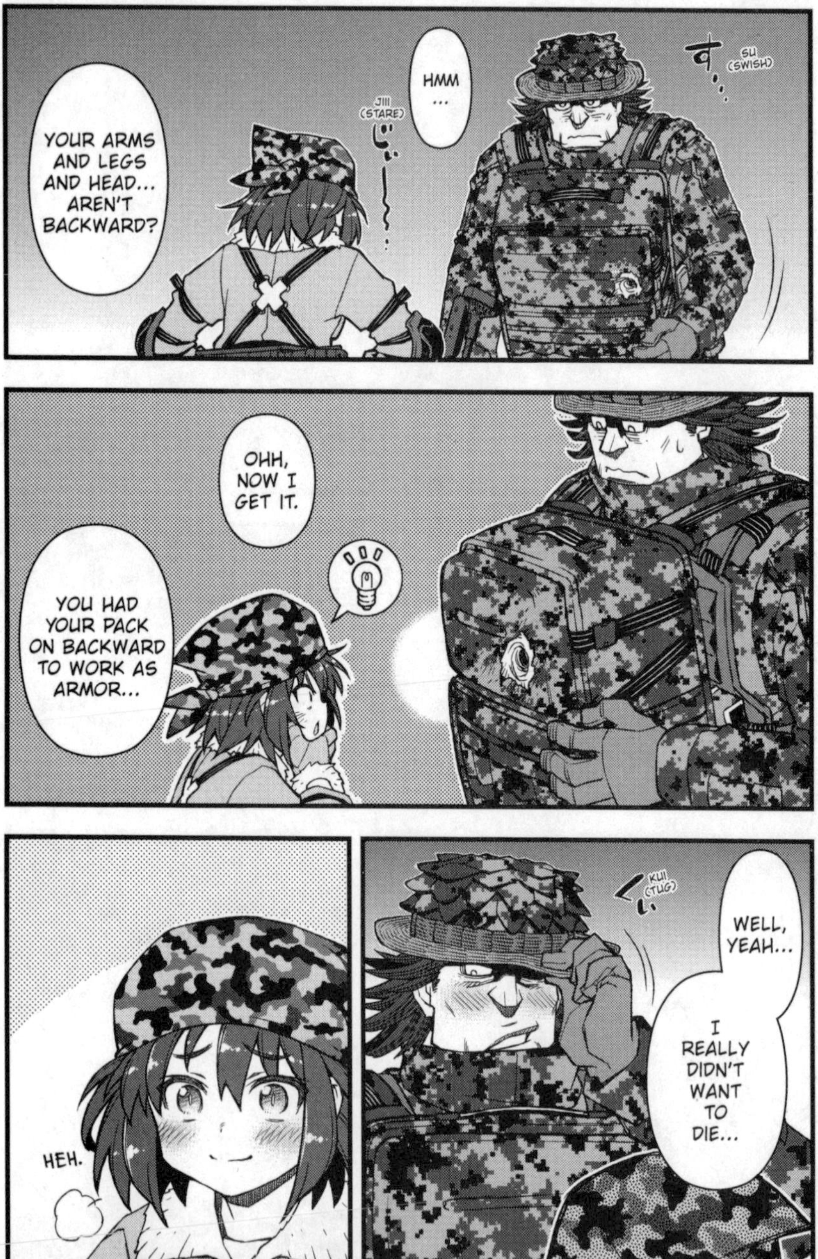

す
SU (SWISH)
HMM...
JIII (STARE)
YOUR ARMS AND LEGS AND HEAD... AREN'T BACKWARD?
OHH, NOW I GET IT.
YOU HAD YOUR PACK ON BACKWARD TO WORK AS ARMOR...
KUI (TUG)
WELL, YEAH...
I REALLY DIDN'T WANT TO DIE...
HEH.

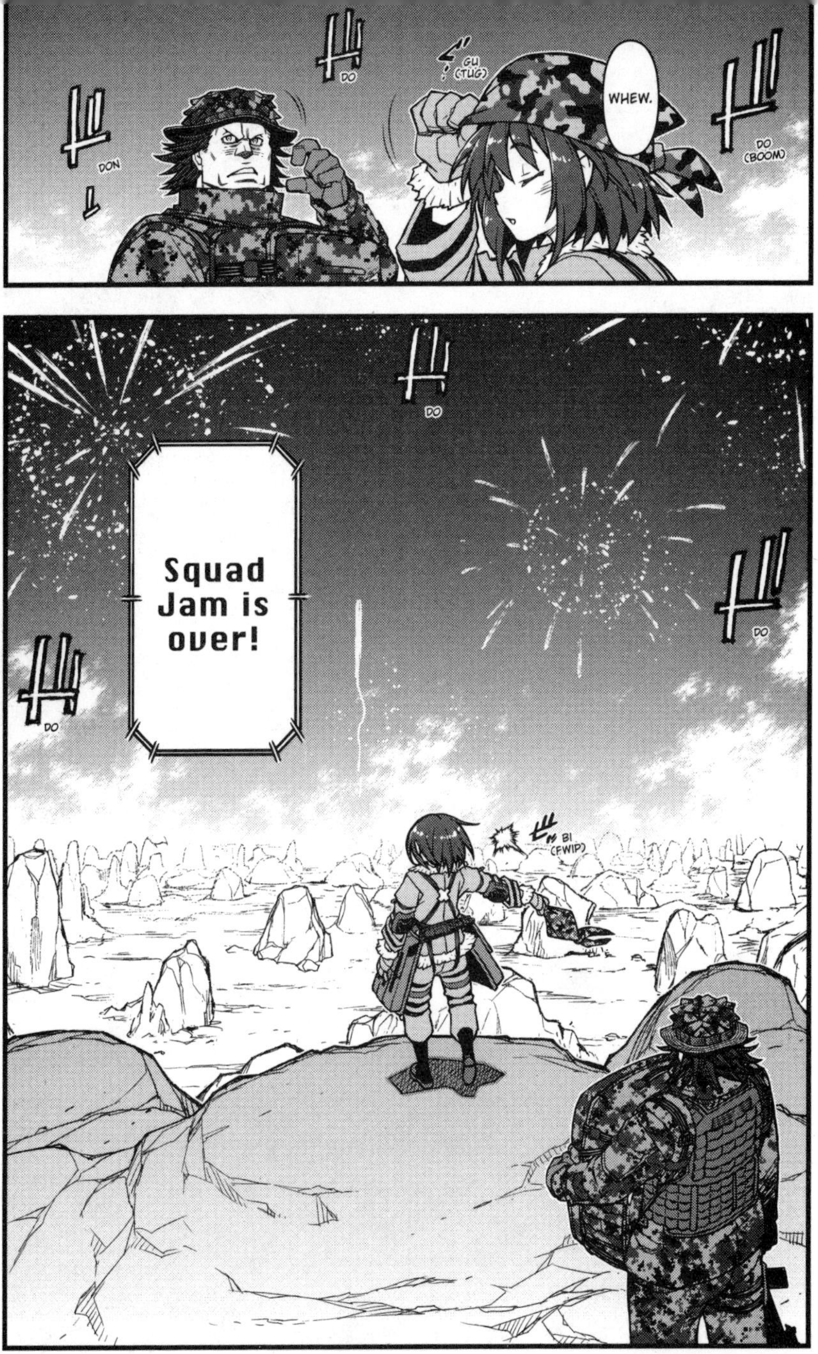
WHEW.
DO (BOOM)
GU (TUG)
DO
DON
DO
DO
Squad Jam is over!
DO
BI (FWIP)

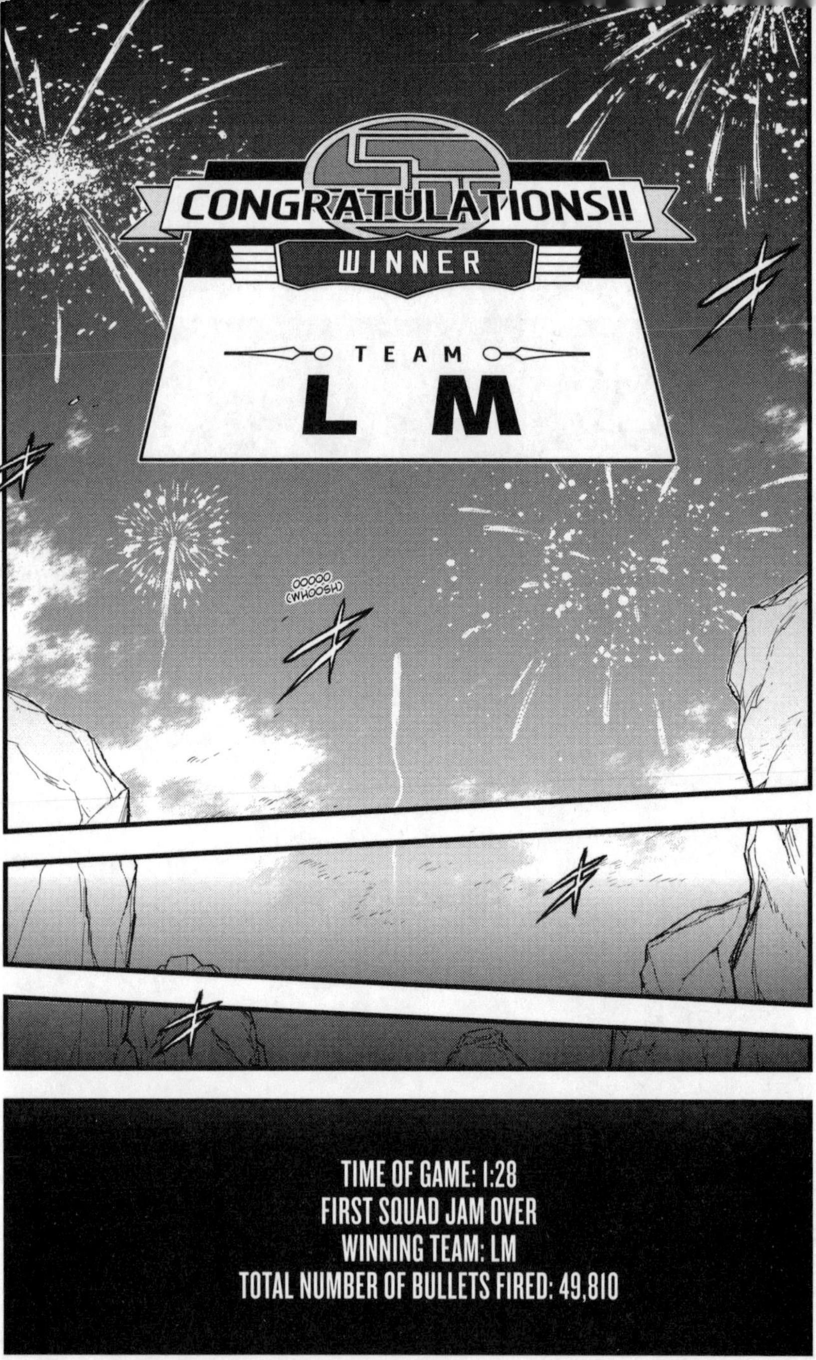
CONGRATULATIONS!!
WINNER
TEAM
L M
OOOOO (WHOOSH)
TIME OF GAME: 1:28
FIRST SQUAD JAM OVER
WINNING TEAM: LM
TOTAL NUMBER OF BULLETS FIRED: 49,810

SWORD ART ONLINE ALTERNATIVE
GUN GALE ONLINE

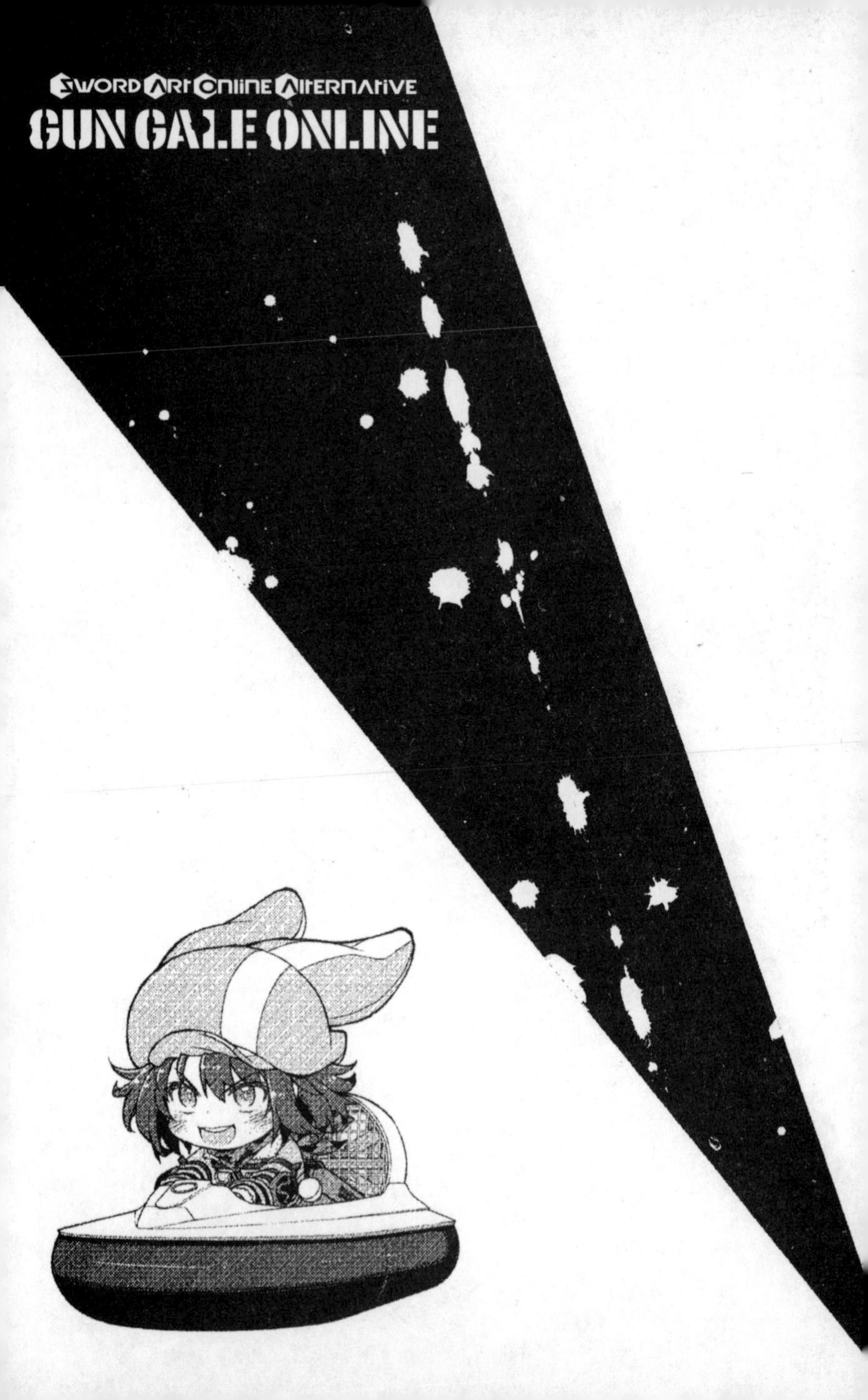
Sword Art Online Alternative
GUN GALE ONLINE

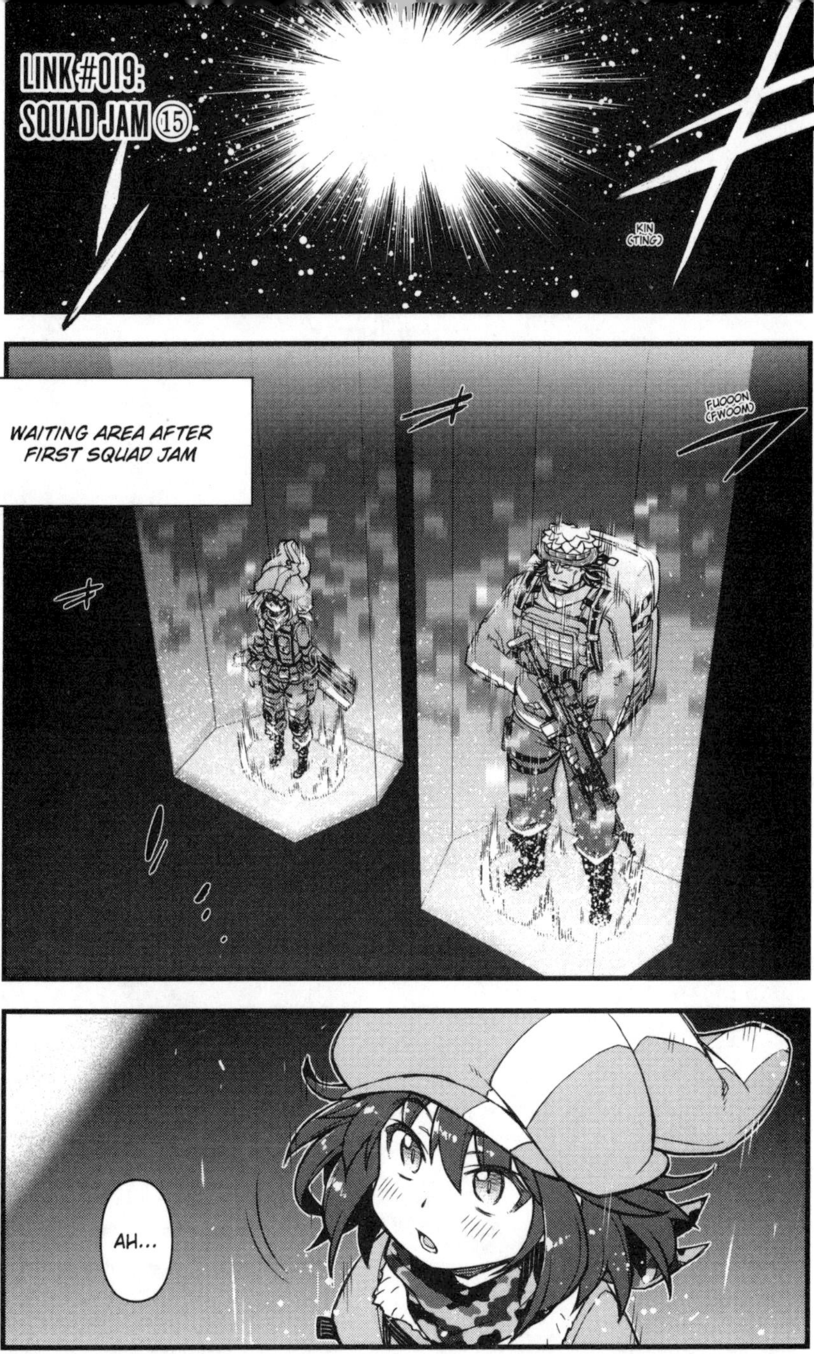
LINK #019:
SQUAD JAM ⑮
KIN (TING)
WAITING AREA AFTER FIRST SQUAD JAM
FUOOON (FWOOM)
AH...

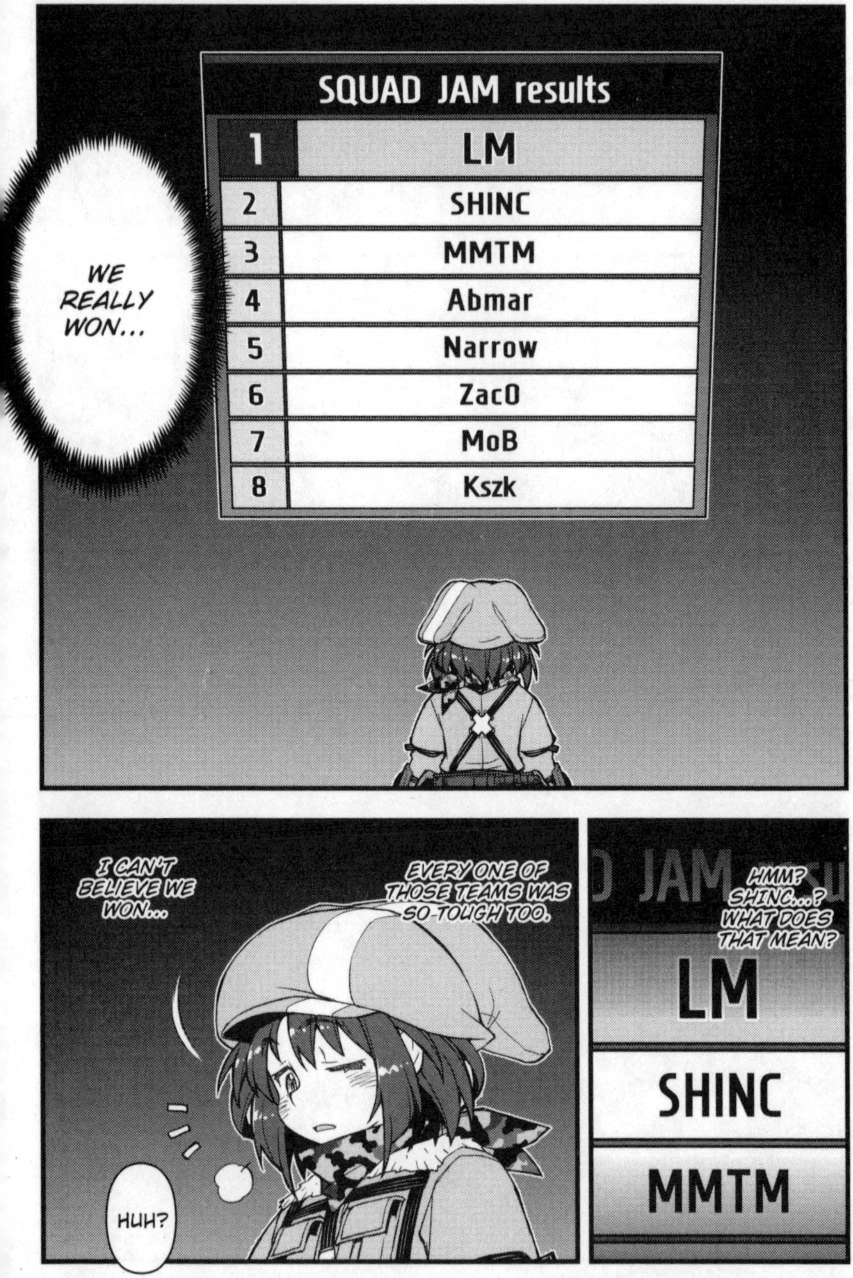

SQUAD JAM results
1 LM
2 SHINC
3 MMTM
4 Abmar
5 Narrow
6 ZacO
7 MoB
8 Kszk
WE REALLY WON...
D JAM
LM
SHINC
MMTM
HMM? SHINC...? WHAT DOES THAT MEAN?
EVERY ONE OF THOSE TEAMS WAS SO TOUGH TOO.
I CAN'T BELIEVE WE WON...
HUH?

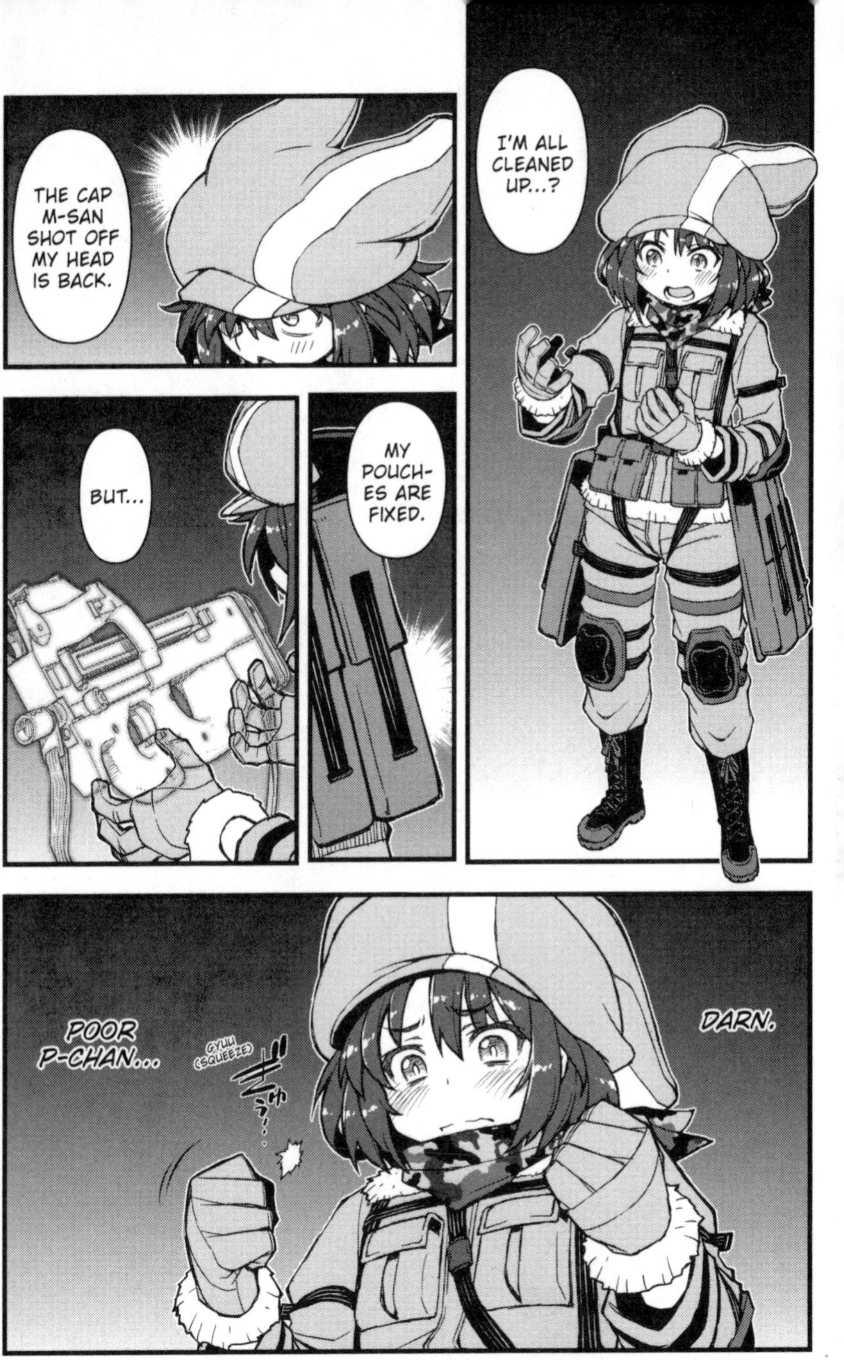
I'M ALL CLEANED UP...?
THE CAP M-SAN SHOT OFF MY HEAD IS BACK.
MY POUCH-ES ARE FIXED.
BUT...
DARN.
GYUU (SQUEEZE)
POOR P-CHAN...

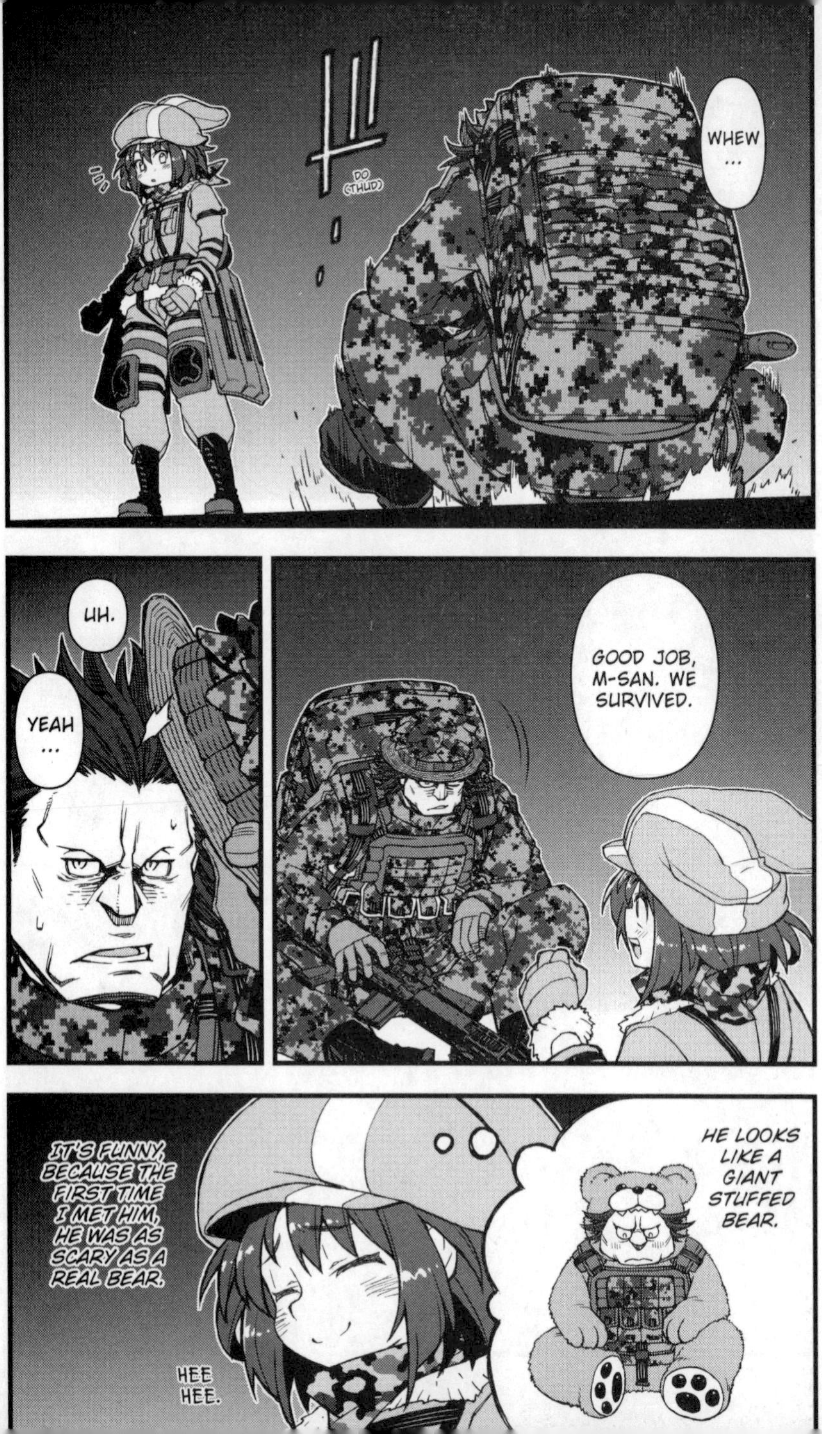
WHEW ...
DO (THUD)
GOOD JOB, M-SAN. WE SURVIVED.
UH.
YEAH ...
HE LOOKS LIKE A GIANT STUFFED BEAR.
IT'S FUNNY, BECAUSE THE FIRST TIME I MET HIM, HE WAS AS SCARY AS A REAL BEAR.
HEE HEE.

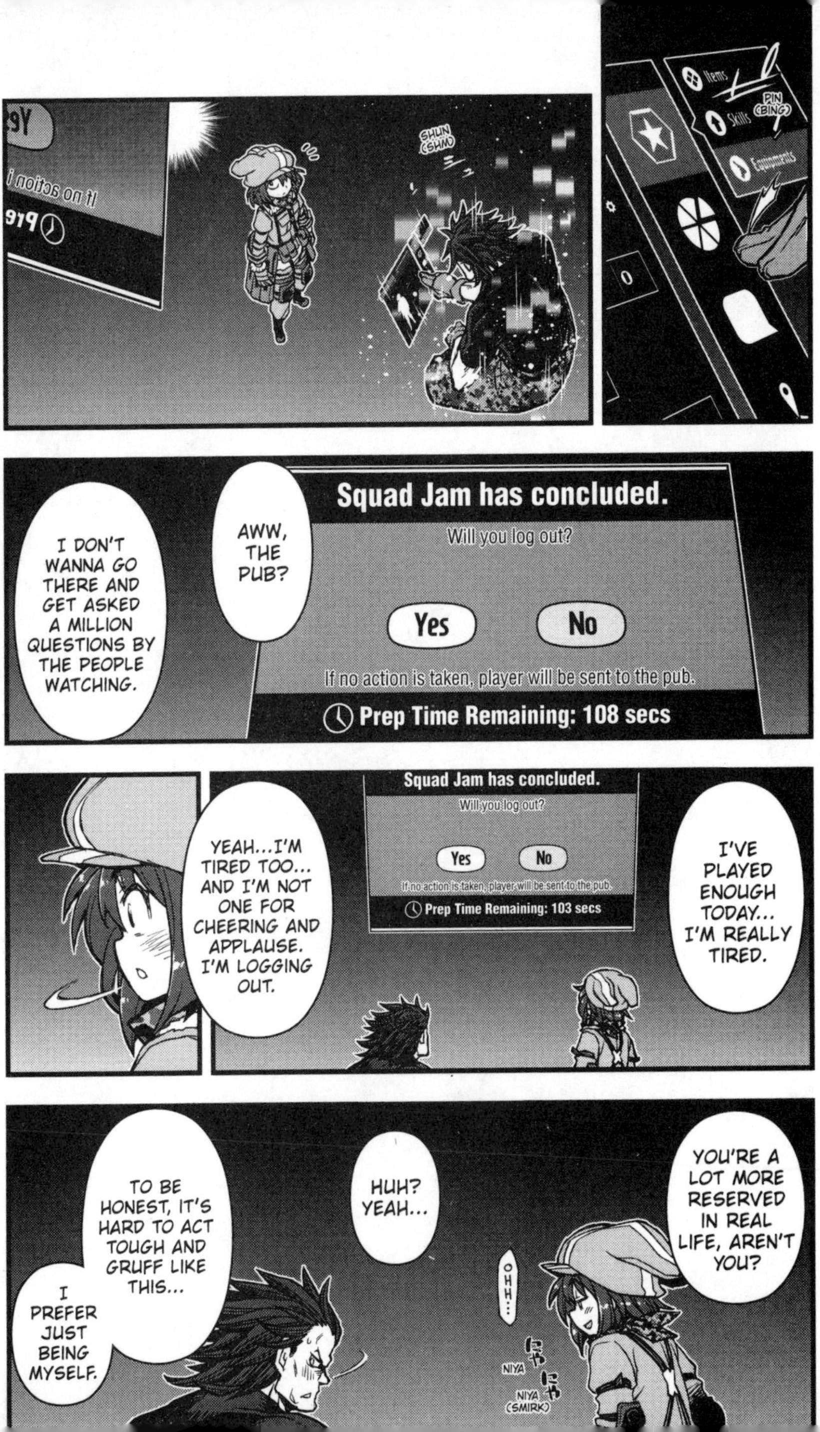
Items
PIN (BING)
Skills
Equipments
SHUN (SHM)
Squad Jam has concluded.
Will you log out?
Yes
No
If no action is taken, player will be sent to the pub.
Prep Time Remaining: 108 secs
AWW, THE PUB?
I DON'T WANNA GO THERE AND GET ASKED A MILLION QUESTIONS BY THE PEOPLE WATCHING.
I'VE PLAYED ENOUGH TODAY... I'M REALLY TIRED.
Squad Jam has concluded.
Will you log out?
Yes
No
If no action is taken, player will be sent to the pub.
Prep Time Remaining: 103 secs
YEAH...I'M TIRED TOO... AND I'M NOT ONE FOR CHEERING AND APPLAUSE. I'M LOGGING OUT.
YOU'RE A LOT MORE RESERVED IN REAL LIFE, AREN'T YOU?
OHH...
NIYA
NIYA (SMIRK)
HUH? YEAH...
TO BE HONEST, IT'S HARD TO ACT TOUGH AND GRUFF LIKE THIS...
I PREFER JUST BEING MYSELF.

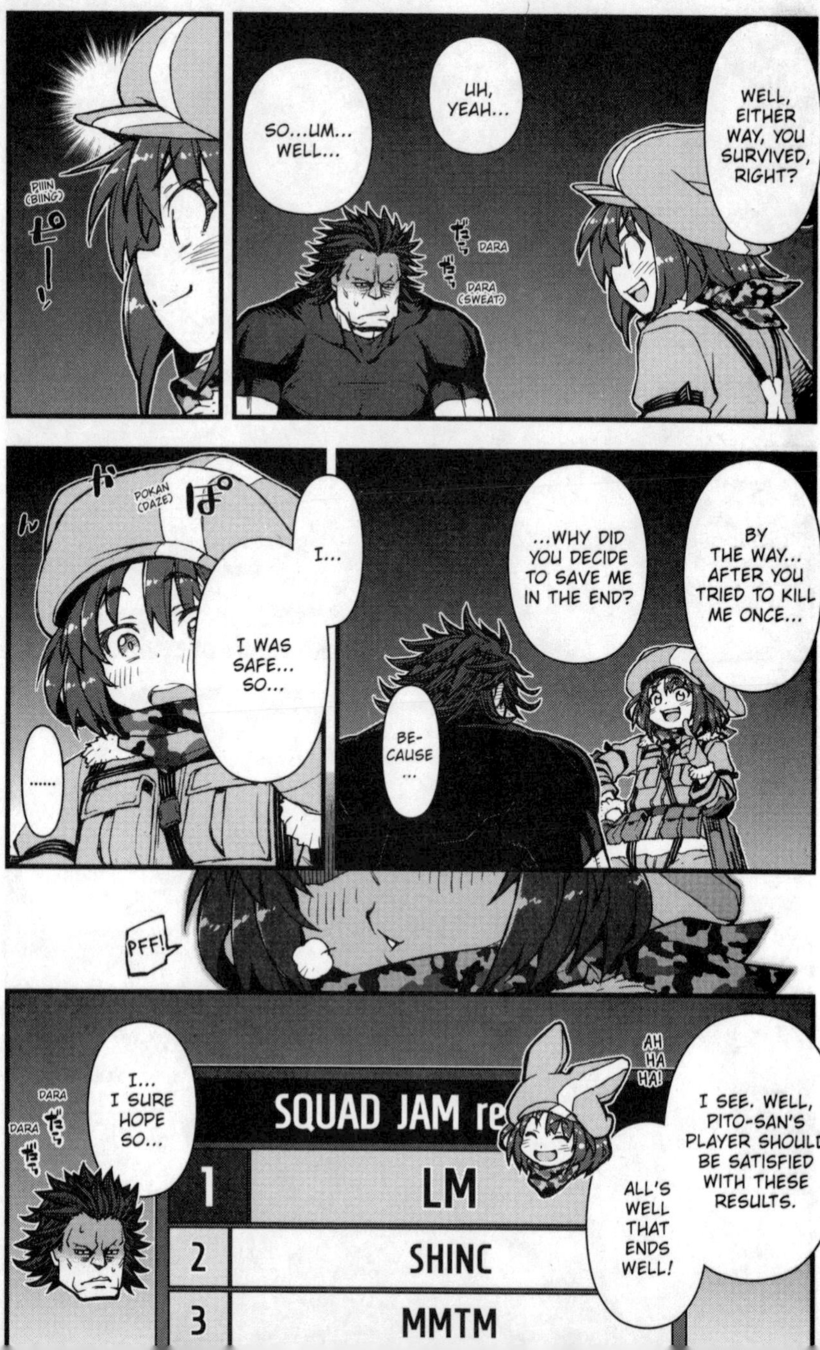
WELL, EITHER WAY, YOU SURVIVED, RIGHT?
UH, YEAH...
SO...UM... WELL...
DARA
DARA (SWEAT)
PIIIN (BIING)
BY THE WAY... AFTER YOU TRIED TO KILL ME ONCE...
...WHY DID YOU DECIDE TO SAVE ME IN THE END?
BE-CAUSE ...
I...
I WAS SAFE... SO...
POKAN (DAZE)
......
PFF!
I SEE. WELL, PITO-SAN'S PLAYER SHOULD BE SATISFIED WITH THESE RESULTS.
AH HA HA!
ALL'S WELL THAT ENDS WELL!
I... I SURE HOPE SO...
DARA
DARA
SQUAD JAM re
1 LM
2 SHINC
3 MMTM

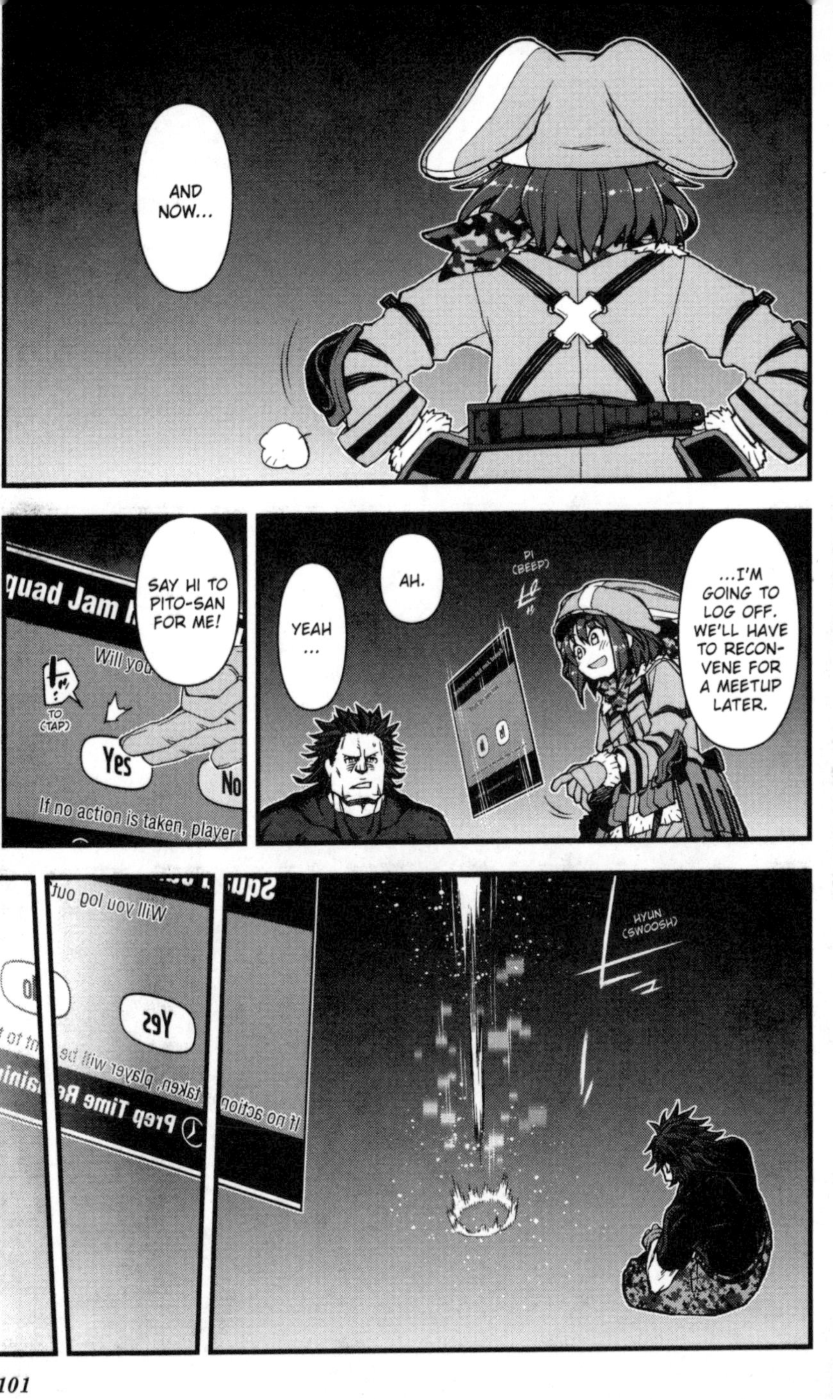
AND NOW...
...I'M GOING TO LOG OFF. WE'LL HAVE TO RECON-VENE FOR A MEETUP LATER.
PI (BEEP)
AH.
YEAH ...
SAY HI TO PITO-SAN FOR ME!
TO (TAP)
Yes
No
HYUN (SWOOSH)

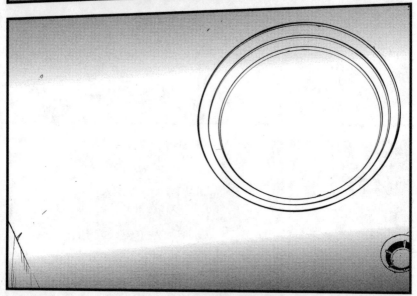

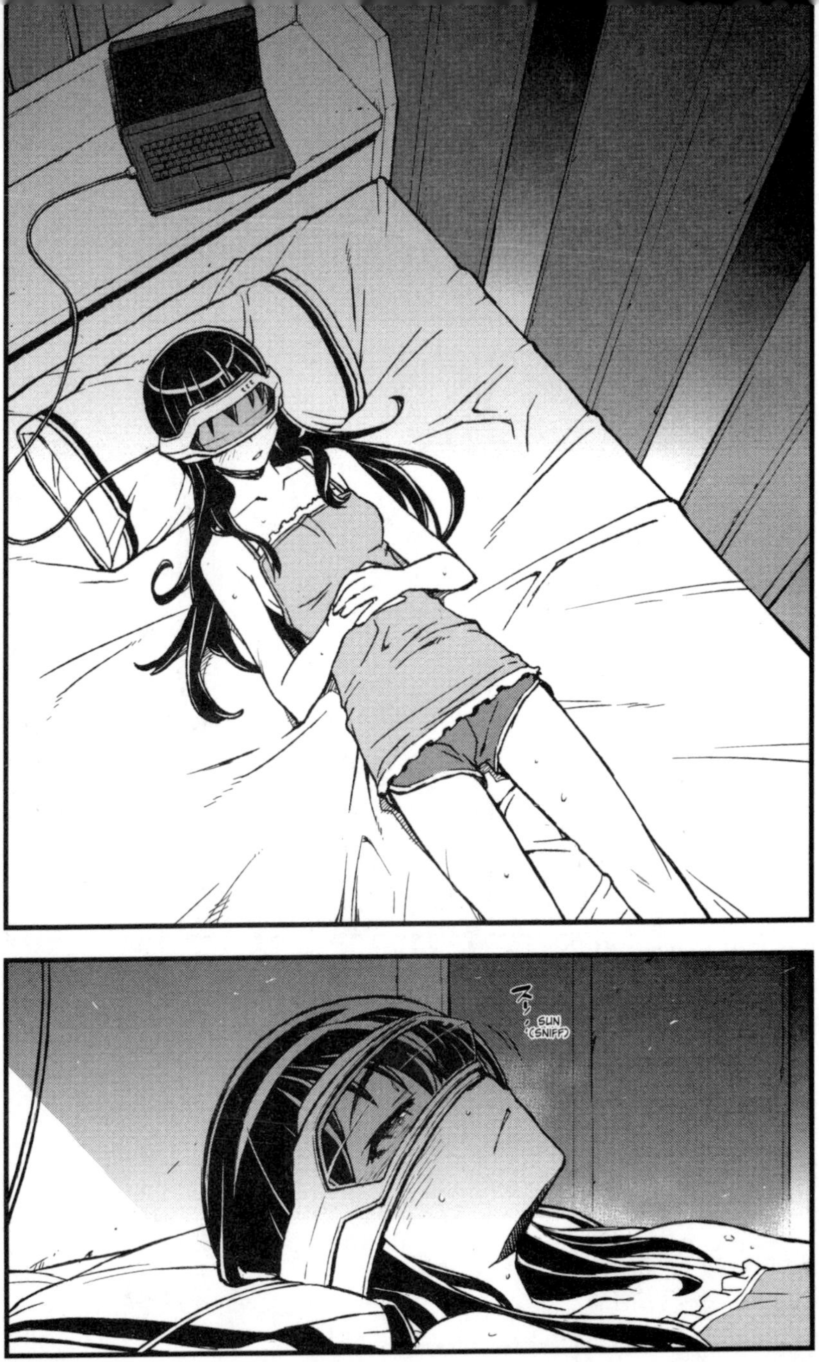
SUN
(SNIFF)

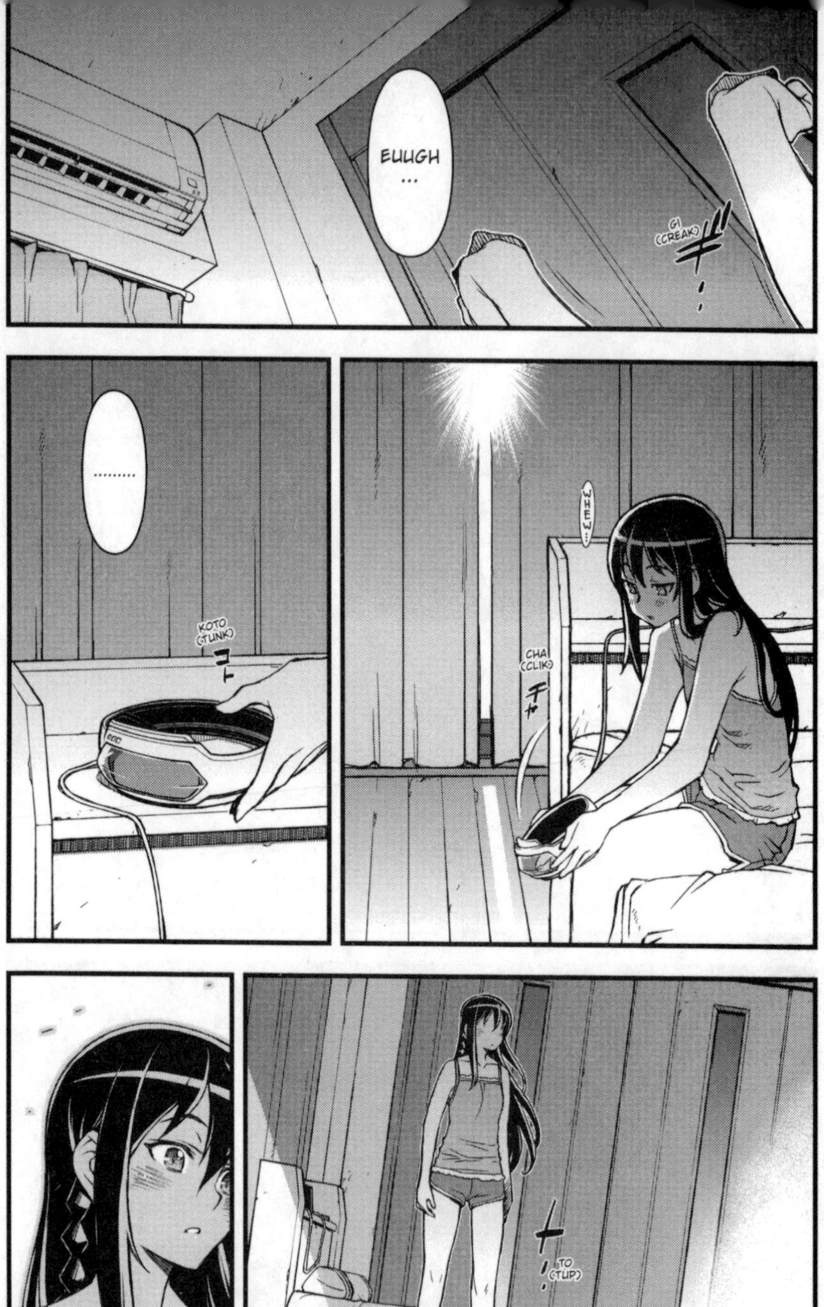
EUUGH ...
GI (CREAK)
WHEW...
CHA (CLIK)
....
KOTO (TUNK)
TO (TUP)

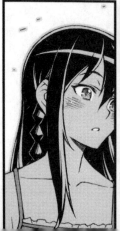

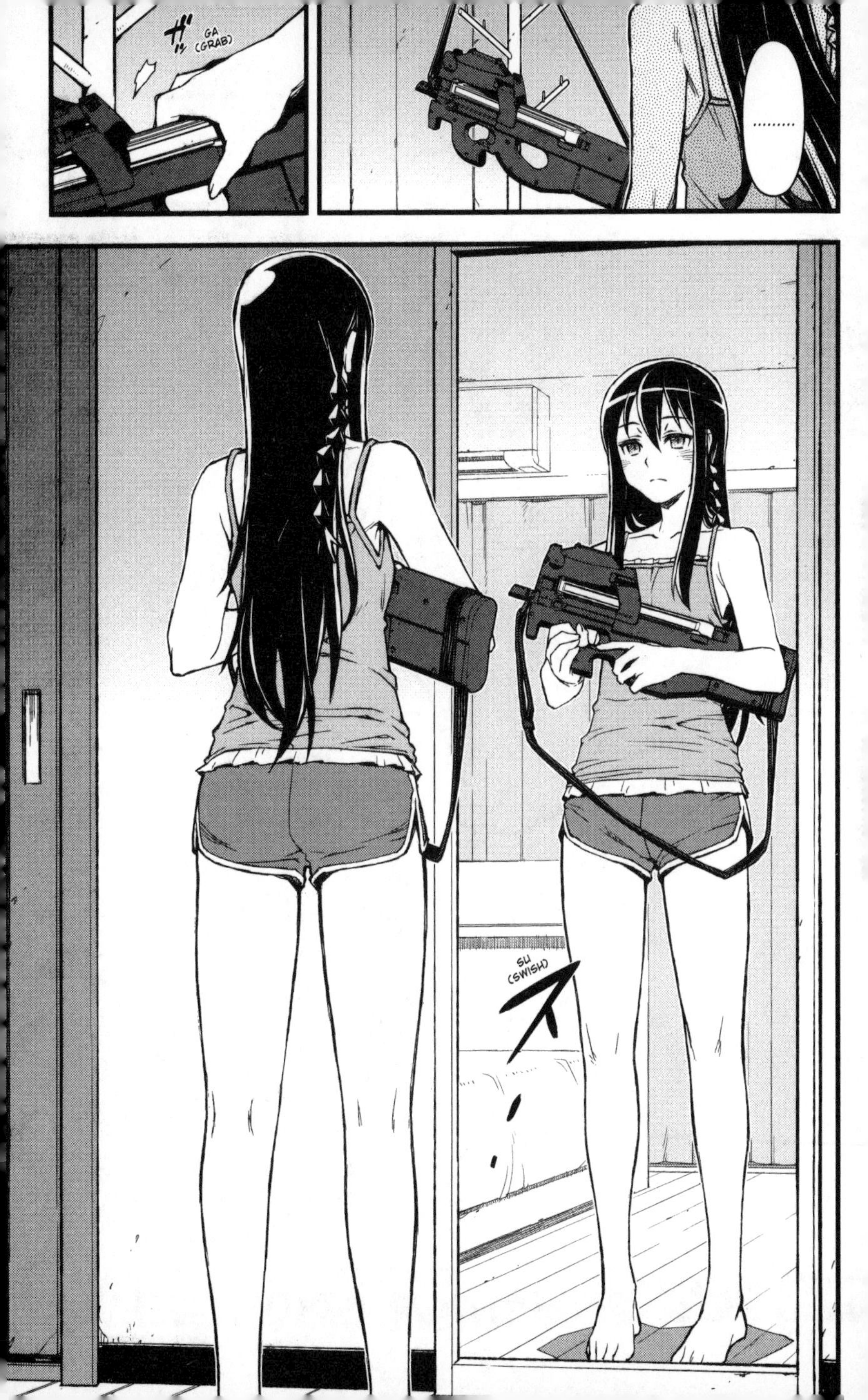
....
GA (GRAB)
SU (SWISH)

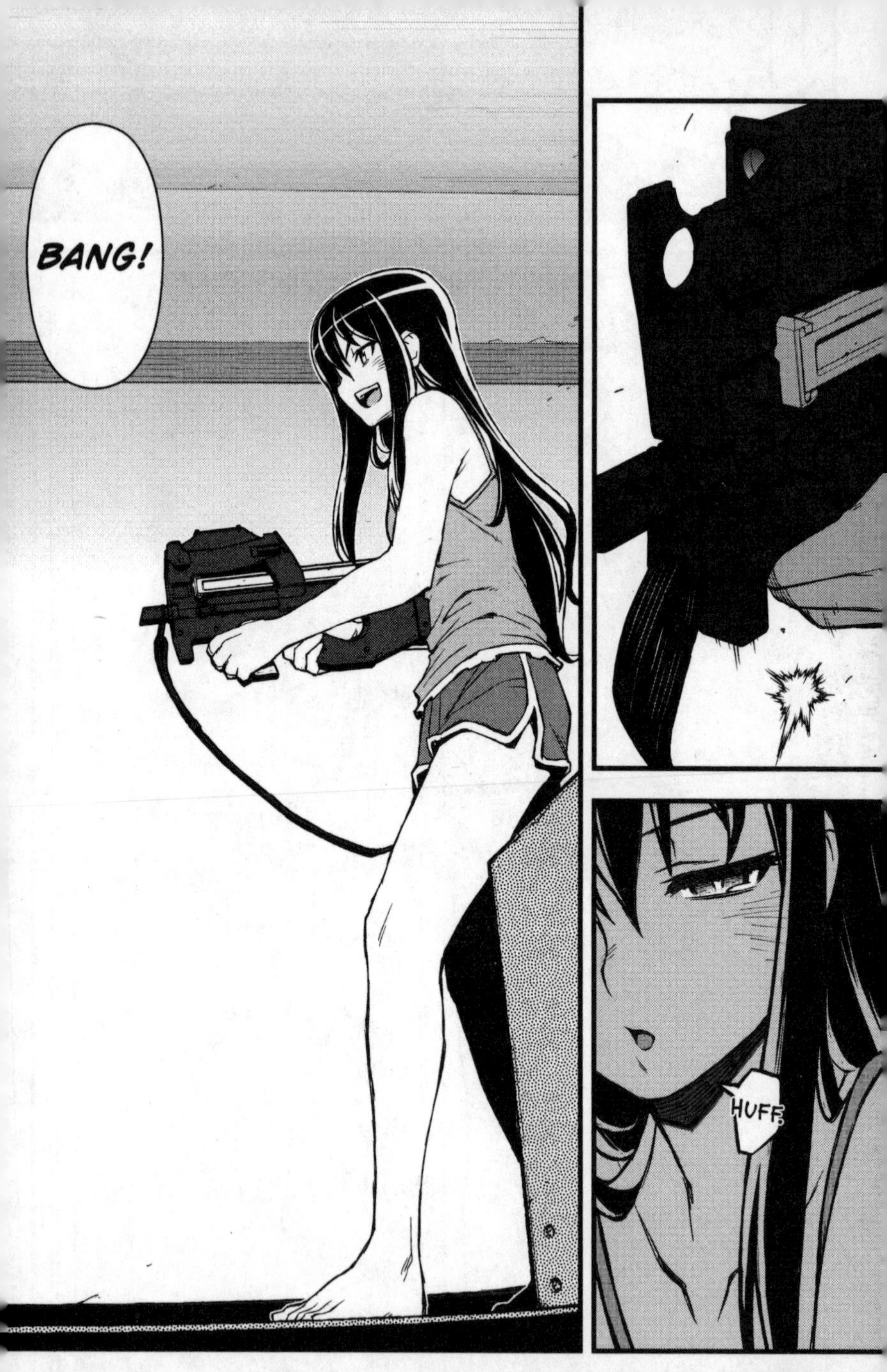
HUFF.
BANG!

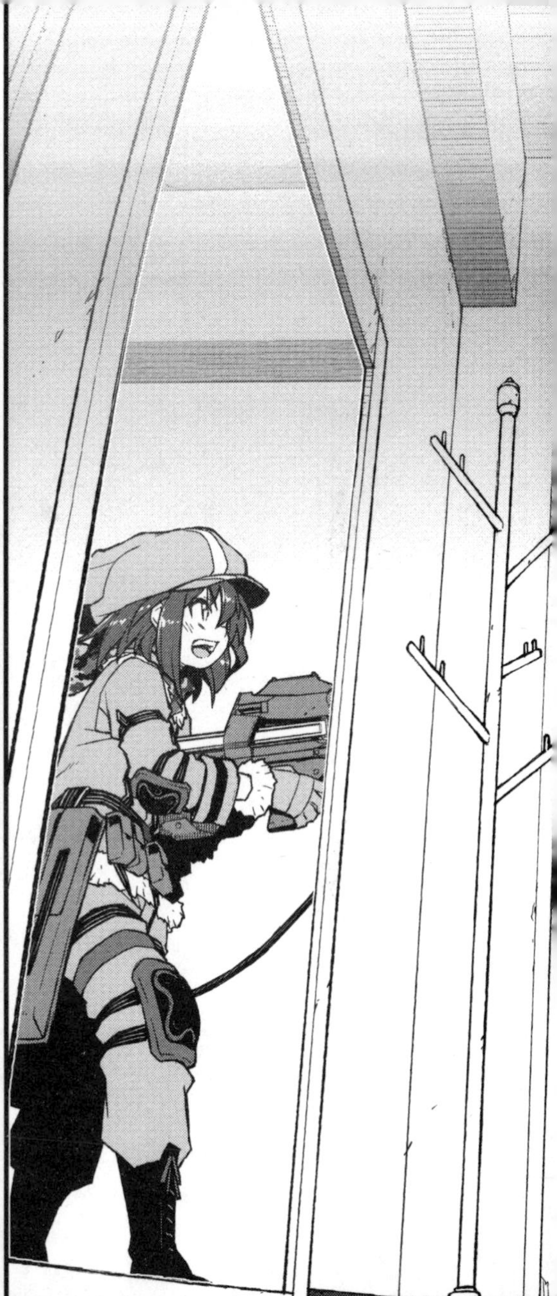
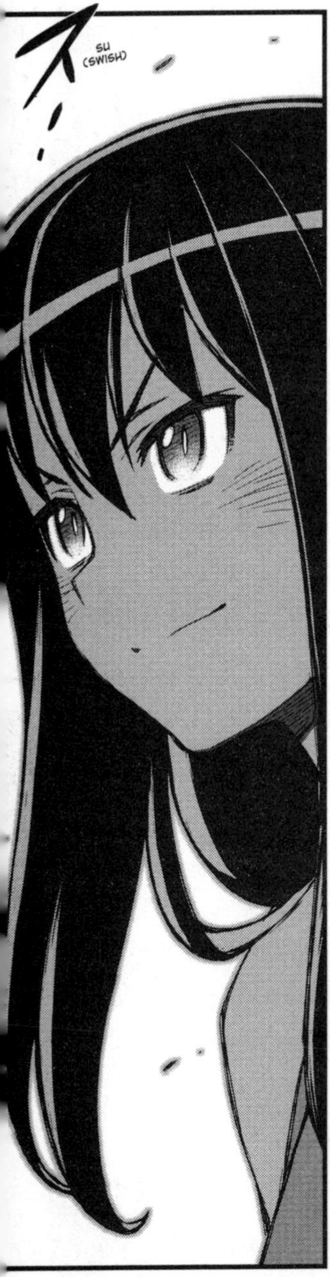
SU
(SWISH)

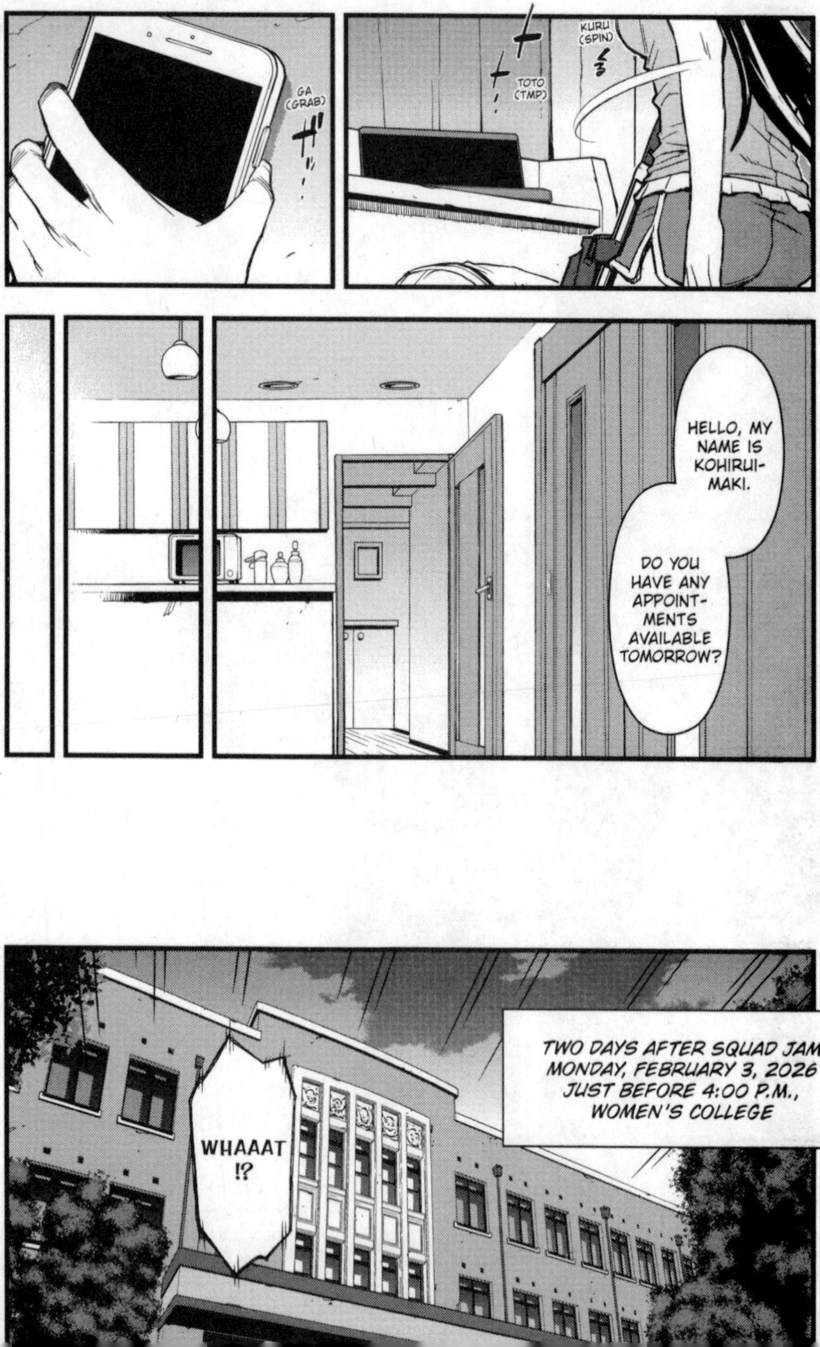
KURU (SPIN)
TOTO (TMP)
GA (GRAB)
HELLO, MY NAME IS KOHIRUI-MAKI.
DO YOU HAVE ANY APPOINT-MENTS AVAILABLE TOMORROW?
TWO DAYS AFTER SQUAD JAM MONDAY, FEBRUARY 3, 2026 JUST BEFORE 4:00 P.M., WOMEN'S COLLEGE
WHAAAT !?

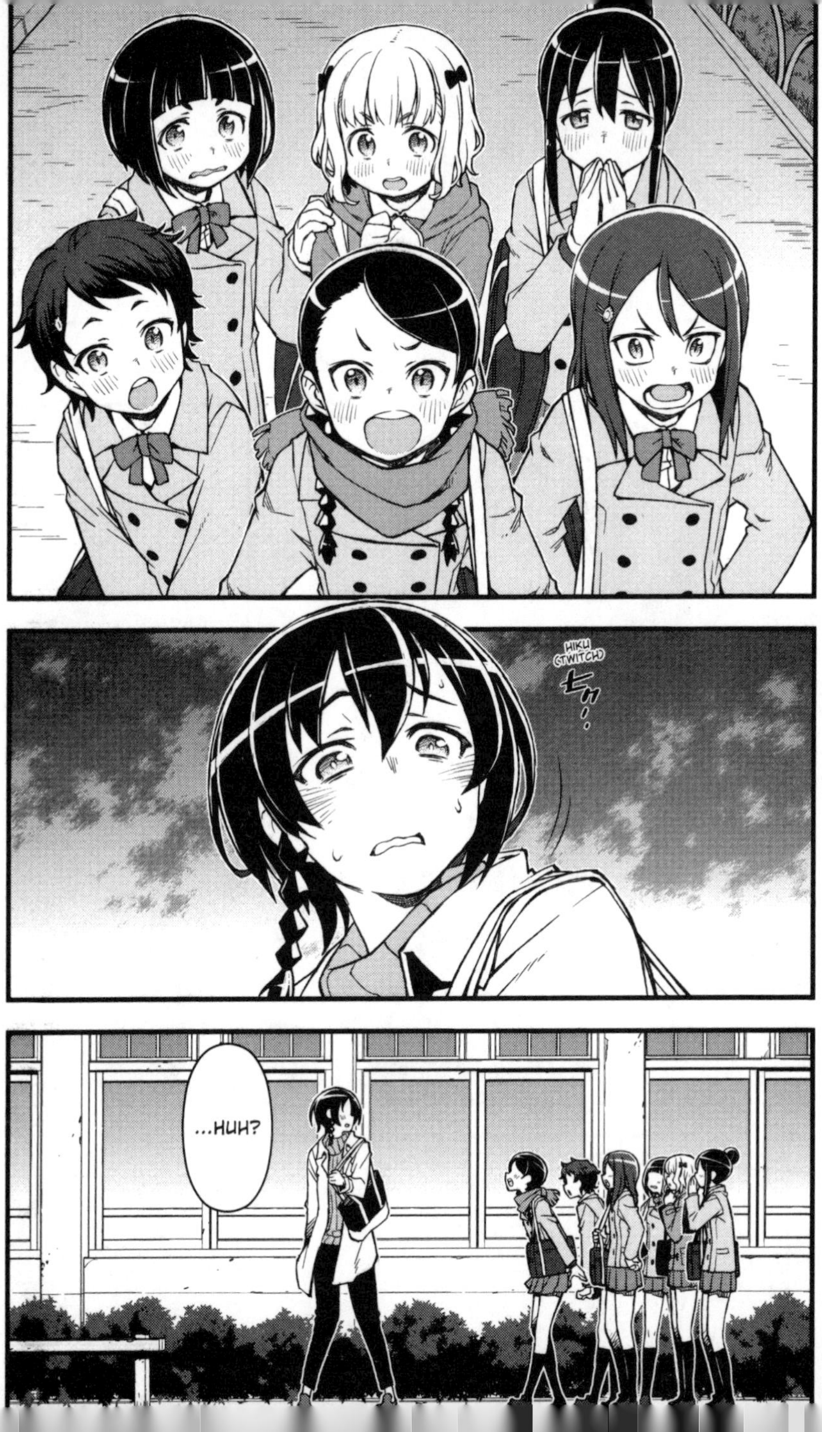
HIKU (TWITCH)
ヒク…
...HUH?

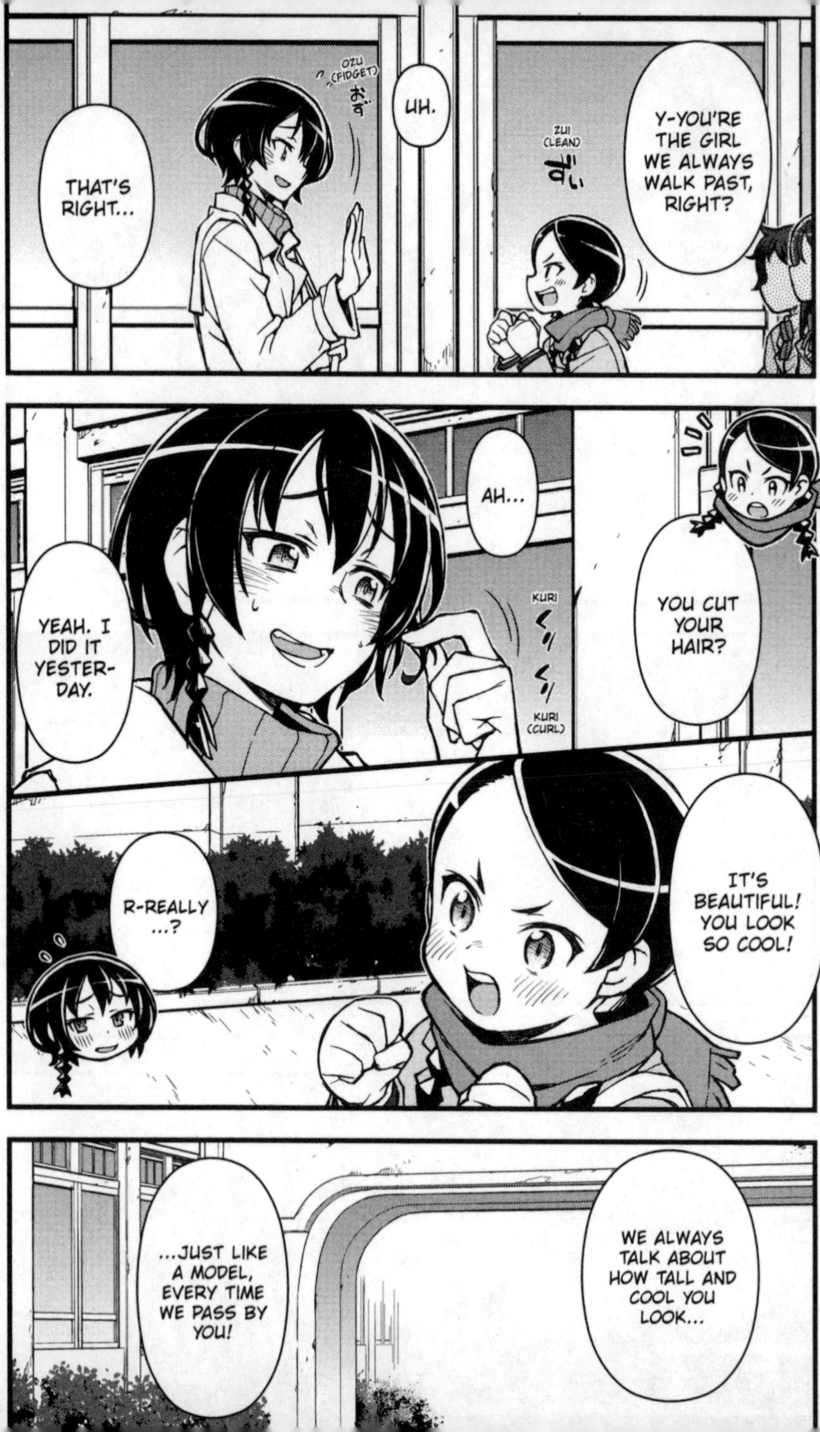

Y-YOU'RE THE GIRL WE ALWAYS WALK PAST, RIGHT?
ZUI (LEAN)
ずい
UH.
OZU (FIDGET)
おず
THAT'S RIGHT...
AH...
YOU CUT YOUR HAIR?
KURI
くり
くり
KURI (CURL)
YEAH. I DID IT YESTER-DAY.
IT'S BEAUTIFUL! YOU LOOK SO COOL!
R-REALLY ...?
WE ALWAYS TALK ABOUT HOW TALL AND COOL YOU LOOK...
...JUST LIKE A MODEL, EVERY TIME WE PASS BY YOU!

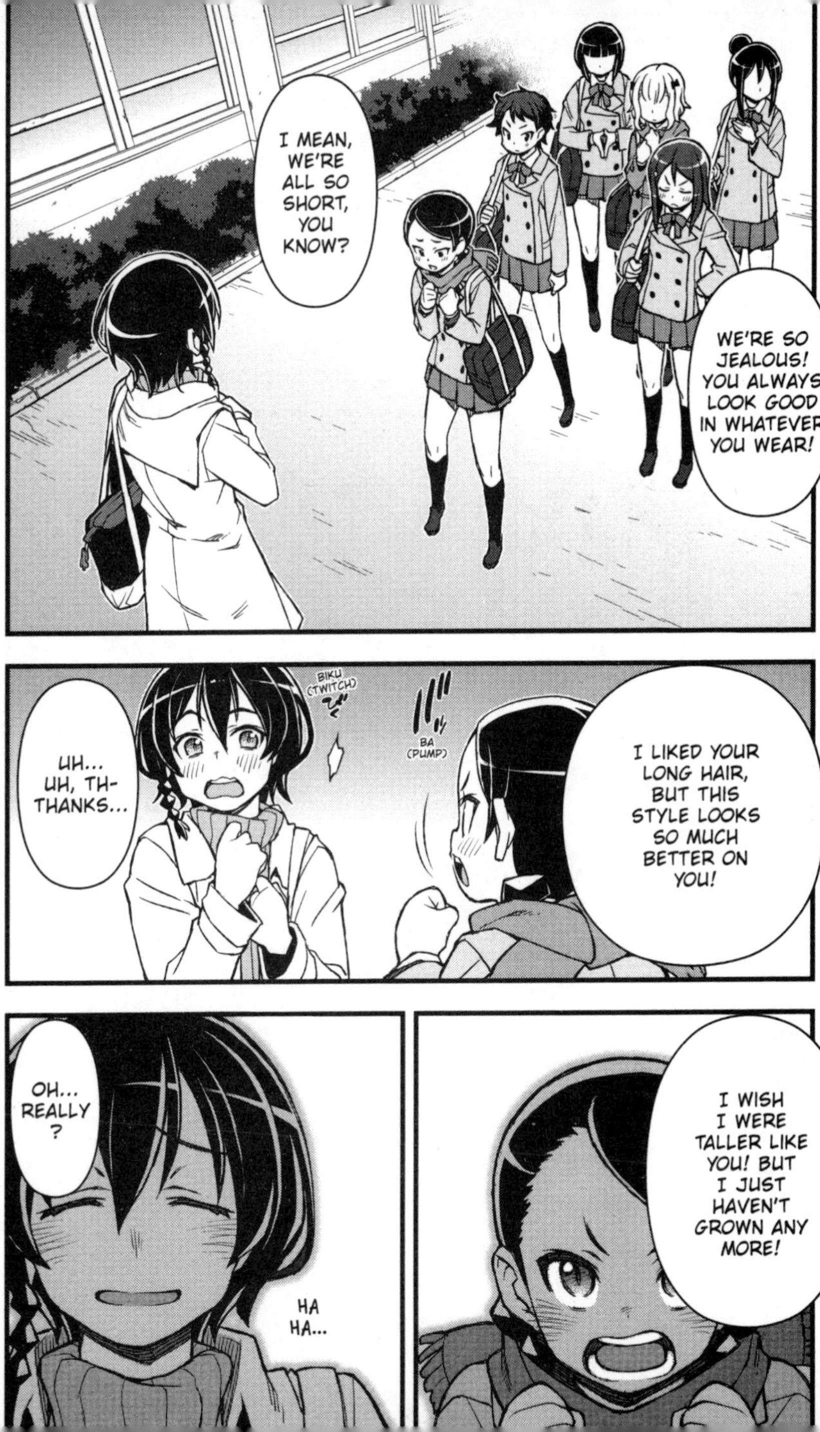
WE'RE SO JEALOUS! YOU ALWAYS LOOK GOOD IN WHATEVER YOU WEAR!
I MEAN, WE'RE ALL SO SHORT, YOU KNOW?
I LIKED YOUR LONG HAIR, BUT THIS STYLE LOOKS SO MUCH BETTER ON YOU!
BA (PUMP)
BIKU (TWITCH)
UH... UH, TH-THANKS...
I WISH I WERE TALLER LIKE YOU! BUT I JUST HAVEN'T GROWN ANY MORE!
OH... REALLY?
HA HA...

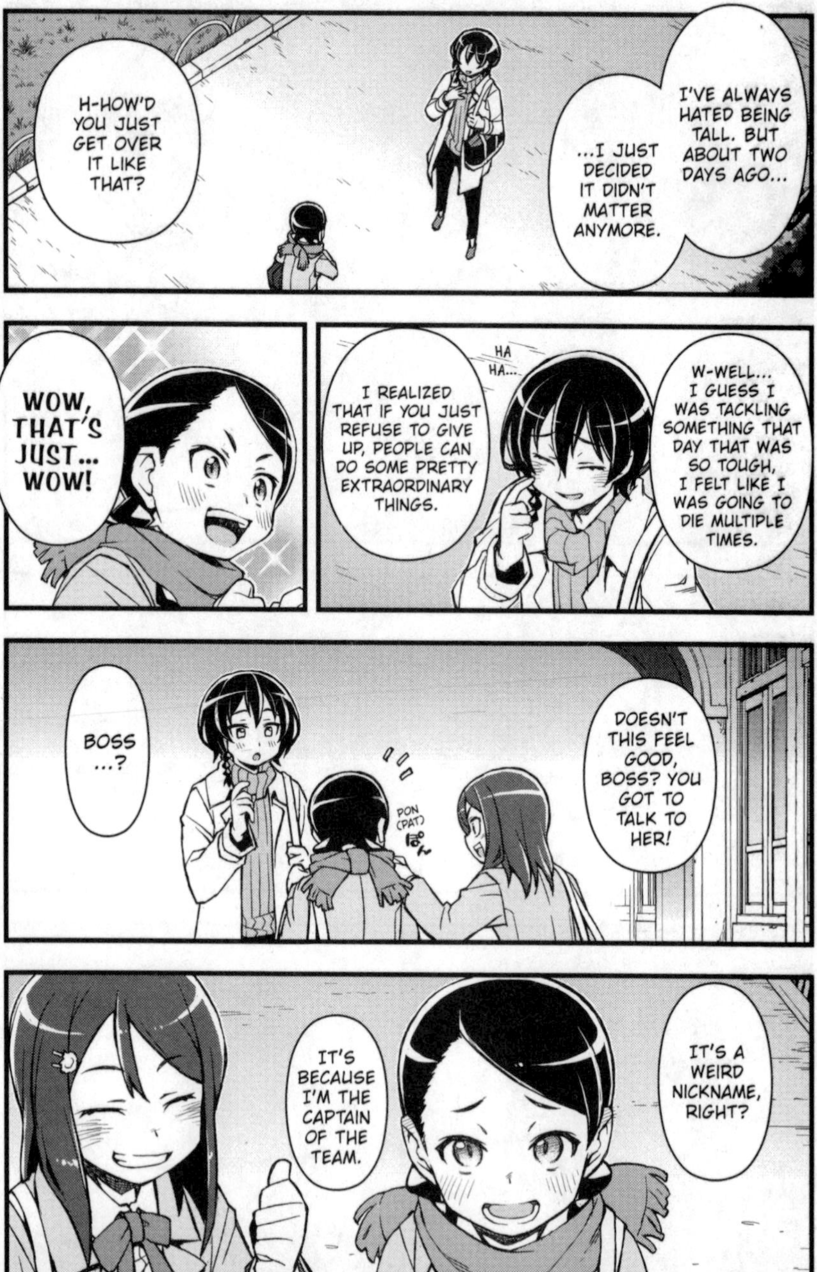
I'VE ALWAYS HATED BEING TALL. BUT ABOUT TWO DAYS AGO...
...I JUST DECIDED IT DIDN'T MATTER ANYMORE.
H-HOW'D YOU JUST GET OVER IT LIKE THAT?
W-WELL... I GUESS I WAS TACKLING SOMETHING THAT DAY THAT WAS SO TOUGH, I FELT LIKE I WAS GOING TO DIE MULTIPLE TIMES.
HA HA...
I REALIZED THAT IF YOU JUST REFUSE TO GIVE UP, PEOPLE CAN DO SOME PRETTY EXTRAORDINARY THINGS.
WOW, THAT'S JUST... WOW!
DOESN'T THIS FEEL GOOD, BOSS? YOU GOT TO TALK TO HER!
PON (PAT)
ぽん
BOSS ...?
IT'S A WEIRD NICKNAME, RIGHT?
IT'S BECAUSE I'M THE CAPTAIN OF THE TEAM.

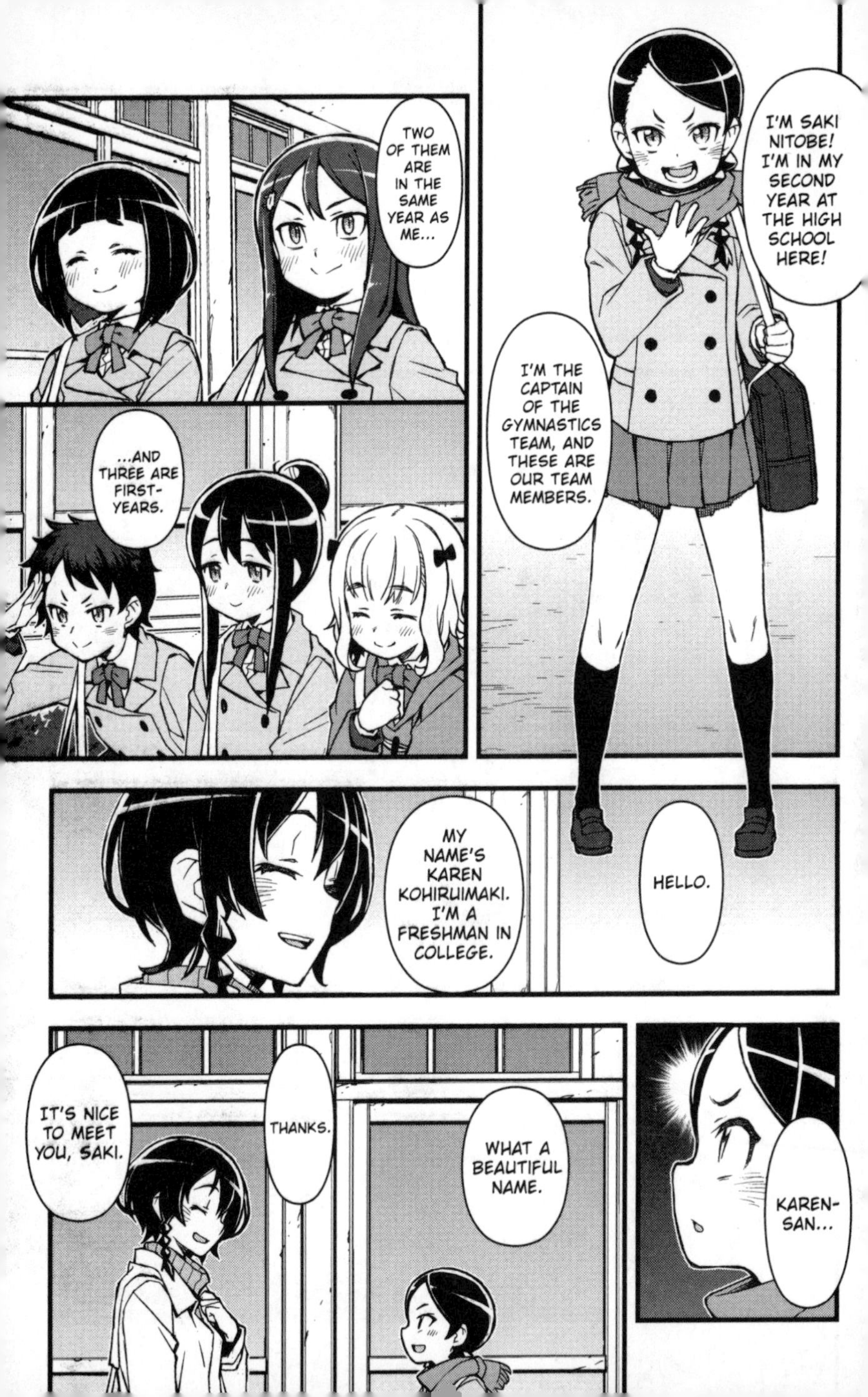
I'M SAKI NITOBE! I'M IN MY SECOND YEAR AT THE HIGH SCHOOL HERE!
I'M THE CAPTAIN OF THE GYMNASTICS TEAM, AND THESE ARE OUR TEAM MEMBERS.
TWO OF THEM ARE IN THE SAME YEAR AS ME...
...AND THREE ARE FIRST-YEARS.
HELLO.
MY NAME'S KAREN KOHIRUIMAKI. I'M A FRESHMAN IN COLLEGE.
KAREN-SAN...
WHAT A BEAUTIFUL NAME.
THANKS.
IT'S NICE TO MEET YOU, SAKI.

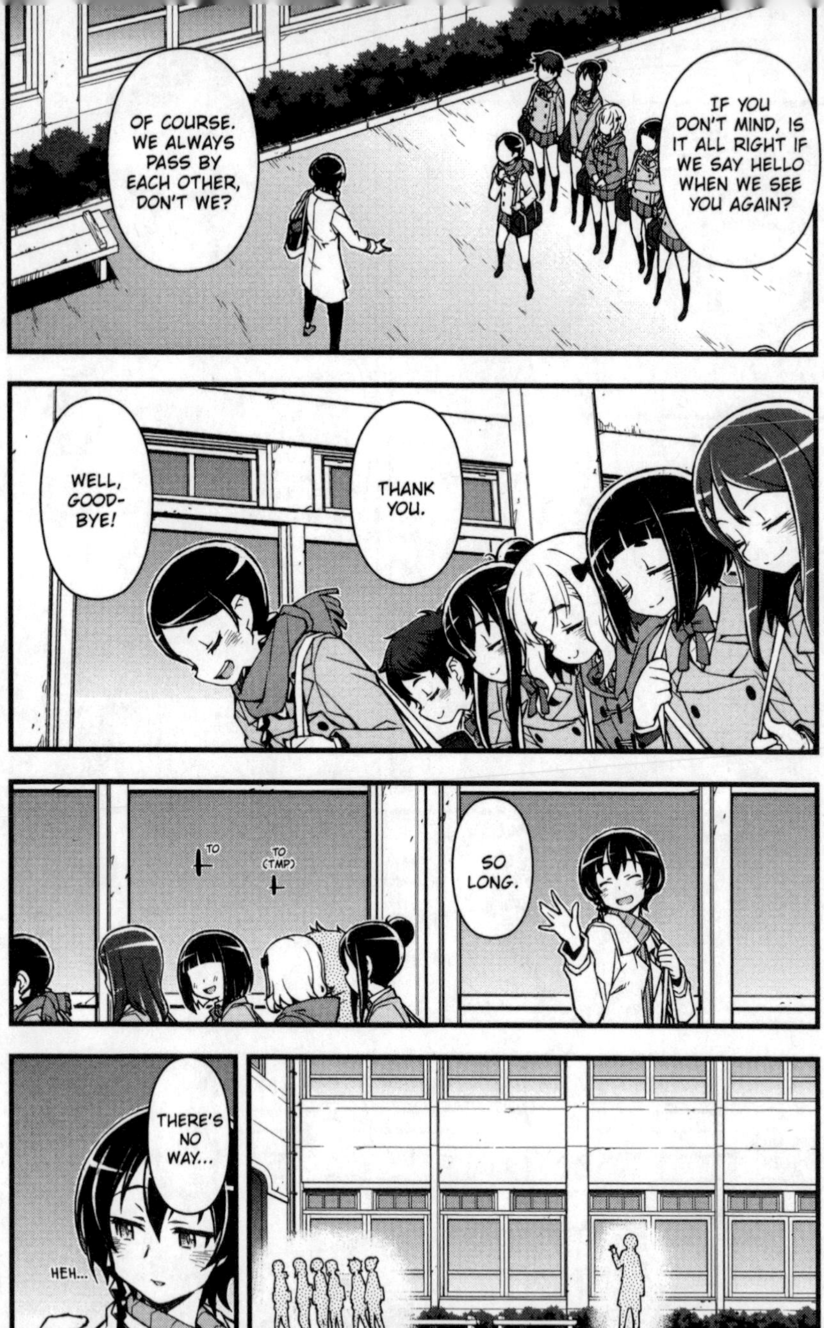
IF YOU DON'T MIND, IS IT ALL RIGHT IF WE SAY HELLO WHEN WE SEE YOU AGAIN?
OF COURSE. WE ALWAYS PASS BY EACH OTHER, DON'T WE?
THANK YOU.
WELL, GOOD-BYE!
SO LONG.
TO
TO (TMP)
THERE'S NO WAY...
HEH...

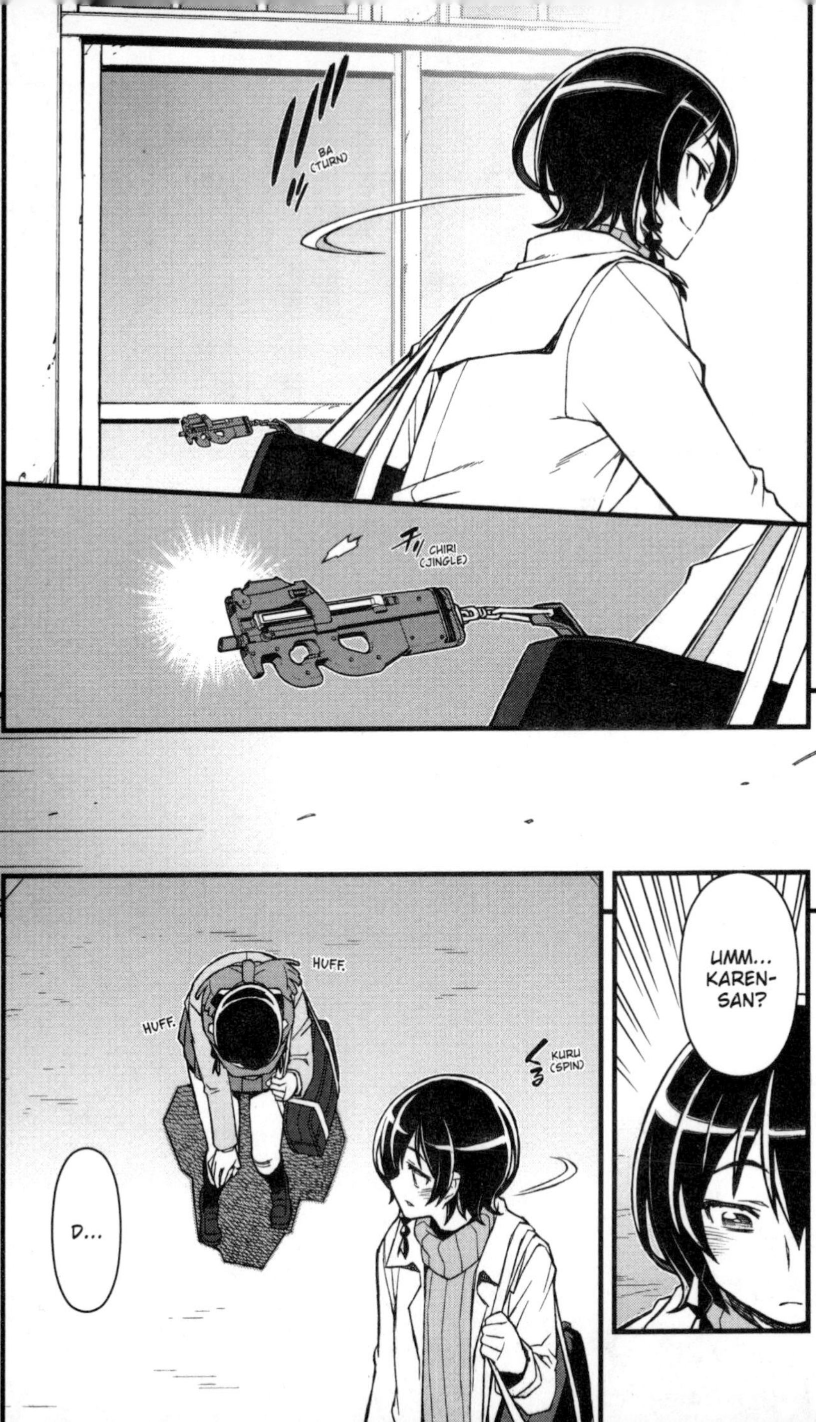
BA (TURN)
CHIRI (JINGLE)
UMM... KAREN-SAN?
HUFF.
KURU (SPIN)
HUFF.
D...

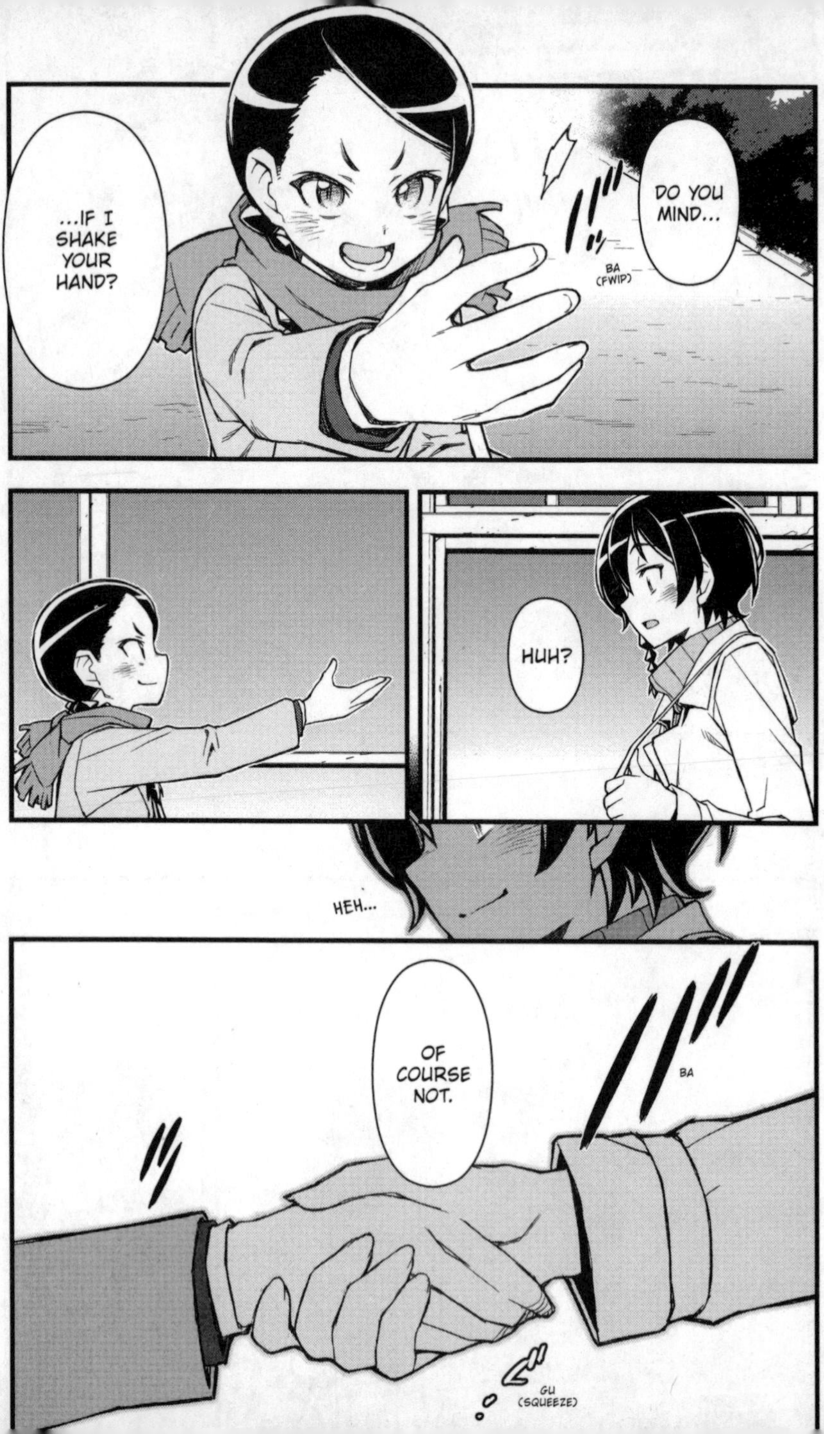
DO YOU MIND...
BA
(FWIP)
...IF I SHAKE YOUR HAND?
HUH?
HEH...
BA
OF COURSE NOT.
GU
(SQUEEZE)

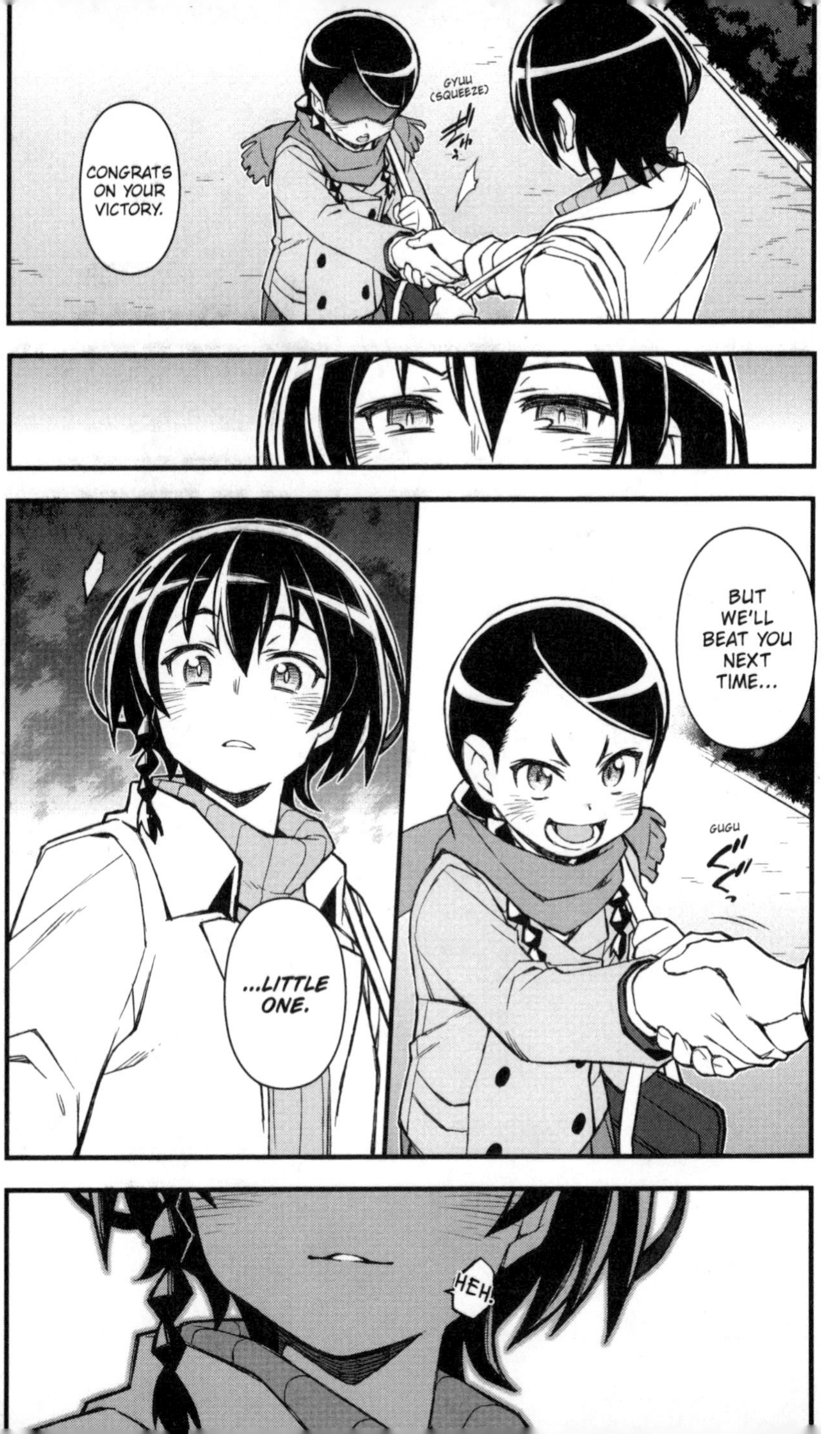
GYUU (SQUEEZE)
CONGRATS ON YOUR VICTORY.
BUT WE'LL BEAT YOU NEXT TIME...
GUGU
...LITTLE ONE.
HEH.

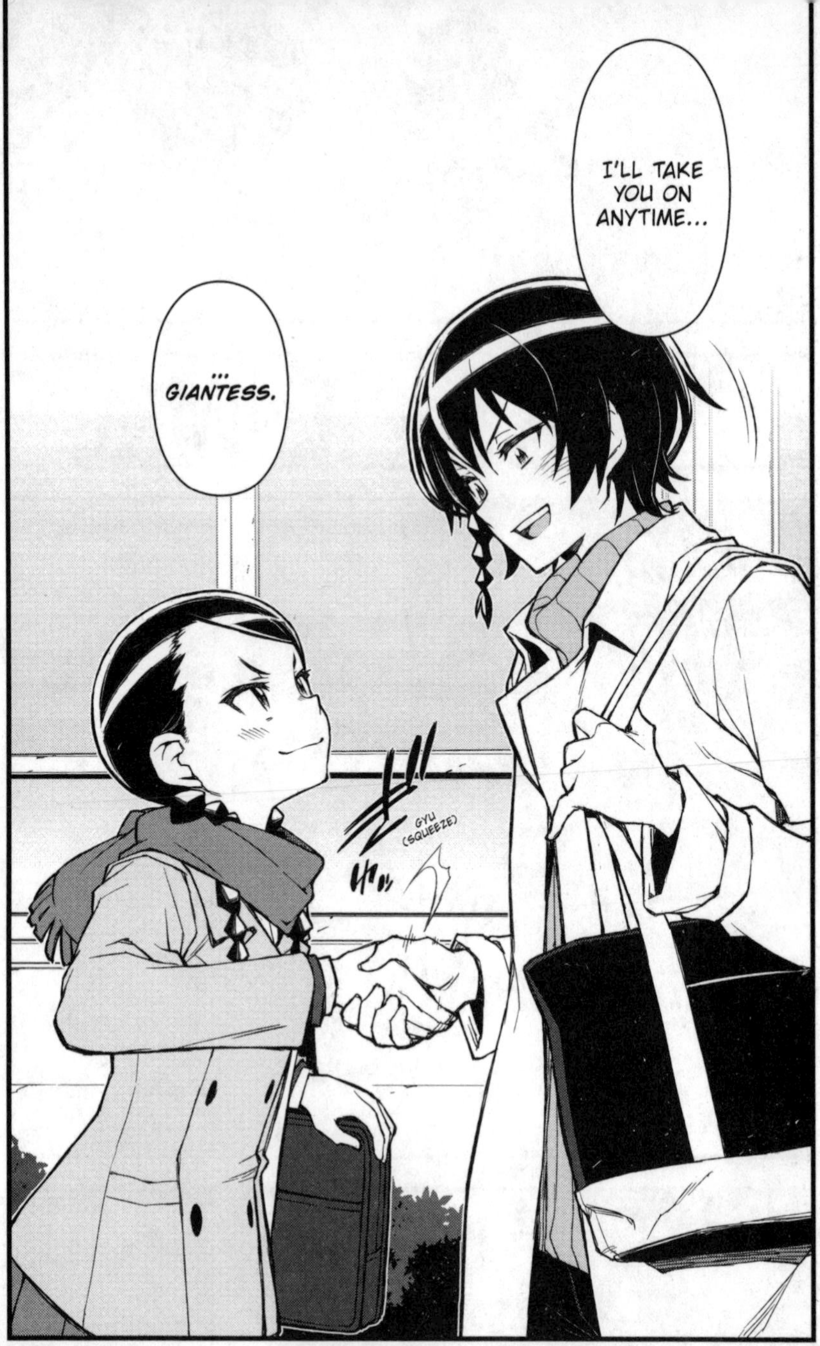
I'LL TAKE YOU ON ANYTIME...
...GIANTESS.
GYU (SQUEEZE)

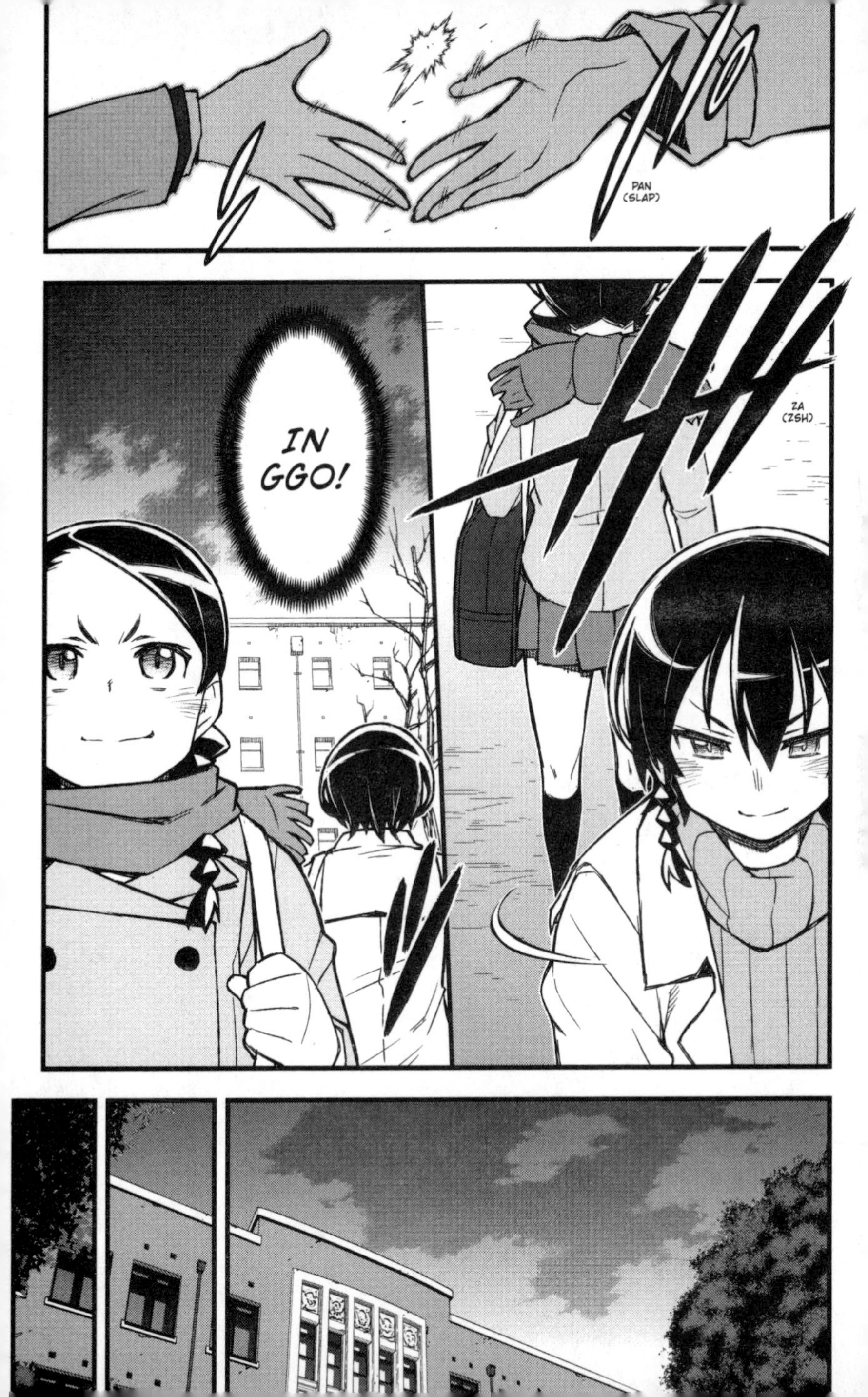
PAN
(SLAP)
ZA
(ZSH)
IN GGO!

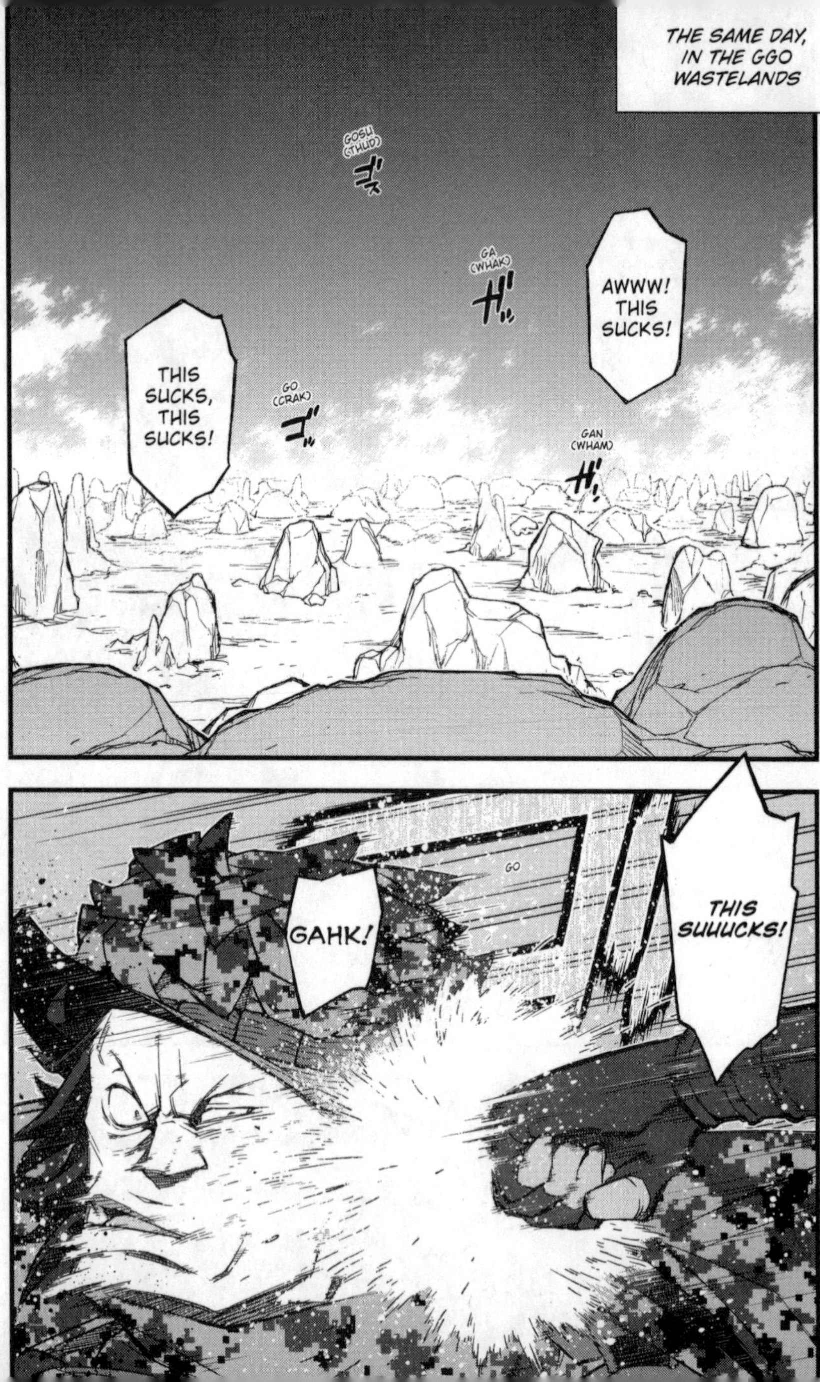
THE SAME DAY, IN THE GGO WASTELANDS
GOSU (THUD)
AWWW! THIS SUCKS!
GA (WHAK)
GAN (WHAM)
GO (CRAK)
THIS SUCKS, THIS SUCKS!
THIS SUUUCKS!
GO
GAHK!

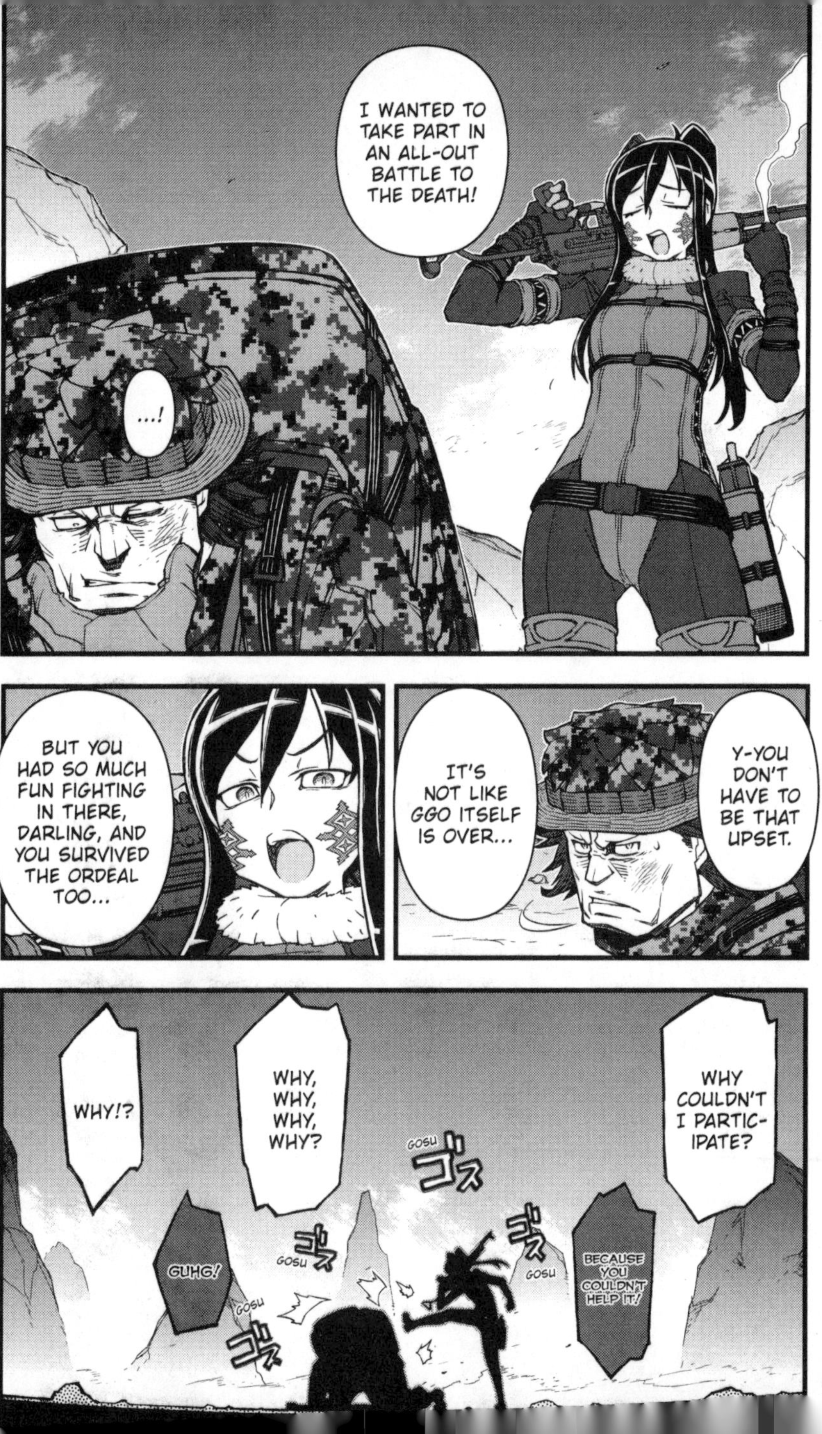
I WANTED TO TAKE PART IN AN ALL-OUT BATTLE TO THE DEATH!
...!
Y-YOU DON'T HAVE TO BE THAT UPSET.
IT'S NOT LIKE GGO ITSELF IS OVER...
BUT YOU HAD SO MUCH FUN FIGHTING IN THERE, DARLING, AND YOU SURVIVED THE ORDEAL TOO...
WHY COULDN'T I PARTIC-IPATE?
WHY, WHY, WHY, WHY?
WHY!?
GOSU ゴス
GOSU ゴス
BECAUSE YOU COULDN'T HELP IT!
GOSU ゴス
GUHG!
GOSU ゴス

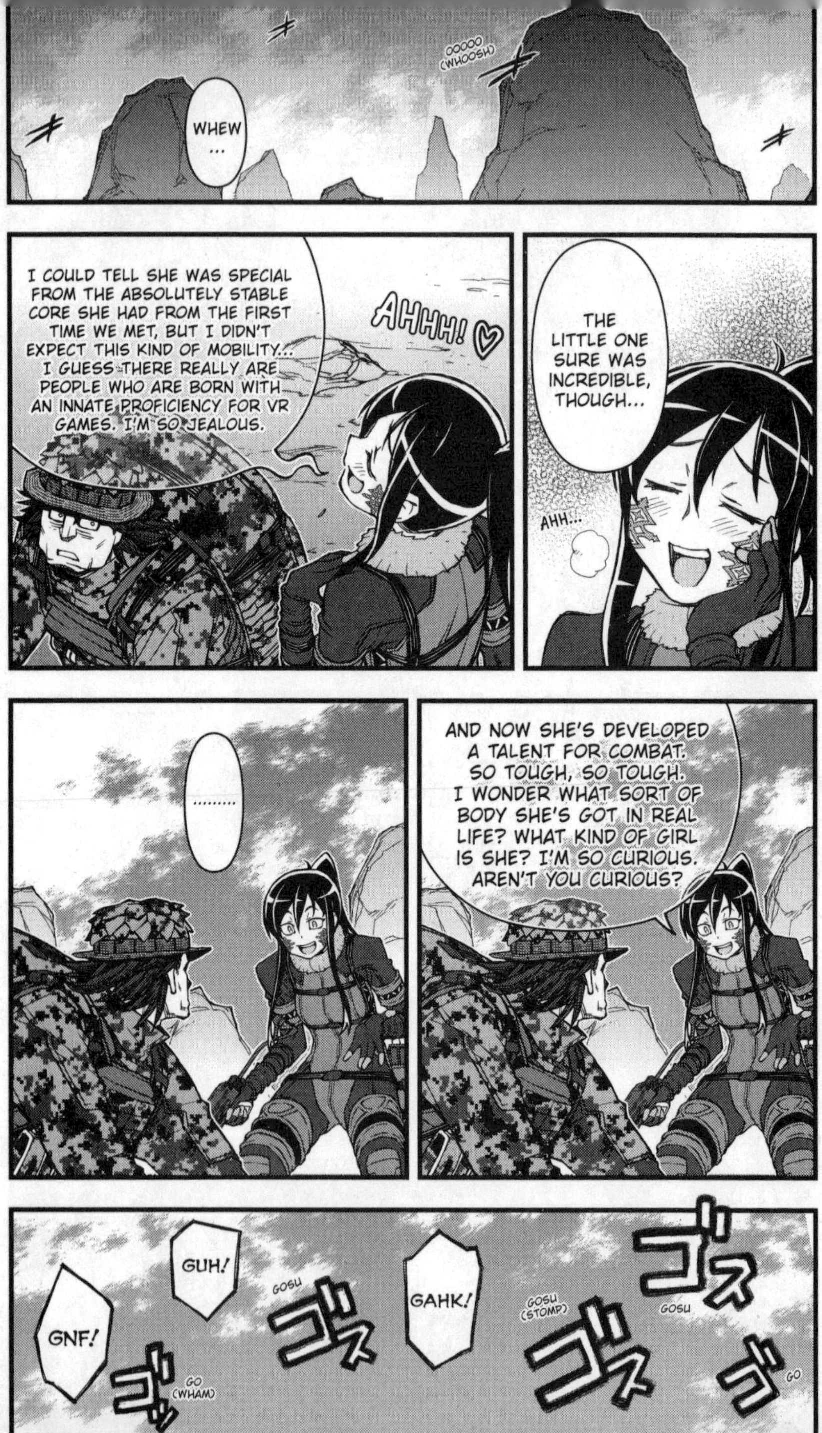
OOOOO
(WHOOSH)
WHEW...
THE LITTLE ONE SURE WAS INCREDIBLE, THOUGH...
AHH...
AHHH! ♡
I COULD TELL SHE WAS SPECIAL FROM THE ABSOLUTELY STABLE CORE SHE HAD FROM THE FIRST TIME WE MET, BUT I DIDN'T EXPECT THIS KIND OF MOBILITY... I GUESS THERE REALLY ARE PEOPLE WHO ARE BORN WITH AN INNATE PROFICIENCY FOR VR GAMES. I'M SO JEALOUS.
AND NOW SHE'S DEVELOPED A TALENT FOR COMBAT. SO TOUGH, SO TOUGH. I WONDER WHAT SORT OF BODY SHE'S GOT IN REAL LIFE? WHAT KIND OF GIRL IS SHE? I'M SO CURIOUS. AREN'T YOU CURIOUS?
....
GOSU
GO
GOSU
(STOMP)
GAHK!
GOSU
GUH!
GNF!
GO
(WHAM)

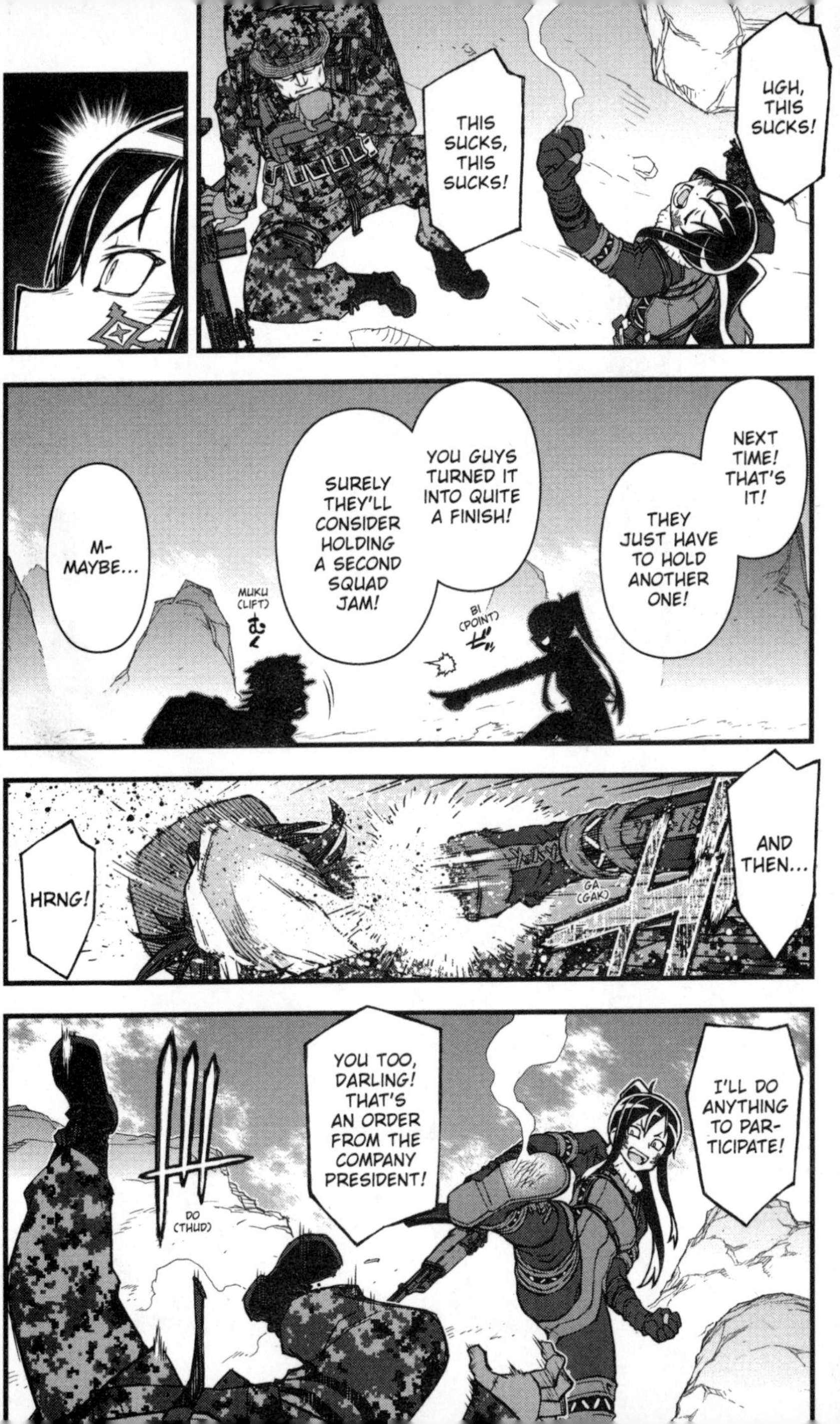
UGH, THIS SUCKS!
THIS SUCKS, THIS SUCKS!
NEXT TIME! THAT'S IT!
THEY JUST HAVE TO HOLD ANOTHER ONE!
BI (POINT)
YOU GUYS TURNED IT INTO QUITE A FINISH!
SURELY THEY'LL CONSIDER HOLDING A SECOND SQUAD JAM!
MUKU (LIFT)
M-MAYBE...
AND THEN...
GA (GAK)
HRNG!
I'LL DO ANYTHING TO PAR-TICIPATE!
YOU TOO, DARLING! THAT'S AN ORDER FROM THE COMPANY PRESIDENT!
DO (THUD)

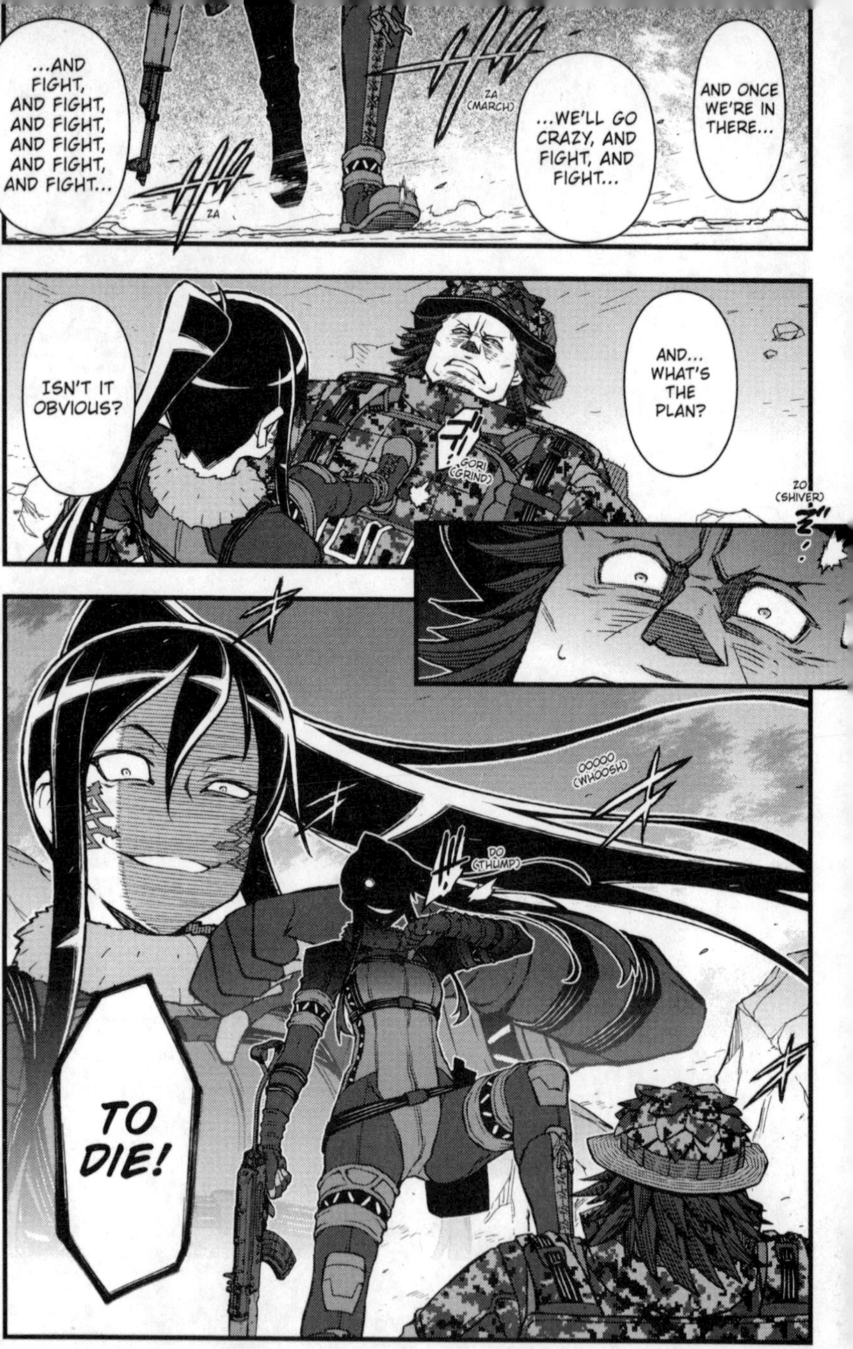
AND ONCE WE'RE IN THERE...
...WE'LL GO CRAZY, AND FIGHT, AND FIGHT...
ZA (MARCH)
...AND FIGHT, AND FIGHT, AND FIGHT, AND FIGHT, AND FIGHT, AND FIGHT...
ZA
AND... WHAT'S THE PLAN?
GORI (GRIND)
ISN'T IT OBVIOUS?
ZO (SHIVER)
OOOOO (WHOOSH)
DO (THUMP)
TO DIE!

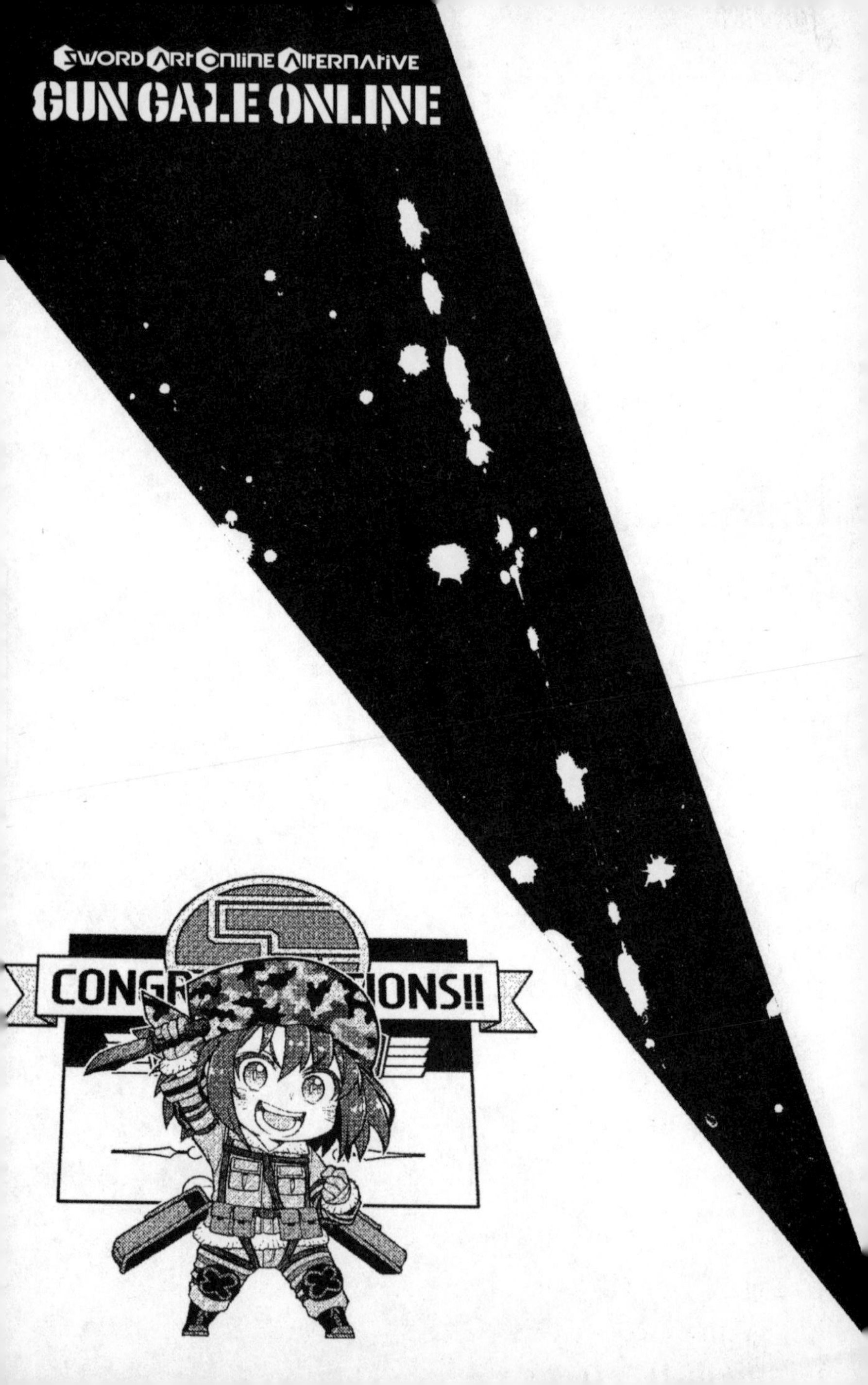
Sword Art Online Alternative
GUN GALE ONLINE
CONGR IONS!!

LINK #020: SECOND SQUAD JAM

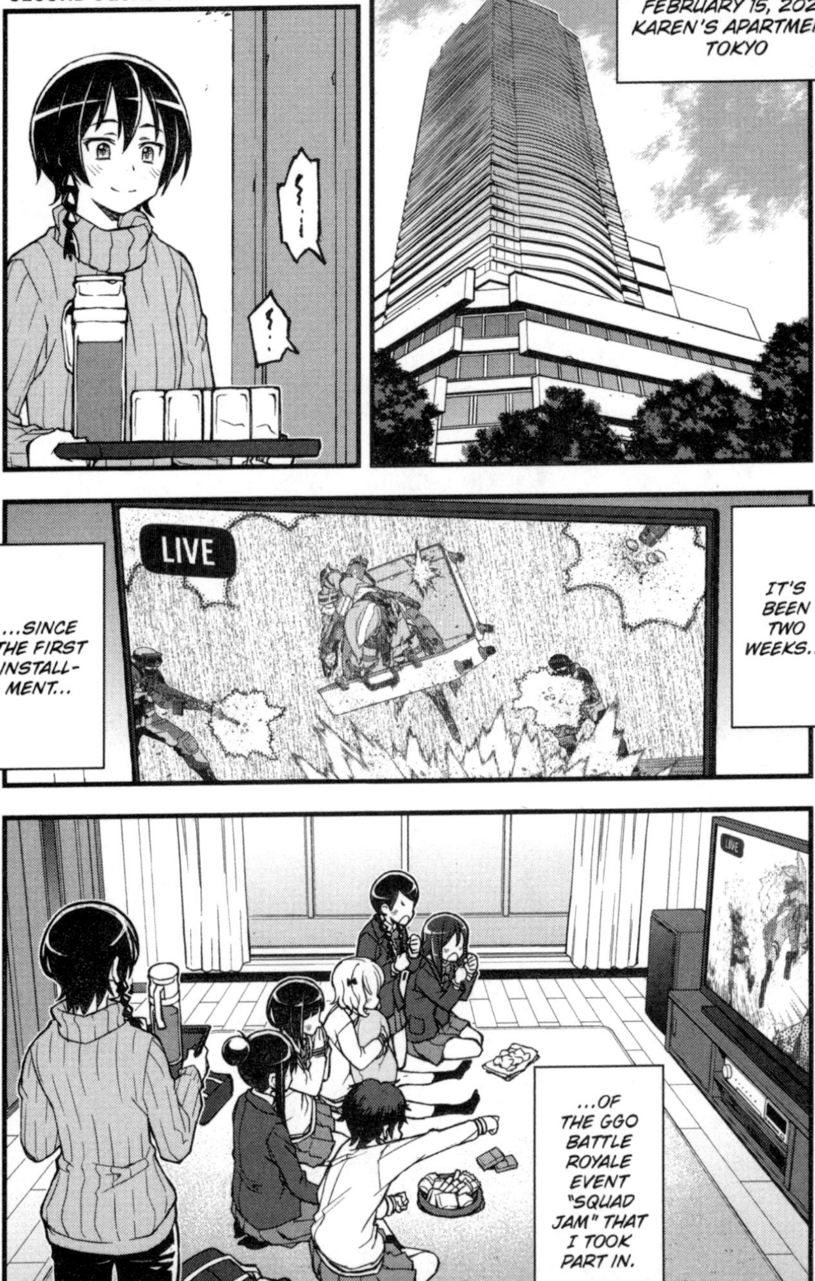

FEBRUARY 15, 2026 KAREN'S APARTMENT, TOKYO
IT'S BEEN TWO WEEKS...
LIVE
...SINCE THE FIRST INSTALL-MENT...
...OF THE GGO BATTLE ROYALE EVENT "SQUAD JAM" THAT I TOOK PART IN.

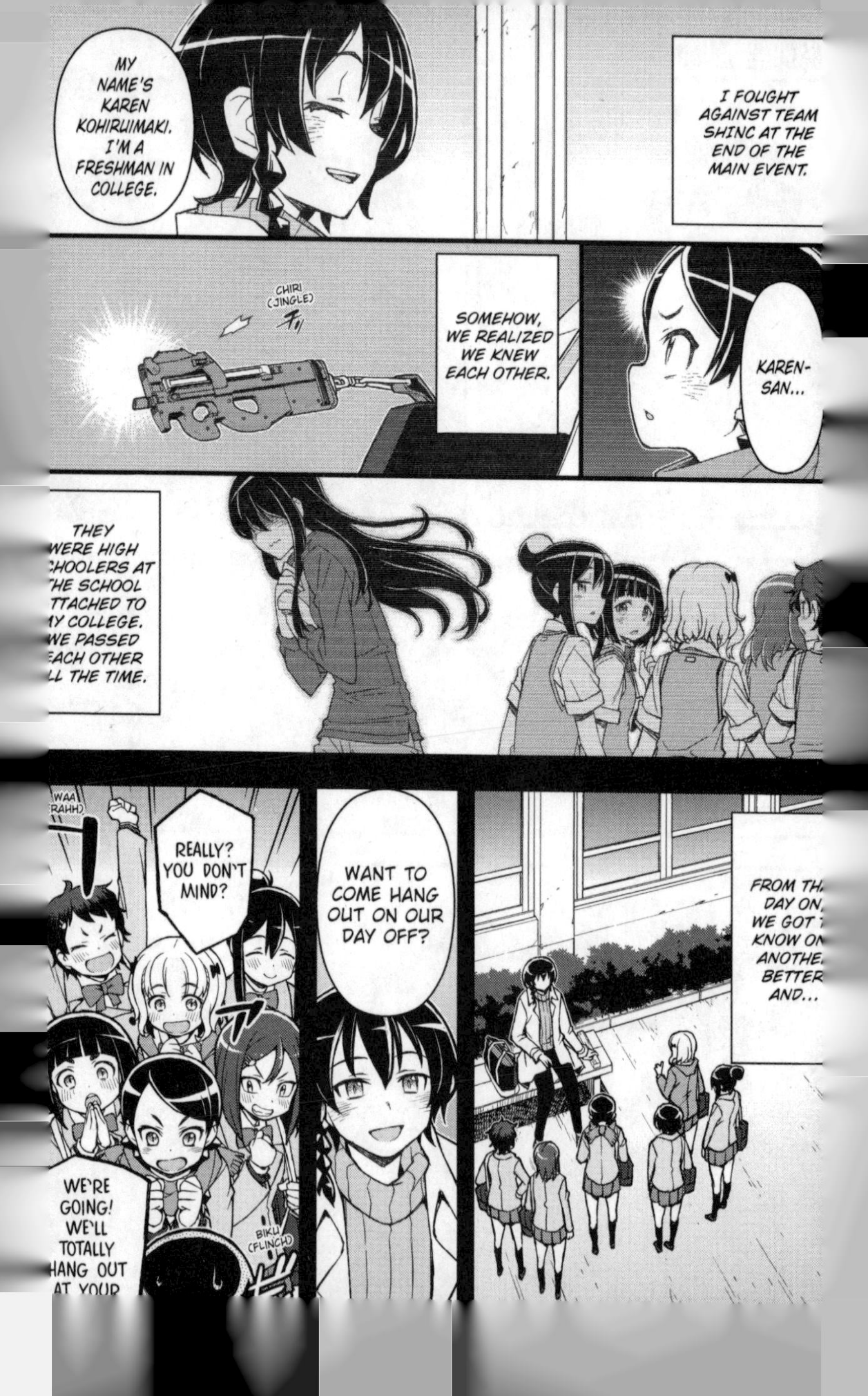
I FOUGHT AGAINST TEAM SHINC AT THE END OF THE MAIN EVENT.
MY NAME'S KAREN KOHIRUIMAKI. I'M A FRESHMAN IN COLLEGE.
KAREN-SAN...
SOMEHOW, WE REALIZED WE KNEW EACH OTHER.
CHIRI (JINGLE)
THEY WERE HIGH CHOOLERS AT THE SCHOOL TTACHED TO MY COLLEGE. WE PASSED EACH OTHER LL THE TIME.
FROM TH DAY ON, WE GOT T KNOW ON ANOTHE BETTER AND...
WANT TO COME HANG OUT ON OUR DAY OFF?
REALLY? YOU DON'T MIND?
WAA (RAHH)
WE'RE GOING! WE'LL TOTALLY HANG OUT AT YOUR
BIKU (FLINCH)

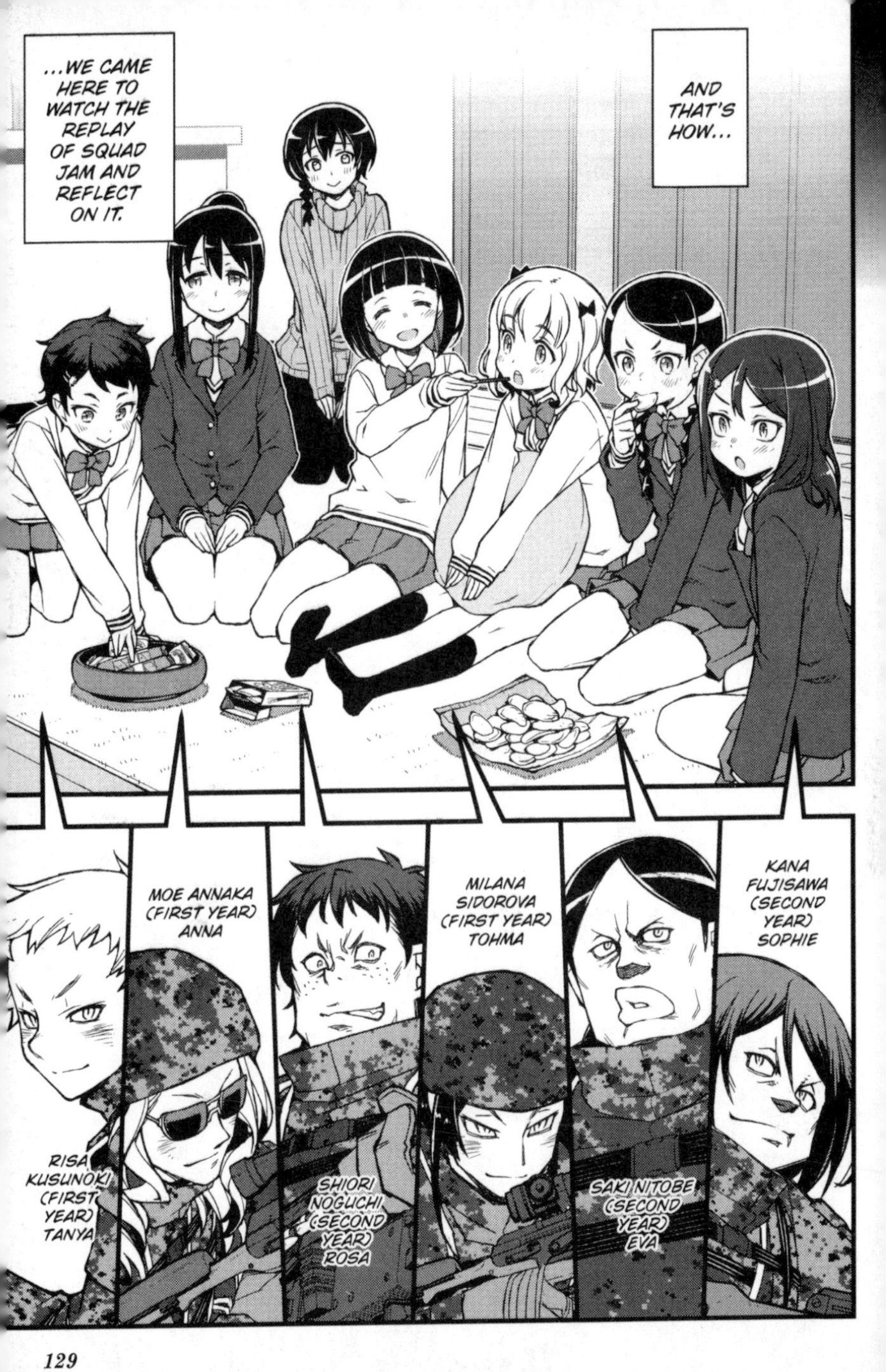
AND THAT'S HOW...
...WE CAME HERE TO WATCH THE REPLAY OF SQUAD JAM AND REFLECT ON IT.
KANA FUJISAWA (SECOND YEAR) SOPHIE
SAKI NITOBE (SECOND YEAR) EVA
MILANA SIDOROVA (FIRST YEAR) TOHMA
SHIORI NOGUCHI (SECOND YEAR) ROSA
MOE ANNAKA (FIRST YEAR) ANNA
RISA KUSUNOKI (FIRST YEAR) TANYA

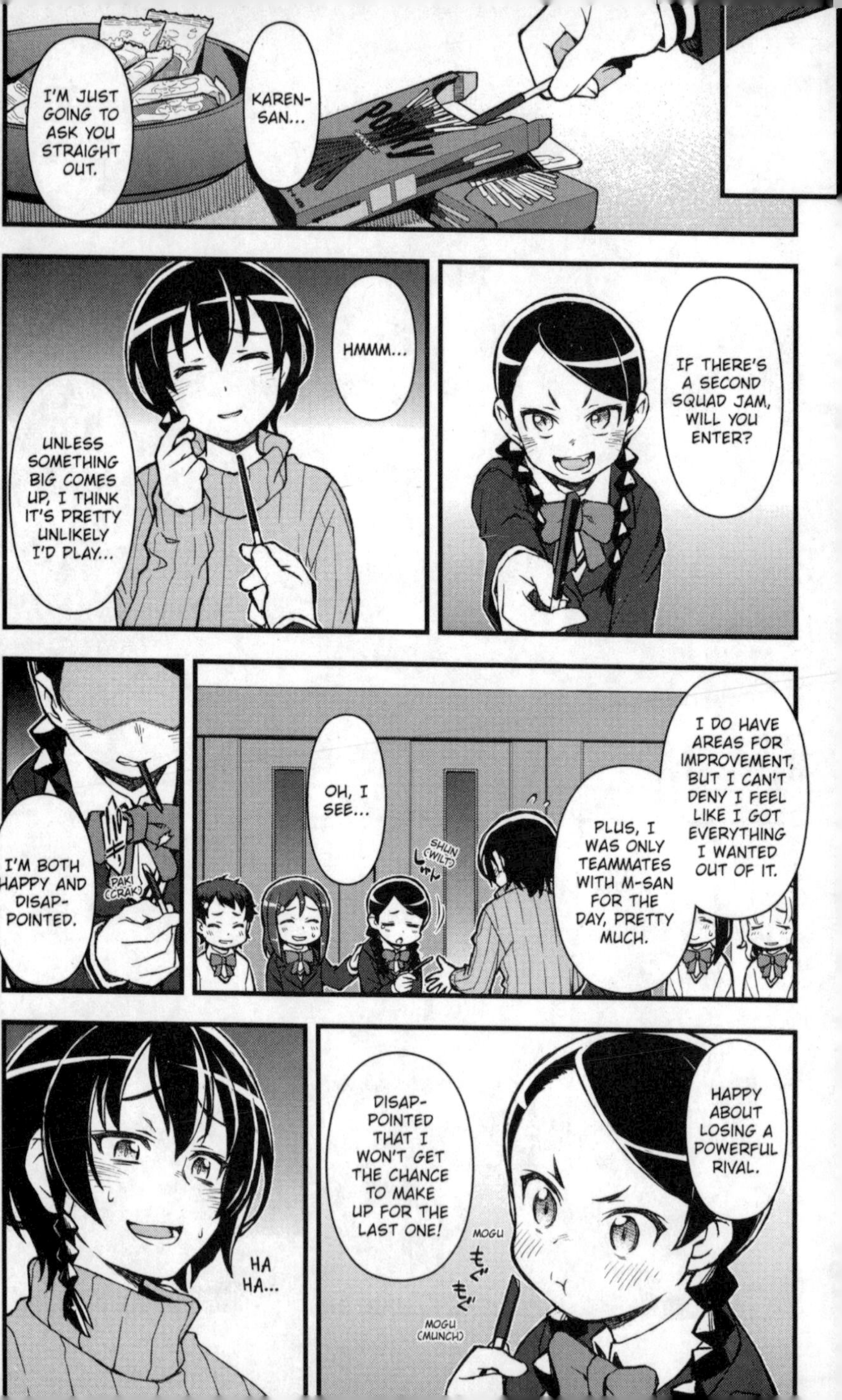
KAREN-SAN...
I'M JUST GOING TO ASK YOU STRAIGHT OUT.
IF THERE'S A SECOND SQUAD JAM, WILL YOU ENTER?
HMMM...
UNLESS SOMETHING BIG COMES UP, I THINK IT'S PRETTY UNLIKELY I'D PLAY...
I DO HAVE AREAS FOR IMPROVEMENT, BUT I CAN'T DENY I FEEL LIKE I GOT EVERYTHING I WANTED OUT OF IT.
PLUS, I WAS ONLY TEAMMATES WITH M-SAN FOR THE DAY, PRETTY MUCH.
SHUN (WILT)
OH, I SEE...
PAKI (CRAK)
I'M BOTH HAPPY AND DISAP-POINTED.
HAPPY ABOUT LOSING A POWERFUL RIVAL.
DISAP-POINTED THAT I WON'T GET THE CHANCE TO MAKE UP FOR THE LAST ONE!
MOGU
MOGU (MUNCH)
HA HA...

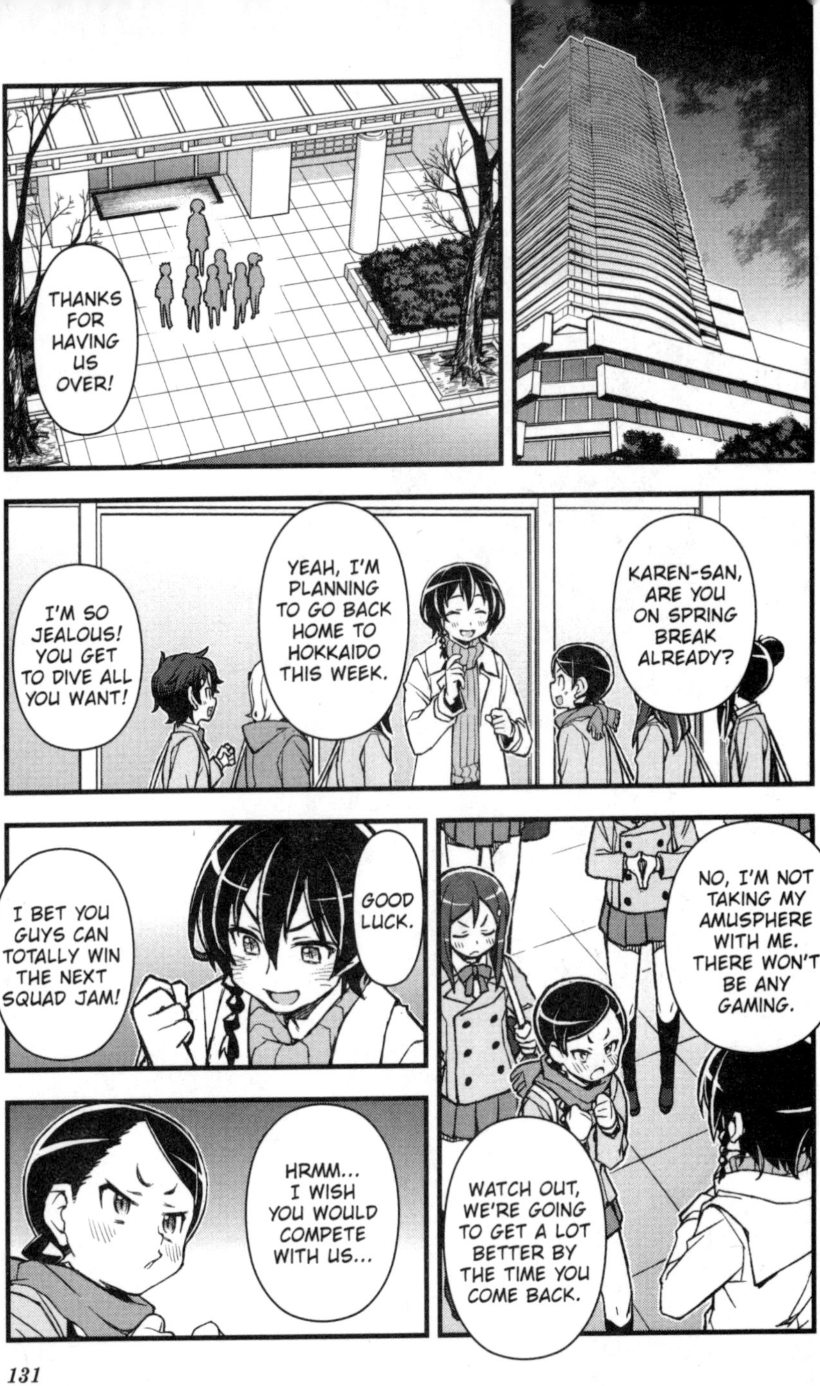
THANKS FOR HAVING US OVER!
KAREN-SAN, ARE YOU ON SPRING BREAK ALREADY?
YEAH, I'M PLANNING TO GO BACK HOME TO HOKKAIDO THIS WEEK.
I'M SO JEALOUS! YOU GET TO DIVE ALL YOU WANT!
NO, I'M NOT TAKING MY AMUSPHERE WITH ME. THERE WON'T BE ANY GAMING.
WATCH OUT, WE'RE GOING TO GET A LOT BETTER BY THE TIME YOU COME BACK.
GOOD LUCK.
I BET YOU GUYS CAN TOTALLY WIN THE NEXT SQUAD JAM!
HRMM... I WISH YOU WOULD COMPETE WITH US...

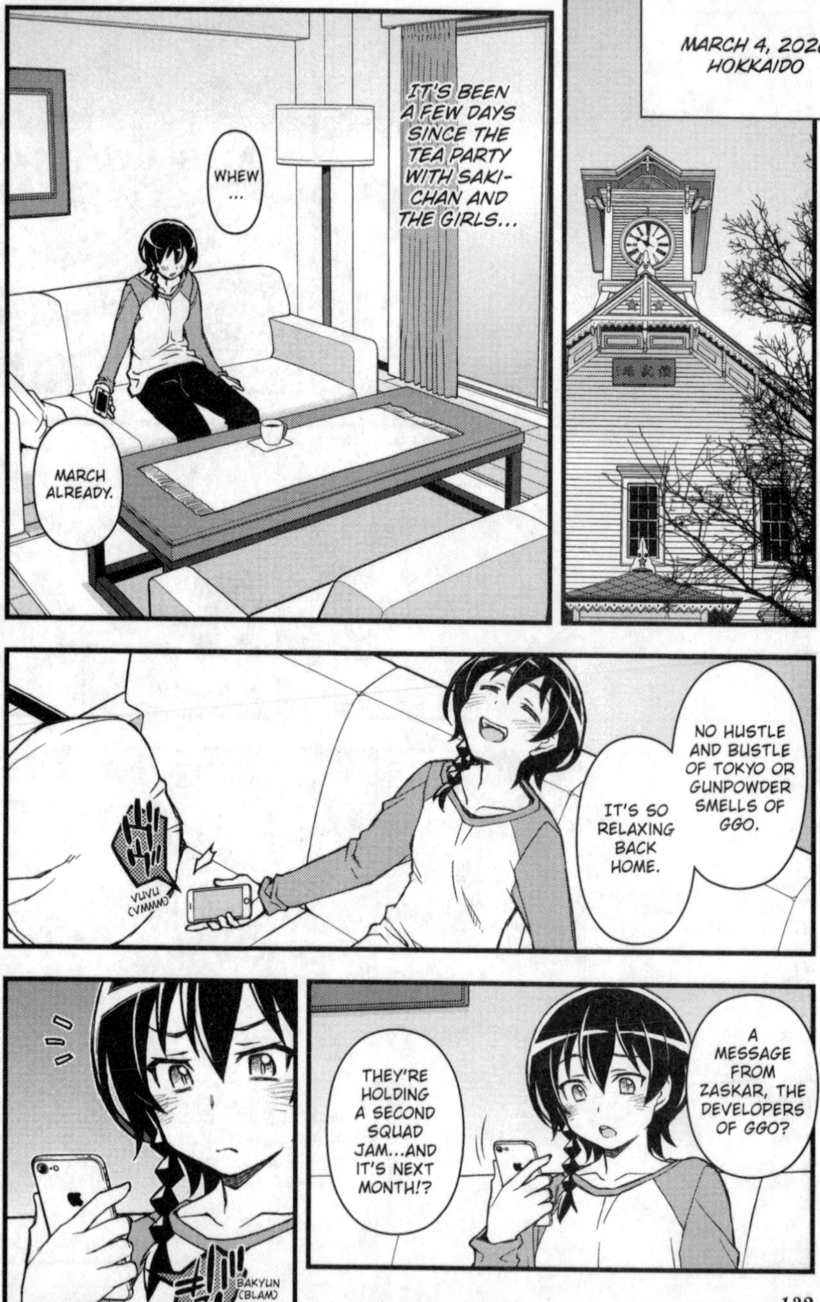
MARCH 4, 2026
HOKKAIDO
IT'S BEEN A FEW DAYS SINCE THE TEA PARTY WITH SAKI-CHAN AND THE GIRLS...
WHEW ...
MARCH ALREADY.
NO HUSTLE AND BUSTLE OF TOKYO OR GUNPOWDER SMELLS OF GGO.
IT'S SO RELAXING BACK HOME.
VUVU (VMMM)
A MESSAGE FROM ZASKAR, THE DEVELOPERS OF GGO?
THEY'RE HOLDING A SECOND SQUAD JAM...AND IT'S NEXT MONTH!?
BAKYUN (BLAM)

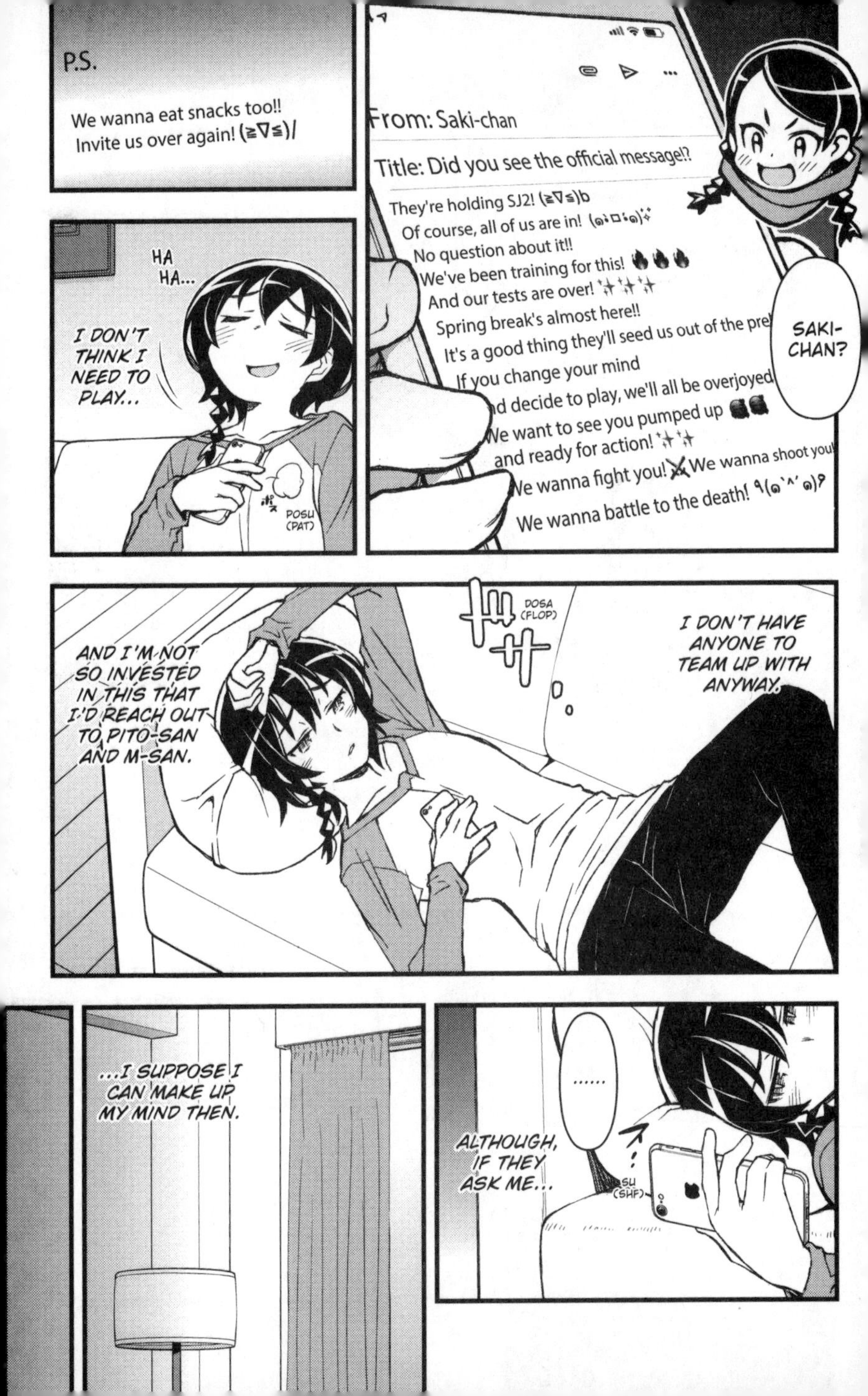
From: Saki-chan
Title: Did you see the official message!?
They're holding SJ2! (≧∇≦)b
Of course, all of us are in! (๑•̀ㅁ•́๑)✧
No question about it!!
We've been training for this! 🔥🔥🔥
And our tests are over! ✨✨✨
Spring break's almost here!!
It's a good thing they'll seed us out of the pre
If you change your mind
nd decide to play, we'll all be overjoyed
We want to see you pumped up
and ready for action! ✨✨
We wanna fight you! We wanna shoot you!
We wanna battle to the death! ٩(๑`^´๑)۶
SAKI-CHAN?
P.S.
We wanna eat snacks too!!
Invite us over again! (≧∇≦)/
HA HA...
I DON'T THINK I NEED TO PLAY...
POSU (PAT)
DOSA (FLOP)
I DON'T HAVE ANYONE TO TEAM UP WITH ANYWAY.
AND I'M NOT SO INVESTED IN THIS THAT I'D REACH OUT TO PITO-SAN AND M-SAN.
......
ALTHOUGH, IF THEY ASK ME...
SU (SHF)
...I SUPPOSE I CAN MAKE UP MY MIND THEN.

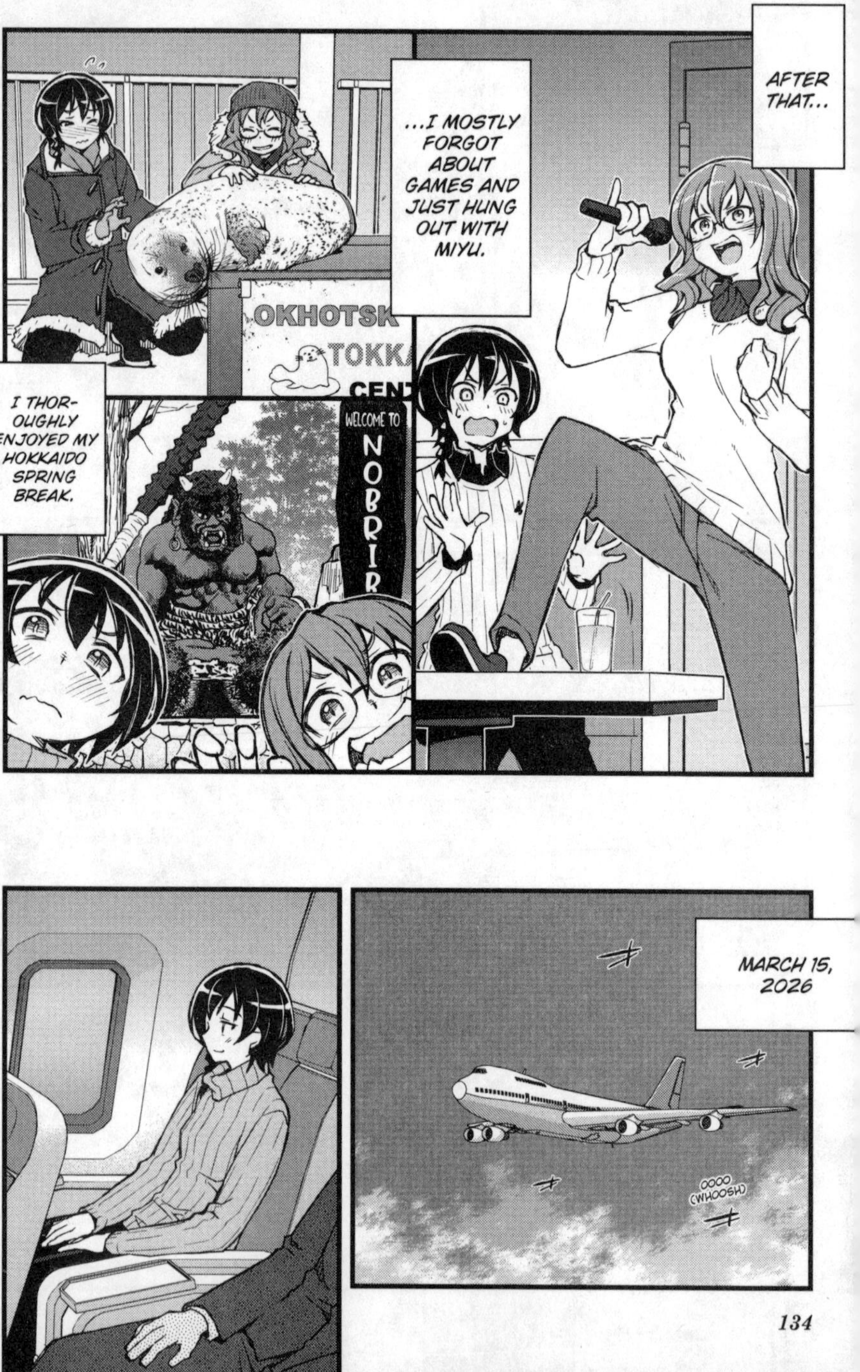
AFTER THAT...
...I MOSTLY FORGOT ABOUT GAMES AND JUST HUNG OUT WITH MIYU.
OKHOTSK
TOKKA
CENT
I THOR-OUGHLY ENJOYED MY HOKKAIDO SPRING BREAK.
WELCOME TO
NOBRIR
MARCH 15, 2026
OOOO
(WHOOSH)

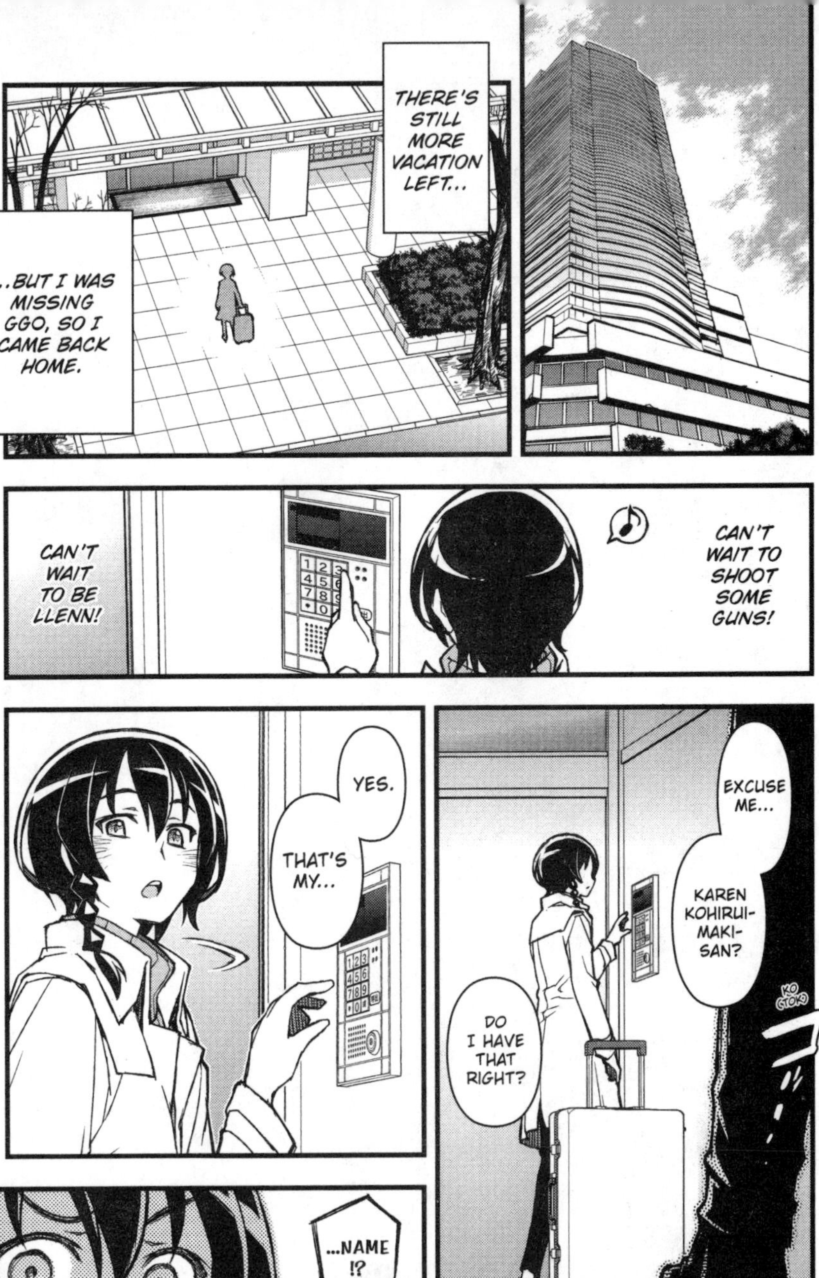
THERE'S STILL MORE VACATION LEFT...
...BUT I WAS MISSING GGO, SO I CAME BACK HOME.
CAN'T WAIT TO SHOOT SOME GUNS!
CAN'T WAIT TO BE LLENN!
EXCUSE ME...
KAREN KOHIRUI-MAKI-SAN?
DO I HAVE THAT RIGHT?
KO (TOK)
YES.
THAT'S MY...
...NAME !?

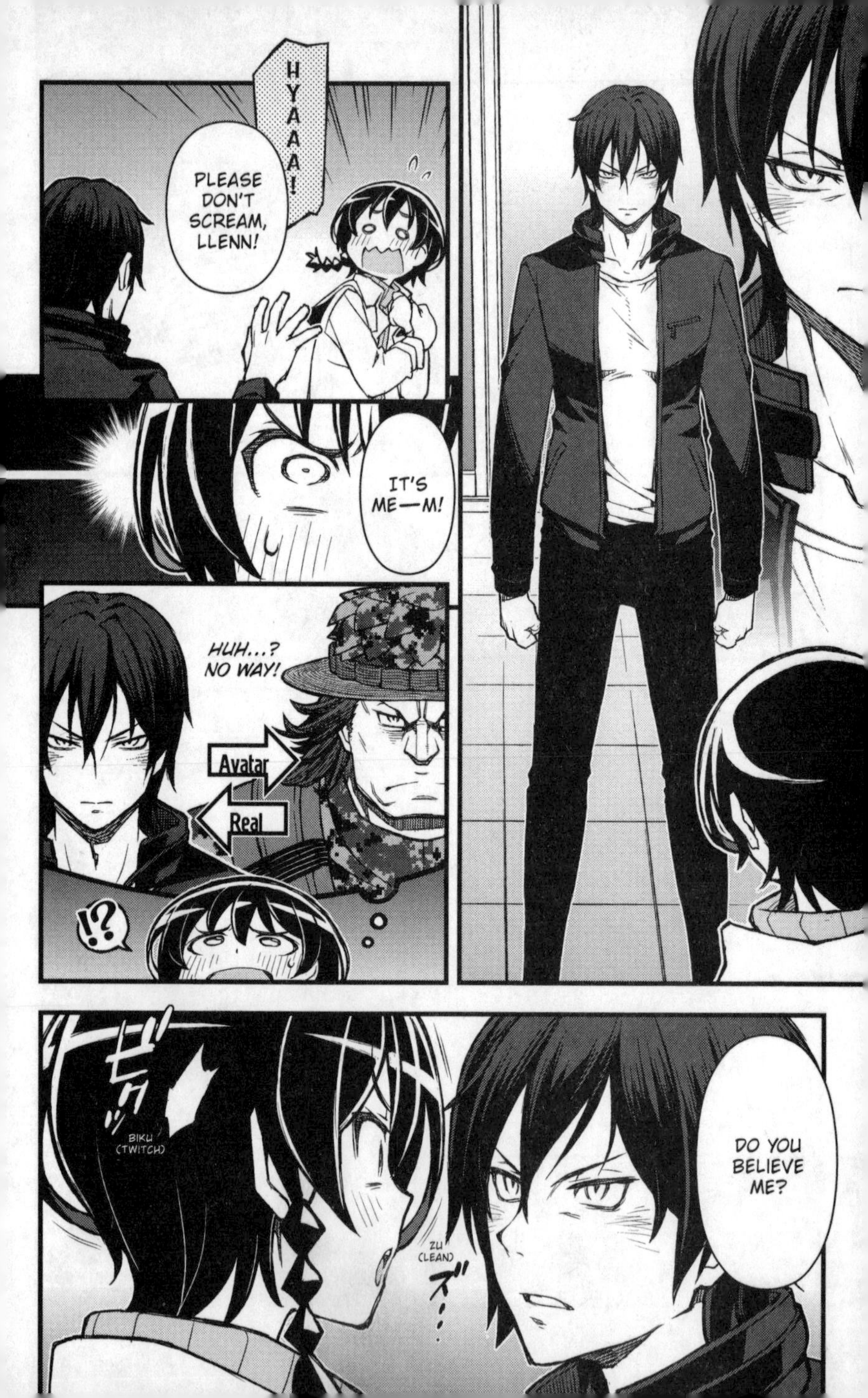
HYAAAA!
PLEASE DON'T SCREAM, LLENN!
IT'S ME—M!
HUH...? NO WAY!
Avatar
Real
!?
DO YOU BELIEVE ME?
ZU (LEAN)
BIKU (TWITCH)

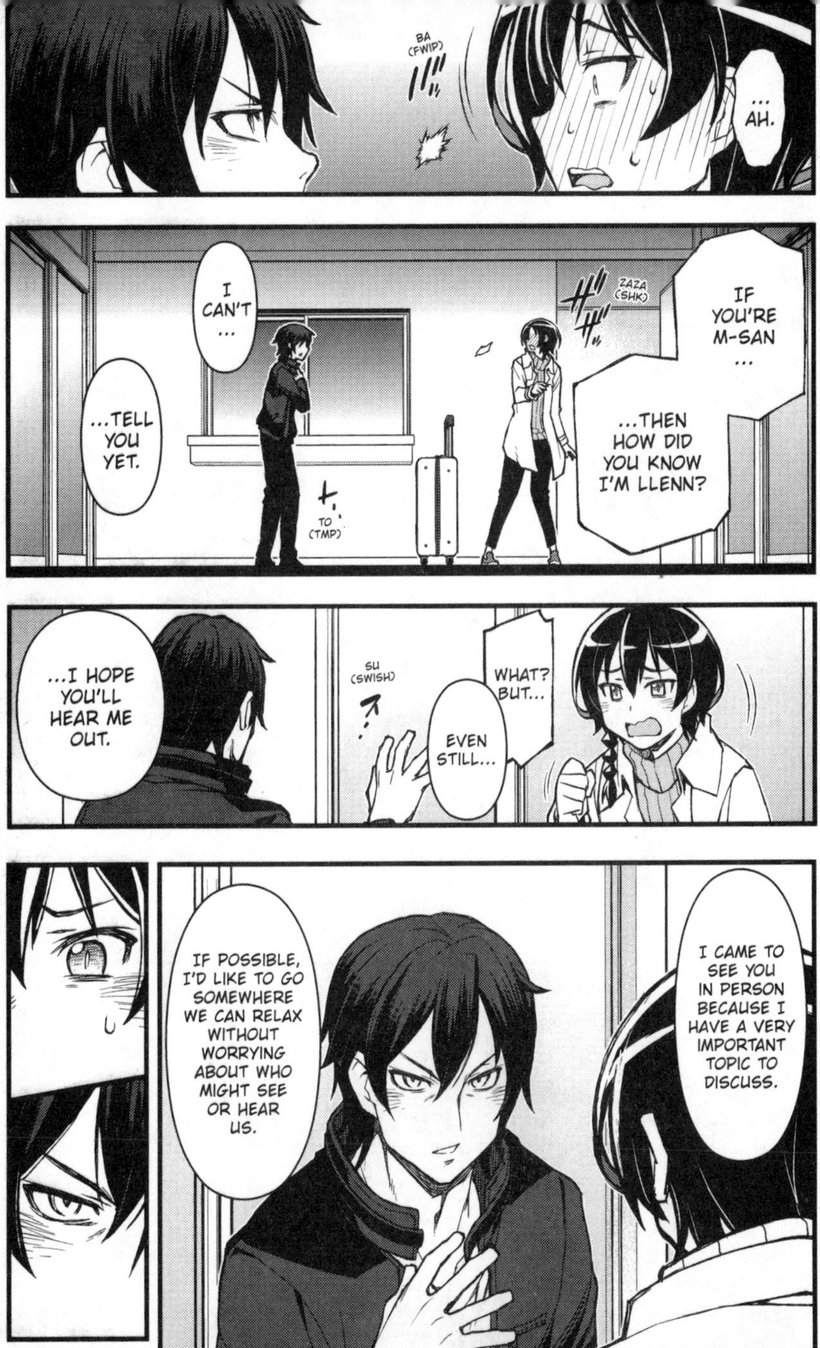
...AH.
BA (FWIP)
IF YOU'RE M-SAN ...
...THEN HOW DID YOU KNOW I'M LLENN?
ZAZA (SHK)
I CAN'T ...
...TELL YOU YET.
TO (TMP)
WHAT? BUT...
EVEN STILL...
SU (SWISH)
...I HOPE YOU'LL HEAR ME OUT.
I CAME TO SEE YOU IN PERSON BECAUSE I HAVE A VERY IMPORTANT TOPIC TO DISCUSS.
IF POSSIBLE, I'D LIKE TO GO SOMEWHERE WE CAN RELAX WITHOUT WORRYING ABOUT WHO MIGHT SEE OR HEAR US.

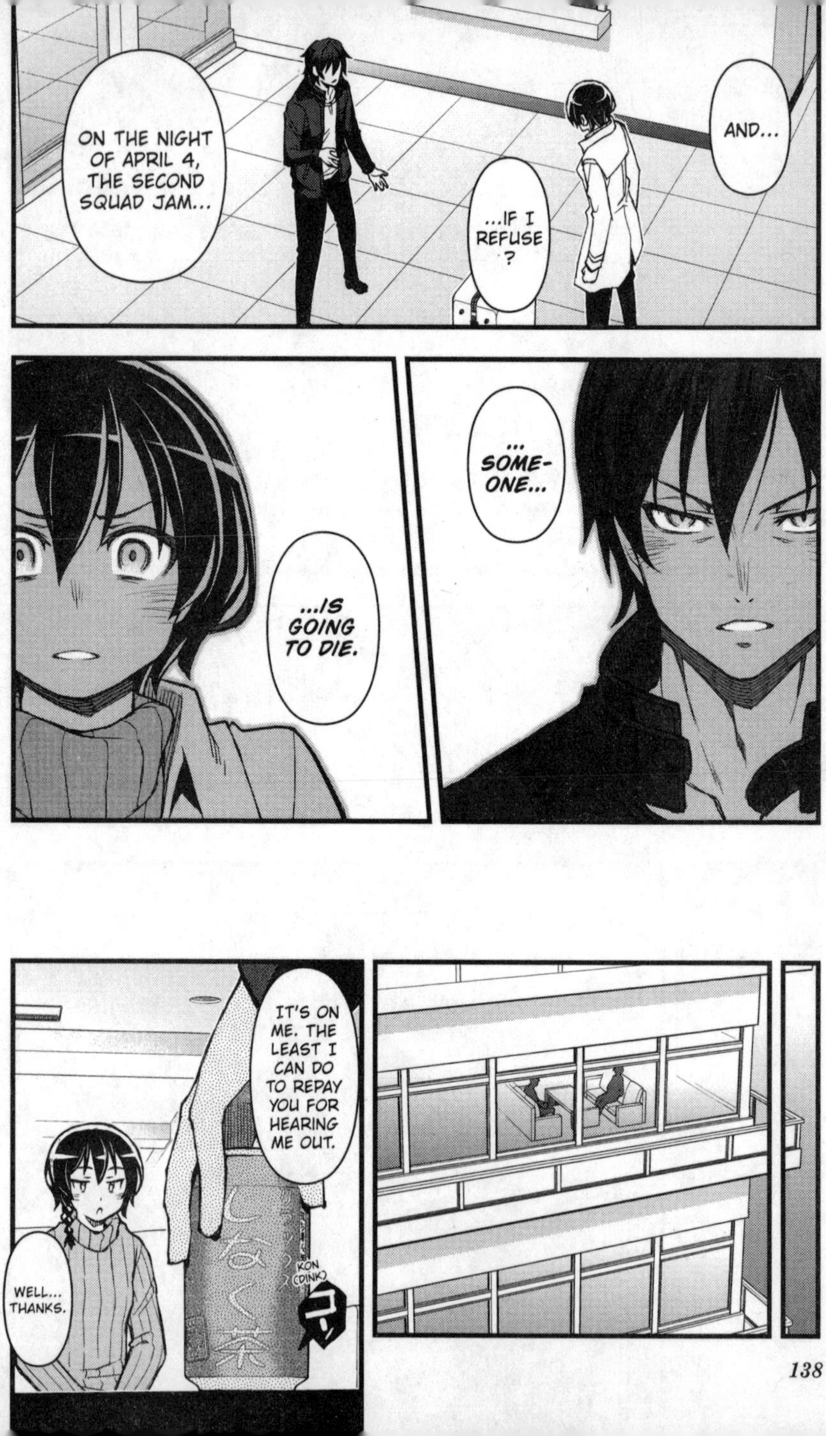
AND...
...IF I REFUSE?
ON THE NIGHT OF APRIL 4, THE SECOND SQUAD JAM...
... SOME-ONE...
...IS GOING TO DIE.
IT'S ON ME. THE LEAST I CAN DO TO REPAY YOU FOR HEARING ME OUT.
KON (DINK)
WELL... THANKS.

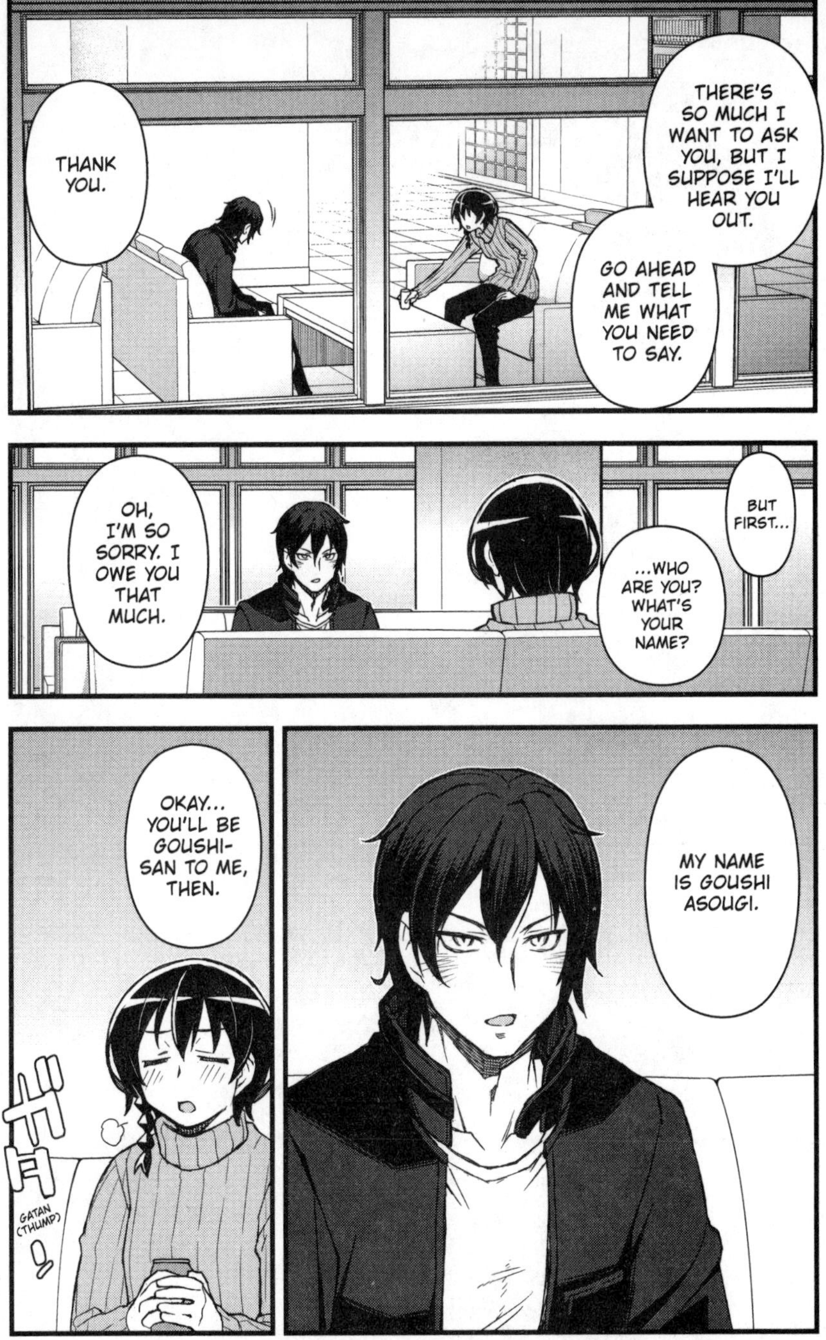
THERE'S SO MUCH I WANT TO ASK YOU, BUT I SUPPOSE I'LL HEAR YOU OUT.
GO AHEAD AND TELL ME WHAT YOU NEED TO SAY.
THANK YOU.
BUT FIRST...
...WHO ARE YOU? WHAT'S YOUR NAME?
OH, I'M SO SORRY. I OWE YOU THAT MUCH.
MY NAME IS GOUSHI ASOUGI.
OKAY... YOU'LL BE GOUSHI-SAN TO ME, THEN.
GATAN (THUMP)

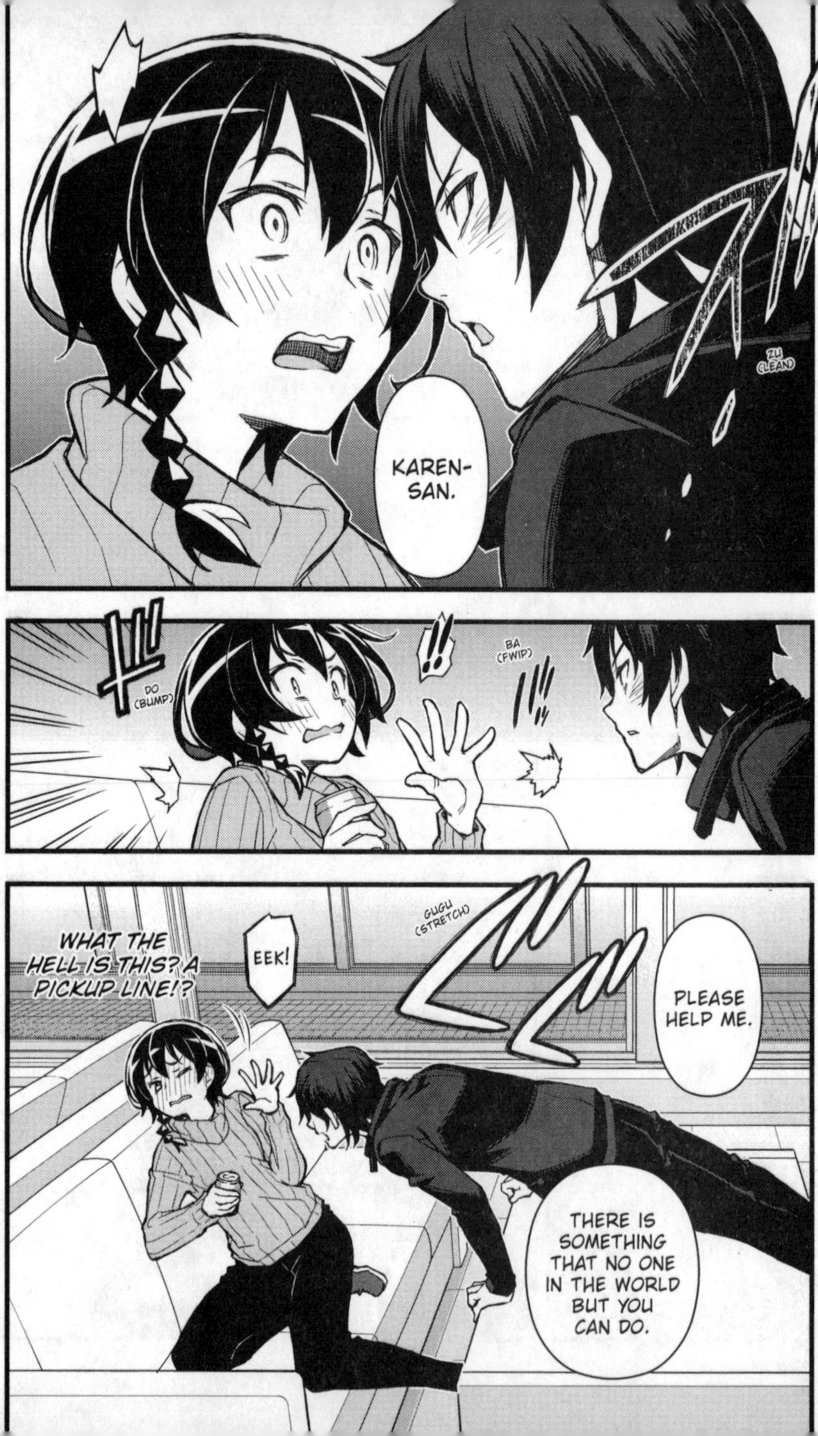
ZU (LEAN)
KAREN-SAN.
BA (FWIP)
!!
DO (BUMP)
PLEASE HELP ME.
GUGU (STRETCH)
EEK!
WHAT THE HELL IS THIS? A PICKUP LINE!?
THERE IS SOMETHING THAT NO ONE IN THE WORLD BUT YOU CAN DO.

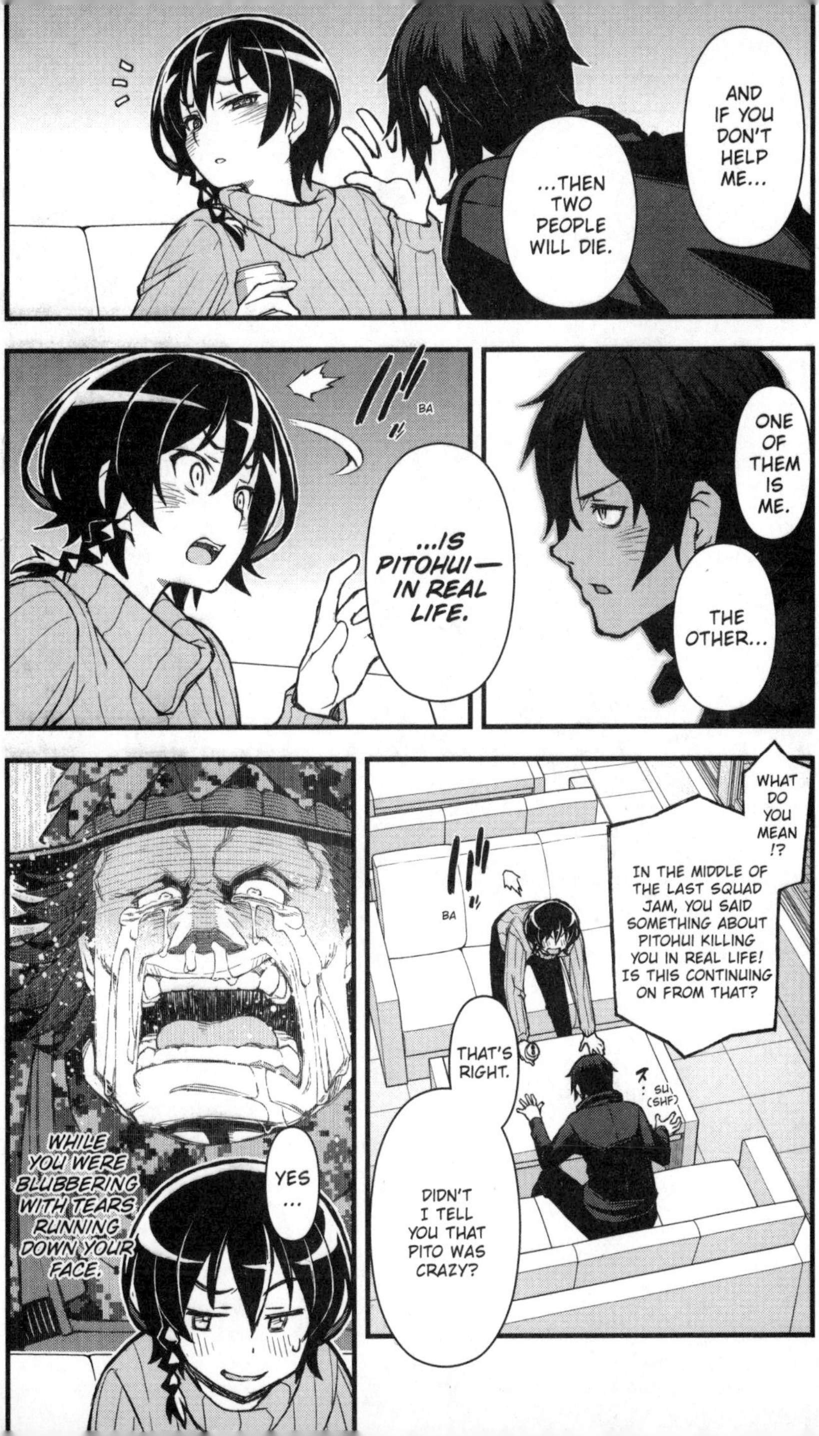
AND IF YOU DON'T HELP ME...
...THEN TWO PEOPLE WILL DIE.
ONE OF THEM IS ME.
THE OTHER...
BA
...IS PITOHUI— IN REAL LIFE.
WHAT DO YOU MEAN !?
IN THE MIDDLE OF THE LAST SQUAD JAM, YOU SAID SOMETHING ABOUT PITOHUI KILLING YOU IN REAL LIFE! IS THIS CONTINUING ON FROM THAT?
BA
THAT'S RIGHT.
SU (SHF)
DIDN'T I TELL YOU THAT PITO WAS CRAZY?
YES ...
WHILE YOU WERE BLUBBERING WITH TEARS RUNNING DOWN YOUR FACE.

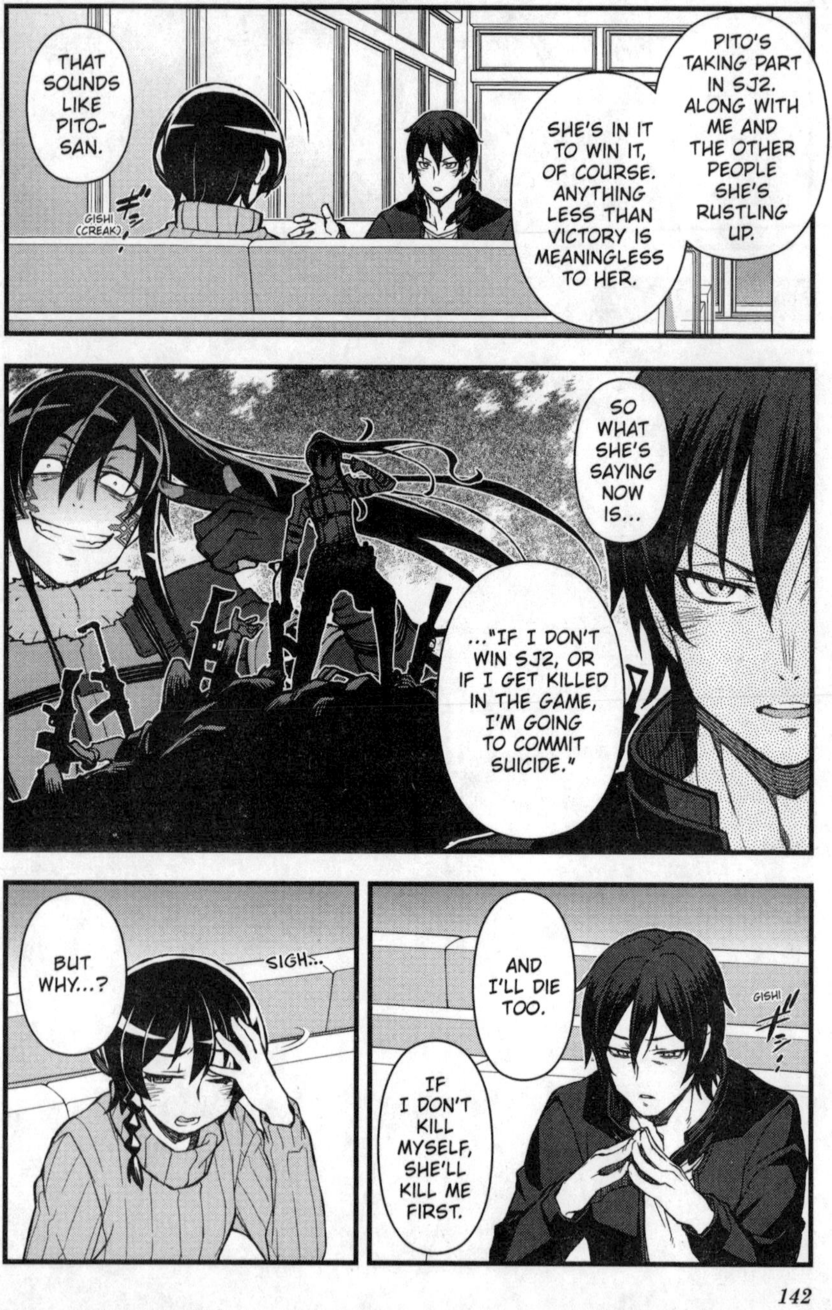
PITO'S TAKING PART IN SJ2. ALONG WITH ME AND THE OTHER PEOPLE SHE'S RUSTLING UP.
SHE'S IN IT TO WIN IT, OF COURSE. ANYTHING LESS THAN VICTORY IS MEANINGLESS TO HER.
THAT SOUNDS LIKE PITO-SAN.
GISHI (CREAK)
SO WHAT SHE'S SAYING NOW IS...
..."IF I DON'T WIN SJ2, OR IF I GET KILLED IN THE GAME, I'M GOING TO COMMIT SUICIDE."
GISHI
AND I'LL DIE TOO.
IF I DON'T KILL MYSELF, SHE'LL KILL ME FIRST.
SIGH...
BUT WHY...?

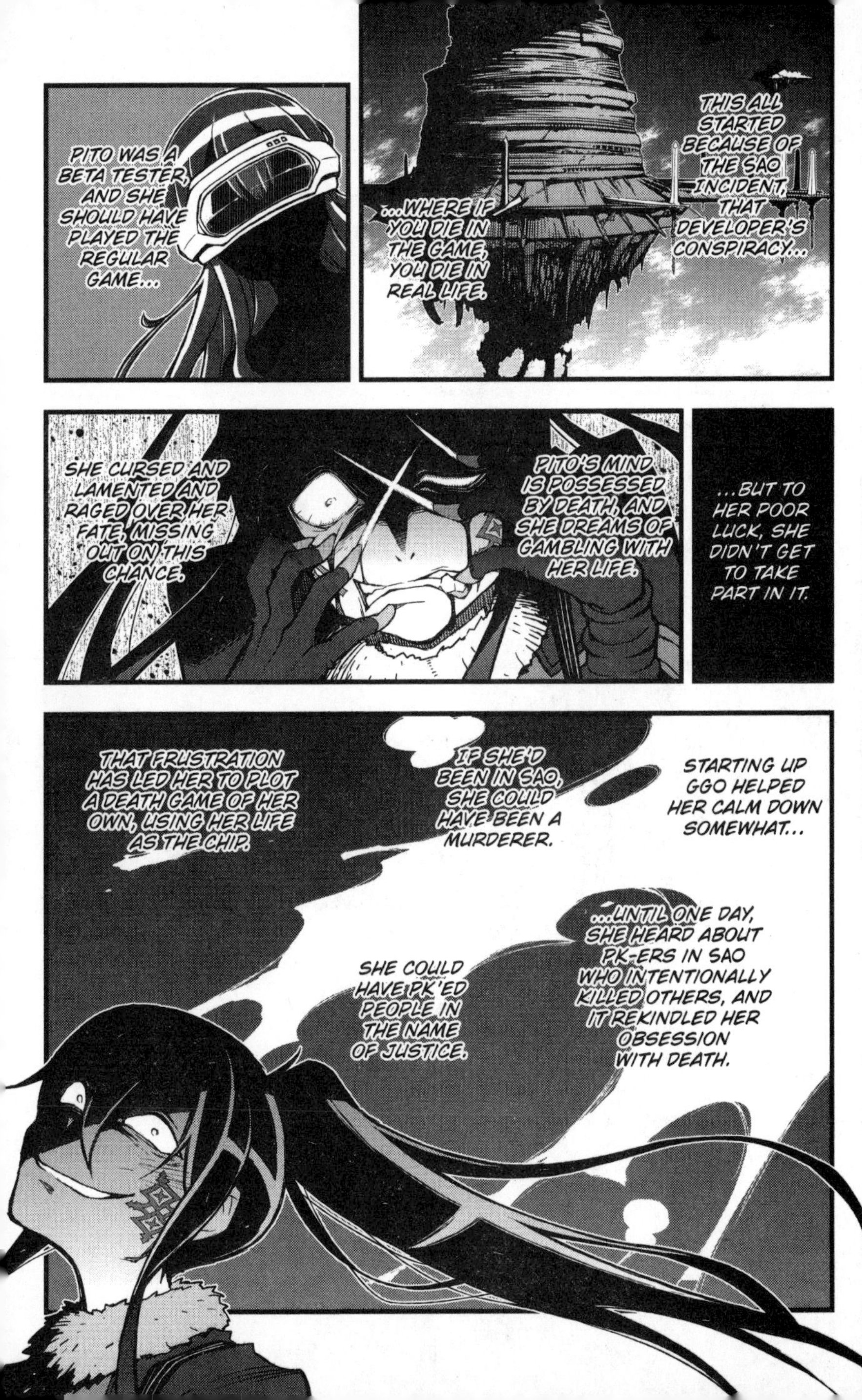
THIS ALL STARTED BECAUSE OF THE SAO INCIDENT, THAT DEVELOPER'S CONSPIRACY...
...WHERE IF YOU DIE IN THE GAME, YOU DIE IN REAL LIFE.
PITO WAS A BETA TESTER, AND SHE SHOULD HAVE PLAYED THE REGULAR GAME...
...BUT TO HER POOR LUCK, SHE DIDN'T GET TO TAKE PART IN IT.
PITO'S MIND IS POSSESSED BY DEATH, AND SHE DREAMS OF GAMBLING WITH HER LIFE.
SHE CURSED AND LAMENTED AND RAGED OVER HER FATE, MISSING OUT ON THIS CHANCE.
STARTING UP GGO HELPED HER CALM DOWN SOMEWHAT...
...UNTIL ONE DAY, SHE HEARD ABOUT PK-ERS IN SAO WHO INTENTIONALLY KILLED OTHERS, AND IT REKINDLED HER OBSESSION WITH DEATH.
IF SHE'D BEEN IN SAO, SHE COULD HAVE BEEN A MURDERER.
SHE COULD HAVE PK'ED PEOPLE IN THE NAME OF JUSTICE.
THAT FRUSTRATION HAS LED HER TO PLOT A DEATH GAME OF HER OWN, USING HER LIFE AS THE CHIP.

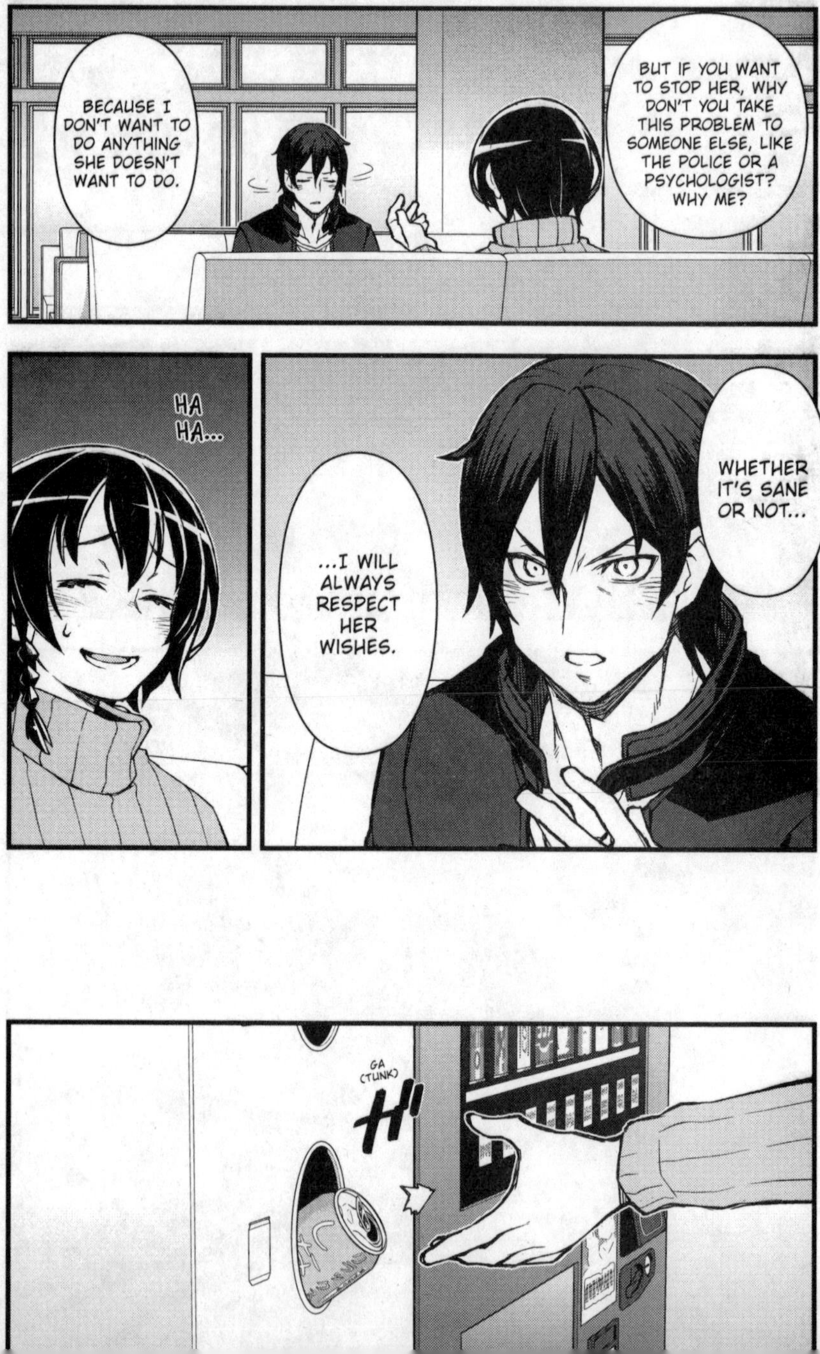
BUT IF YOU WANT TO STOP HER, WHY DON'T YOU TAKE THIS PROBLEM TO SOMEONE ELSE, LIKE THE POLICE OR A PSYCHOLOGIST? WHY ME?
BECAUSE I DON'T WANT TO DO ANYTHING SHE DOESN'T WANT TO DO.
WHETHER IT'S SANE OR NOT...
...I WILL ALWAYS RESPECT HER WISHES.
HA HA...
GA (TUNK)

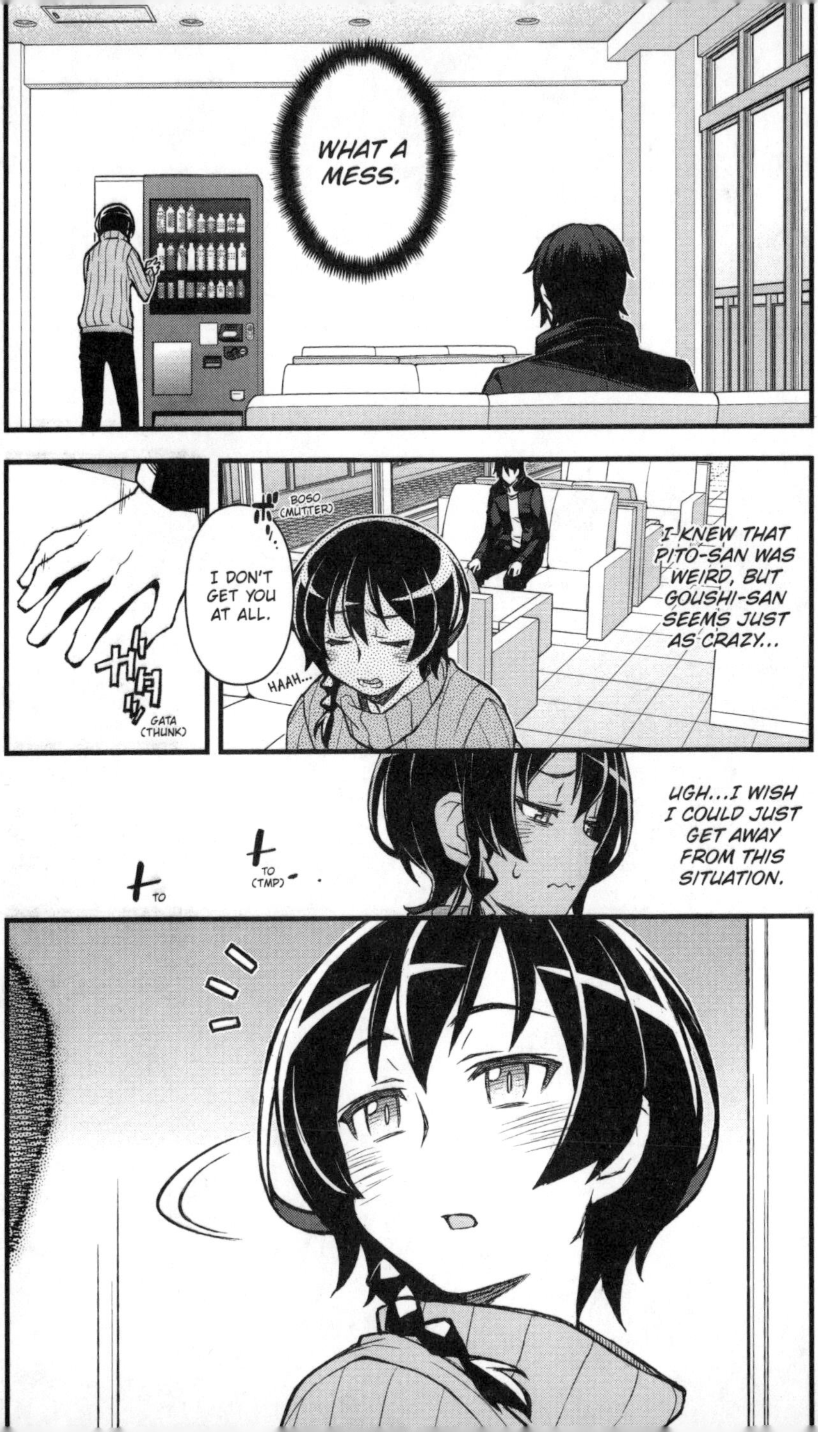
WHAT A MESS.
I KNEW THAT PITO-SAN WAS WEIRD, BUT GOUSHI-SAN SEEMS JUST AS CRAZY...
BOSO (MUTTER)
I DON'T GET YOU AT ALL.
HAAH...
GATA (THUNK)
UGH...I WISH I COULD JUST GET AWAY FROM THIS SITUATION.
TO (TMP)
TO

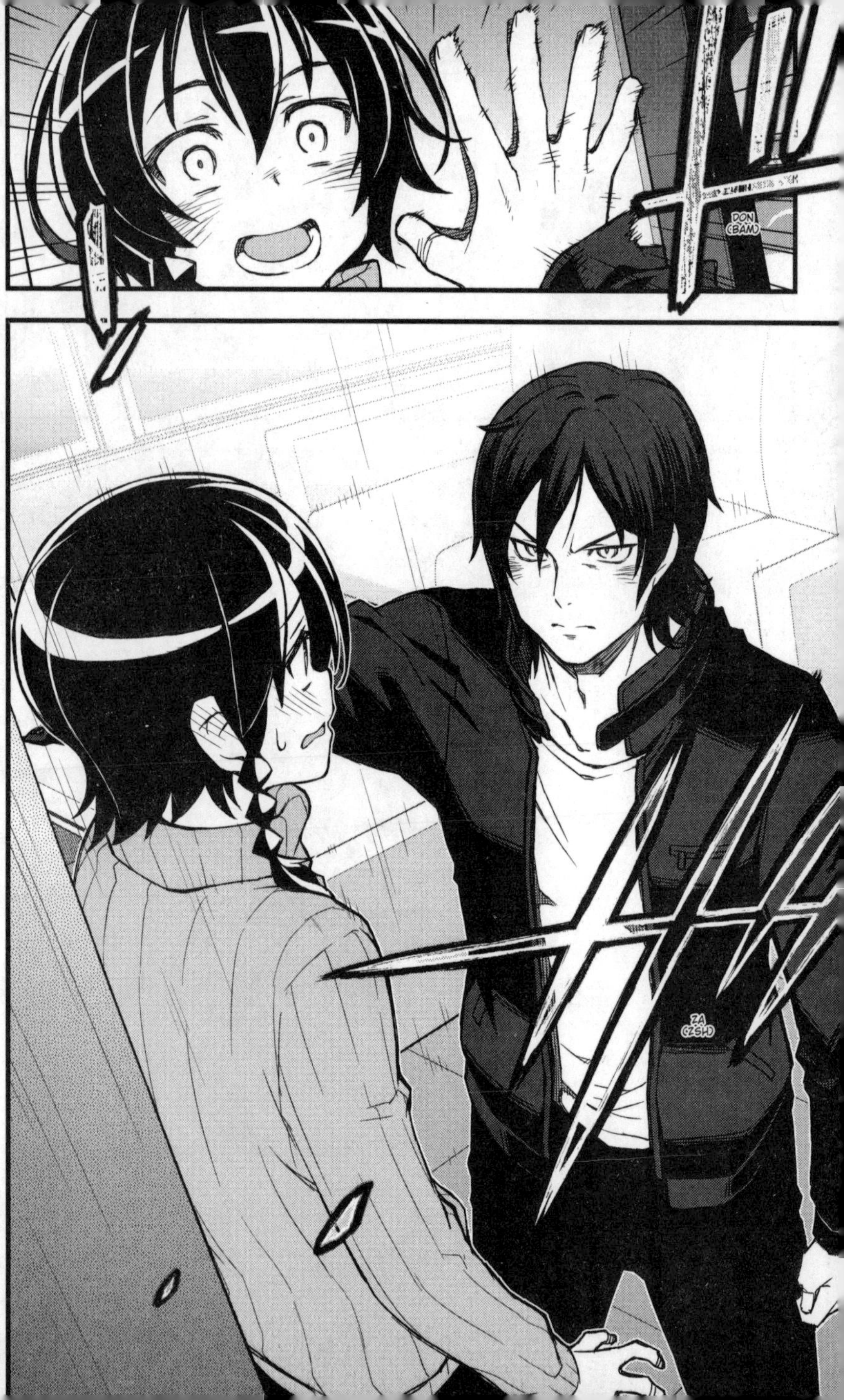
DON (BAM)
ZA (ZSH)

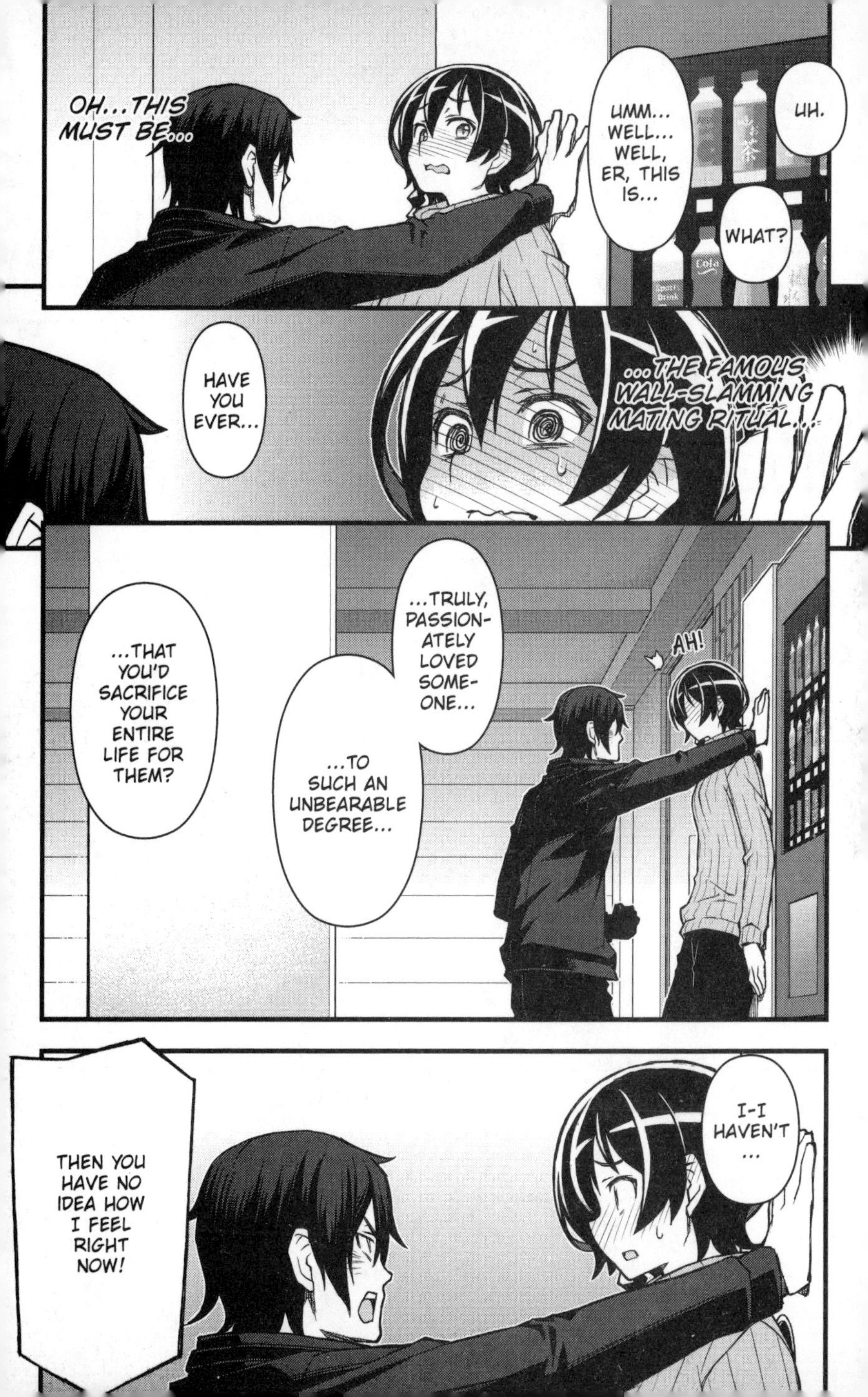
UH.
WHAT?
UMM... WELL... WELL, ER, THIS IS...
OH...THIS MUST BE...
...THE FAMOUS WALL-SLAMMING MATING RITUAL...
HAVE YOU EVER...
AH!
...TRULY, PASSIONATELY LOVED SOMEONE...
...TO SUCH AN UNBEARABLE DEGREE...
...THAT YOU'D SACRIFICE YOUR ENTIRE LIFE FOR THEM?
I-I HAVEN'T ...
THEN YOU HAVE NO IDEA HOW I FEEL RIGHT NOW!

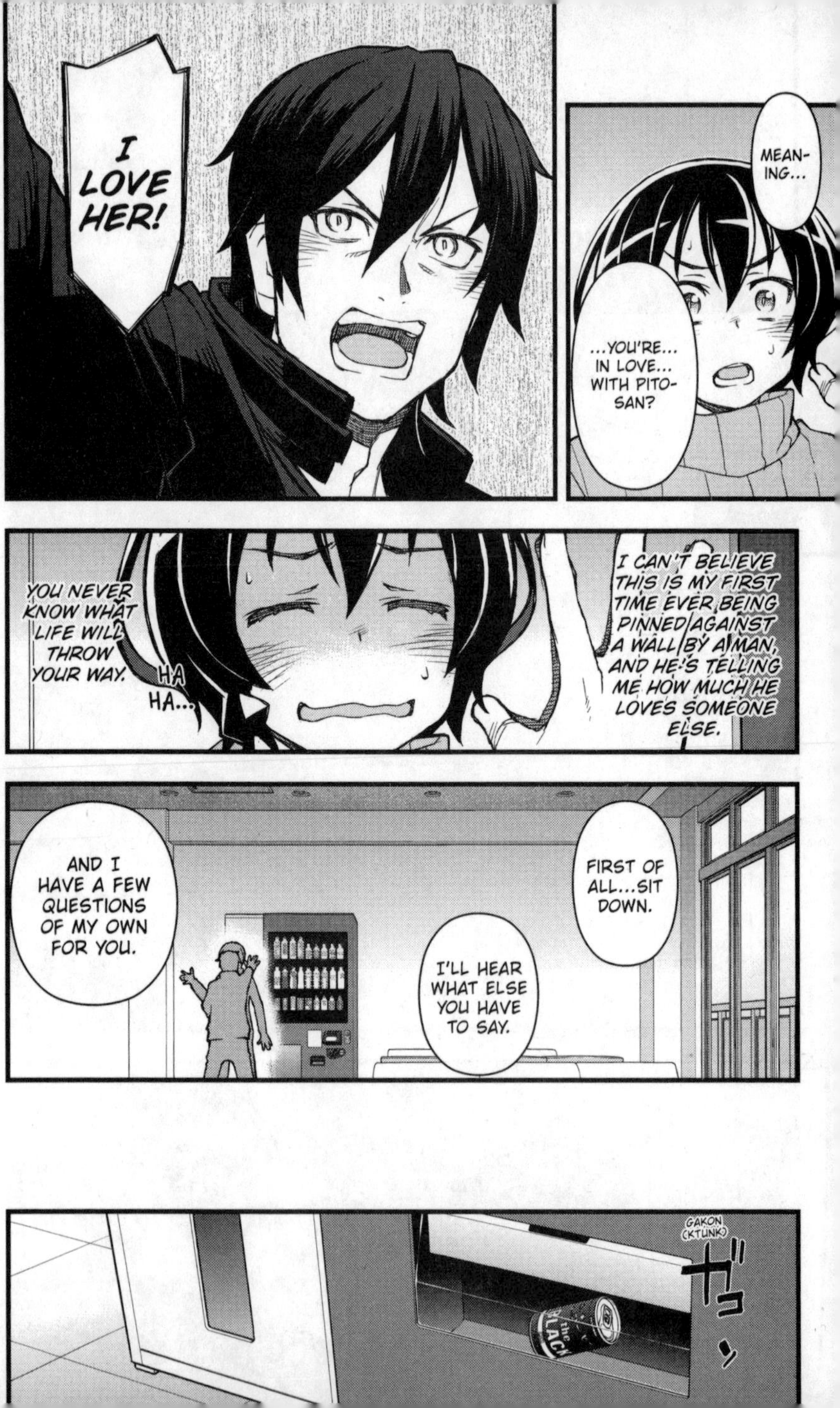
MEAN-ING...
...YOU'RE... IN LOVE... WITH PITO-SAN?
I LOVE HER!
I CAN'T BELIEVE THIS IS MY FIRST TIME EVER BEING PINNED AGAINST A WALL BY A MAN, AND HE'S TELLING ME HOW MUCH HE LOVES SOMEONE ELSE.
YOU NEVER KNOW WHAT LIFE WILL THROW YOUR WAY.
HA HA...
FIRST OF ALL...SIT DOWN.
I'LL HEAR WHAT ELSE YOU HAVE TO SAY.
AND I HAVE A FEW QUESTIONS OF MY OWN FOR YOU.
GAKON (KTUNK)

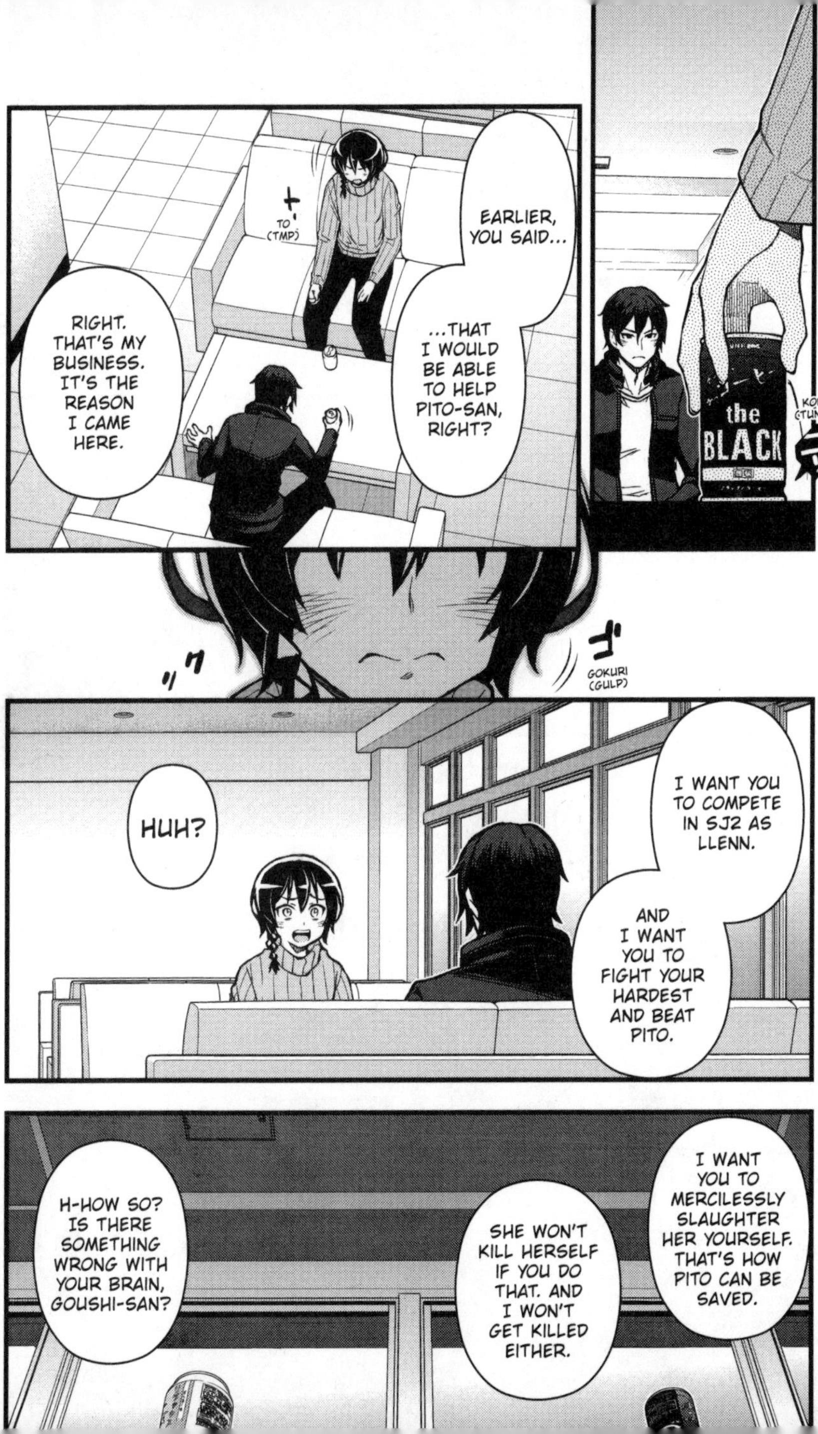
KON (TUNK)
EARLIER, YOU SAID...
TO (TMP)
...THAT I WOULD BE ABLE TO HELP PITO-SAN, RIGHT?
RIGHT. THAT'S MY BUSINESS. IT'S THE REASON I CAME HERE.
GOKURI (GULP)
I WANT YOU TO COMPETE IN SJ2 AS LLENN.
AND I WANT YOU TO FIGHT YOUR HARDEST AND BEAT PITO.
HUH?
I WANT YOU TO MERCILESSLY SLAUGHTER HER YOURSELF. THAT'S HOW PITO CAN BE SAVED.
SHE WON'T KILL HERSELF IF YOU DO THAT. AND I WON'T GET KILLED EITHER.
H-HOW SO? IS THERE SOMETHING WRONG WITH YOUR BRAIN, GOUSHI-SAN?

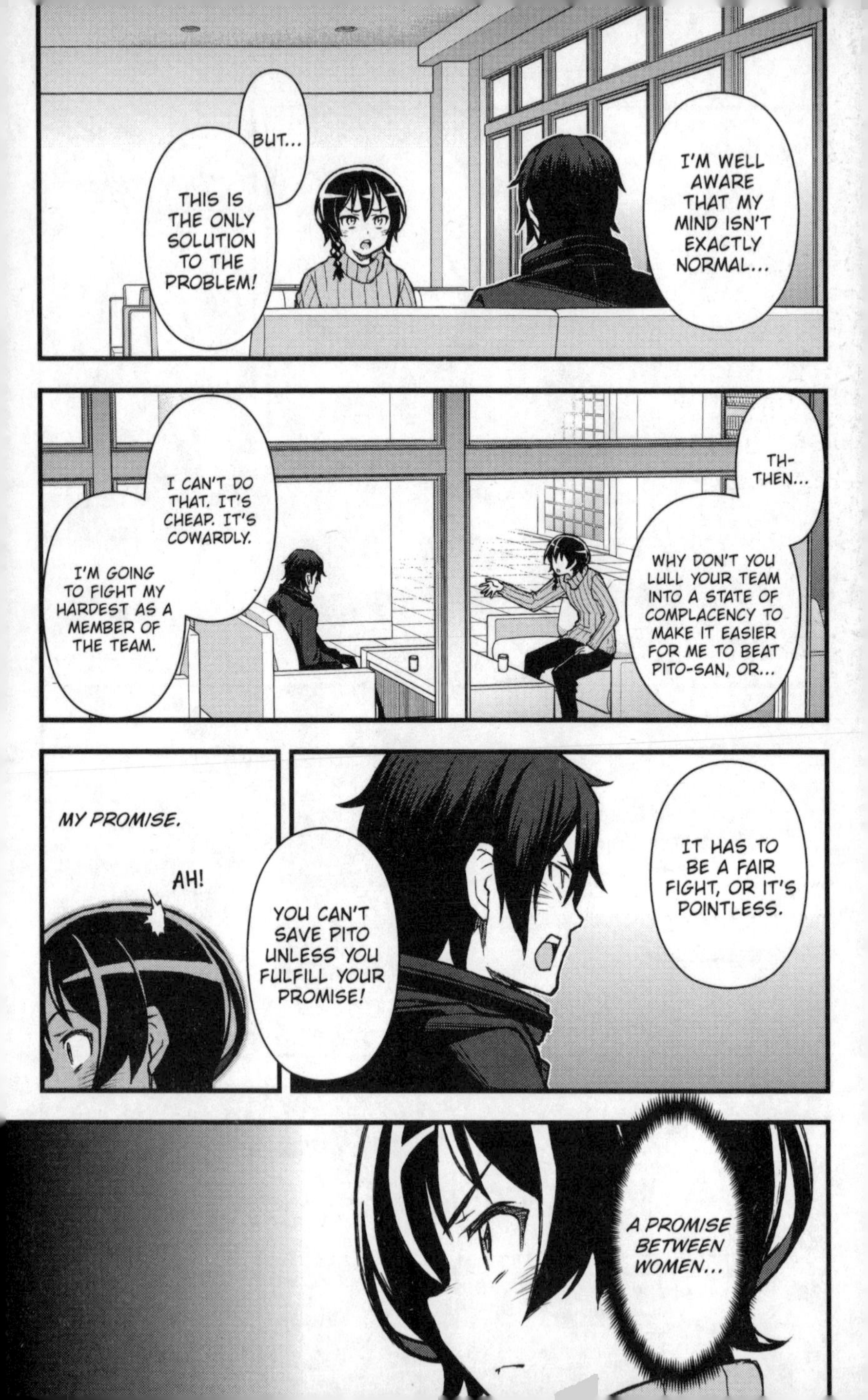
I'M WELL AWARE THAT MY MIND ISN'T EXACTLY NORMAL...
BUT...
THIS IS THE ONLY SOLUTION TO THE PROBLEM!
TH-THEN...
WHY DON'T YOU LULL YOUR TEAM INTO A STATE OF COMPLACENCY TO MAKE IT EASIER FOR ME TO BEAT PITO-SAN, OR...
I CAN'T DO THAT. IT'S CHEAP. IT'S COWARDLY.
I'M GOING TO FIGHT MY HARDEST AS A MEMBER OF THE TEAM.
IT HAS TO BE A FAIR FIGHT, OR IT'S POINTLESS.
YOU CAN'T SAVE PITO UNLESS YOU FULFILL YOUR PROMISE!
MY PROMISE.
AH!
A PROMISE BETWEEN WOMEN...

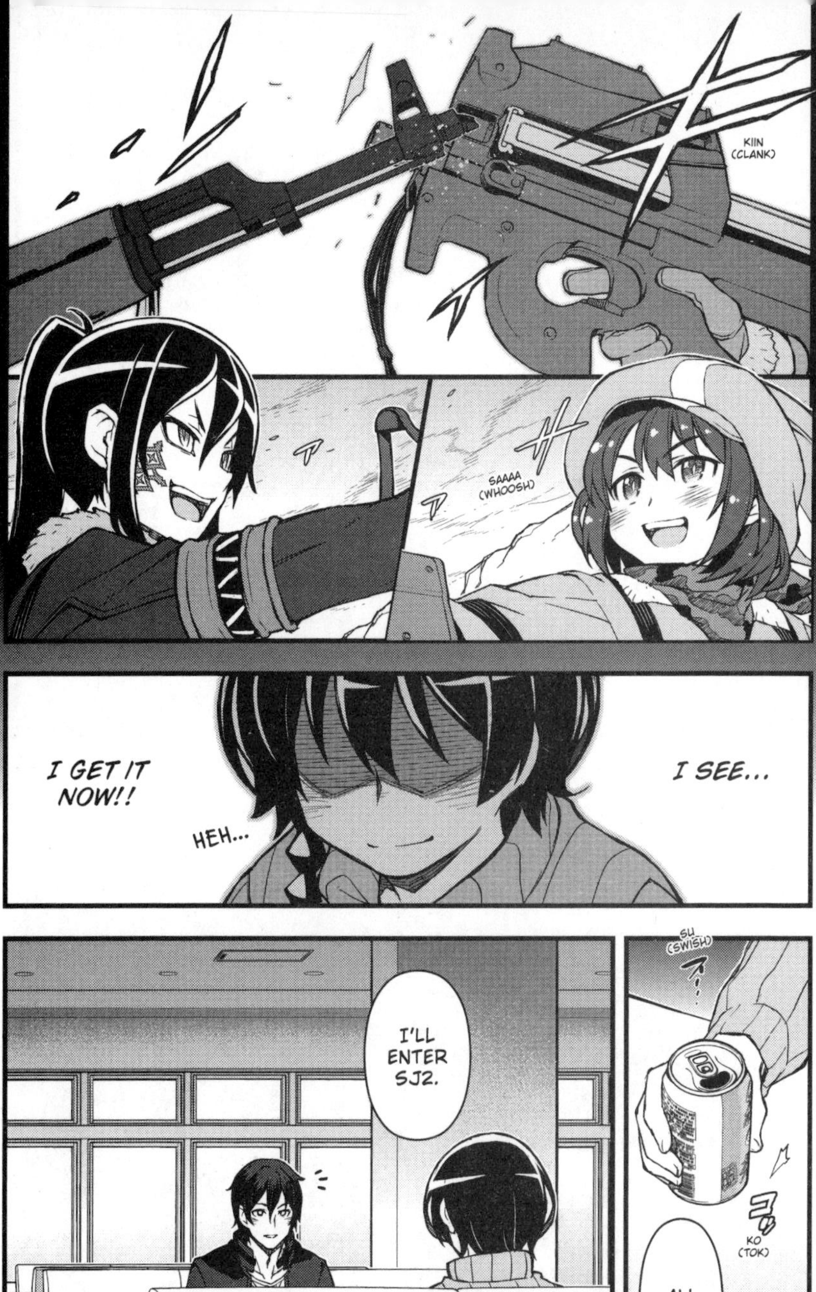
KIIN (CLANK)
SAAAA (WHOOSH)
I SEE...
I GET IT NOW!!
HEH...
SU (SWISH)
KO (TOK)
ALL RIGHT...
I'LL ENTER SJ2.

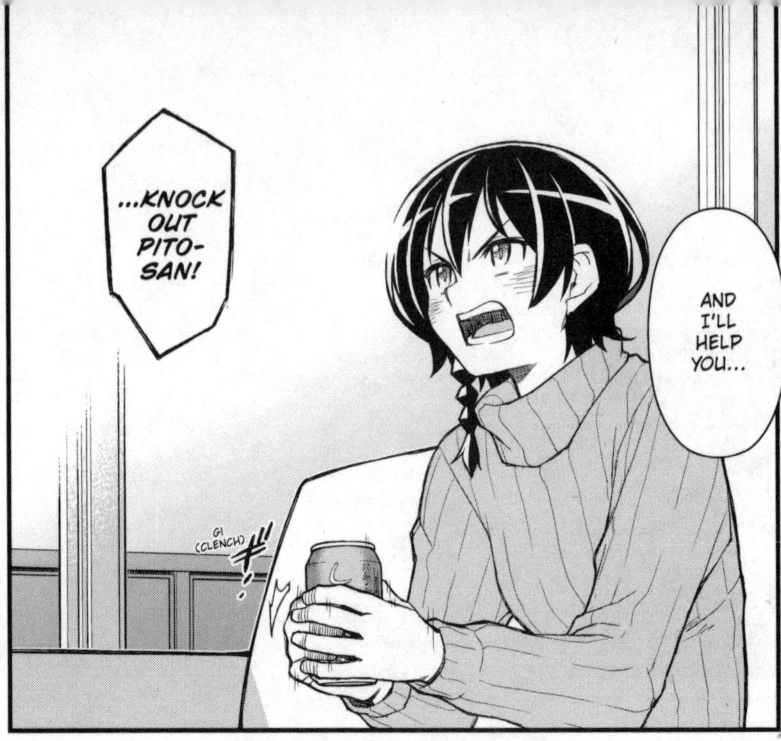
AND I'LL HELP YOU...
...KNOCK OUT PITO-SAN!
GI (CLENCH)

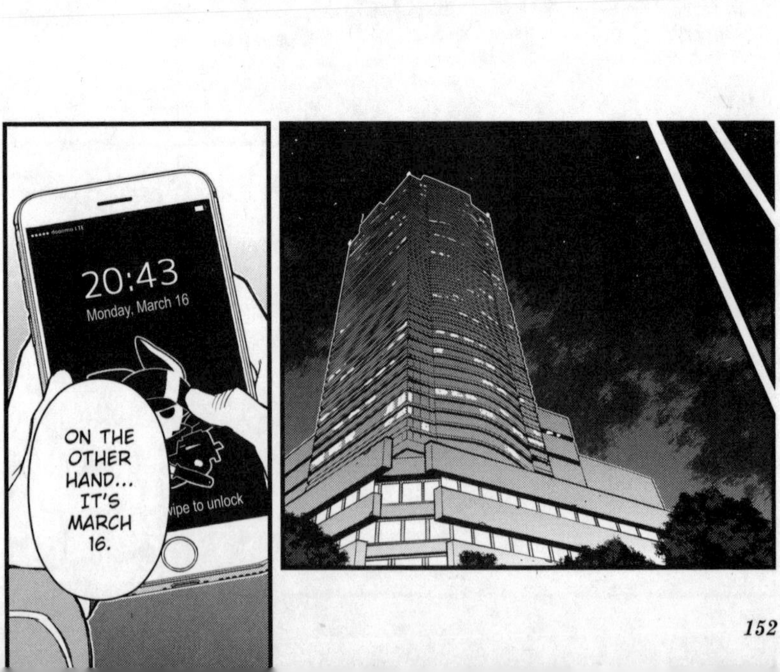
20:43
Monday, March 16
wipe to unlock
ON THE OTHER HAND... IT'S MARCH 16.

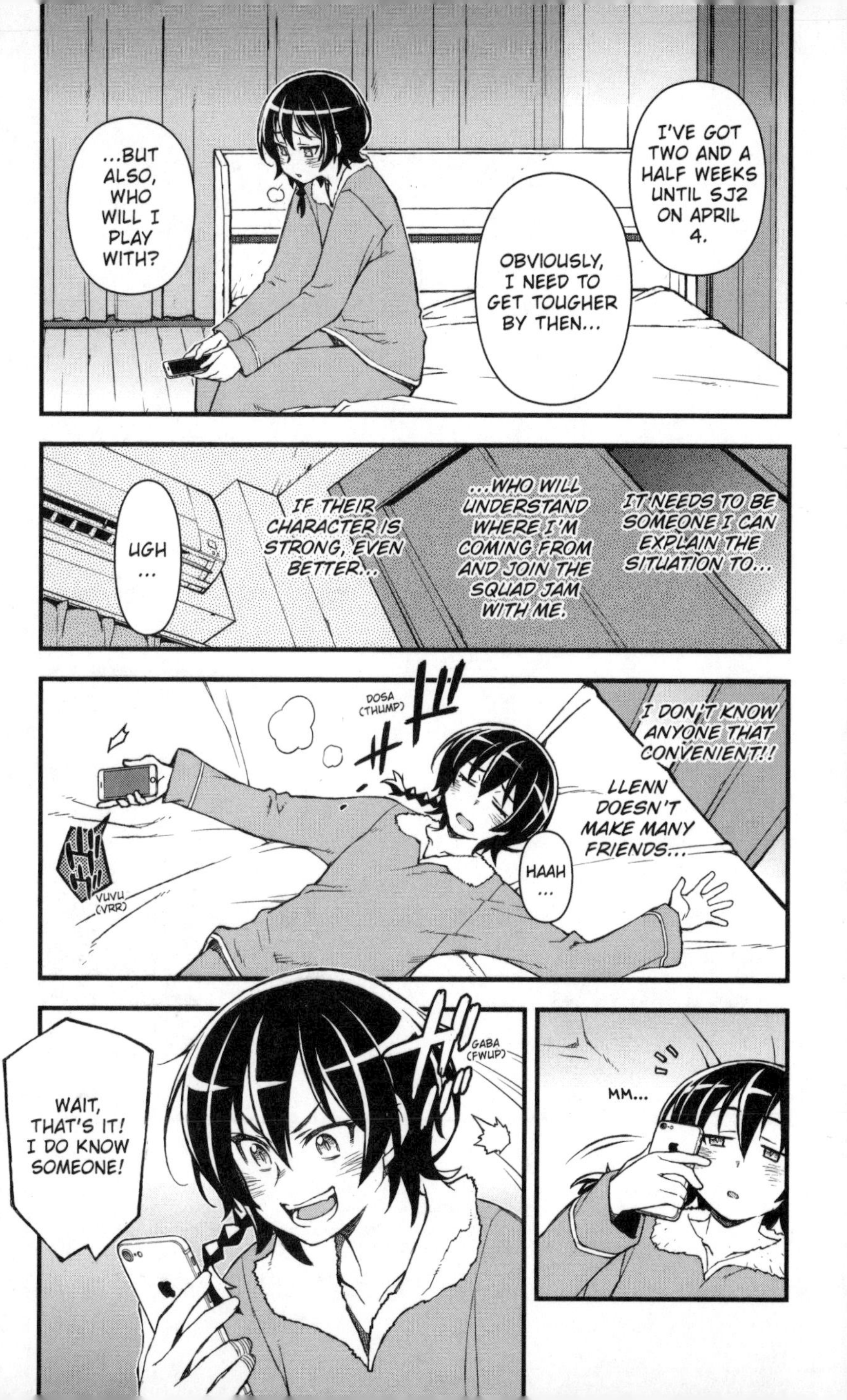
I'VE GOT TWO AND A HALF WEEKS UNTIL SJ2 ON APRIL 4.
OBVIOUSLY, I NEED TO GET TOUGHER BY THEN...
...BUT ALSO, WHO WILL I PLAY WITH?
IT NEEDS TO BE SOMEONE I CAN EXPLAIN THE SITUATION TO...
...WHO WILL UNDERSTAND WHERE I'M COMING FROM AND JOIN THE SQUAD JAM WITH ME.
IF THEIR CHARACTER IS STRONG, EVEN BETTER...
UGH ...
I DON'T KNOW ANYONE THAT CONVENIENT!!
LLENN DOESN'T MAKE MANY FRIENDS...
HAAH ...
DOSA (THUMP)
VUVU (VRR)
MM...
GABA (FWUP)
WAIT, THAT'S IT! I DO KNOW SOMEONE!

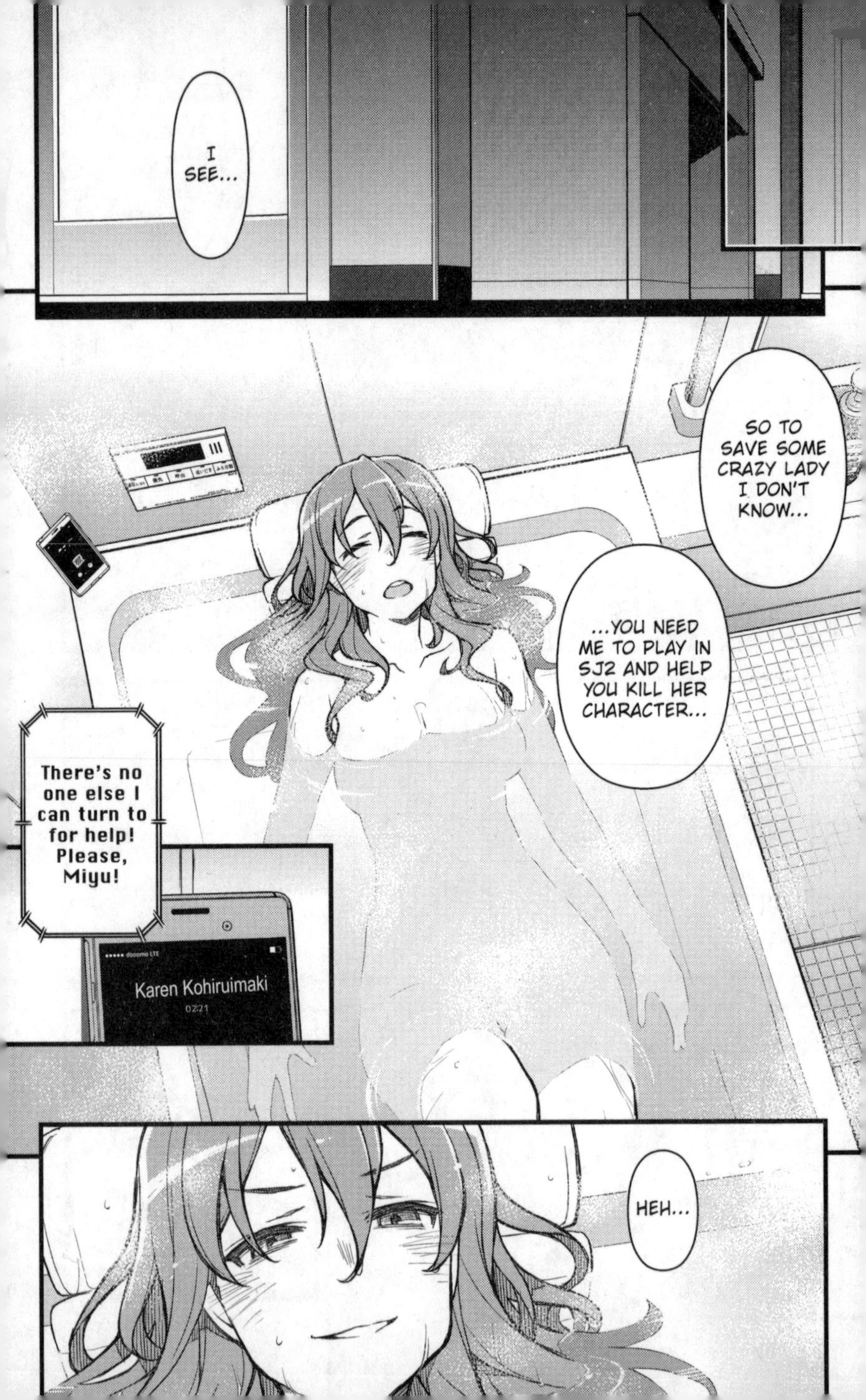
I SEE...
SO TO SAVE SOME CRAZY LADY I DON'T KNOW...
...YOU NEED ME TO PLAY IN SJ2 AND HELP YOU KILL HER CHARACTER...
There's no one else I can turn to for help! Please, Miyu!
Karen Kohiruimaki
02:21
HEH...

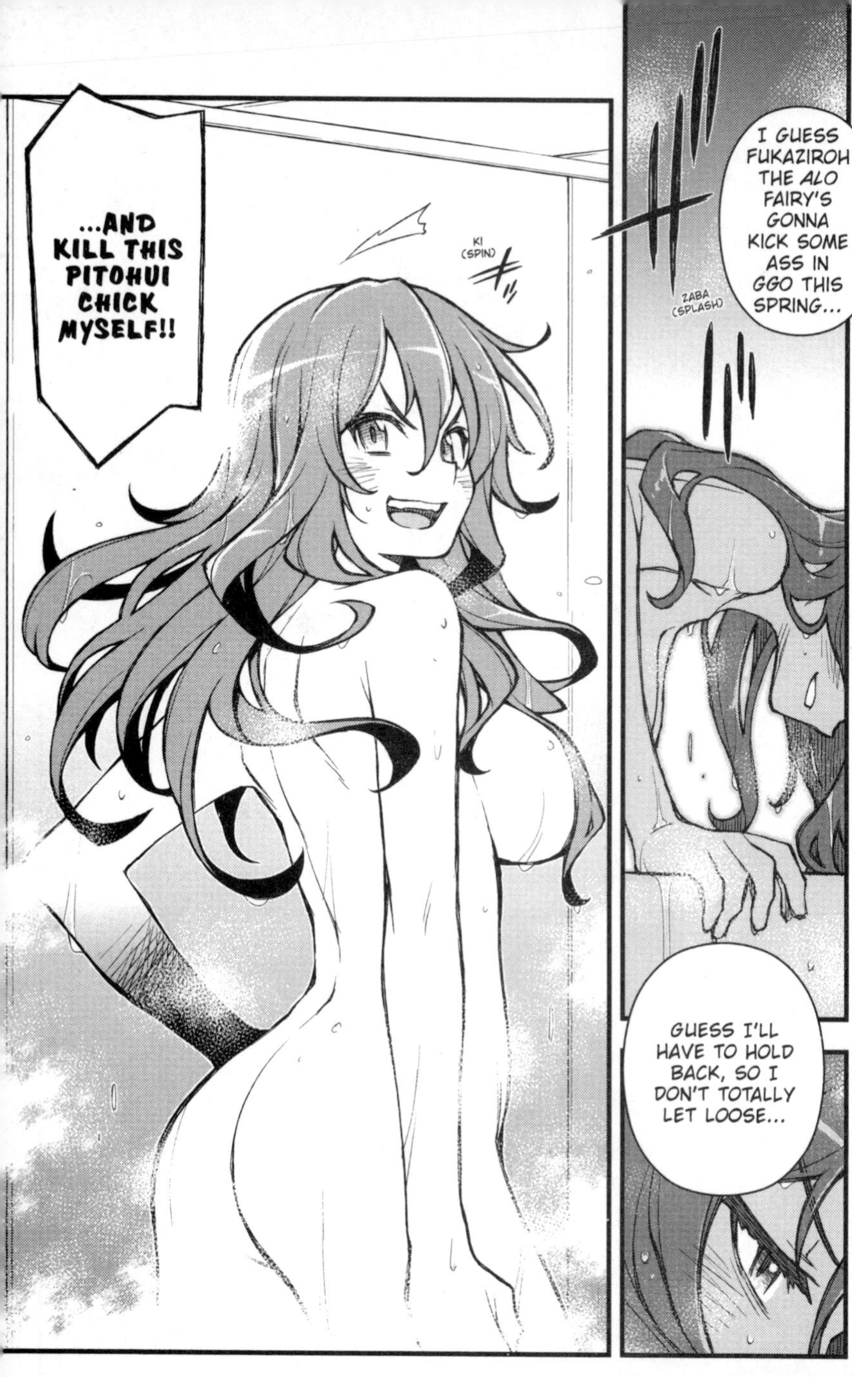
I GUESS FUKAZIROH THE ALO FAIRY'S GONNA KICK SOME ASS IN GGO THIS SPRING...
ZABA (SPLASH)
GUESS I'LL HAVE TO HOLD BACK, SO I DON'T TOTALLY LET LOOSE...
KI (SPIN)
...AND KILL THIS PITOHUI CHICK MYSELF!!

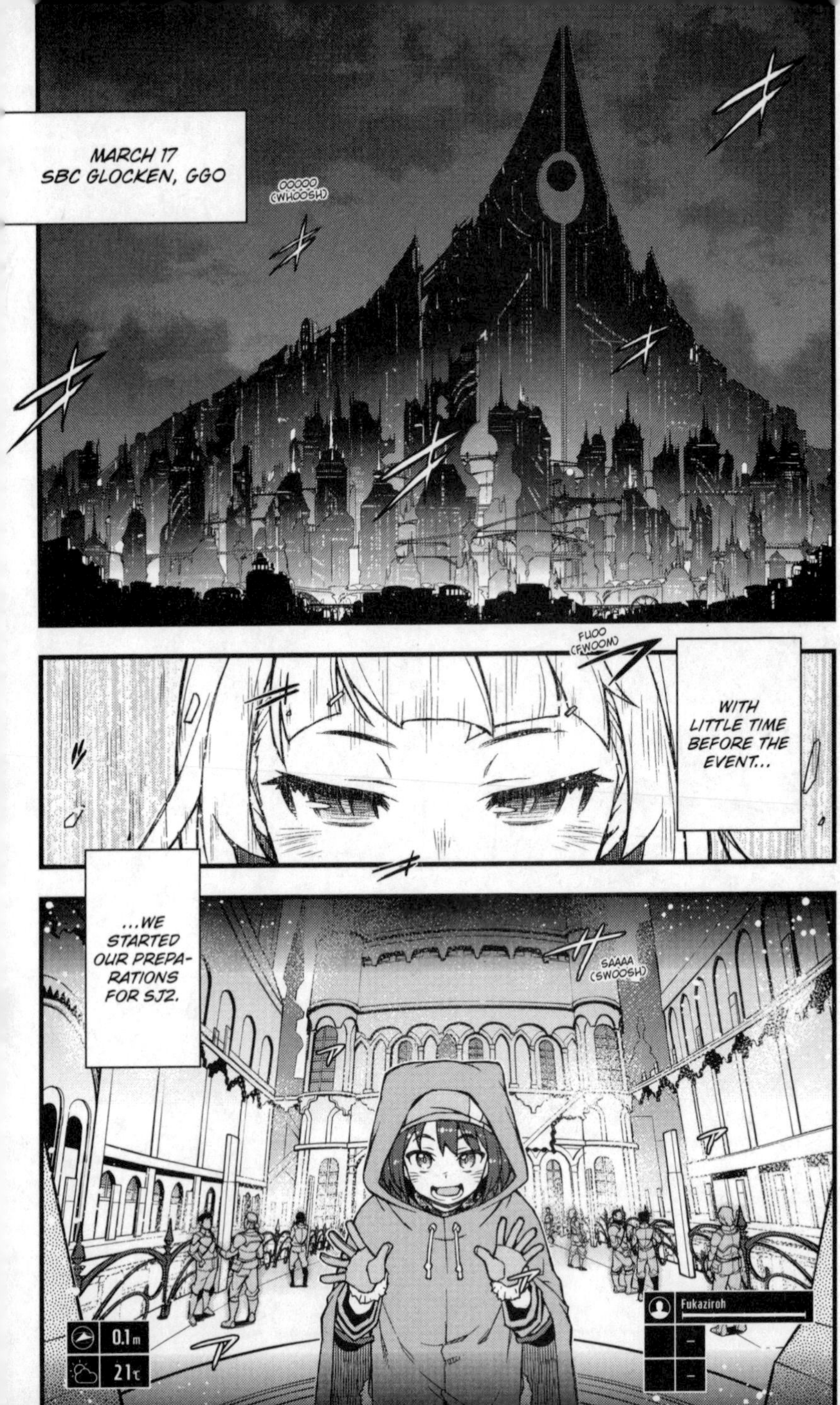
MARCH 17
SBC GLOCKEN, GGO
OOOOO (WHOOSH)
FUOO (FWOOM)
WITH LITTLE TIME BEFORE THE EVENT...
...WE STARTED OUR PREPA-RATIONS FOR SJ2.
SAAAA (SWOOSH)
Fukaziroh
0.1m
21℃

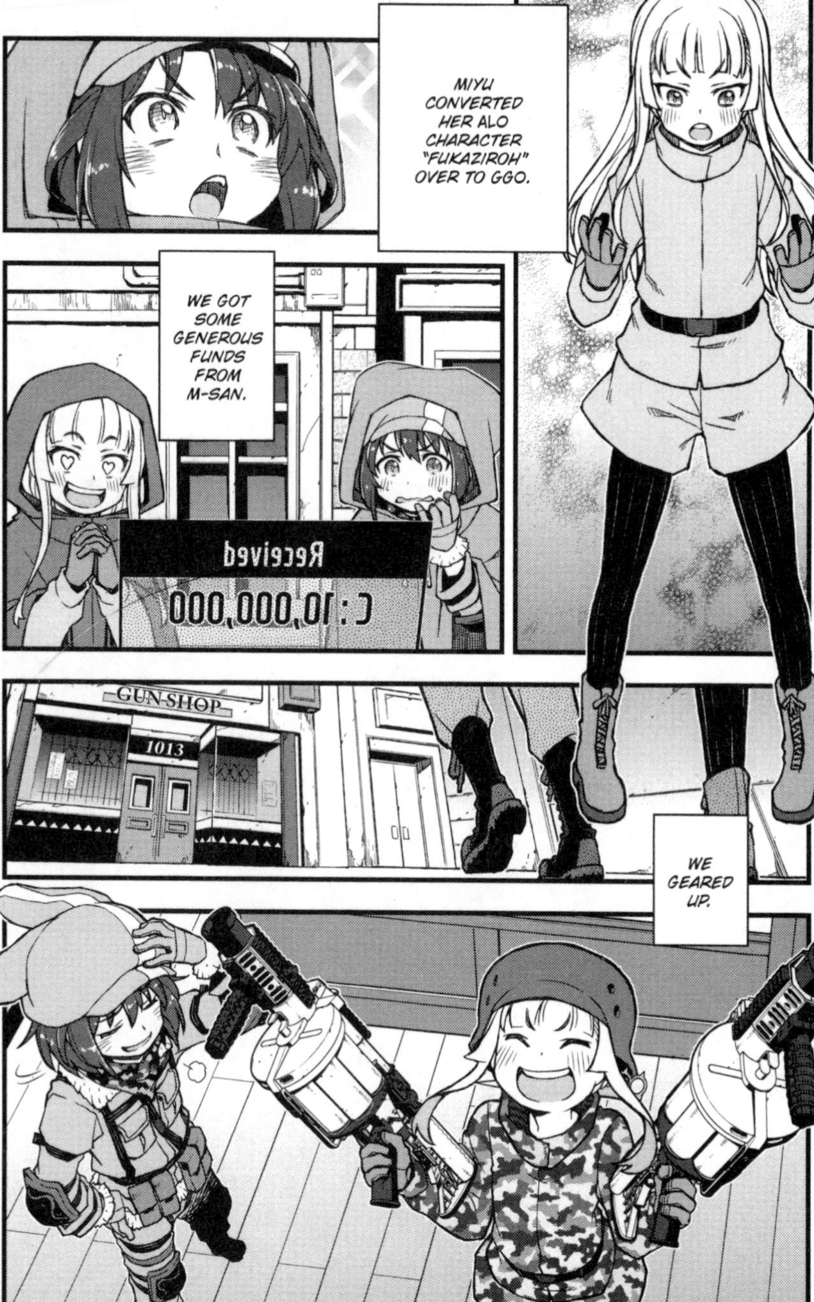
MIYU CONVERTED HER ALO CHARACTER "FUKAZIROH" OVER TO GGO.
WE GOT SOME GENEROUS FUNDS FROM M-SAN.
Received
C : 10,000,000
GUN SHOP
1013
WE GEARED UP.

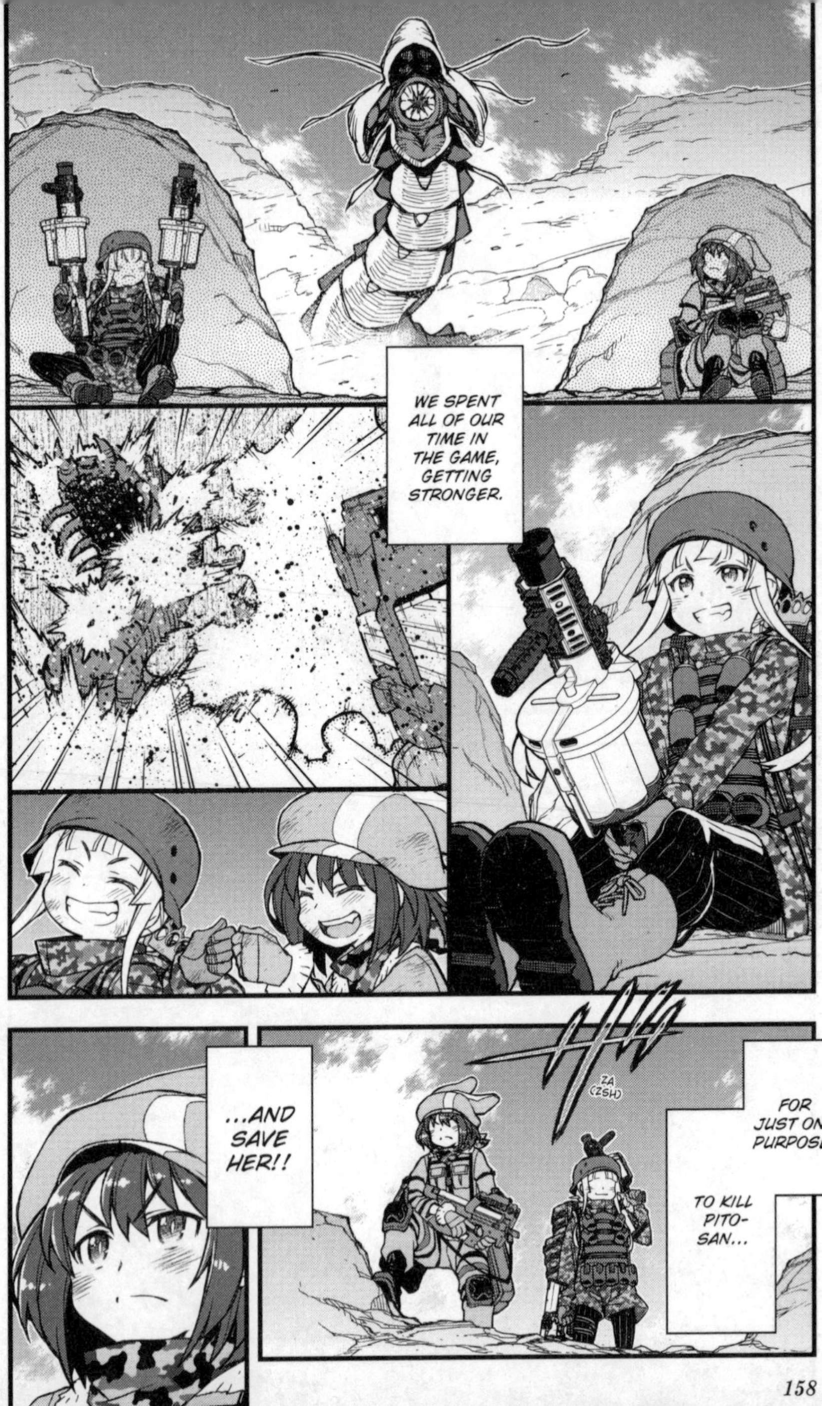
WE SPENT ALL OF OUR TIME IN THE GAME, GETTING STRONGER.
FOR JUST ONE PURPOSE.
TO KILL PITO-SAN...
ZA (ZSH)
...AND SAVE HER!!

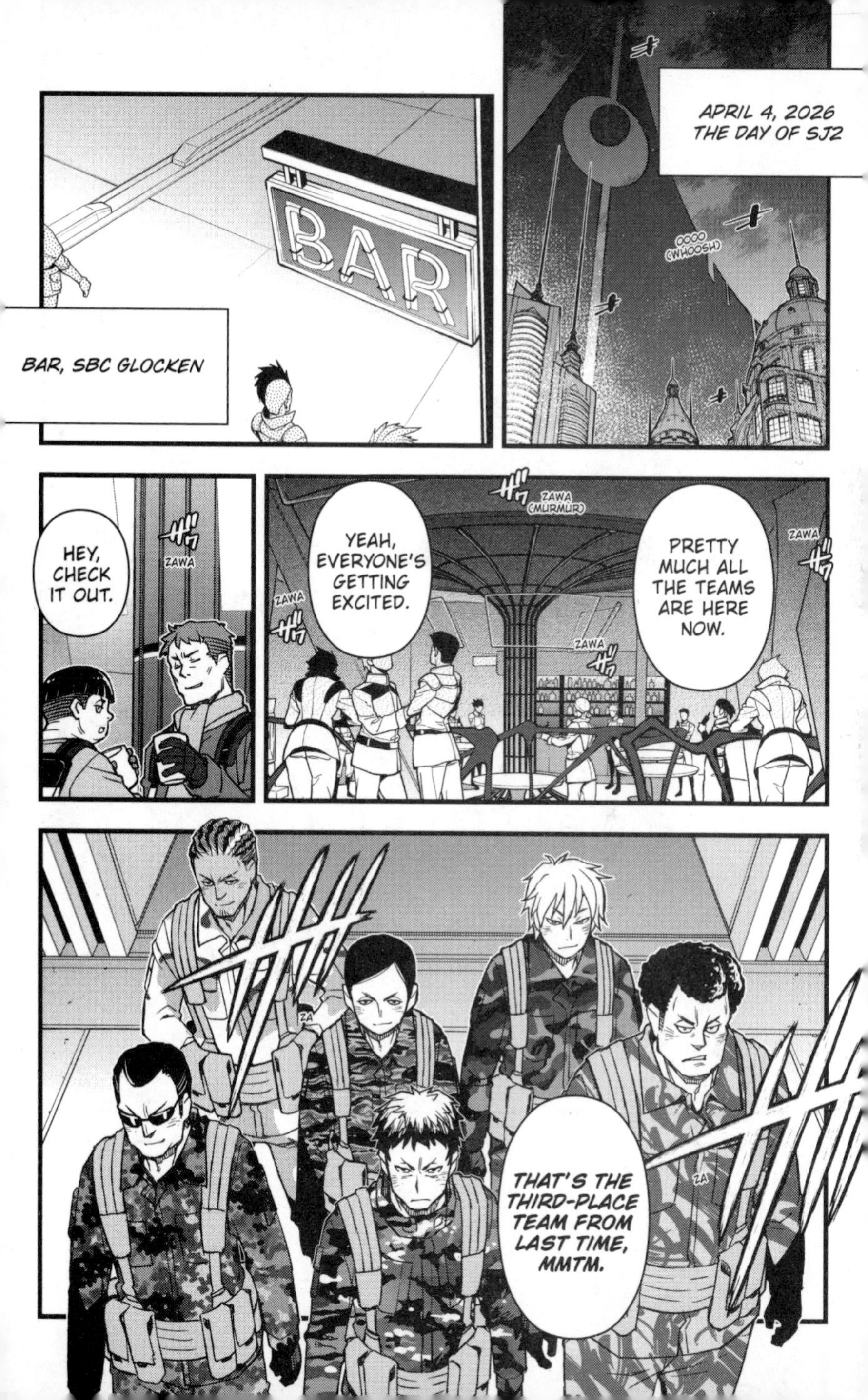
APRIL 4, 2026
THE DAY OF SJ2
OOOO (WHOOSH)
BAR
BAR, SBC GLOCKEN
ZAWA (MURMUR)
PRETTY MUCH ALL THE TEAMS ARE HERE NOW.
ZAWA
ZAWA
YEAH, EVERYONE'S GETTING EXCITED.
ZAWA
ZAWA
HEY, CHECK IT OUT.
ZA
ZA
THAT'S THE THIRD-PLACE TEAM FROM LAST TIME, MMTM.

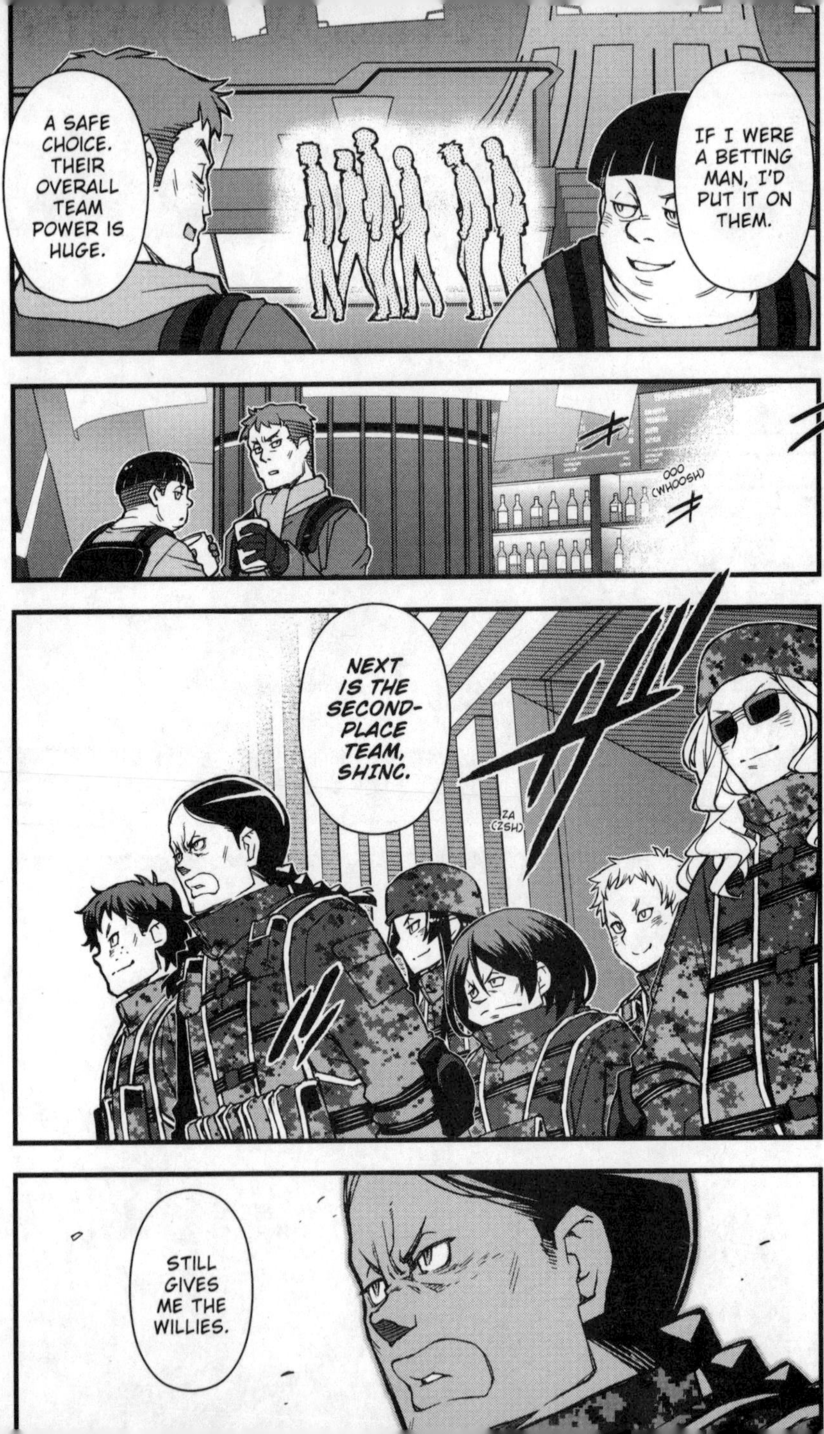
IF I WERE A BETTING MAN, I'D PUT IT ON THEM.
A SAFE CHOICE. THEIR OVERALL TEAM POWER IS HUGE.
OOO (WHOOSH)
ZA (ZSH)
NEXT IS THE SECOND-PLACE TEAM, SHINC.
STILL GIVES ME THE WILLIES.

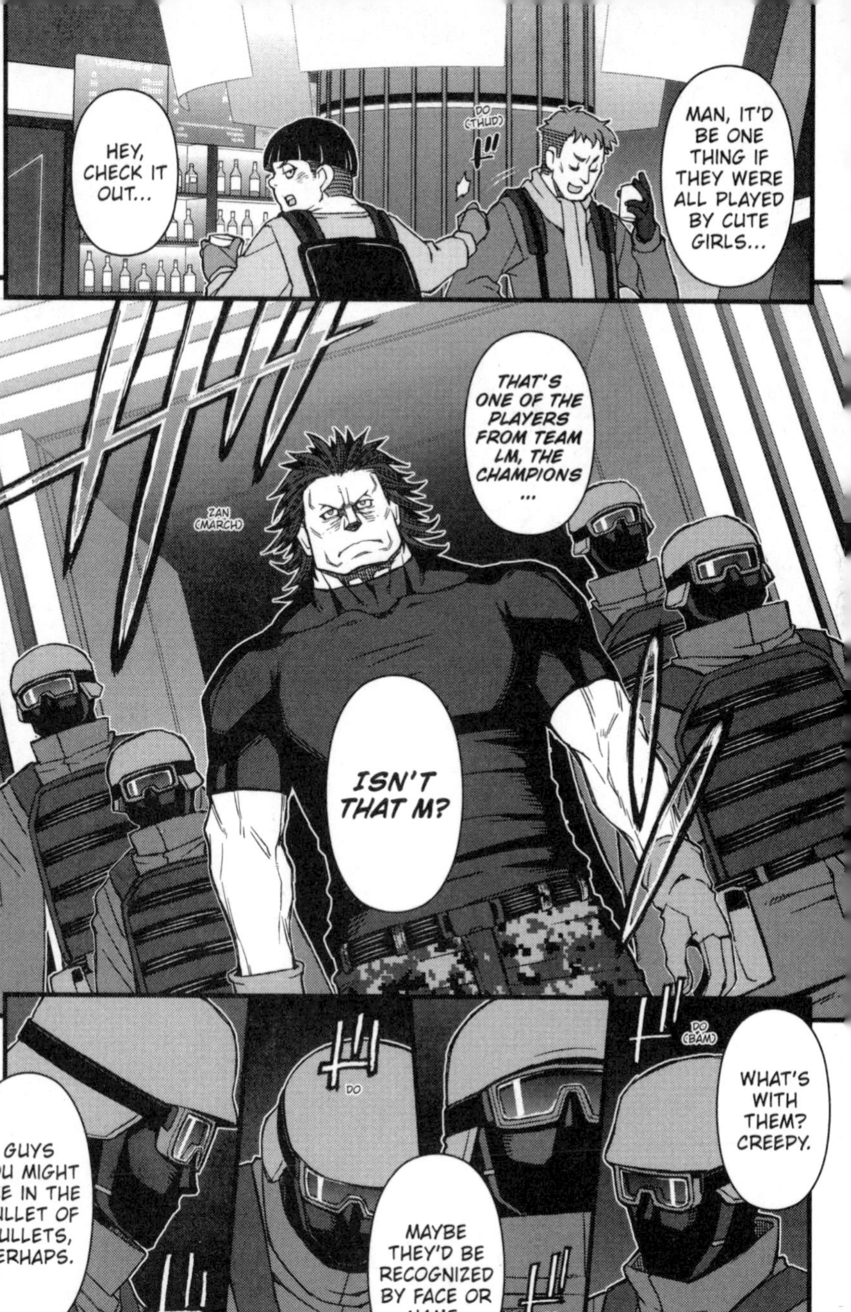
MAN, IT'D BE ONE THING IF THEY WERE ALL PLAYED BY CUTE GIRLS...
DO (THUD)
HEY, CHECK IT OUT...
THAT'S ONE OF THE PLAYERS FROM TEAM LM, THE CHAMPIONS ...
ZAN (MARCH)
ISN'T THAT M?
DO (BAM)
WHAT'S WITH THEM? CREEPY.
DO
MAYBE THEY'D BE RECOGNIZED BY FACE OR NAME.
DO
GUYS YOU MIGHT SEE IN THE BULLET OF BULLETS, PERHAPS.
DO

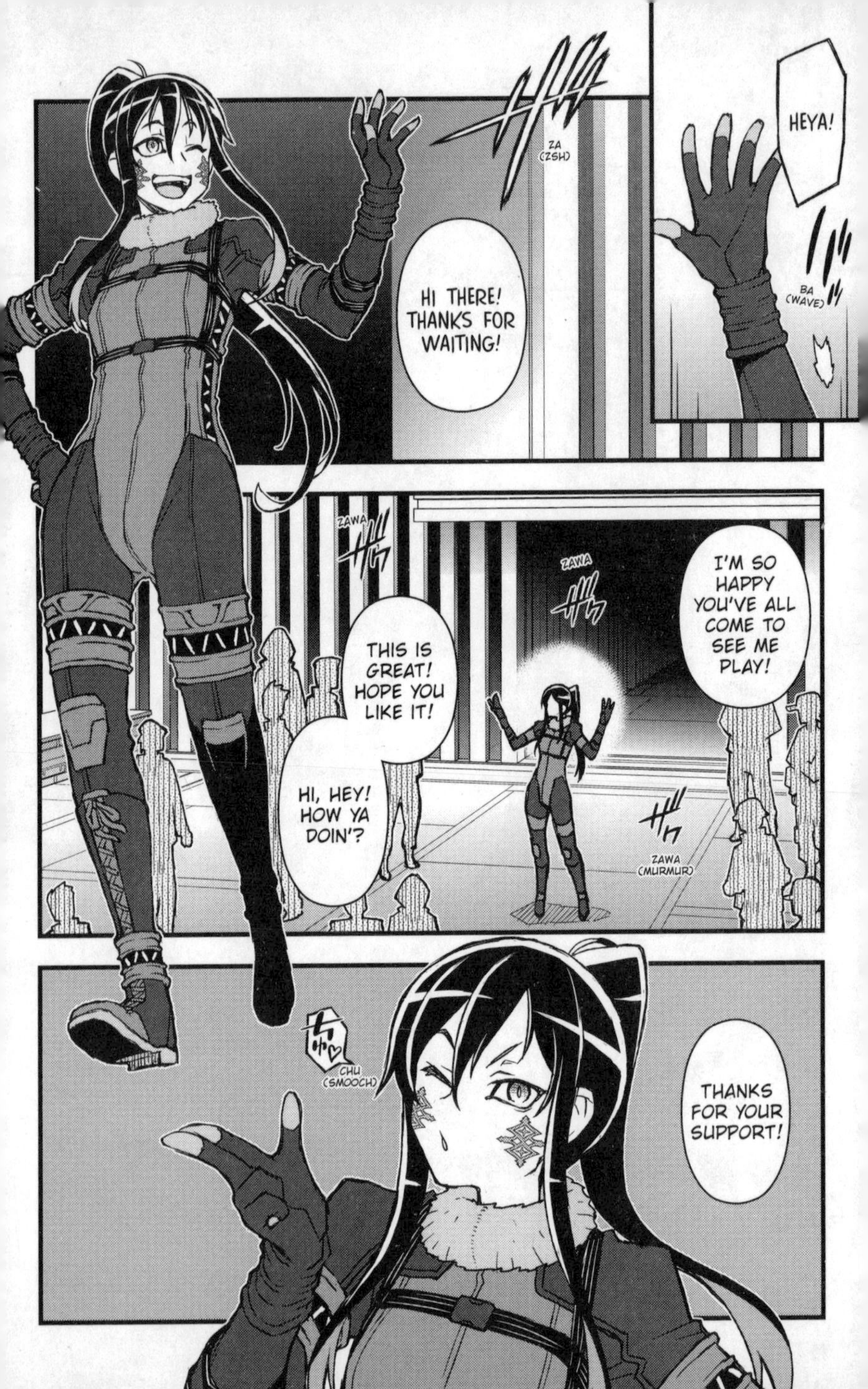
HEYA!
BA (WAVE)
ZA (ZSH)
HI THERE! THANKS FOR WAITING!
I'M SO HAPPY YOU'VE ALL COME TO SEE ME PLAY!
ZAWA
ZAWA (MURMUR)
THIS IS GREAT! HOPE YOU LIKE IT!
ZAWA
HI, HEY! HOW YA DOIN'?
THANKS FOR YOUR SUPPORT!
CHU (SMOOCH)

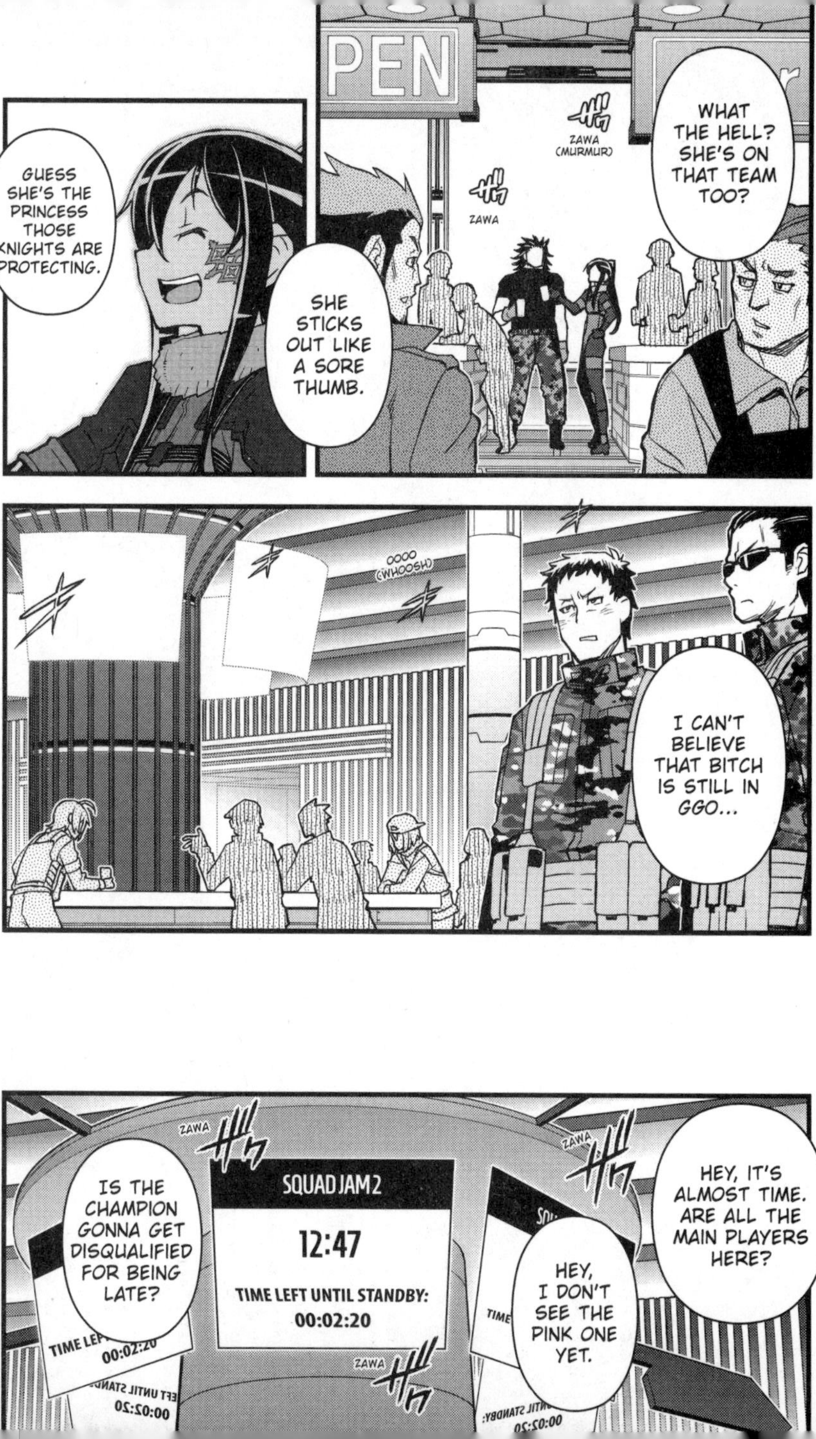
WHAT THE HELL? SHE'S ON THAT TEAM TOO?
ZAWA (MURMUR)
ZAWA
SHE STICKS OUT LIKE A SORE THUMB.
GUESS SHE'S THE PRINCESS THOSE KNIGHTS ARE PROTECTING.
OOOO (WHOOSH)
I CAN'T BELIEVE THAT BITCH IS STILL IN GGO...
ZAWA
HEY, IT'S ALMOST TIME. ARE ALL THE MAIN PLAYERS HERE?
HEY, I DON'T SEE THE PINK ONE YET.
SQUAD JAM 2
12:47
TIME LEFT UNTIL STANDBY:
00:02:20
ZAWA
IS THE CHAMPION GONNA GET DISQUALIFIED FOR BEING LATE?
ZAWA

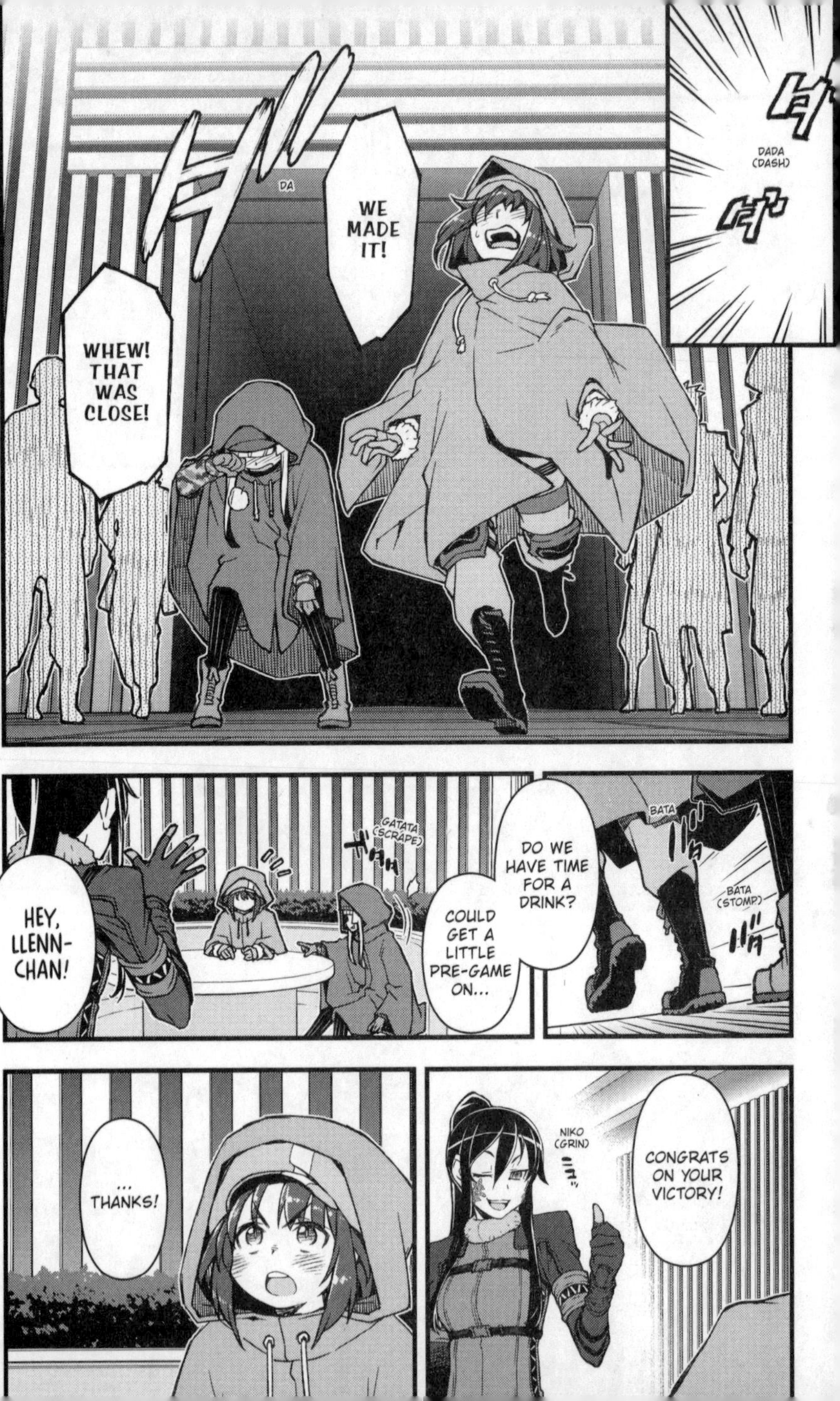
DADA (DASH)
WE MADE IT!
DA
WHEW! THAT WAS CLOSE!
BATA
BATA (STOMP)
DO WE HAVE TIME FOR A DRINK?
COULD GET A LITTLE PRE-GAME ON...
GATATA (SCRAPE)
HEY, LLENN-CHAN!
CONGRATS ON YOUR VICTORY!
NIKO (GRIN)
... THANKS!

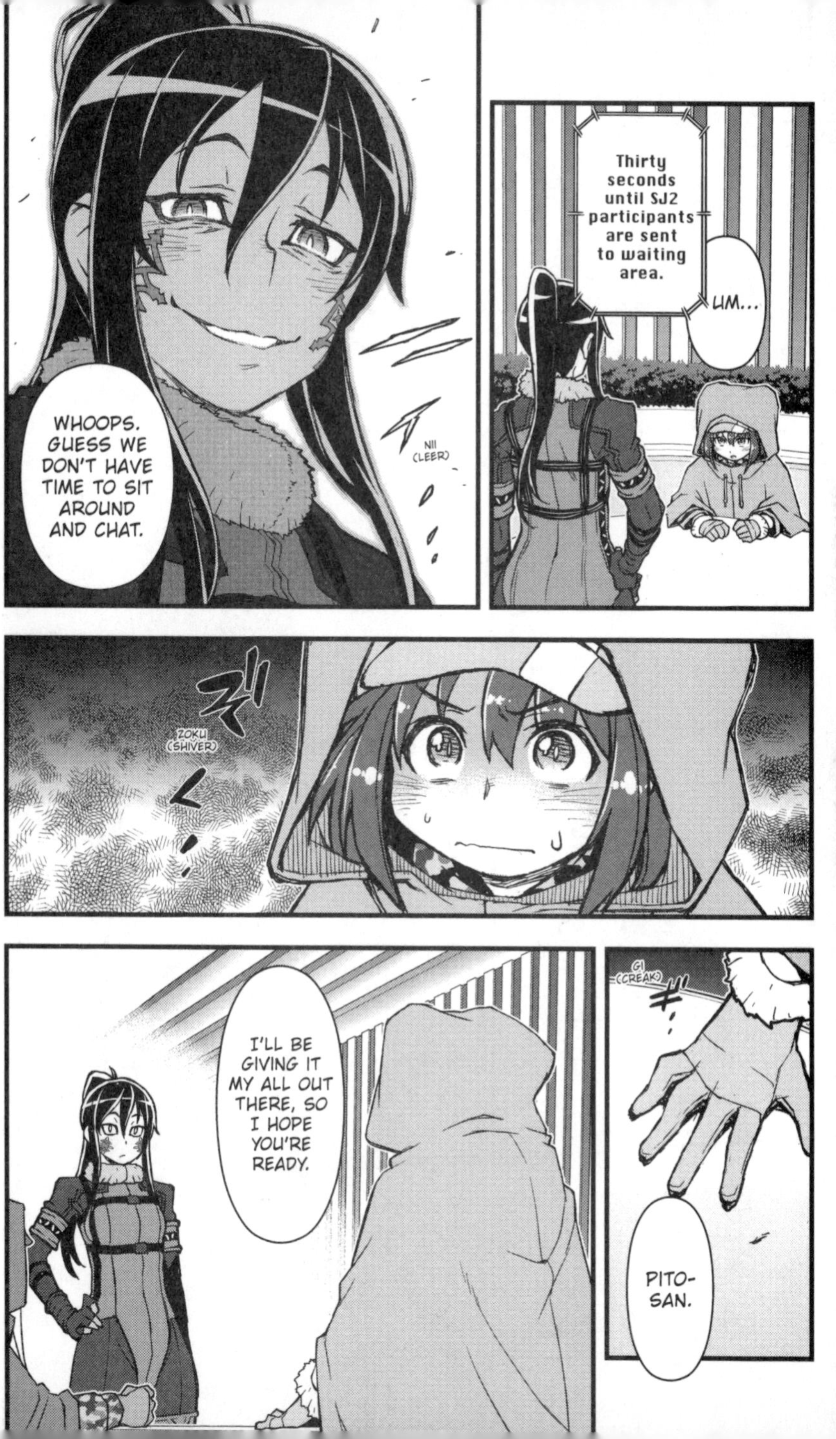
Thirty seconds until SJ2 participants are sent to waiting area.
UM...
WHOOPS. GUESS WE DON'T HAVE TIME TO SIT AROUND AND CHAT.
NII (LEER)
ZOKU (SHIVER)
GI (CREAK)
PITO-SAN.
I'LL BE GIVING IT MY ALL OUT THERE, SO I HOPE YOU'RE READY.

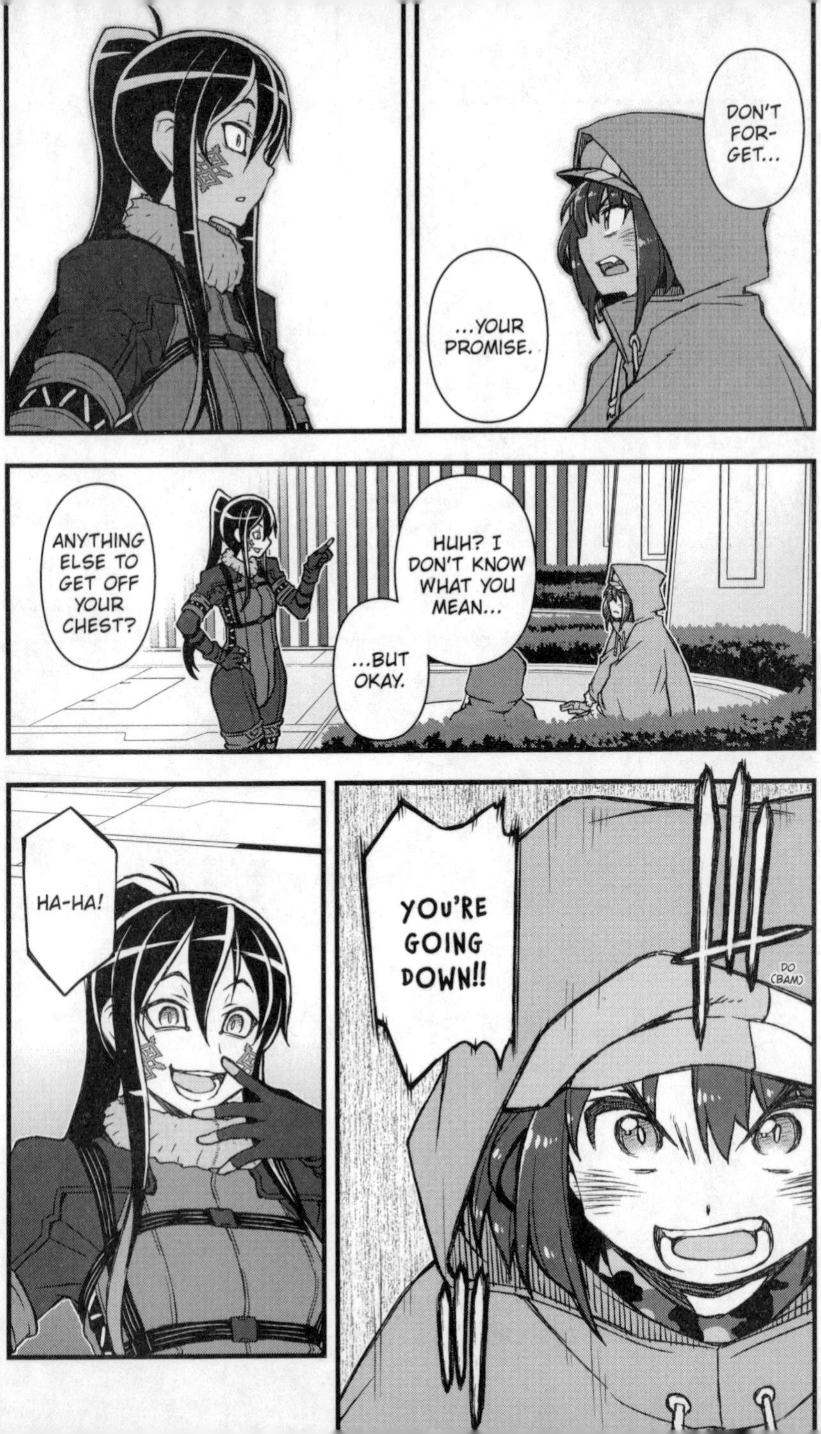
DON'T FOR-GET...
...YOUR PROMISE.
HUH? I DON'T KNOW WHAT YOU MEAN...
...BUT OKAY.
ANYTHING ELSE TO GET OFF YOUR CHEST?
YOU'RE GOING DOWN!!
DO (BAM)
HA-HA!

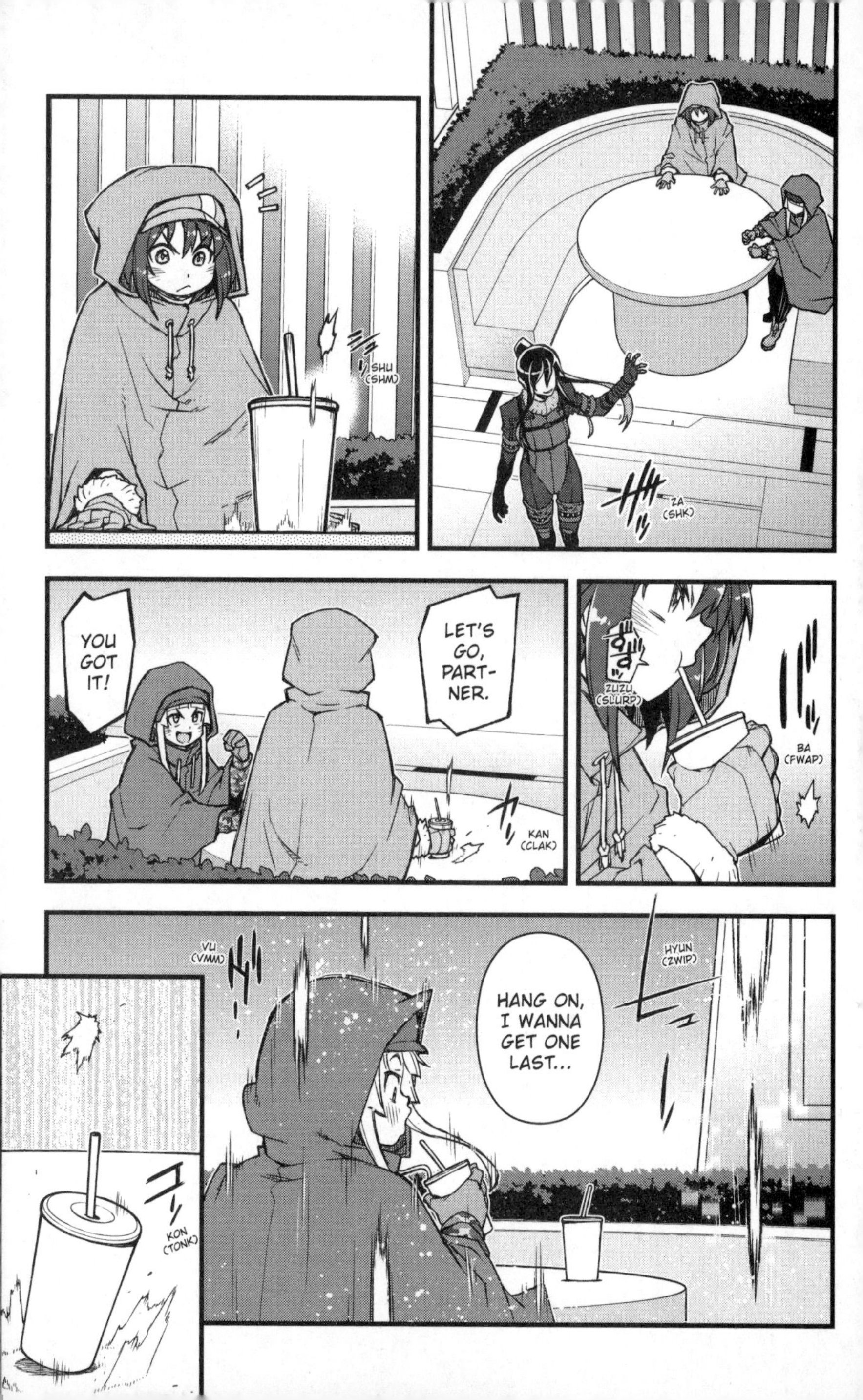
ZA
(SHK)
SHU
(SHM)
ZUZU
(SLURP)
BA
(FWAP)
LET'S GO, PART-NER.
YOU GOT IT!
KAN
(CLAK)
HYUN
(ZWIP)
HANG ON, I WANNA GET ONE LAST...
VU
(VMM)
KON
(TONK)

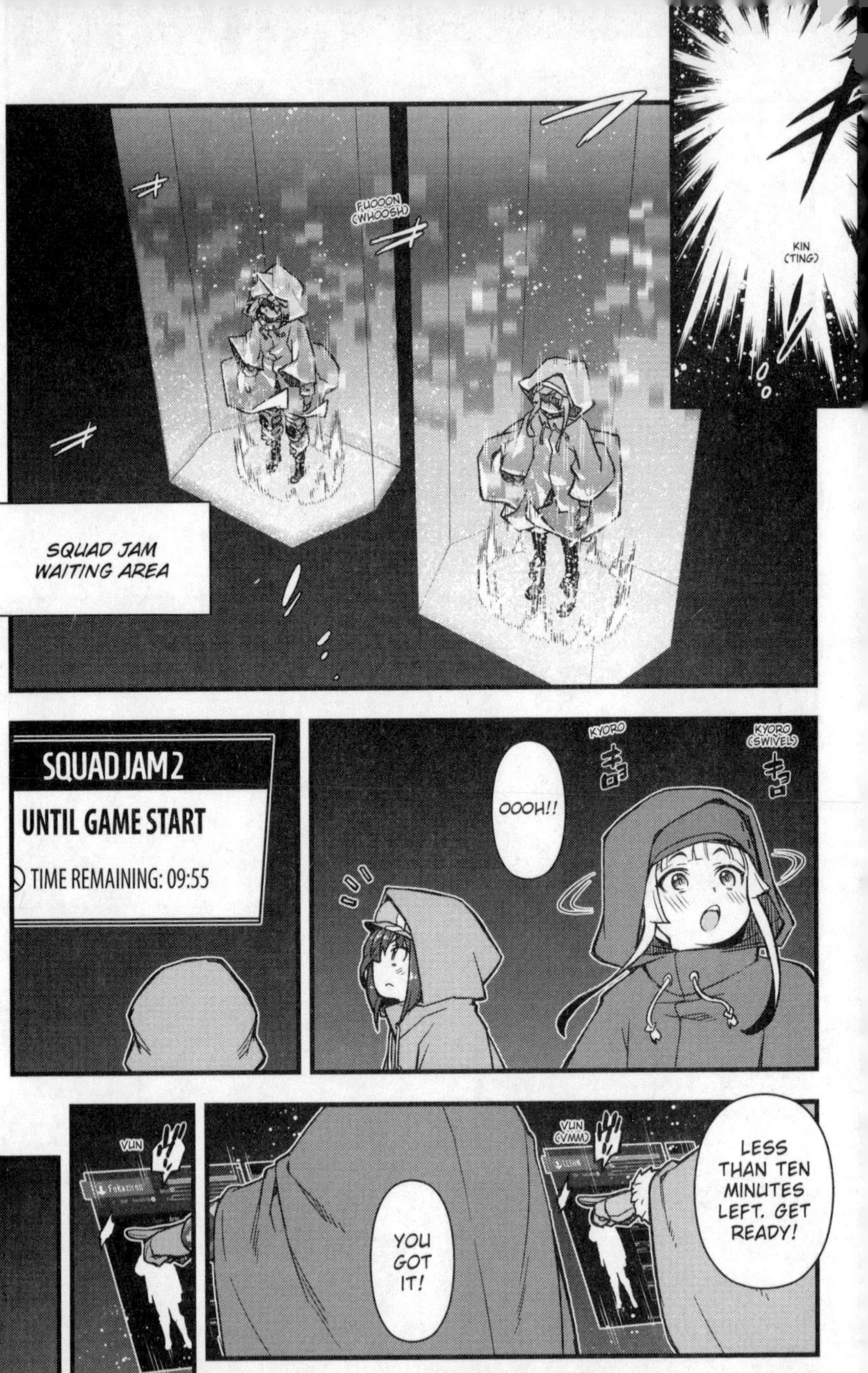
KIN (TING)
FUOOON (WHOOSH)
SQUAD JAM WAITING AREA
KYORO
KYORO (SWIVEL)
OOOH!!
SQUAD JAM 2
UNTIL GAME START
TIME REMAINING: 09:55
VUN (VMMM)
LESS THAN TEN MINUTES LEFT. GET READY!
YOU GOT IT!
VUN

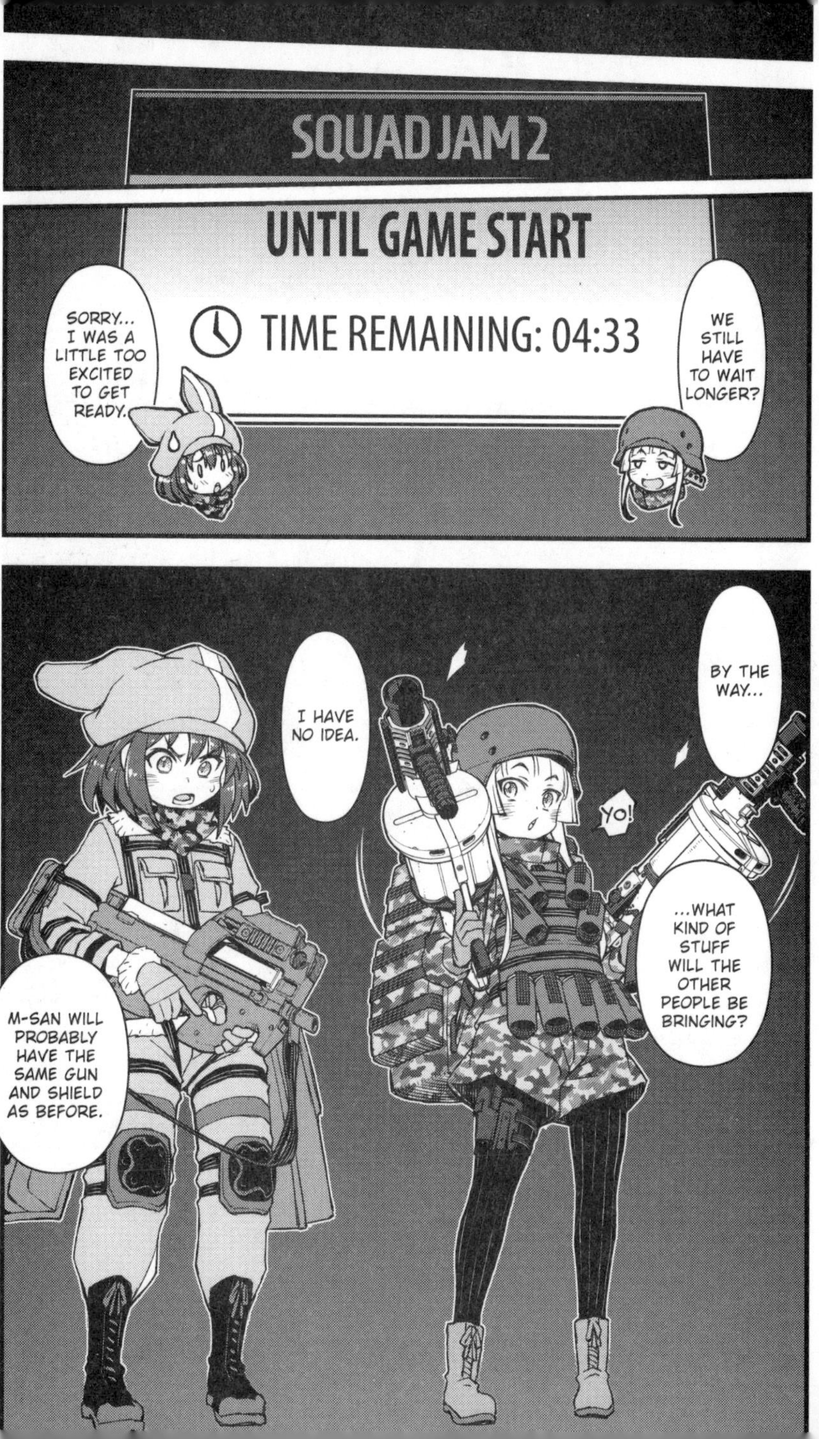
SQUAD JAM 2
UNTIL GAME START
TIME REMAINING: 04:33
WE STILL HAVE TO WAIT LONGER?
SORRY... I WAS A LITTLE TOO EXCITED TO GET READY.
BY THE WAY...
YO!
...WHAT KIND OF STUFF WILL THE OTHER PEOPLE BE BRINGING?
I HAVE NO IDEA.
M-SAN WILL PROBABLY HAVE THE SAME GUN AND SHIELD AS BEFORE.

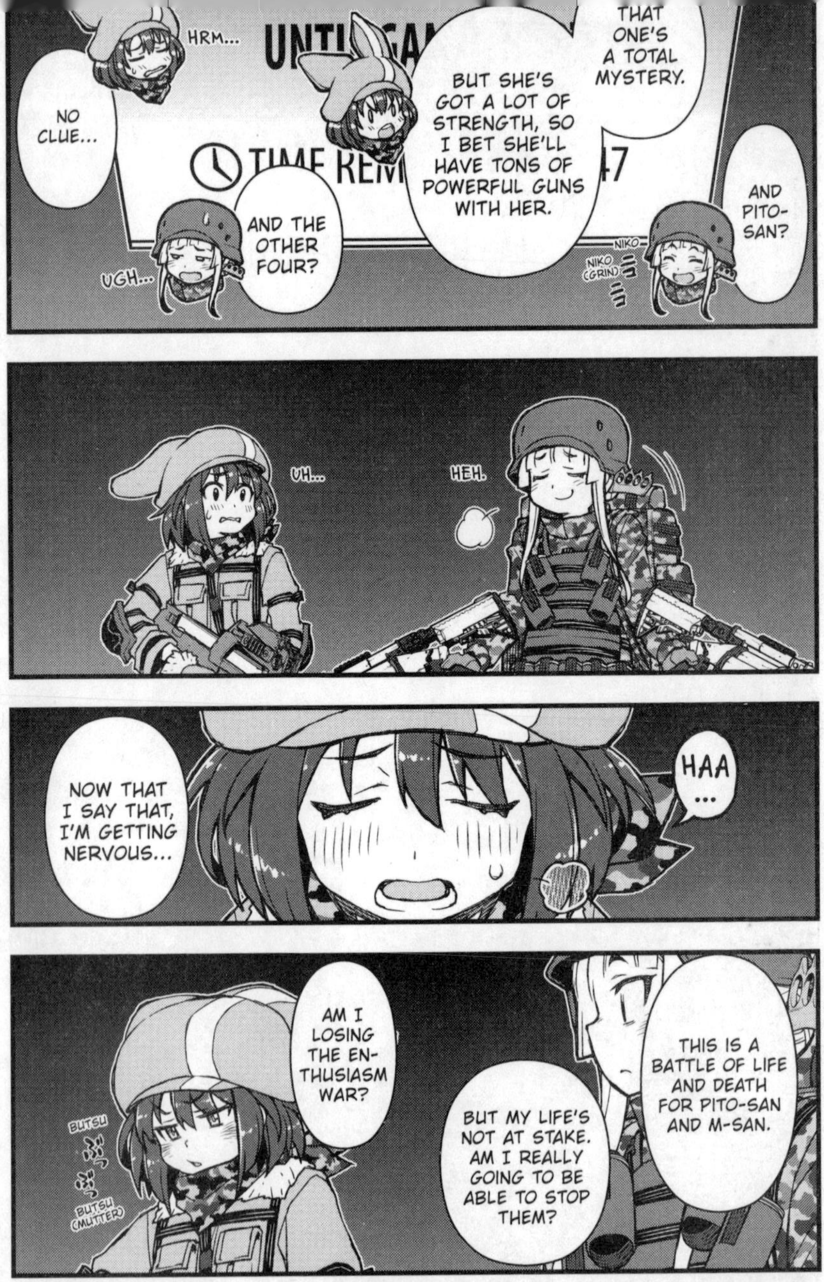
AND PITO-SAN?
NIKO NIKO (GRIN)
THAT ONE'S A TOTAL MYSTERY.
BUT SHE'S GOT A LOT OF STRENGTH, SO I BET SHE'LL HAVE TONS OF POWERFUL GUNS WITH HER.
AND THE OTHER FOUR?
UGH...
HRM...
NO CLUE...
HEH.
UH...
HAA...
NOW THAT I SAY THAT, I'M GETTING NERVOUS...
THIS IS A BATTLE OF LIFE AND DEATH FOR PITO-SAN AND M-SAN.
BUT MY LIFE'S NOT AT STAKE. AM I REALLY GOING TO BE ABLE TO STOP THEM?
AM I LOSING THE EN-THUSIASM WAR?
BUTSU BUTSU (MUTTER)

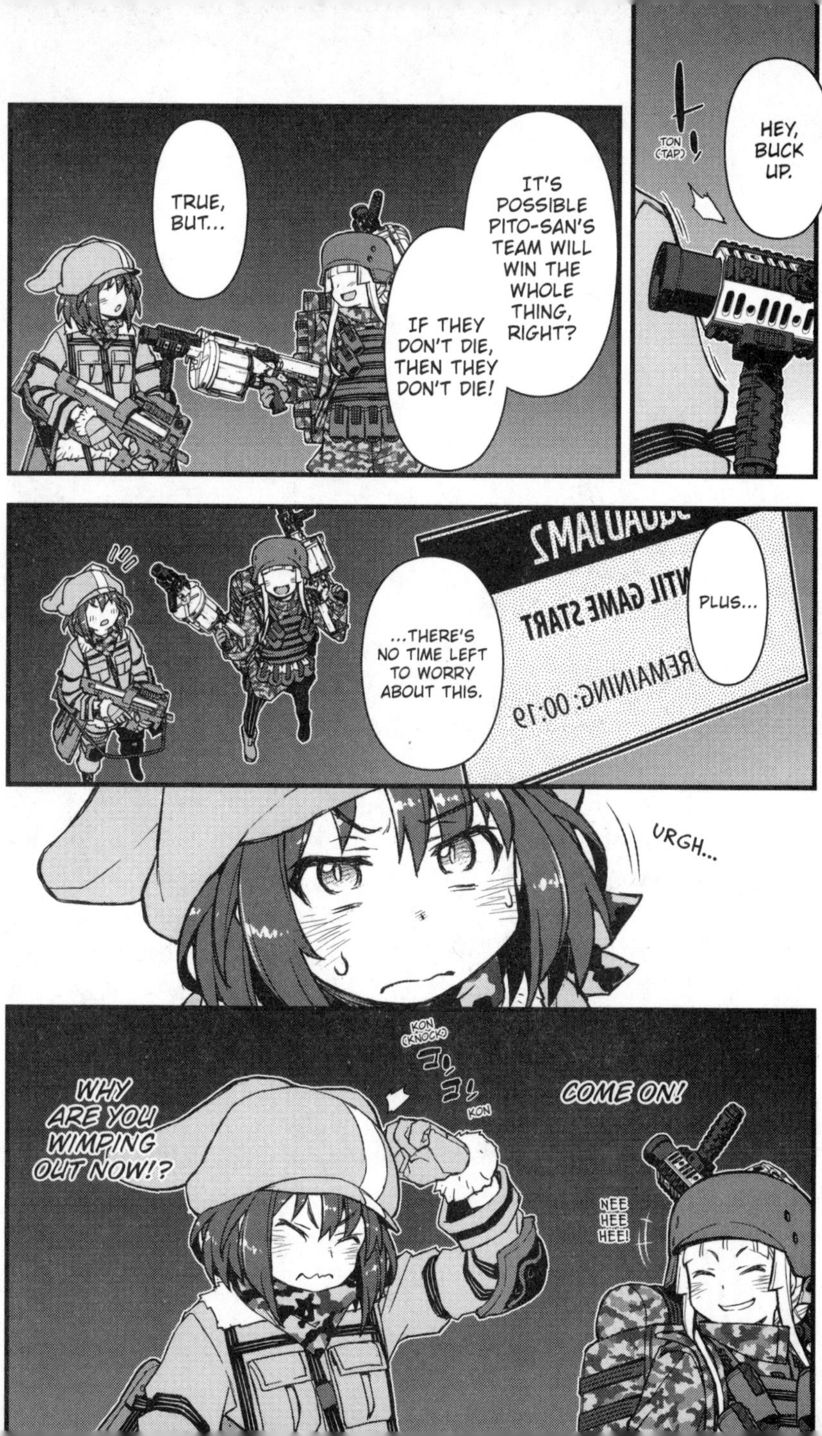
HEY, BUCK UP.
TON (TAP)
IT'S POSSIBLE PITO-SAN'S TEAM WILL WIN THE WHOLE THING, RIGHT?
IF THEY DON'T DIE, THEN THEY DON'T DIE!
TRUE, BUT...
PLUS...
...THERE'S NO TIME LEFT TO WORRY ABOUT THIS.
URGH...
COME ON!
NEE HEE HEE!
KON (KNOCK)
KON
WHY ARE YOU WIMPING OUT NOW!?

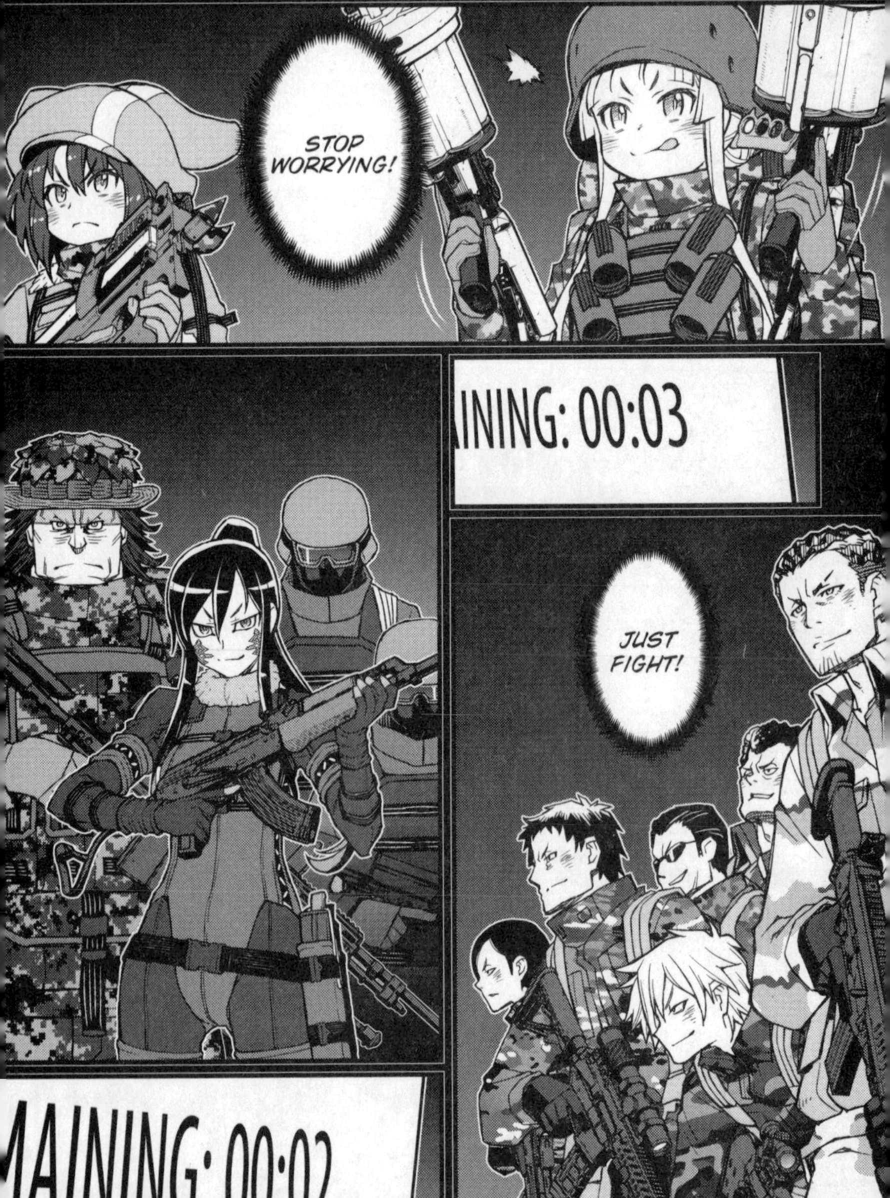
STOP WORRYING!
AINING: 00:03
JUST FIGHT!
MAINING: 00:02

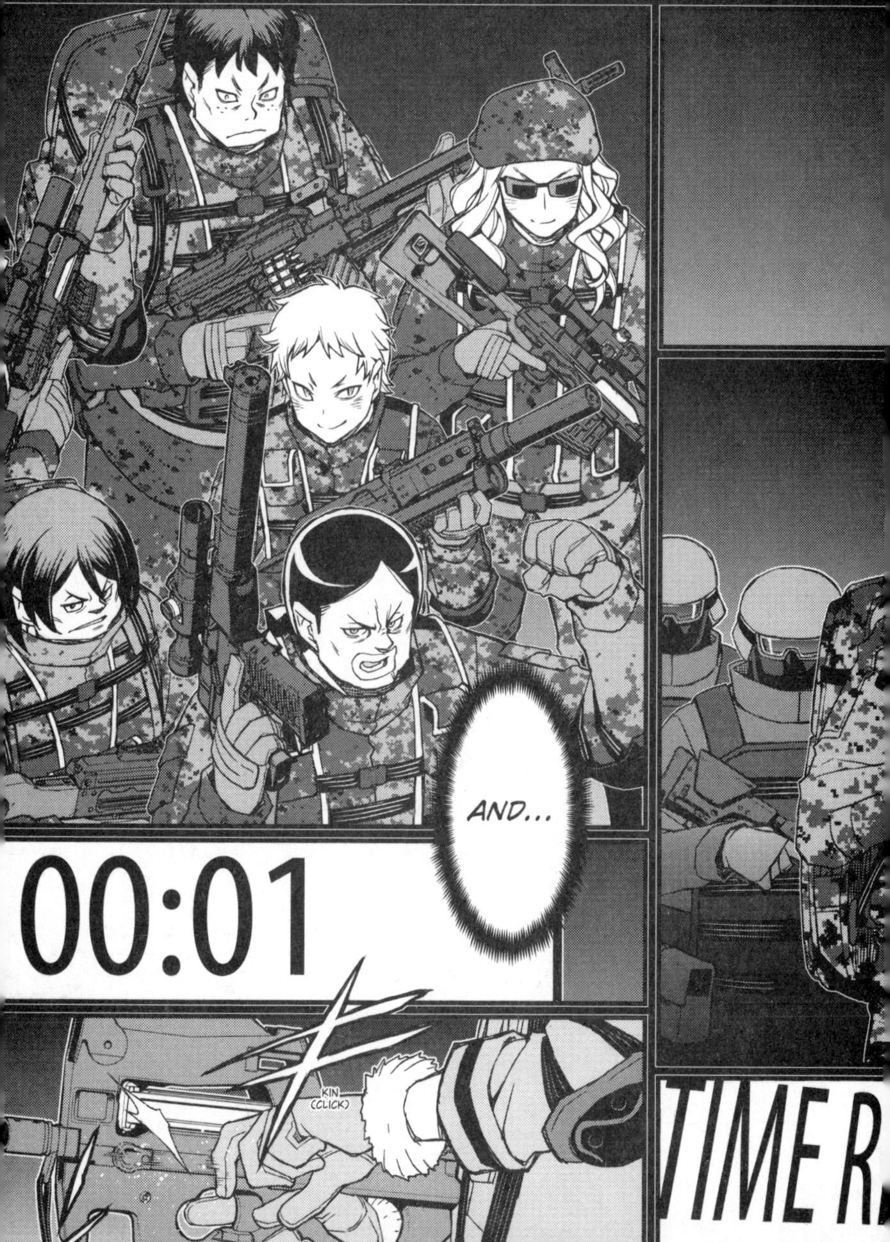
TIME R
AND...
00:01
KIN
(CLICK)

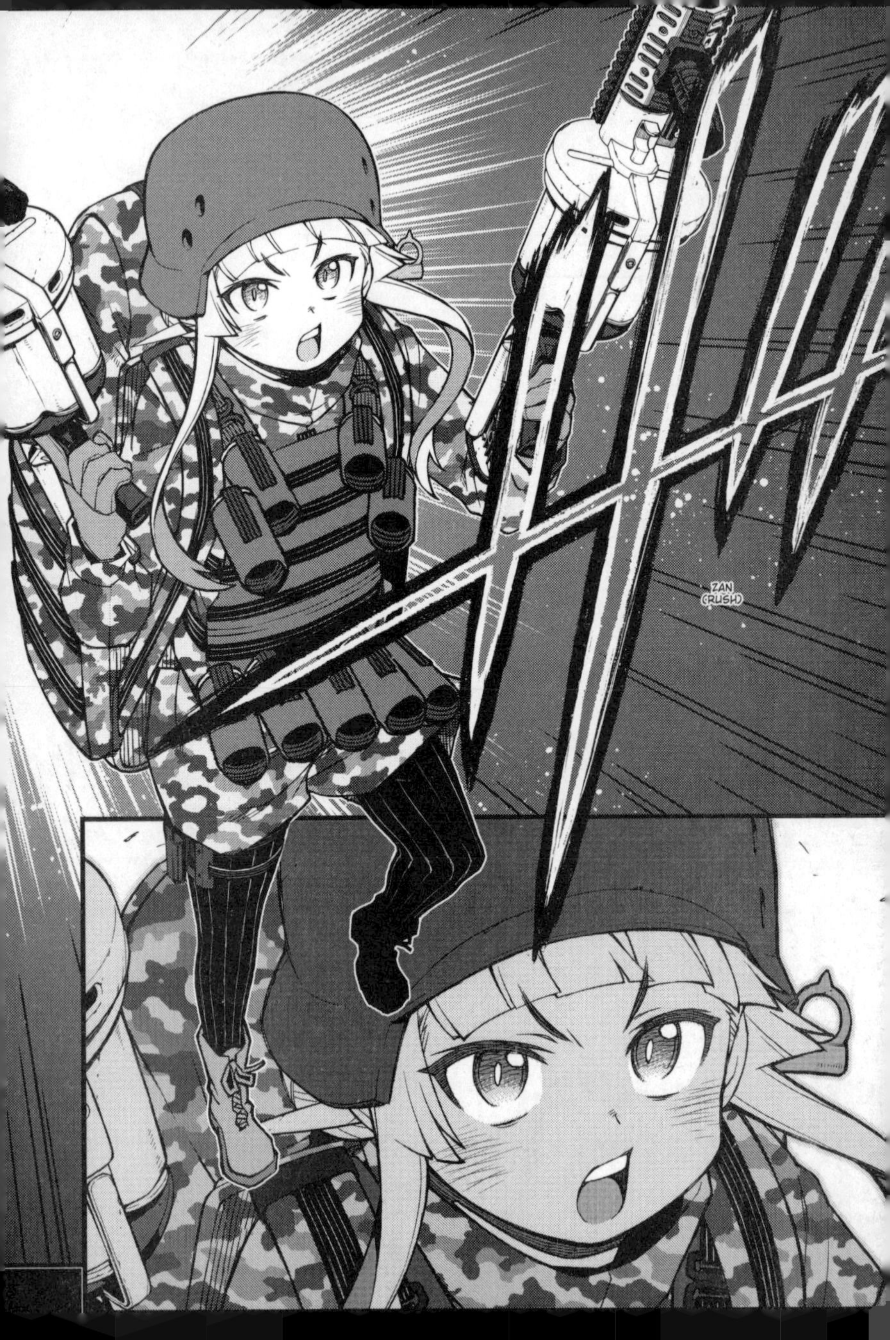
ZAN
(RUSH)

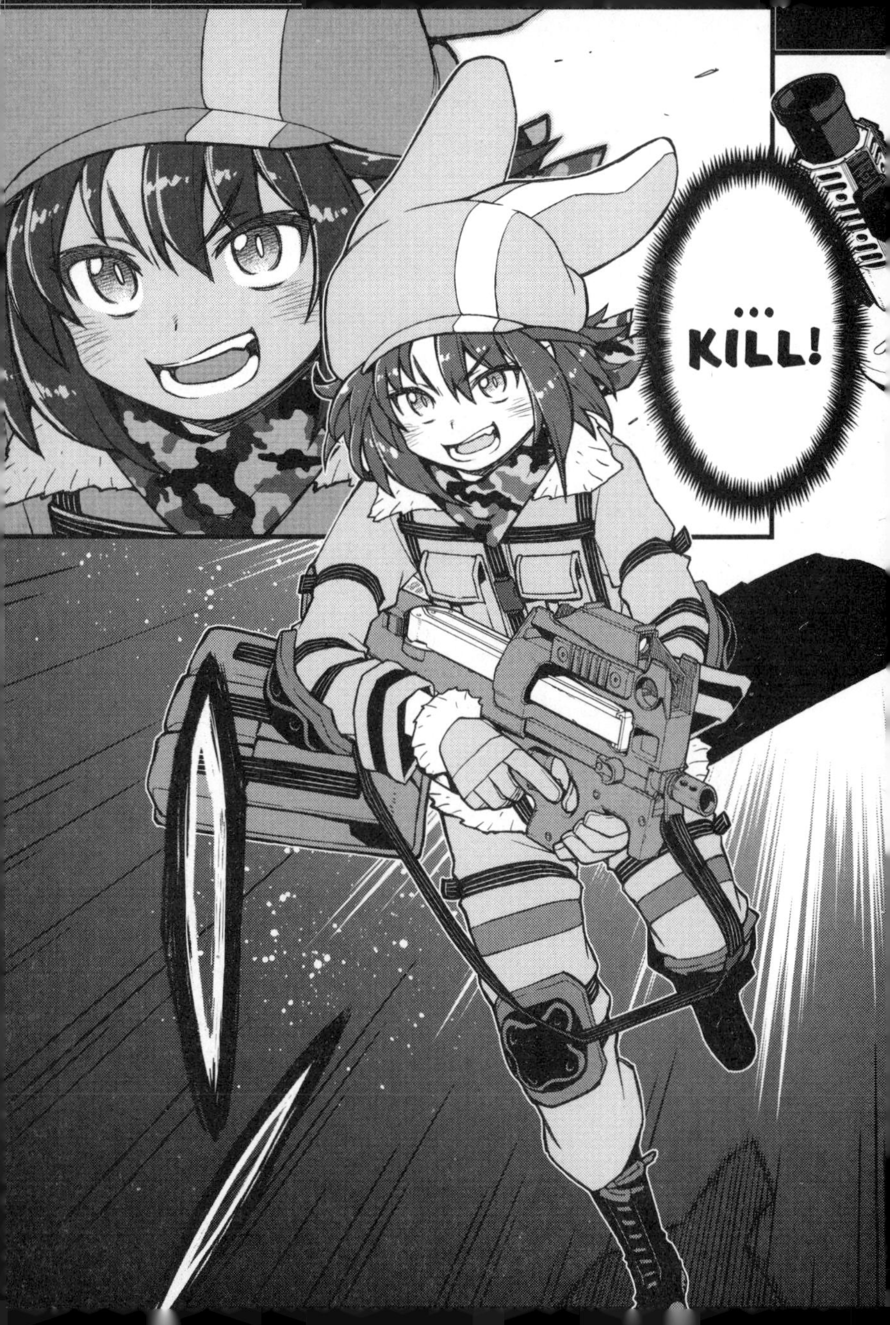
...KILL!

WANT TO KNOW WHAT HAPPENS NEXT?

PICK UP THE STORY IN THE NOVELS:

SWORD ART ONLINE ALTERNATIVE

GUN GALE ONLINE, VOL. 2

2ND SQUAD JAM: START

FROM CHAPTER 6, "BOOBY TRAP"

The final volume!
Tamori-san's Llenn was a sharp, aggressive Llenn with a different touch to her than Kuroboshi-san's soft Llenn in the novels, or the cute and lively Llenn in the anime.
As the gun-obsessed author, I found my body temperature elevated by the ferocious depictions of firearms and battles. Your splendid manga adaptation of my story was a thorough delight! Thank you for everything!

Keiichi Sigsawa

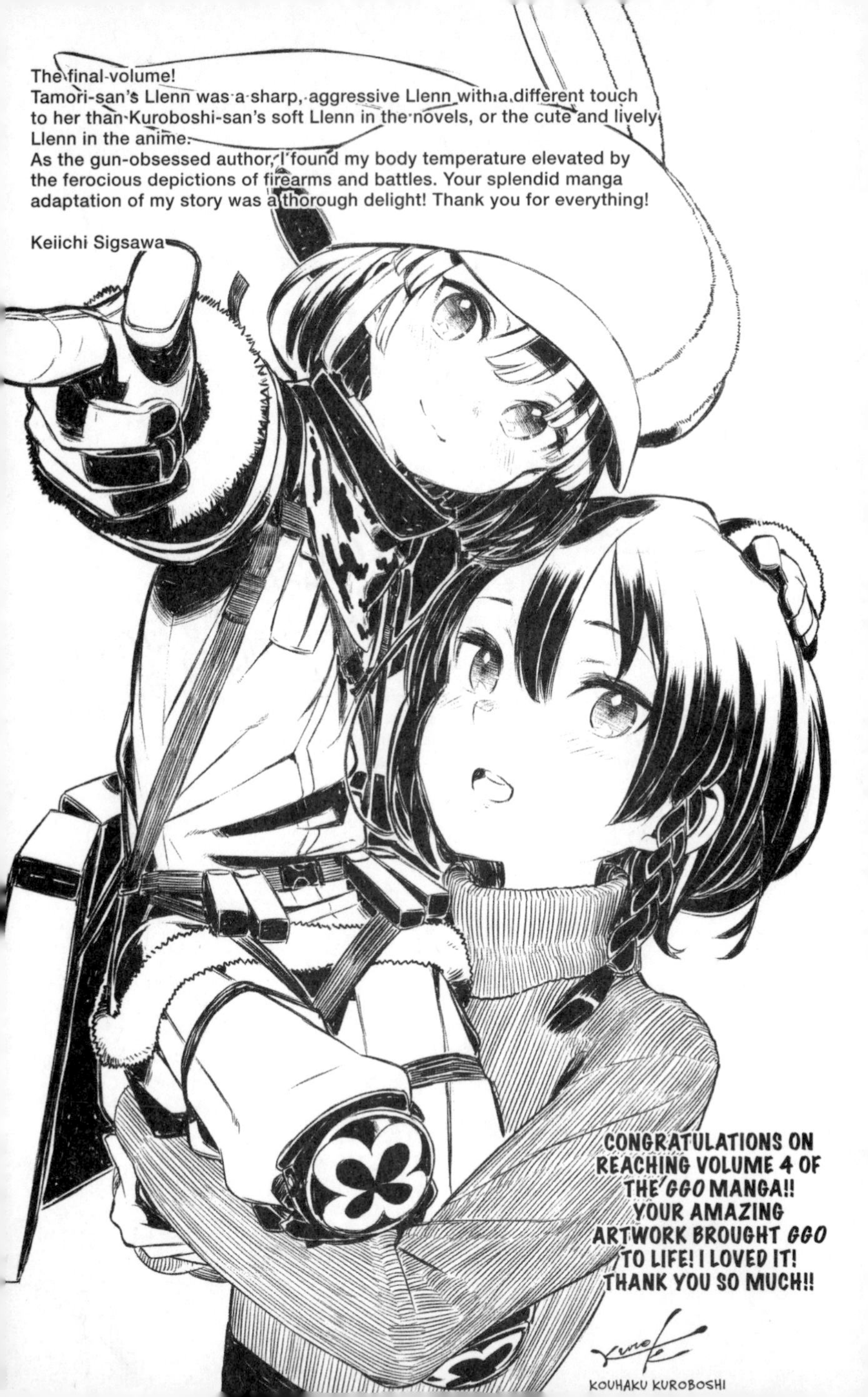
CONGRATULATIONS ON REACHING VOLUME 4 OF THE *GGO* MANGA!! YOUR AMAZING ARTWORK BROUGHT *GGO* TO LIFE! I LOVED IT! THANK YOU SO MUCH!!
KOUHAKU KUROBOSHI

SWORD ART ONLINE ALTERNATIVE: GUN GALE ONLINE 4

ART: TADADI TAMORI
STORY: KEIICHI SIGSAWA
ORIGINAL STORY: REKI KAWAHARA

Translation: Stephen Paul   Lettering: Barri Shrager

SWORD ART ONLINE ALTERNATIVE GUN GALE ONLINE
© Keiichi Sigsawa 2021 © Reki Kawahara 2021 © Tadadi Tamori 2021
First published in Japan in 2021 by KADOKAWA CORPORATION, Tokyo.
English translation rights arranged with KADOKAWA CORPORATION, Tokyo,
through Tuttle-Mori Agency, Inc., Tokyo.

English translation © 2022 by Yen Press, LLC

Yen Press
150 West 30th Street, 19th Floor
New York, NY 10001

Visit us at yenpress.com
facebook.com/yenpress
twitter.com/yenpress
yenpress.tumblr.com
instagram.com/yenpress

First Yen Press Edition: January 2022

Yen Press is an imprint of Yen Press, LLC.
The Yen Press name and logo are trademarks of Yen Press, LLC.

The publisher is not responsible for websites (or their content) that are not owned by the publisher.

Library of Congress Control Number: 2017954143

ISBNs: 978-1-9753-1406-4 (paperback)
         978-1-9753-1405-7 (ebook)

10 9 8 7 6 5 4 3 2 1

WOR

Printed in the United States of America